C: ation
ar annel
4, strip
ca *fe*, an
ar vards
ar that
C il she
w Peryl,
sh *sco on*
ar

JUST A LITTLE DISCO ON AN OPEN-TOP BUS

An Illustrated Year in the Life of
Edie Dudman, Girl in a Rut, 1982–3

CANDY GUARD

PENGUIN BOOKS

PENGUIN BOOKS

Published by the Penguin Group
Penguin Books Ltd, 80 Strand, London WC2R 0RL, England
Penguin Group (USA) Inc., 375 Hudson Street, New York, New York 10014, USA
Penguin Group (Canada), 90 Eglinton Avenue East, Suite 700, Toronto, Ontario, Canada M4P 2Y3
(a division of Pearson Penguin Canada Inc.)
Penguin Ireland, 25 St Stephen's Green, Dublin 2, Ireland (a division of Penguin Books Ltd)
Penguin Group (Australia), 250 Camberwell Road, Camberwell, Victoria 3124, Australia
(a division of Pearson Australia Group Pty Ltd)
Penguin Books India Pvt Ltd, 11 Community Centre, Panchsheel Park, New Delhi – 110 017, India
Penguin Group (NZ), cnr Airborne and Rosedale Roads, Albany, Auckland 1310, New Zealand
(a division of Pearson New Zealand Ltd)
Penguin Books (South Africa) (Pty) Ltd, 24 Sturdee Avenue, Rosebank 2196, Johannesburg, South Africa

Penguin Books Ltd, Registered Offices: 80 Strand, London WC2R 0RL, England

www.penguin.com

First published 2006
2

Copyright © Candy Guard, 2006
All rights reserved

The moral right of the author has been asserted

Set in Garamond MT
Printed in England by Clays Ltd, St Ives plc

Every effort has been made to trace copyright holders and we apologise in advance
for any unintentional omission. We would be pleased to insert the appropriate
acknowledgement in any subsequent edition.

Contents

I

The Devil Makes Work for Idle Brains

I had noticed that all I did was do things and then immediately regret them. Sometimes I regretted them before I'd even done them, but I still went ahead and did them anyway. Being twenty, nearly twenty-one, was part of the problem as I felt any decision I made was going to have profound consequences on the rest of my life. Like taking a job – any old job – and then missing the opportunity of a lifetime whilst doing it. I had delusional thoughts about people recognizing my intelligence and talent just by spotting me on the street and offering me glamorous jobs like Ice Skater or Playwright. So I found it much easier to sit in a paralysed state, drinking tea and smoking and worrying, 'What am I Going to Do?'

I was doing this one morning whilst staring at my cup of tea, which I had placed precariously on the edge of the kitchen table. The washing machine had just gone into spin and my cup of tea was dancing about noisily.

'That cup of tea's going to fall off any second, I shouldn't just sit here staring at it, I should move it, it's going to fall off any second . . .'

After my cup of tea had fallen off, I mopped it up with a pair of pants – I was too depressed to reach for a cloth. I was thinking, 'Why do I do things that I know I shouldn't?' When my flatmate Lucille came stomping in, a white lacy bra dangling from her manicured finger. It was the sort of philosophical question Lucille would've enjoyed debating when we were spiky-haired fifteen-year-olds sharing a joint on her Mum's balcony. So I said, 'Why do I do things that I know I shouldn't?' but Lucille just stared at the washing machine and tutted.

'Do you do that?' I added needily.

'Do what? Can you take your stuff out? I want to wash this.'

'Things that you know you shouldn't.'

'Of course I don't.'

Her words were like a dagger in my lonely heart. And then she twisted the blade by turning her critical gaze on the huge pile of washing up. All of which was mine – 14 plates covered with crumbs and crusts, 23 tea- and coffee-stained mugs, 3 ashtrays and 11 bowls with cornflakes in various stages of rigor mortis welded to their rims

Lucille's one mug

– the remnants of days of unemploy. She washed the one cup that was hers as I declared, 'I'm going to do it. It's on my list.'

I read out today's list: '1) Post Office – cash Giro 2) Washing up liquid – see! – 3) Floodlight/prospectus – I've decided to get my act together – retake my A levels – maybe go to art school! 4) Library – classic novels . . .'

'Did you go into Crusties?' Lucille demanded. Another twist of the blade. I wanted to fling myself at her fluffy mules and beg her to be as crap as I was – like she used to be.

'No, I didn't! I don't want to get stuck in another crappy job. I want to be something exciting.'

'Wouldn't it be better to be doing something rather than lying around and obsessing about Steve?'

'I'm not obsessing about him!'

'Good.'

I covered my list with my hand and crossed out 5) Phone Steve. There was a pause whilst Lucille sipped at her herbal tea (what *had* happened to her?)

'I haven't seen him for a week! I've called him and left messages and he doesn't ring – I don't know what to do!' I wailed.

'You're too available, Edie. Next time he calls you just say . . .'

'But he never calls me, he just turns up, hangs about and then goes. He never makes any arrangements.'

'OK, next time he comes round just say you're busy.'

'Yeah! "Hello you bloody bastard,"' I rehearsed, '"I'm busy. Now you know what it feels like, hurting, day in and day out . . ."'

Lucille interrupted my outburst.

'No. Not aggressively. Be jolly and nice.'

'Jolly and nice? But . . .'

'Say in a bright voice, "Oh! It would've been lovely to see you but I've made other plans! Bye!"'

'But he might think I'm happy without him and never come round again.'

Lucille sighed and paused for about the amount of time it might take someone to count to ten.

'Just try it, Eed.'

'Is that what your Mum tells you? You're so lucky having a Mum who tells you tricks to keep men. My Mum's hopeless.'

We both glanced at some photos magnetted to the fridge – one of Lucille and Barry laughing with her Mum and her Mum's boyfriend Frank, all glammed up at a wedding and one of me and my Mum in my Mum's living room, my Mum cackling in her Parker Knoll, with a piece of crisp in her teeth, and me looking daggers. No men in sight, just Flopsie, my enormous buck rabbit, behind us on the balcony, a figure made more tragic-looking by being out of focus and having red-eye.

'But I don't know what's happened – he was nice before, why can't he be nice again? Last time I saw hi–' I began.

'Oh, look, Eed, I've got to dash.'

Though crushed, I stood up. 'Me too!'

Minutes later Lucille dashed past the doorway smelling of employment and normality and that new perfume Barry bought her, 'Blazé'.

'Barry's picking me up and we're having a quick breakfast before work!' she boasted.

'How come you get the nice boyfriend and I get the horrible one?' She didn't answer so I called, 'I think I've got angina!' Slam!

She'd gone. I clutched my heart disease and watched Lucille trotting across the quad to Barry's car, muttering to myself.

'The trouble with you, Lucille, is you're selfish. When you were single and I was first with Steve I always included you. I could've gone to Boxford Grammar for Girls but I went to the comp to be with you.'

She might've been happy being a temp at the *Boxford Gazette* but it wasn't enough for me. She was holding me back from the life I deserved – exciting, stimulating friends, intellectual pursuits, travel etc etc.

I sat back down, lit a B&H and wrote '5) Change Life.' Then I phoned Steve's flat and let it ring 34 times (he might've been in the bath).

I got out my old portfolio and started sifting through all my photos I took for Photography A level. I was starting to cheer up – they were really quite good – when I came across one of Steve and I on the beach at Brighton. I slung it aside and felt an urgent need to do something with a hair product. I chose Lucille's Henna for Blondes. My hair is brown but I knew there was some blonde just busting to get out.

Within seconds of opening the pot, adding water and starting to mix the henna into a paste, the bathroom was completely covered with splatters of brown mud. I 'massaged' it into my hair and then read the instructions. 'Wrap hair in a warm towel, cover in cling film and leave for 45 minutes.' Forty-five minutes! Now they tell me! Oh well, *Pebble Mill*'s on in five minutes.

'Brrring!' The doorbell. I went on tiptoes and peeped out of the tiny bathroom window. A crash helmet with Steve underneath it.

'I don't believe it! Don't let him in, don't let him in, it's a very bad idea to let him in!' I chanted as I ran down the stairs, whipped a Miss Selfish plastic bag on my head and opened the door.

'Come in!'

'What's that on your head? Shit?' he said, barging in and plonking himself on the sofa.

'I was just henna-ing my hair,' I said, trying to sound jolly. 'I'm a bit busy.'

Steve took a large joint out of his pocket and lit up.

'What you got all this crap out for?' He picked up the photo I had slung aside of us on the beach at Brighton the day I messed up my Photography A level.

'D'you remember that?' I asked.

'No.'

'Yes, you do, that was that day we went to Brighton – I was supposed to be in my Photography theory exam. Mr Howard told me I was ruining my life.'

'You should've told him to *ferck erff.*'

This was Steve's answer to everything. And every story he ever told always ended with him saying 'Ferck erff ' in a druggy 'I don't care' way to figures of authority, blokes in pubs – anyone really. But I knew that he never really said it. He just thought it. He passed me the joint.

'No, for God's sake don't have any,' I warned myself, but self-destructively took a big puff.

'You remember,' I said. 'We had sex under the pier.'

'Oh yeah.'

'It was a lovely day.'

'Yeah, I remember, you had that purple flying suit on with the zip right up the front. Phwoargh! Come here my little Whale Pup.'

'What?' I lied.

I was playing for time. For a thicko he had a surprisingly sophisticated line in cute nicknames and one second later I was sitting on his lap receiving a blow-back from his beautiful shapely lips, his hand creeping into my dressing gown.

I still had the plastic bag on my head as we lay in post-coital bliss. Well, actually I was in post-coital anxiety as I was rehearsing my 'Steve I think we should talk about the relationship' speech and worrying about the henna all over my sheets. Steve was droning on scintillatingly about his job as a tree surgeon.

'And then, right, Gaffa said to me and Dave, right, "Get out of the van and get those logs loaded" and I said, "Oh, ferck erff Gazza!"'

I laughed fakely. He was so thick I couldn't follow any of his work 'stories'. But his looks confused me. I stared at the blond hairs at the edge of his hairline, his long eyelashes, his full mouth, perfect small teeth and pink gums and thought,

'Oh well,' closed my eyes (my ears would've been more appropriate) and went to nibble his lower lip.

But he was up and zipping his fly.

'I'd better shoot off.'

'Hang on!' I protested.

'Things to do.'

'What?'

'People to see.'

'Who?'

Why did I let him in? Why did I get stoned? Why did I have sex with him? It was too late to rectify the situation – or was it?

I caught up with him halfway along the balcony, Jervis's dog, Kenneth, yapping at my heels.

'Young lady!' Jervis called.

'Hang *on a minute*, Jervis! Steve! Come back!' I shouted, chasing him along the balcony.

'I suppose you're not going to make any arrangement? Is it at all possible for me to know when I'm seeing you again?'

He'd already put his helmet on and I was tugging at his leather jacket when my Mum's front door flung open.

'What's going on?' she demanded, but then as she clocked Steve she muttered 'Oh God' and retreated back into the flat. Typical. If Dad was around he'd have challenged Steve, asked him what his intentions were, told him never to darken our doorstep again.

'You bloody bastard! I never ever want to see you again!' I screamed. 'Come back!'

And I heard Mum turn the volume up on her TV as the lift doors closed on Steve.

I stomped back along the balcony, leaning over the railings for a few seconds to watch Steve sauntering across to his Honda 250 Silver Dream, nodding to Buster as he passed. Buster, estate gardener, ex-boyfriend (very ex, we were fifteen and lasted five weeks) and Annoying Person Number One, bristled like a dog at Steve and glanced up at me.

'Nice hat, Edie!' he called.

I felt my hat area, remembered I still had the Miss Selfish plastic bag on my head and hurried towards my Mum's flat, rang the doorbell twice and looked through the letter box. I could see my Mum's feet sticking out from her Parker Knoll and resting on the pouffe. The fire was on, it looked very cosy.

'Mum! I'm worried about you!' I yelled. 'That you might be lonely, bored and confused!'

She turned the volume up even more. 'She can't be that deaf,' I thought, pushing away the thought that even my Mum found me too available.

As I approached my flat Jervis was positioned just outside, his wheelchair blocking my way.

'Edna!'

'You know full well it's Edie.'

His fake senility was just an attention-grabbing device. As was the theatrical coughing fit he proceeded to enact.

'Did you get my prescription, love?'

'No Jervis, I'm sorry, I've been really busy – I will get it.'

He did a particularly graveyard cough and for pathos added, 'That's a nice dress, love.'

I glanced down at my dressing gown covered with henna and slammed into the flat. After rinsing the henna off my hair I tried to see if there were any honey glints. Despite my suicidal state, I knew that waiting for my hair to dry and have honey glints would give me a reason to go on living.

I added '6) Jervis's prescription' to my list and '7) Start New Life – properly this time'. Clearing up the living room and my ransacked portfolio and cleaning the henna off the bathroom would have to wait until later.

I was charging across the quad when Buster appeared from behind a bush.

'Hi Edie, is that you? Fancy a coffee?'

'I can't, Buster, I'm really busy.' Why was it so easy to tell everyone but Steve that I was busy?

'Doing what? Come on, just a quick one!'

'No!' I said, pushing past him.

'Your hair looks nice!'

Damn, he knew me so well. He knew any mention of my hair would intrigue me.

'Really? Can you see any honey glints yet?'

'Yeah, loads.'

'Really?' I looked into Buster's eyes. He looked different, sort of piggy. Pig*gier*. He wasn't wearing his bottle-bottom glasses – he was lying about my glints, he was blind as a bat!

Minutes later I had re-re-started on my New Life and was standing in the rain (my hair would *never* dry!) in a distressingly disorganized gaggle at the bus stop. I was pretty sure I was fifth in gaggle, behind the old lady with the green hat and in front of the man with the glasses. I had a creeping feeling that he thought he was already there when I got there but he definitely wasn't. This, and the five coffees, were giving me a panic attack and I was already mentally rowing with the man in the glasses when I checked my purse and realized I only had the ten-pound note Mum had lent me. The palpitations really set in then. Did I have time to dash to the shop? It was one of those life or death decisions so common in my life. Miss the bus or make the driver cross? Too much time to think made every decision of vital importance. Having nothing to do – the long, lonely hours of mind-nattering – had drained me of the confidence to make simple choices.

I dashed to Ali's (even though lately I tended to walk miles to unfamiliar shops rather than face familiar chat with the locals – even saying 'hello' and drawing attention to myself held terror and shame for me), bought a Mars bar, told poor lonely Ali that I was in a hurry as I had a job interview, felt guilty when he called 'good luck!' and watched three buses whizz past. Not so fast that I didn't see the man with the glasses in the best seat, at the front on the top, smile smugly at me.

Why? Why? Why? Why? Did I go to the shop? Did I not go earlier? Did I just buy a Mars bar? Did I mess up my A levels? Did I give up French? Did I not go to gymnastics that night when I was twelve? Lucille and I had waited at the bus stop for fifteen minutes and then gone back to hers and became toast addicts instead of gymnasts. I might've been able to do a backward walkover by now. I hate Lucille. It's all her fault.

I debated, 'Maybe I should walk, it'll do me good. But if I walk a bus will come. Oh I don't know.' I took one step, 'Oh I'll walk it'll do me goo– no I'll wait – no I'll walk . . .' I found myself distractedly staring at the small ads in Ali's window:

I was just jotting the number of the puppies down when I stopped myself, 'Don't be ridiculous!' I glanced up, still shaking my head madly, and saw Ali grinning at me through the window. I pretended to look at my watch (I haven't got one) and started walking quickly towards my 'job interview'. Immediately a bus roared past and through a huge puddle which splattered my black stretch jeans. I bent to wring them out and noticed a dog and two old ladies staring at me maliciously.

'It's alright!' I called, 'I'm fine! Don't worry about me. I'm just soaked!'

and hurried on.

The Mars bar made the walk into town more bearable — one bite every three hundred yards and I'd be at the Post Office.

The woman in the Post Office noticed I'd done something to my hair and, as I counted my dole money outside, I felt a cheery sense of achievement and took my list out to tick off number 1. But it wasn't my list, it was my Mars bar wrapper and my heart skipped a beat as a flashback flitted across my dim-witted brain: my stupid hand flinging the list in a bin and putting the Mars bar wrapper in my pocket.

'Oh well,' I thought, 'I can't do anything now, without my list – if I rush back I'll be in time for *Young Doctors*!' Oh God, I sounded like Mother, and as I stood on the pavement with

the self-consciousness of the unemployed person with nowhere to hurry my eyes alighted on:

Crusties the Bakers.
Sales people required.

2

Why, Why, Why, Why, Why, Why, Why?

'Yeah, right, so I ses to 'im, I ses look you total arsehole type of a person, they's your kids as well . . . yeah, can I help you?'

'Um, the job? Is it still available?'

'Yeah, hang on. Moi! Get your fat arse out here! She's out doing the bins, she won't be a minute. Yeah, so's anyway, what was I saying? Yeah, so I ses I'm only eighteen, you knocked me up, I'm going out clubbing, you're babysitting.' Then she laughed like a machine gun.

Kerry's hair was straight and brown for the first two inches below her nylon hat and then broke out into a very blonde, very curly bubble perm that stayed completely static as she waved her freckly face around animatedly.

I took in the brown and white checked nylon dress and hat and thought: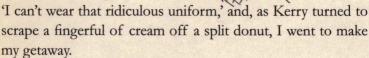
'I can't wear that ridiculous uniform,' and, as Kerry turned to scrape a fingerful of cream off a split donut, I went to make my getaway.

'Oi! Where you legging it?'

'Um . . .' I explained.

14

'Fill this out,' she said commandingly, and shoved an application form in front of me. This is how I filled out the form:

CRUSTIES
APPLICATION FORM FOR THE POST OF SALES ASSISTANT.

Name: Edie Dudman *D.O.B:* 30.09.61
Address: 24 Kent House, Boxford.
Tel: 748 2259
Why do you want to work for Crusties? I don't.
What relevant catering experience do you have? None.
What other work experience do you have? Harrods lamp department Summer sales job. Education Officer Boxford City Farm (in charge of small caged animals) Saturday job. Lyric Theatre Coffee Bar (not catering) 6 months, sales assistant. Ali's General Store (not relevant) 6 weeks.
What character traits do you have that you think would make you a good employee for Crusties? Clumsy, innumerate, kleptomaniac, binge eater.

And I rushed out and straight into Miss Selfish feeling another undeserved sense of achievement – I mean I had *applied* for a job. And if I was going to get a job (not that one, obviously) I would need a new outfit. I felt my excitement mounting as I surveyed the rows of tantalizing items. Ten minutes later, with no blood in my arms from flicking hangers along the rails, I was in the bowels of the shop thinking, 'What am I doing here?' when a voice said:

'Alright, Edie?'

It was Julie Fitchebauer from my needlework CSE class at school.

'Oh, hi Julie.'

'I've got those trousers, they look fab on.' Though she said so herself.

'Oh, OK, I'll try them on.'

'You still with Steve?'

'Yes.'

'Oh, well if you ever get fed up with him pass him over. He's gorgeous. I think he looks like John McEnroe.'

As I squeezed the black stretch drainpipes on I worried, 'What did she mean? She's heard something. She was looking at my too-short trousers and my Mum's dyke shoes and wondering what he's doing with me.' She'd always fancied Steve. It's things like that that make it hard to split up with someone.

'How you doing?' Julie swished the curtain open.

'Um, OK, it's just . . .'

'They look great!'

'Well, this 12's got a funny sticky-out bit here and this 12 goes a bit up my bum. Have you got another 12?'

'No, last two pairs. *They* look great!' she said, pointing at the up-the-bum ones and then whisked the curtain shut.

Then I heard another voice,

'Not more black trousers. I hate you in black trousers. Why don't you wear a nice short skirt?' It was Steve trying to dominate me again through telepathy.

'I don't give a shit what you think,' I said, obviously out loud, because the curtain whisked open again.

'What?' said Julie.

'Um, I'll take them,' I said. 'Thanks for the advice.'

'What advice?'

'You said they looked great.'

'Did I?' she said, looking genuinely amazed.

'Why, why, why did I buy these trousers?'

I was back at home, in front of the mirror, red in the face and tugging at the funny sticking-out bit. 'They go right up my arse! It's all that Julie's fault. She wants me to look horrible so she can steal Steve away from me.' Then I saw one of Steve's large joint butts in the ashtray like a beacon of light in my mental hell and lit up, dropping ash all down the trousers.

Lucille came bustling along the balcony, high heels cloinking, slammed the front door, whisked past the living room door, M&S carrier bags rustling efficiently. She had stopped to stare disbelievingly at my prostrate shape on the sofa as I woke up from a sleep that was unravelling my huge trouser leg of care.

'Sorry about the mess,' I croaked.

Then I heard her tut at the washing up in the kitchen.

'I'm going to do it! I'm going to do it!' I shouted.

Lucille trotted upstairs and tutted at the henna-ed bathroom – it's amazing how loudly that girl could tut – and then appeared in the doorway again to tut at me and the sea of photos all over the floor.

'It smells of dope in here,' she said, wrinkling her snub little nose.

'Does it? Steve came round.'

'And?' she said aggressively.

'And then he left.'

'Did you do what I said? Were you unavailable?'

'Yes.'

'And cool?'

'Kind of. Yes I was.'

'Did you say you had other plans?'

'Yes. I said I had other plans for the rest of my life,' I announced proudly.

'Oh Edie, you didn't? That sounds desperate.'

'It's OK, I don't think he heard me – he had his crash helmet on.'

'Hmm,' she said critically.

Lucille trotted back up the stairs with a large Chelsea Girl bag. I trailed her, brooding on the fact that I now had to tell her white lies whilst in the past, when we were fat and fifteen and Thatcher wasn't in power yet, I could tell her anything. Michael Foot and I had been left behind in the soft and caring seventies. It felt so lonely in the eighties. I had to tell her the truth. I leant casually on Lucille's bedroom door frame and droned on:

'I know I should've rinsed my hair but I was trying to be myself. To suddenly not henna my hair would've been false – when I'd read the instructions and everything. I mean it's better to be myself, isn't it?'

'God, no. Definitely not.'

'Why not?'

'Oh, look Edie, I've got to get ready.'

I remembered I was still wearing my new trousers.

'D'you like my trousers?'

'They're your old ones, aren't they?'

'No, they're new. I hate them and they go up my bum.'

'What did you buy them for if you don't like them?'

Lucille was holding a dress up against her ample bosom. A black velvet cocktail dress with a huge bow on the back. Her natural blonde highlights were gleaming on her natural waves and every one of her twenty-three cuddly toys was neatly in its place on her bed.

'Going somewhere with Barry?'

'Why do you always say "Barry" like that?'

'I don't. Like what?'

I did a funny nasally Northern accent when I said 'Barry', hoping to keep the bitterness and jealousy out of my voice.

'We're going to the theatre with his parents to see *Othello*.'

'Really? I think I'd faint with joy if Steve offered to take me to the theatre with his parents . . . you're so lucky with Barry!' I said, forgetting to do my nasally voice.

Lucille smiled pityingly and as I busied myself looking for non-existent honey glints in her three-way dressing table mirror, I had a vision of me and Steve coming out of the theatre having just seen *Othello*. Steve was wearing a cravat just like Barry and put his arm round me protectively as I said:

'But don't you think the breakdown between Othello and Desdemona was really well observed?'

And Steve said, 'Yeah it reminded me of the mind games that you and I play, both afraid to show our true feelings.'

'What?' I said.

'He should have told her to ferck erff,' he said.

The doorbell woke me from my fantasy nightmare.

'There's no point me thinking still waters run deep with that idiot,' I blurted and noticed that Lucille's panda, Binky, was staring at me intently, but Lucille had gone. I was transfixed by Binky's penetrating button eyes. I hadn't quite mentioned the sex bit of the Steve story to Lucille but Binky's eyes were saying:

'I'm going to tell Lucille what you were up to this morning, I can see straight in your room from here.'

Telling myself I was still stoned from that roach I smoked earlier, I heard Lucille opening the front door and saying, 'Come in, then,' in a not-very-friendly way. Maybe it was Steve! I poked my tongue out at Binky victoriously and ran downstairs.

But it was Barry. Lucille nearly always spoke to him in an unfriendly way but still he hung on her every chilly monosyllable.

In the living room Lucille said, 'Edie, you know there's about a thousand messages from Crusties on here.'

She was pointing at her new fangled answering machine, yet another present from Barry, whose dad worked for BT.

'Are you going to ring them back?'

'I'm thinking about it.'

'They sound very keen,' she enthused.

'I know, it's a bit off-putting.'

'Crusties the bakery?' said Barry. 'Great! I get my cheese and onion bap in there every lunchtime.'

That was the nail in the coffin for Crusties as far as I was concerned.

'I'm just going to put my face on,' Lucille said. Put her face on? Lucille had turned into an alien adult. And she went upstairs, leaving me in the living room with *Barry*. (Said in nasally Northern accent.)

'Hi Barry.'

'Hi Edie,' Barry laughed.

He was so gormless. We sat and stared at the telly. Barry kept glancing at the doorway hoping Lucille would appear in it. That made me even more depressed, as even though Barry is the most boring man in the world I wasn't good enough company for him. He worked in the council in Parks so had vague links with the tree gang and Steve the Bastard. I was always thinking that he might have secret information about Steve, which actually promoted him to only second most boring man in the world. There was always the chance he might say, 'Saw Steve today. That man adores you, never stops talking about you – Edie this, Edie that – that cool dude stuff is just a front. He's obsessed with you.'

Barry was looking at my slippers. They were actually slippers that I had bought for Jervis for Christmas last year, forgetting that he only had one leg; so I kept them even though they were brown tartan and size 11.

Barry snorted unattractively.

'What?' I said.

'Your slippers,' he chortled.

'Oh right, yes, very funny, so I'm wearing men's slippers. Hee, hee, hee, hee, hee.'

'They look cute on you.'

It was pathetic how, in a compliment desert, something so small could cheer you up. Immediately I saw Barry in a new light. I was almost falling in love with him! But then Lucille appeared, dressed up to the nines, and Barry's attention was completely focused on her, even though she was either ignoring him or bossing him about. I decided to go round my Mum's.

'I'm going round my Mum's. If anyone calls can you tell them I'm there.'

'Like who? Steve?' Lucille said nastily, in the same way as I said things nasally, nail varnish lid between her teeth.

'No!' I said. 'Don't be silly.'

I did a little pirouette down the communal balcony in my 'cute' men's slippers and felt a warm glow as I anticipated seeing my Mum. My lovely cuddly Mum.

'I love my Mum, love her, love her, love her,' I thought. 'I won't go on about Steve, I'll be really nice, tell her she looks nice . . .'

As my Mum opened the door I said, 'God Mum, I can hear your telly all along the balcony,' in a not very loving tone.

'Sorry I . . .'

'Parker Knoll hair, Mum!' I added.

She made a feeble attempt to flatten her hair at the back to match the flatness on top. Why couldn't she have big fluffy hair like Lucille's mum, Wendy?

I trailed her into the kitchen and saw she was getting a Liver, Bacon and Mash Gas mark 4 meal from M&S out of the oven.

'Is that a meal for two?' I asked accusingly.

'Um, no, it's a meal for one. But you have it.'

'No! You have it.'

'Honestly dear, I'm full.'

'You haven't eaten any yet.'

'I've gone right off it. I want you to have it, you sounded so keen.'

'Mum, I don't want it.'

'Are you sure?' she said.

22

'Positive,' I replied.

Pleased but guilty-looking she hurried into the lounge, sat back down in her Parker Knoll and settled the plate on her cushion tray on her lap. I was just resolving to be really nice again – my dear lovely Mum – when I opened the fridge and saw the splayed open milk carton. At the same time my bionic ears tuned into the munching noise of Mum eating. I could feel my blood rising.

'Mum,' I shouted, 'I *showed* you how to open the milk, you have to fold back these wings and pull the spout . . .'

'Sorry, dear. I will next time,' she called, as milk cascaded all over the sideboard.

As I came in with the tea Mum glanced at me. 'They're nice tights, dear.'

'No, they're not, they're horrible trousers.'

'Haven't you already got some like that?'

'I'm taking them back tomorrow.'

'What's that stain? Chocolate?'

'Leave me alone!' I'd now managed to get henna on them from the uncleaned bathroom.

Later on, settled on the leatherette sofa drinking my tea, I was just starting to enjoy myself – *Coronation Street* was on – when the phone rang and, stupidly thinking it might be Steve, I picked it up.

'Oi, d'you mind?' Mum snatched it off me. '748 2259?' She always tried to say the number because in the days when Distant Dad first left and was being particularly nasty he would do a terrifying silence if she simply said, 'Hello.'

'Edith? Oh yes. Edie, it *is* for you, dear.'

I felt a surge of excitement. Only Steve ever called me Edith.

'Hello?!'

A woman's voice said, 'Hello, Edith Dudman? It's Moira here, the manageress of Crusties.'

I couldn't have felt more gutted. 'Hello.'

'Um, hello dear. I received your application form. Everything looks fine. Could you start tomorrow?'

'Well, um, I've never worked in a bakery before.'

'That's OK, we'll train you.'

'I can only do part-time.'

'That's fine, love.'

Why couldn't she take a lie for an answer?

'Um,' (fake coughing fit) 'can I call you back? I'm not feeling very well.' I slammed the phone down. I felt really depressed and looked across at Mum.

I thought, 'Look at Mum. The way she juts her lip out when she's watching TV! It's because she's crap with men that I'm crap with men. Don't say it though, you'll hurt her feelings.' I glanced towards the (filthy!) mirror to check my golden highlights and saw with horror that I was jutting my lower lip out just like Mum.

'It's your fault I'm crap with men,' I blurted, 'because I don't know the tricks! Lucille's mum teaches her tricks about how to keep men.'

'What tricks?' Mum said, talking with her mouth full.

'See, you don't know them, so how am I supposed to know them?'

'I know some. Keep your nails and hair clean and your clothes nice.' She had liver and bacon for at least one down her jersey.

'Hopeless!' I spat.

'And be yourself.'

'That is the *worst* thing you can do, Lucille said Wendy said.'

'Oh is it?' My Mum looked so anxious and eager to learn that I felt guilty but then she blew it by saying, 'Did you have a fun time with Steve earlier?'

'No I didn't!' I shouted and threw myself on the leatherette sofa, sobbing. 'I was all demanding! I've probably completely frightened him away. I hate him, I hate him, he's ruined my life! You should never have let me go out with him! You should've let me move in with him when he asked me! If I had a big strong Dad he would've asked what his intentions were, and maybe he'd treat me with some respect!' I then wailed for a few more minutes into the sofa. When I came up for air from my fake leather vale of tears Mum was looking frostily out of the balcony doors.

'I'm nearly twenty-one! I should be out clubbing showing off my young bottom not sitting in with my Mum, bored, on a Friday night wearing old men slippers!'

'If you're so bored why don't you get some straw and clean out poor old Flopsie?' she said, gesturing with a fork at the balcony.

'I'm twenty, not twelve!' I whined, unconvincingly.

'Old enough to clean out your rabbit then.'

I glanced at Flopsie, who was staring guilt-makingly from his hutch on the balcony. Even in real life and without the aid of red-eye, he still managed to look like he'd just been crying.

'Oh thanks!' I screamed. 'I'm having a nervous breakdown about my life, no job, an ex-best friend, a bastard boyfriend and you mentioning Flopsie – and you know Steve gave him to me for my nineteenth! – is just the last stra–'

Mum paused nervously then burst out laughing. It was

funny and I wanted to laugh but I was proud and mean and she had gravy in the corner of her mouth so instead I said severely:

'OK straw, yes, very funny. I said straw . . . See you around!'

And I stormed out just in time to see Lucille and Barry giggling across the quad towards Barry's parents' car.

'Oi, young man!' It was Jervis lurking in his doorway.

'It's me Jervis, I . . . Why, do these trousers make me look masculine?'

'Did you steal those pants off my line?'

'No I did not.'

'Well, I've got a pair of long johns exactly like that, somewhere,' he said accusingly.

That was it. I was definitely going to take them back.

3

An Answer for Everything

The next morning (11.59 a.m.) I wrote my list.

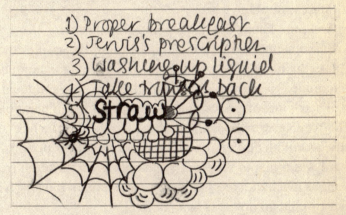

I laughed to myself as I doodled round 'straw'. 'That was really mean of me not to laugh with Mum, I'll regret that when she's dead.'

The doorbell rang. It was Steve! I recognized the shape of his crash helmet through the frosted glass of the front door. I resolved to tell him to Ferck Erff. That was the only language he understood. I opened the door, and my heart sunk so deep I knew I wouldn't have told Steve to F— off. It was Buster, holding his spade upside down (deliberately, I felt) to look like Steve's helmet.

'Don't let him in. Don't let him in,' I told myself.

'Come in Bust,' I said.

'You know Ken Jefferson?' he said, sitting himself down at the kitchen table.

'No.'

'That bloke from school in the year above you, his brother swam the Channel.'

'What did he look like?'

'I don't know. Anyway he's dead. Car crash. Only twenty-one. Makes you think.'

'Makes you think what?'

'Well, you know, what's the point of it all?'

Buster slumped on the table and read my list upside down. I swear he enjoyed making things difficult for himself. I determined to stay bright and not let Buster drag me down.

'There's lots of points to it all!' I said in a fake, flutey voice. The trouble with Buster was that his downbeat nature and obsession with death tapped in to some part of my personality that I was trying to suppress. I was only a hair's breadth from being as much of a mess as Buster and if I spent too long with him I would go downhill fast. 'Coffee?'

'Two sugars please.' He stared at my list again '"Evening class"?'

'Yeah, I'm going to do a class or two.'

'You said that last year,' Buster said.

'Yes, well,' I said dropping my egg into the boiling water hoping it wouldn't break. But it did and white of egg started bulging out of the crack like that yellow stuff in attics.

'And the year before.'

'Well I'm going to do it this year. I might learn massage. You can make loads of money massaging actresses and stuff in their houses.'

'But you might get funny pervy blokes or hunchbacks.'

I ignored him stoically. I'd already thought of that.

'And photography. I'm going to take my A level again.'

Buster stirred his coffee. 'You know sugar's carcinogenic?'

'Really. That's nice.'

'I'll do a class with you. I was going to do one anyway.'

'You've just made that up.' He was always copying me.

'In computers. There's loads of money in it.'

'No, I don't want to do that.'

'I could do the massage class with you, we could practise on each other.'

'It's massage for women,' I lied.

Buster slumped into his chair and drained his cup.

'Oh, what's the point anyway? I'm too old to go to college. I'd never stick to it. I'm just going to have to remain an undiscovered genius.'

'Oh come on, Bust! We're young, we can do anything!' It was funny how being with someone more miserable than you really did make you take up the role of the cheery one in a quite convincing way. I tapped the top of my exploded boiled egg and sang to myself.

'Hen's period.'

'What?' I said.

'That's all an egg is,' Buster said, 'if you think about it. A hen's period.'

'Anyway,' I said, gagging, 'I'm going to get my life sorted out before my twenty-first birthday.'

'Oh yeah, your mum mentioned that.'

'Did she? She's not trying to organize a surprise like last year, is she?'

Buster shrugged unconvincingly, looked at my list and read:

'"Warts?" Have you got that wart coming up on your nose again?'

'No, I haven't! It says Straw. For Flopsie.'

'I can get you some straw. From the depot.'

'Really. That's great, Bust. Anyway I must get on. Things to do!'

'What?'

'People to see!'

'Who?'

'So see you later!'

'When?'

Suddenly I could see why Steve was finding me so unappealing. I resolved to be even cooler with Steve.

'Yeah, I'd better get back to my weeding. And I need to do diarrhoea after that coffee,' and Buster rushed out.

'I'm not chatting to Buster in the mornings anymore,' I thought. 'And I've got irritable bowel from all those coffees he made me have. And he ruined my breakfast. Undiscovered genius?! In what field of the Arts or Sciences exactly?' We were yet to be told.

I flung my new jeans in an old wrinkled Top Shop bag and set off. I was going to take them back today. It was my big task for the day and I had been rehearsing half the night. I had sponged off the ash and the henna stain and was feeling fairly confident. As I came out of the front door Jervis was pretending to be dead in his wheelchair outside his flat. But there was a steaming cup of tea next to him on the wall and I knew he was far too mean to die before drinking it so I ignored him and walked off.

'Oi! Ethel! I need my prescription! Now!'

'Yes, yes, it's on the list! I have got a life to live you know, Jervis.'

Approaching my Mum's flat I could hear the telly blaring from the kitchen and her window flew open as I passed.

'Darling, you couldn't get me the *Radio Times*, could you?'

'Can't you get it?'

'*Young Doctors* is just starting.'

I glanced at my nonexistent watch. 'Is it? Tut! You shouldn't be watching TV in the day. No wonder I'm so unmotivated.'

Then my Mum took ages fumbling about in her giant purse and counting the money in coppers.

'How am I going to make my way in life, if I can't even make it along the balcony?'

'24, 24 and a half, 25, 25 and a half. Could you sub me half a p? Is that alright dear? Oh no, I'll go and check down the side of the sofa, I don't want to see you short . . .'

'No! No! It's alright!' and I fled.

As I marched across the quad I looked back to see Buster hunched dejectedly over his spade weeding, Jervis coughing on the balcony and my Mum anxiously waving something which I assumed must be a ½ p. And with that confusing mix of guilt and rage that people who are closest to us bring out I hurried off to the bus stop.

Once again I was at the bus stop churning away about my new life. I was imagining hiring a double decker bus and taking all my friends on it for my birthday. Maybe down to Brighton to a disco. Or I could have a disco on the bus. Or what about a disco on a boat? Oh Jesus. What was wrong with me? I resolved to completely ignore my birthday.

As the rain gently spat on our expectant faces, the rest of the bus gaggle and I stared towards the spot where we hoped the 88 bus would appear. Thirty-five minutes we'd been waiting!

'Right, that's it!' I thought. 'When the bus arrives, I'm going to have words with the driver. I'm going to tell him that because he's late I'm going to miss the interview for the job, the wages from which were going to pay for my Mum's life-saving operation.' That would make him sorry.

Just then the old clichéd three buses came at once. We all tutted in unison before our war spirit camaraderie melted away and we started shuffling territorially. I elbowed the old lady in the purple mohair hat out of the way and stepped on the bus ready to deliver my guilt-making speech. But the driver was Dean Rumble from school, the one who squeezed my bottom in third year assembly and shouted out 'Urgh! Edie Dudman's wearing a jam rag!' I didn't want to risk a repeat performance, even though there's no way he could've reached my bottom from his booth, so instead of the operation speech I said 'thirty-p please'. Even that seemed to annoy him, so I hurried in, thanking God I'd had the right change.

Floodlight cost £3.95!! So I thought I'd have a quick glance in Maider's Newsagents and was scribbling down some photography evening classes on my list when I heard Mrs Maider tut loudly.

Why isn't 'tut' in the English dictionary? Surely it is the most overused word in Britain. Trouble is, it has so many meanings it would need a whole volume to define it. In this case it meant:

Tut: Latin, Thinks it's a library.

I turned proudly towards Mrs Maider, determined to show I had purchasing power. 'Have you got any Polos?'

'Polos?' she said.

'Yes, the ones with the holes in them. People like them.'

'No.'

'You haven't got any Polos?' I said, unable to disguise my disbelief.

'No, we haven't.'

'I can't believe it!'

As I left she tutted to Mr Maider.

Tut: thinks I'm a liar.

He tutted back.

Tut: you can tell she's unemployed and crap with blokes.

Confidence dented, I braced myself. Next on the list was Miss Selfish, to take the black stretch drainpipes back.

Standing outside, occasionally glancing in at Julie, who was filing her nails, I did a bit more rehearsing. I was determined to have an answer for everything.

An Answer for Everything

'*I'd like to exchange these trousers,*' I rehearse.
'*Have you worn them?*'
I have Julie say suspiciously.
'*No,*' I say. '*Well, only round the house, I didn't sit down, or eat in them or anything.*' No, no, no! Don't over-explain!

I had a vision, then, of Julie examining the crotch area.

'*I don't know what that is,*' I interject, '*it was on them when I got home . . . funny . . .*'

But Julie is on the ball in these dress rehearsals.

'*Looks like mud.*' She sniffs the crotch and looks up at me. '*Your hair's got honey glints which I don't remember from before. Have you been henna-ing your hair?*'

Back in real life, I glanced inside the shop. Julie was still filing her nails and looking gormless but in my head she continues:

'*Wearing these trousers?*'

'*No, I swear!*' I say.

It was no good.

'I can't do it today, I'm too mentally ill,' I thought.

I still had ten days to take them back. Why do today what you can torture yourself worrying about doing for another week or so? As I sloped away I saw Julie craning her neck to look up at something, and followed her gaze and oh my God, it was Steve the Bastard lounging on the branch of a large London plane tree, wearing manly-looking straps and ropes, headphones on and smoking a big joint, 'doing' some tree surgery.

I tossed my hair back (golden glints hopefully glinting in the sunshine), sucked my cheeks in and stopped casually to look in a shop. What a weird thing a cream horn is, I thought. Then, seeing something moving beyond the cream horn, my eyes refocused – on that Kerry-with-the-perm! Mouthing something to, presumably, that Moira-the-manageress-with-the-fat-arse. I was staring into Crusties! Moira came looming towards me, grinning and waving. I turned and ran away, aware all the time of Steve's eyes boring into my back, no doubt thinking 'Look at her, she runs like a gazelle, she is so beautiful and courageous, what have I done? I love her and I want her back.'

I could see Lucille typing away in the window of the *Boxford Gazette* office and waved up at her. She looked a bit annoyed but when I mimed eating and drinking motions she nodded and disappeared from the window.

In the café I was buying a large builders tea to take away, but I couldn't find my fiver and had to take everything out of my purse.

'I just feel so confused,' I said to Lucille.

'Maybe you'd feel less confused if you tidied out your purse.'

'I didn't mean that! Anyway I like having a purse stuffed with bus tickets and receipts – it makes me feel a sense of mystery about my life, like random events might befall me; the chaos means I'm living on the edge, that anything could happen.'

'Like not being able to find your fiver.'

Oh, what was the point of discussing philosophy with Lucille?

'I *meant* I feel confused about Steve.'

On a bench in the graveyard off the High Street, Lucille nibbled at her anally retentive packed lunch. She even wrapped her orange in silver foil.

'So I thought maybe I should just phone Steve and ask him to the theatre to see *Othello* for my twenty-first,' I ventured.

Lucille chewed and her eyes had a faraway look.

'I mean I could say it in a casual way, say I happen to have two tickets . . .'

'No, Edie, don't phone him. He should be calling you. Just let him stew for a bit.'

'Is that what your mum says?'

'Hmm. Actually I'm going to have to do a bit of that with Barry.'

'What? But it all seems so perfect with Barry!'

'Yes it is, but we've been together nearly a year and we're not talking about commitment. So I'm going to cool off a bit.'

'Does that mean we can do something on my birthday, just you and me?'

'Yeah, maybe,' she sighed.

'Poor you,' I said.

What I meant was 'Hurray!!'

I was obviously not a true friend to Lucille because I was instantly cheered up. I needed her to have a problem too. It gave me the energy to get the bus to our old school, Boxford Comprehensive, where the photography evening class was, and pick up a prospectus. I started glancing through it – there was so much I could do! Photography, ceramics, American history – my new life was about to begin! I felt really excited; I was going to forget about Steve, get my life on track before my twenty-first birthday and have a proper friendship with Lucille again.

I bought a giant bottle of red wine on the way home to celebrate.

4
Playing Hard to Get

Lucille and I were all snug together in the living room. I was still studying the prospectus, biting my nails to the quick with excitement and she was doing a French manicure.

'Isn't this great, just like the old days!' I enthused.

'Can you move your head, Eed? I can't see the telly.'

'What would you do, ceramics or acrobatics?' I asked.

'Neither.'

'What do you fancy? We could do one together.'

'No thanks. I've had enough of school.'

'But we never went,' I reminded her.

'Can you pass the remote?' she said, dangling her hand towards me, but staring resolutely at the telly. The phone rang. Lucille motioned me not to answer. The answer machine beeped fourteen times. It was Barry – his fourteenth call of the night.

'Lucille babe, are you there yet? I'm worried sick.'

'Lucille,' I said, 'you're being really nasty to Barry. How could you be so cruel?'

'Because it'll get results,' she said, filing aggressively at a nail. 'And he'll be happier for it and so will I.'

'But he might get fed up and stop calling.'

'Then it's not meant to be,' she sighed.

'Oh, right,' I said, pleased. 'So, if I'm doing dressmaking I should do basic pattern cutting immediately before and yoga afterwards to relax.' I added these to the timetable I had drawn out on a big sheet of paper.

'And I should do French as well, that'll be useful for the fashion industry. And Japanese, there's a big media industry over there and they like Western stuff. Gosh, that's nearly half my week full. I won't have time to fit in a job at this rate!'

'Don't be ridiculous, Edie,' said Lucille.

Poor Barry! He was nearly in tears the next time he called.

'I've rung your mum's, Edie's mum's, Sandra's, work … Please babe, pick up the phone. Edie, are you there?'

I looked at Lucille for permission to answer and she shook her head.

'I was really nasty to Steve and he hasn't called at all,' I said.

'Because he knows you don't mean it.'

'I do mean it. If he heard me. What about Early Bird Japanese on a Wednesday morning?'

'Look, Edie, I don't care what you do as long as you pay your rent. You can do Ancient Egyptian Mummy-making if you like,' and she did a horrible high pitched giggle. I covered up Ancient Egyptian Mummy-making on my timetable. She'd be giggling on the other side of her face when I won *Mastermind*.

The phone rang *again*.

'Eeeeedie! Helloooooooo!'

'It's Steve doing a funny voice!' I cried and I leapt to answer the phone.

'Don't!' Lucille yelled.

'Edie,' the answer machine began, 'how could you be so cruel to me when you know I wuv you so very, very much.' My heart started to beat faster. 'Please clean me out! And Mumsie said did you get her *Radio Times*, she needs it now! Love Flopsie. Kiss, kiss, kiss.'

Though deeply disappointed I managed to be brave.

'Thank God! It's only Flopsie!' I laughed gaily and, fuming internally, went down the balcony to my Mum's, to inform her of the latest news on the straw front.

By eleven o'clock Lucille was tucked up in bed with that bastard Binky and his horrible friends. I was adding the finishing touches to my timetable and polishing off the two-litre bottle of screw-top red wine. I had made the same mistake again of buying fizzy red and Lucille had refused to drink it. I was pissed and had hardly noticed that Barry was on the answer machine again ... I just caught the tail end of his message, 'So call me as soon as you get in ...'

I looked guiltily towards the stairs and grabbed the phone.

'Hi Barry!'

'Edie, thank God, what's happened?'

'Nothing! Don't worry, Lucille's in bed, she's fine, I didn't want you to warry, Borry ... I mean worry, Barry ... heh, heh.'

Suddenly Lucille reared up behind me looking like a raging bull in a pink dressing gown.

'What the hell d'you think you're doing?' she growled and snatched the phone off me before heading off to the hall.

'Yes? Oh hi. Have you? I didn't hear the phone ...' she began cordially and banged the door shut behind her.

I drained my wine and looked in the mirror.

'I bet Barry secretly prefers me because I'm soft and muddled up,' I thought.

I was just leaning in to eavesdrop at the door when Lucille came bursting back in, clanking me on the head with the doorknob.

'Edie, maybe if you had more of your own life you wouldn't take such an unhealthy interest in everybody else's.'

'WooOOoo!' I retorted.

Lucille ignored this remark and turned to me, hands on hips. 'Did you call Crusties back?'

'Stop putting pressure on me!' I wailed, rubbing my head. 'I think I might be having a brain haemorrhage!'

'Oh come on, Edie, why don't you just call them tomorrow?'

'I don't want to say no or yes and then regret it. I'm keeping my options open.'

'Like Steve's doing with you?' she said, and left the room.

By 4.35 a.m. I was still tossing and turning in bed, unable to sleep in anticipation of all the fantastic things I would soon be doing. I had pinned the timetable to the wall so I would see it as soon as I woke and kept leaping up to make minor amendments to it, or to add another activity. I was projecting myself more and more into the future. I virtually had my whole life worked out; soon I would be working on my funeral arrangements . . . maybe a disco on a boat across the Channel and a party in Paris?!

'After art school I could go to Spain and paint for a while! I'll need to do Spanish then.' I leapt up, referred to my already dog-eared prospectus and added Spanish on Wednesdays at 8 p.m.

Back in bed my mind continued whirring.

'What about jewellery making? I could get a little shop and

sell my own designs. My Japanese will be useful with the tourists. I could set up a snazzy hotel . . . everyone could come and stay in the holidays!'

I was back at the timetable adding Jewellery Design and Hotel Management and was considering whether Teaching English as a Foreign Language might not be useful when I spotted Tree Surgery.

'Maybe I should do that! Steve and I could set up our own business, get a Jack Russell, live by the sea . . . Stop it! Stop it! Stop it!' I ranted, banging my forehead with my fist, trying to beat my brain into submission. I shook thoughts of Bastard-Features out of my head, wrote 'swim' in a few early morning slots and fell asleep eventually at 6.13 a.m.

My eyes flashed open two hours later. The first image that crossed my mind was Steve, and my stomach slumped. I pushed the image away and as the verbal part of my brain chugged into action the first thought that entered my head was:

'At least I take an interest in other people, and I'm not just part of the new Me, Me, Me generation.'

It was my belated riposte to Lucille from last night, accompanied by a gnawing sensation in my gut. I glanced at the huge timetable in the dimness of my room and thought,

'What's that large poster with writing all over it?'

And then I remembered and started to cry. What was the point? Why was I like this? Why couldn't I just be like everyone else and not do any evening classes, instead of wanting to do 100 million. Still crying self-pityingly, I took my biro to the timetable and crossed nearly everything off, leaving nine classes and a couple of swims. At least that was slightly more realistic.

TIMETABLE Sep '82 — June '83   E. Dudman.

(Mille!!)

	MON	TUES	WED	THURS	FRI	SAT	SUN
6-9	SWIM	Sauna	EARLY BIRD TAI?	Sauna	SWIM	Swim	
9.30-11.00	ASSERT-IVENESS ✓	Biology O'level / ORNATHOLOGY	Assertiveness? Counteracting your potential.	Sculpture	ACROBATICS ✓	Swim	
11.30-2.00	military MIME MOSAICS counting dance	Anger Management counting dance	Pottery ✓ Fulfilling your potential. Pottery ✓	STAIN GLASS FRENCH FRENCH FRENCH ✓	16mm film making / video?	Finish Jumper Photos → Albums Patchwork
1-2	L	C	N	C	H	Salad	Fruit
2.30-4.00		LIFE DWG Best of INT?	meditation	Pattern Cutting or Design ✓ Jewellery	EUROPEAN CINEMA	JOG RAMBLERS? Join
4.30-6.00 (10ish)	screen writing	SPANISH FRENCH SPANISH ✓	PIANO * gardening?	DRESS MAKING In FLORISTRY	HAIR DRESSING (2) ✓	STACC! PORTOBELLO
6-7	YOGA TEACHER TRAINING ✓	Hotel Management or Sign Language (MUM) for people with mental health difs.	French ✓	6-7 YOGA	BUS KIDS? other centre	LONELINESS ALONENESS + CREATIVITY?
7-9	EGYPTIAN MUMMY MAKING AEROBICS	MASSAGE FOR WOMEN.	8 SPANISH GREEK?	PHOTOG ✓		DRESS UP! GO OUT!
9-11	RELAX					CLUBS?

READ CLASSIC NOVELS — 1 a week!!!

Edie Dudman

L.M.F.H   EDITH DUDMAN   STEVE BONIFACE   Love!   P.33

I felt like shit. People think you can't feel ill at twenty but I am living proof that you can feel ill virtually all the time at twenty. Physically *and* mentally. Lucille was always poo-pooing my major physical illness. My brain tumour she dismissed as 'just a headache', my strokes as 'tiredness', my blackouts as 'momentary losses of concentration', my rheumatoid eczema as 'dry skin', my kidney stones as a 'stitch' and my angina as 'wind'. But she wasn't so quick to dismiss my mental illnesses – like my multiple personality disorder, my paranoid schizophrenia or my manic depression. I was feeling very ill, obviously, but I was also feeling very cross so I decided today was the day to take my black stretch jeans back. I took out my 3rd draft script I had been working on and started rehearsing my lines. 'Look, Bitch . . .' I began.

In the bathroom I stood at the sink as it slowly filled up with hot water. I did one brush of my teeth and then spotted the mascara. Leaving the toothbrush in my mouth, I picked up the mascara, took the lid off and began to apply it. I caught sight of myself in the misted-up mirror. A blob with fine flat brown hair, a toothbrush sticking out of my mouth, mascara on one set of eyelashes, water overflowing onto my feet.

Tears pricked again at my eyes.

'Oh, for God's sake do one thing at a time! That's the trouble with me, I want to do everything, so I don't do anything. I hate myself!'

And I slumped onto the loo to pee. I tried to do some more crying but suddenly, miraculously, I felt better. A calm feeling flooded through me. I glanced in my knickers. A speck of blood. So that was it! That explained the enthusiastic planning of a new life, either in Spain or Scotland, inexplicably combined with feelings of futility and pointlessness. And now the rapid evaporation of both. My period.

I looked across at Lucille's mini chest of drawers. The drawers were marked 'Light Flow', 'Medium Flow', 'Heavy Flow' and 'Night-time Pads'.

There is such a thing as being *too* organized, you know, Lucille, I thought.

But quite useful too, and I nicked two super tampons and a night-time pad and went back to bed.

The phone rang and the answer machine clicked on. Lucille and I both waited for poor Barry's plaintive tones. But 'A message for Edith' a voice said. My heart leapt. 'It's Steve, *definitely*, doing a funny voice, no one else calls me Edith!' I cried.

'Don't!' Lucille shouted.

But it was too late.

'Hello?' I said casually.

Lucille was mouthing, 'Be unavailable'.

'At this time of night?' I said into the phone.

Lucille did a thumbs-up sign.

'That would have been lovely but I've got a few other things lined up. Tomorrow morning? That's impossible, I'm afraid.'

Lucille was nodding her encouragement.

'Er, no, the thing is, I've slipped my disc.'

Lucille looked unsure; maybe I was going too far?

'OK, I'll try and hobble down there,' I said.

'That's marvellous,' said Moira from Crusties. '7.45 tomorrow morning then.'

I had been *genuinely* hard-to-get with Crusties and it had worked. They were keener than ever. My being pretend hard-to-get hadn't worked on Steve at all.

'That wasn't bad at all,' Lucille said. 'It was a shame you agreed to meet him, but still, you sounded pretty disinterested.' It was the nicest thing she'd said to me in months.

'It wasn't Steve,' I reluctantly admitted.

Lucille looked disappointed.

'It was Crusties. I'm starting tomorrow.'

Her face lit up again. 'That's brilliant Edie! That's great! You'll feel so much better having some routine to your days.'

'It's only part-time.'

'Oh well, maybe they'll like you and give you a full-time post!'

She didn't understand me at all.

5

She's My Best Friend and I Hate Her

Next morning, there I was, in the brown and white checked nylon dress and hat with the Crusties logo. Moira was fussing round me. Kerry had just come in, late, and was sitting at one of the tables, feet up, smoking a fag and reading the *Mirror*.

'Now Edith, love. Could you go on the snack bar? It's very easy. Mornings it's mainly tea and coffee and then lunchtime, rolls, sarnies, hot pies and sausage rolls etc and soup. I'll show you the ropes. Kerry, can you do the rolls and sarnies?'

'Oh Moi, do I have to? I'm knackered.'

'Oh, OK, I'll do them, you supervise Edie.'

Kerry settled back down. Moira set off for the preparation area and kitchen at the back of the shop, calling back, 'Mr Pollock's coming in after lunch so I want it spick and span!'

'Moi's having a thing with Mr Bollock so she gets a bit flustered. He's a right tosser, treats her like shit,' Kerry said without looking up from the *Mirror*.

'Is he really called Mr Bollock?'

'Yeah, weird name, isn't it? I think it's South African.'

By lunchtime I was having a nightmare behind the snack bar. I was very agitated as there was a huge queue and someone had just asked for a large tomato soup and a sausage in a soft roll. I'd done the soup in its Styrofoam cup and there was sandwich paraphernalia on every surface so I put it in front of the till. 'I must move that soup before I ring up the till' I mentally chanted as I negotiated the sausage into the soft roll. I then rang up the till without moving the soup and the drawer thwacked orange gloop all down my uniform.

Kerry fired machine gun laughter at me from behind the bread counter. 'I always did that, didn't I, Moi? First couple of years!' she yelled.

'Yes,' Moira said anxiously. Had she got another klutz on her hands?

Moira handed me a damp cloth that smelt of old vegetables and bleach and took over the snack bar whilst I daubed ineffectually at my brown, white and orange uniform, tears pricking my eyes.

'Greg!' Moira warbled. I looked up.

A man in his forties had appeared in the doorway, all suspicious glassy eyes, beige mac and trimmed beard.

'Greg,' Moira repeated. And then said proudly, 'This is our new girl, Edith. Edith, this is the area manager.'

He looked at my soupy dress.

'Nice to meet you, Mr Bollock.'

There was a silence with something funny going on in it.

'What did you say?' he said.

'Nice to meet you,' I repeated and then, losing my confidence, 'Mr . . . Bollock?'

'PPPPollock . . .' he spat. 'And get that uniform washed, girl!'

Kerry burst out laughing and a few people in the queue tittered as a vision flashed across my brain of taking the vat of soup and pouring it over Mr Bollock's head. But I didn't have the nerve and it would be one of my bigger regrets later in life.

Instead I just smirked like a schoolgirl whilst he stalked into the back like a bloodhound in a mac, sniffing for things to complain about. Moira scurried after him.

'I've saved you a donut, and cut it up how you like it, Greg.'

'"Mr Pollock" in shop hours, Moi.'

'Sorry Gre– Mr Pollock.'

By the end of my first shift I was absolutely dropping; I felt like I'd been there a week. I fell asleep on the bus, a delicious, head-bobbing, dribbling slumber. I decided I deserved a hot bath when I got in. Luckily the immersion was switched on. I looked in Lucille's cupboard of juicy cosmetics and sploshed some of her Fenjal into the bath water.

I was just dozing off, foam up to my ears, when three loud thuds sounded on the door.

'Edie! You'd better not be in the bath? I programmed the water to come on because I've had an exhausting day!'

I stayed very still and didn't answer. Eventually she cloinked away and I heard her tut at the still unwashed pile of washing up. It was simply not exhausting to be Lucille! I ran through in my mind a typical Lucille day:

'Walk, walk, walk, not investigating anything or having fearful thoughts, type, type, type, munch, munch, munch, ooh, do the crossword, spend, spend, spend, no doubt, no analysis, type, type, type, tut, laugh, laugh, head empty so can plan baths, meals, tidy out purse etc.'

OK, I may not be a nurse or anything but my day at Crusties *had* been very demanding.

'*I've* had an exhausting day as well,' I pronounced as I entered the kitchen. 'Crusties was exhausting, my rheumatoid eczema has come up. I had to have a bath . . .'

'I thought Fenjal would be bad for your eczema?'

I was speechless. For a nano-second.

'Any messages?'

'None from Steve.'

'Maybe I . . .?' I reached for the phone.

'Don't phone him.'

'At least I'd have a boyfriend for my birthday. He's still nice sometimes.'

'When?'

'When he calls me Whalepup or Woolly Monkey.'

'Hmm.'

'OK, we don't communicate very well verbally but we still have quite exciting sex – we were really happy for the first six months.'

'And miserable for the last eighteen.'

'Maybe it's me, *I* messed it up.'

'*Edie.*'

'You're right, I won't phone him. Anyway I don't care. I think we should have fun being single again. I mean we're young, we should. You're right, Steve is a bit of a wanker and let's face it Barry's really boring. We can have another girly night in, get a curry. There's a juicy night on telly . . .'

Then I noticed Lucille had a bulging bag of food from M&S.

'Ooh, what are we having?'

'Um, Edie . . .'

'What?'

A tap at the kitchen window alerted me to Barry, face pressed Cubist-style against the frosted glass, hands clutching a large bunch of flowers and a bottle of champagne.

49

'Barry and I met for lunch today and well . . .'

Lucille held out her manicured hand to me. Stupidly I went to shake it, even though I'd met her many times before. Barry was still grinning inanely through the window.

'Ri–ight,' I said, still shaking Lucille's hand. 'What did you have?'

'Edie! Look!' she said, snatching her hand away from my enthusiastic shaking and proffering it again.

I looked. A giant ring sparkled in the strip lighting.

'Why don't you have a glass of champers with us?' she chirruped.

'Traitor, traitor, traitor,' I ranted as I stomped along the balcony.

'Oi, young woman, you short-changed me for my prescription yesterday!' Jervis called.

'No I did not!' I yelled, and on I stomped.

'Edie, come back!'

'Oh, you remember my name now!'

As I crossed the quad, there was my Mum, lying on her sun lounger quaffing wine, and Buster sitting on his spade. They looked thick as thieves.

'There she is! Edie!' Buster yelled.

'What's wrong, dear?'

'Nothing!' I screeched.

Ali's grumpy wife was serving in the shop, which was good. I could keep my murderous expression on and slam the washing up liquid on the counter without any niceties. As I stormed back past my Mum and Buster something horrible dawned on me.

'If you're plotting anything to do with my birthday you can forget it!'

They both looked like they had no idea what I was talking about. Yeah, good one.

In the kitchen I slammed the washing up liquid down as hard as I could on the table but still Lucille and Barry didn't look up from their love huddle on the sofa. It was an outrage!!

'Pretending to cool off with Barry, and now they're engaged! Engaged at twenty! How ridiculous! Like playing grown-ups. I'm much happier anyway. Lucille just holds me back. She'll probably want to move Barry in now which is good, it'll force my hand. I'll have to move on and start my new life.'

I drained the rest of the champagne.

'Traitor, traitor, traitor,' I ranted as I did the entire pile of washing up, crashing and banging and hoping the noise would keep Lucille and her *fiancé* (said in nasally Northern accent) awake.

6

Just a Little Disco on an Open-top Bus

I woke up with the manic excitement one sometimes experiences after a bitter blow. It's nature's way of keeping you going. I felt energized by Lucille's traitordom. I felt like ME again. This was the debate that had been raging about my birthday – IGNORE IT vs MAKE GREAT BIG FUSS.

I had neither casually ignored it nor managed to organize anything. Why was I always choosing between two things? Two things that were either almost exactly the same – like two pairs of the same trousers both in a size 12, one a bit twisty on the seamline, the other a bit bulgy on the pocket – or two things that are so different that they shouldn't be in the same thought process. Like a Barn Dance on a Double Decker Bus versus An Early Night. I decided I was going to organize something simple for my birthday *and* I was going to enrol for the nine classes I had more realistically opted for. I only worked at Crusties four four-hour shifts a week; temporarily it was giving me a sense of normality. I could organize my new life around it like clothes on a dummy and then get rid of the dummy.

'I thought you said you were ignoring your birthday,' said

Buster, who had managed to wheedle his way in for a coffee again.

'Yes, yes, but I was thinking I could invite everyone out for a drink – or a meal and then a drink? What about the theatre? After all it is my twenty-first. Then a meal then a drink. No, the theatre's not very sociable . . .'

'I think I've got piles,' was Buster's contribution.

'Maybe I should have a huge party? I could hire the upstairs of a pub . . . or a hall. A meal in a restaurant could be nice . . . or everyone meet in a club? What d'you think, Buster?'

'I think the drink idea's easier. My fucking arsehole!' he growled, shifting his potential piles around on his chair.

'Maybe I should do something really exciting? What about one of those river boats? Or I could get a DJ and have a disco? Or hire a double decker bus and drive everyone down to Brighton? Or a disco on a double decker bus to a boat then a boat round the coast to Brighton?' I took a deep breath. 'After all it is my twenty-first.'

In my head I pictured myself laughing with a glass of champagne on top of a double decker bus. My hair was blonde and I was wearing a vaguely familiar black velvet cocktail dress with a big bow on it. I was surrounded by a crowd of people, but their faces were blurred.

'I think you should just stick with the drinks. After all, isn't your birthday tomorrow?' Buster said.

'Oh don't try and put a damper on it, can't you be encouraging for once?'

'Who's everyone?'

'What?'

'"Everyone down to Brighton", you said.'

'Well,' I said, looking around in my head for the list of

names to match the numbers on the people-shaped outlines on top of the bus. 'You. Um, Lucille and Barry, I s'pose, though I could do without them there. Um, that's three, potentially. Not Steve, because we've split up. Mum, my brothers Pat and Mark. Oh god, Mark won't like anywhere smoky. Er, Jervis, that's seven ... Oh no, that means somewhere with disabled access ... Oh, and the gang from work! Kerry, Moira and Mr Pollock maybe. Ten. That won't fill a bus. It'll be awful!'

My vision dissolved – my terrible 'everyone', in all their garish detail, popped off the bus. I no longer laughed with champagne on the bus – I was alone in the gutter, crying into half a bitter, contemplating throwing myself under the bus.

'It's too late, my birthday's tomorrow, for God's sake. I'm going to ignore it.'

'The drinks idea's OK though, isn't it?'

'No!' I snapped.

'But you said . . .'

'Stop reminding me of what I said, I wasn't in my right mind, it's irrelevant now! The whole thing's off!'

'What about a theme party?' I thought as I arranged the tomato in the cheese baps in the back of Crusties. 'Or maybe

I should organize a drink after work? That's what normal people do.'

'Kerry?' I said out loud.

She was busy coughing over a crate of cream cakes. 'Yeah?'

'D'you fancy coming out tomorrow night for my birthday? Just a drink. Or that quiz night at the George the IV?'

'Oh yeah! Quiz night! I could do with a night out. Blinding! I'll get Fuckface to babysit.' Fuckface was her term of endearment for Fred, father of Blaize, two, and Curtis, one.

'Ooh, that'd be lovely, wouldn't it Kerry?' Moira said when I invited her. 'A quiz night! Greg loves quizzes.'

Well that was it! I'd organized something now. There was no going back. But I did allow myself a weeny vision of myself, Kerry, Moira and Mr Pollock at the quiz night and it was a bit Half a Bitter and not very Champagne.

I had my Top Shop bag containing my black stretch jeans in one hand – hoping I might get the urge to face Julie on the way home – and my dog-eared prospectus in the other. I'd seen it was the last possible day to enrol for classes and it was now 6.27. Three minutes left. I stood on the steps of my old school and stared at the double doors. Gritting my teeth, I pushed them open and stepped in.

'Oh God, it smells like school. I'm too old to go to college. By the time I've got my A levels and stuff I'll be ancient, like twenty-two!' Just then, I heard a motorbike roar past. 'Steve?!' Maybe he had come to rescue me? 'Maybe it's better to stay with your first love. If I get any cleverer it'll be hopeless, Steve's so thick. Maybe if I could get him to stop smoking dope . . .' Just then I spotted someone familiar – greying hair, dandruff on polyester shoulders, tortoiseshell glasses . . .

Mr Howard! My old English teacher! He was going to see that his premonition about me ruining my life was right! I turned away ashamed. He was chatting to some sixth formers, trendy seventeen-year-olds giggling and clutching folders and sports bags.

'I can't do it! I can't do it!' and I was just about to run out when I heard a voice. A shaky old lady's voice.

'Oil Painting for Beginners, love. I wish I'd done it when I was younger, but my Bert didn't like it . . .'

I looked round at the enrolment desk. A tiny, trembly old lady stood there, yellowing blue eyes gleaming with excitement. I strode over to the desk and joined the queue.

The bloke in front of me was enrolling when I tuned into the woman at the desk saying, 'Oh, yes, love, you're OK. One place left on Photography A level.'

'Oh no!' I blurted, pushing forward. 'That's the one I wanted!'

She stared at me. 'Please wait till I have served this gentleman. So, Sir, is there—'

But 'Sir' had turned to me. He was tall and potentially handsome, but grubby-looking with round glasses, and a blinking twitch. He had no sense of personal space and leaned in towards me, grinning.

'You can go on a reserve list. I did that last year with Drumming for Health and got on . . .'

'Tut! If I hadn't spent so long looking through the catalogue and just come straight down . . .'

He laughed fruitily, his eyes creasing up. 'Catalogue!' he said. 'That's sweet.' Then he said, 'I know you. You're Edie Dudman. We were in the sixth form together. You were really good at photography, I remember . . . those brilliant pictures of people in the High Street. You had a really good eye. I'm Ralph. Ralph Buchanan.'

Oh yes! Ralph! He played Romeo in the school play and everyone called him a poof for ever more. He was the only Classics student in the sixth form and was known to be brilliant. He was an eccentric loner.

'Anyway, good luck!' he continued. 'Maybe see you in the class!' and he trundled off, dropping papers on his way.

Eileen the enroller cleared her throat.

'So shall I put you on the reserve list for Photography A then?'

'Yes, please.'

She glanced at her watch.

'And there were a few others as well,' I asserted.

She sighed.

'Um, Spanish on Wednesdays.'

'Full.'

'Pottery Thursday.'

'Full.'

'OK, Acrobatics.'

'Full.'

'Early Bird Japanese Wednesdays, that can't be full.'

'You're right.'

'Thank God.'

'Cancelled,' she said.

'And one more. Massage. I was going to make money doing it while I'm at college doing my degree. I had it all planned.'

'Hang on. No, sorry, Macramé, full.'

'Massage I said.'

'No you didn't.'

'How would I make money at macramé?'

She ignored me. 'There's some space left in Massage and Relaxation for Women.'

'Hallelujah!'

'However you've missed the first class, Backs, but the second class, Fronts, is about to start, you could go straight in now.'

'But,' I looked at my watch. I had my whole evening planned. *Coronation Street* and *Dallas* with a huge pile of steaming dinner. Then I saw the massage students filing into the main hall. They looked decidedly pervy, and one had a hunchback. I had a horrific vision of them all massaging my front. One of them was saying, 'Let me massage your aching boozies for you, Miss!'

'Oh what a shame, I can't. I'm due at work in twenty minutes. I'm a nurse, you see.'

I was going for the sympathy vote but Eileen just stared at me. I could tell she didn't totally believe I was a nurse.

'So I'll just stick with being on the reserve list for Photography please.'

I arrived home feeling secretly relieved and very much looking forward to my steaming dinner in front of *Coronation Street*. But Lucille and Barry were ensconced on the sofa tittering.

Lucille glanced at my prospectus. 'Did you enrol in your classes?'

'They were all full.'

'What, even Ancient Egyptian Mummy-making?' Lucille said, smirking.

Barry sniggered.

'Some classes were cancelled.'

'Ah, Edie that's awful,' Lucille said and they both did that trying-not-to-laugh throat noise.

'I only got on the reserve list for the photography,' I said.

'Oh well, you'd never've stuck with it anyway,' Lucille said, fondling Barry's ear.

'I would've done! I desperately wanted to do that photography class. I'd set my heart on it!'

'Maybe someone will drop out and you *will* get on the course,' Barry added helpfully.

'I won't, I won't! I never ever get the things I really, really, really want!' and I stormed out of the room dramatically, stomped upstairs to my room and flung myself on my bed. I waited for Lucille to come up after me. After fifteen minutes – at last! – she called up.

'Edie!'

'What?' I croaked expectantly.

'Me and Baz are just popping out to the Dervish Kebab! See you later!' and the front door slammed. And then I heard them laugh. Laugh! When *I* was on the verge of a breakdown.

'I should never have cooled off with Steve. Why did I listen to Lucille? It's not in my nature to not phone Steve. Dear Steve, my first love, he can't help being dim about relationships.'

REASONS WHY I SHOULDN'T PHONE STEVE
1) He is horrible.
2) He is a bit thick.
3) He never phones me.
4) He is the reason why I failed my A levels and work in Crusties.
5) He'll make me more, not less, lonely.

REASONS WHY I SHOULD PHONE STEVE
1) I'm going to.

In my bedroom I snatched up the phone and dialled. He answered almost straight away.

'Yeah?'

'Hi, it's me, Edie, how are you?'

'Cool.'

'Sorry, what was that? How am I? I'm a bit down actually. Thanks for asking. Lucille and Barry are engaged and it made me feel a bit funny.'

'We're not getting engaged,' he said.

'I know! God. It's just that I feel she's not my friend any more . . . she's gone all grown up.'

'Just tell her to ferck erff.'

'Hmm,' I said, 'I could try that. Er, d'you want to do something for my birthday?'

'When?'

'On my birthday,' I said. 'Tomorrow.' I attempted a gay laugh.

'Yeah maybe.' I could hear him lighting a joint. His voice was doing that strangled-holding-smoke-down thing. 'Could get a quick curry I s'pose.'

'Er,' I said. 'Well, I thought maybe we could go to *Othello*?'

'Nah, the Delhi Princess.'

'OK. Shall we meet in the Packhorse first? About seven?'

'OK. See you around,' he drawled.

'Well, tomorrow night?'

When I put the phone down I tried to feel pleased. But rage was bubbling up. Why did I do that? All that self-control, and then Poof!

I knew I couldn't go and meet him. I had to cancel. Or not turn up. That was the best thing to do. Not go. He didn't give a shit about me – he could suffer waiting for me in the pub all night. What I would do was cancel Kerry and Moira – they would be desperately disappointed but, well, I had to think about Number One. That's what Thatcher and all the stripy-shirted yuppies said. I was pretty sure Mum would've organized a 'surprise do' so I would make her and the others happy, make a brave appearance and then go home, curl up in a ball and wait for my birthday to be over. I phoned Steve back but it just rang and rang. Where had he gone? It was quarter past midnight!

7

Trying to Think of Me, Me, Me on this Special Day

On the 30th of September I woke up, remembered who I was and wanted to die. That's not a nice way to feel on your twenty-first birthday. I resolved to phone Steve as soon as I got up and cancel our 'arrangement'. Lucille stood over me with a tray with a flower (a yellow and brown carnation bud from Barry's bouquet), a card and a cold cup of tea.

'Is that the post?'

'No, it's only 10 past 8,' she said and sat on my bed.

'I haven't had enough sleep,' I said accusingly. 'The day's ruined already.'

'Why don't you spend tonight with me and Baz, we're going out with his parents for a meal. Why don't you join us?'

'No, it's OK, I'm going out with the crowd from work.'

'Oh, that's nice Edie! It's great you've made friends there.' She had yet to meet Kerry and Moira and her look of relief that she didn't have to deal with me was very hurtful.

'It's not nice at all. I'm going to cancel it and spend the evening on my own. It's what I want.'

'Oh OK! You should do what you want on your birthday,' she said. Couldn't her unimaginative brain see that I was crying out for help?

* * *

As I made myself a cup of tea there was a ring on the doorbell. I could see a large square shape through the frosted glass.

I couldn't believe it! 'It's Steve with a great big present!'

My not-ignoring-him technique had worked! Lucille was wrong ... he just needed reminding, encouragement, reassurance, love, warmth – all the techniques that came naturally to me.

I flung open the front door and was greeted by a haystack on legs.

'What do you want, Buster?' I asked obtusely.

'Got you the hay for Flopsie! Happy birthday!' and he handed me a leaf with 'Luv and x's Buster' on it in Magic Marker.

I sat in front of Buster at the kitchen table being vile, sifting through my birthday cards without bothering to open them. 'Auntie Evelyn, Dad and Pam – they can fuck off – Mum, Flopsie, brothers. Nothing from Wank Features.' But Buster didn't seem to want to 'shoot off' or 'see me around'.

'There's still the second post,' he said kindly.

'Oh yeah!' I said excitedly, then amended my tone back, 'Oh well, there'll be nothing from him in that post either. Hopefully.'

Round my Mum's I was quickly cleaning out Flopsie on the balcony. Buster stood over me claustrophobically, slurping his tea.

'So! twenty-one!' Buster said.

'Yeah,' I sniffed.

'Twenty-one's a good age.'

'Did you enjoy it?'

'No, but you might.'

'I won't.'

'Yeah, I s'pose we've had our best years. And they weren't very good.'

'My favourite birthday was my nineteenth because I'd just met Steve and he was still all romantic. We went to Virginia Water, "where the trees are nice in Autumn" he said, on his motorbike and drank champagne up a tree, it was amazing.'

'I was sick with jealousy. Of that bike.'

'And he gave me this gold bracelet with "All My Love Steve" on it.'

What had happened? Why didn't he give me 'all his love' any more? What had I done? Surely I could make him love me again.

'Why don't you . . .?' Buster broke in.

'What?'

Buster was trying and failing to sound bright.

'Why don't you take the day off? And I'll take you to Virginia whatever – on the train, obviously – and we could take a picnic.'

'Er, we could.'

I imagined me and Buster up a tree. He was sitting too close and doing loud eating, not unlike the loud eating of a biscuit he was doing right then in real life.

'Um, that's sweet of you Buster, but I've got to go to work.'

'Yeah, it probably wouldn't be any good with me anyway. I'd probably just get on your nerves,' he said, crumbs in his stubble.

'Of course you wouldn't! Jesus!' I snapped.

We leant over the balcony and stared mournfully into our

coffees.

'Sorry, Buster.'

'S'alright', he said.

'Look, don't make me feel guilty!'

'I'm not.'

'Sorry, Bust.'

I looked through the balcony doors at my Mum in her Parker Knoll with Flopsie on her lap, staring with her mouth open, trying to hear our conversation. Though how she was going to hear through her mouth God alone knows.

I was very tempted to wait for the second post but I was already late for work. I phoned Steve from a phone box on my way to Crusties but he hadn't answered after three rings and there was a threatening-looking man waiting to use the phone.

When I got to Crusties the closed sign was on the door but all the buns, cakes and bread were present and correct in the window. I peered in. No one. I banged on the door. Nothing. So I got down on my hands and knees and screamed through the cat-eye level letter box, 'Moira!!!!!!' Moira came scurrying out from the back, drying her hands on her apron, and let me in.

'Happy birthday, love!' she said, leaning behind the snack bar and producing a huge pink envelope. Brilliant! One of those giant birthday cards with loads of signatures on. I'd always wanted one of those! I ripped the envelope open, glanced at the bunny clutching a gold embossed 21 on the front and heaved it open.

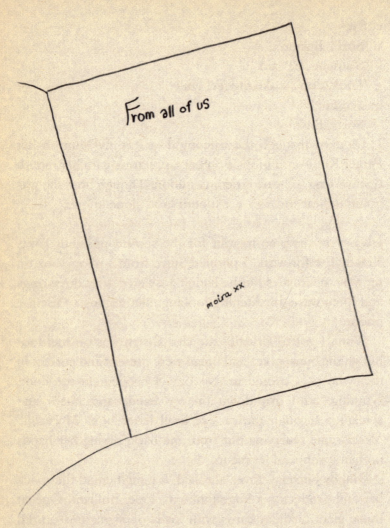

From all of us

moira xx

'Sorry, love. I meant to get everyone to sign it but no one's been in. I've no idea where Kerry's got to.'

'For fuck's sake, you two ignoramuses! What's been going on? I'm fucking soaking!' Kerry came literally steaming in.

'Moira,' I explained. 'You didn't open up.'

'Didn't I?' Moira's eyes filled with tears. 'Oh, you clever girl! What would I do without you? You're a little angel sent from heaven.'

'Oh that's nice!' yelled Kerry, scrunch-drying her perm over the heater. 'What about me?'

'You're both my little angels!' and she pulled us towards her ample bosom. Kerry winked at me and mouthed, 'Bollock must be due in,' and then, in her sweetest baby voice, 'Moi? Can we have a weeny liccle cweam cake?'

'Course my little dears, you can have whatever you like!' she said dreamily. 'And I've got a special birthday present for you, pet!'

She handed me a parcel. It was big and squidgy and probably clothing. Always exciting! And usually disappointing. But this took the biscuit. It was a brand new Crusties' uniform! In a size *14/16*! The cheek!

But then I thought maybe this is just what I need. A nice normal job. A nice – OK not nice but *a* – boyfriend and just be normal and get on with it. Then I felt a warm glow as I imagined Steve's shapely lips coming towards mine. Tonight, if I didn't cancel.

'At least I can get a thick jumper under my new uniform in the winter!' I told myself positively and I kissed Moira on the cheek. But then I remembered – I'd arranged to go out with Moira and Kerry tonight. Oh God, they were so excited about it! They would be really disappointed. Kerry would be cross – she'd probably call me something really horrible, she'd got a babysitter and everything. Moira would be gutted – she loved me so much, she was lonely, this was probably her social event of the year. But I had to metaphorically put on a stripy shirt and red braces. I had to think of Me, Me, Me. I cleared my throat nervously.

'Um, Moira, Kerry?' I said.

'Yeah?' said Kerry.

'Oh, look I'm really sorry. It's about tonight. Steve's planned a surprise meal for me, you see. Straight after work. Immediately after work. So unfortunately we can't go for a drink.'

'Eh?' Kerry said.

'Drink?' Moira said.

'No, no drink, Moi. Sorry.'

'Oh right! I . . . don't understand?'

'I'm sorry, I can't make the drink for my birthday tonight. We could go tomorrow instead?'

'I need more notice than that, Edie, I've got two kids.'

Neither of them were in the least bit gutted – they had both forgotten!

'So Edie, love, where's Steven taking you?'

'Oh, it's a surprise!'

'Up town?' Kerry asked.

'Yeah, probably.'

'You lucky bitch!'

Maybe I *was* lucky, I thought. Maybe I was too fussy? Maybe I was really happy but I just didn't realize it? Maybe I could still make a go of it with Steve after all?

At lunchtime, feeling more excited about my date after my fake telling of it to Moira and Kerry, I popped into Miss Selfish to finally take back my black stretch drainpipe 'tights'.

I had all my answers to everything Julie might say ready.

But she said 'Credit or refund?' with only a cursory glance at my trousers.

I was quite disappointed, as I had enough adrenaline

pumping round my body to fuel at least a heated debate, if not a full physical fight. I was tempted to point out the henna stain myself so I could deny it was henna or chocolate and see if she noticed my honey glints.

'Credit please,' I said. 'I'll choose something now.'

'Goin' out?'

'Yeah, Steve's taking me out later, for my birthday.'

'Oh, when's your birthday?'

'Well. Today.'

I ignored a niggling feeling that Steve and Julie's similar powers of deduction meant they were made for each other.

'Oh,' she said, and a most satisfying jealous look flashed across her big green eyes.

In the changing room I was struggling into a 'pretty dress' as Mum would describe it, when Moira came in with the same dress but, obviously, a gianter version.

'Oh, hello Edie, love,' she gushed. 'I'm entertaining Gre– Mr Pollock – tonight – if he can get away – we're going over some figures.'

Aha! so that explained the distraction, the forgetting of my birthday drinks and the gooey goodwill to all sales assistants. I knew what figure Bollock would be going over tonight and it was rather large for that size 14 dress. But Moira squeezed the dress on to the accompaniment of the sound of seams splitting and admired herself in the mirror. It looked ridiculous.

'What d'you think?'

'It looks nice,' I lied. I definitely wasn't going to buy my version.

'I'm going to splash out! Mr Pollock likes me in feminine dresses. See you back at the ranch!' she said excitedly and was gone.

'God, she really is a woman who loves too much,' I thought, as a rejected red leather mini-skirt caught my eye on the other side of the changing room. I stared at it. I glanced at myself. Why not? I was young, I was slim, it was my twenty-first birthday and after all, Steve liked me in short skirts.

'Did he phone you then?' Lucille said in an amazed voice, staring at my new mini-skirt.

'Yup,' I said. 'He's taking me out tonight.'

'Gosh! So the being cool actually worked.'

'Yeah.'

'I told you. Make sure you don't slip into your old ways though.'

'What do you think of the new outfit?'

'Looks great,' she said.

Barry looked at me anxiously. 'It doesn't seem right seeing you in a sexy outfit, Eed. I prefer you in those men's slippers and that old man's cardi. You look cute.'

'Lucille wears sexy outfits,' I reminded him.

They both smiled patronizingly at me.

'You look great, Edie,' Lucille said, smacking Barry's hand mock reprimandingly and managing to make me feel very silly.

'Sorry, darling,' my Mum said later, as she handed me her present. Not wrapped. Still in the plastic bag. The 'Wanda's Women's Outfitters' bag.

'You can take it back, the receipt's in there. Wanda's expecting you,' she gabbled.

I held up the beige blouse against myself and Mum put on her glasses hopefully.

'What a fiasco! I made loads of hints about ice skates.'

'Did you?' Mum said. 'Dear, that skirt's awfully short.'

'Oh, you never want me to look sexy!'

'Don't I?' she said, as though she hadn't realized I *did* look sexy.

She looked extra anxious; there was some sort of split screen effect going on, like through an SLR camera focus finder. Her eyeballs were all jumbled up so the top half was all skewhiff from the bottom.

'What are those glasses?' I demanded.

'Oh, they're new. They're bifocals. They're marvellous! Look! Look down to see the *Radio Times* and then up to see the telly!'

'It's no good being jolly about your glasses, it won't cheer me up. So when are the others arriving?'

'What others?'

'Don't tell me you haven't arranged the usual thrilling surprise tea party with Mark and Pat and Sandy, Georgie and the kids?'

'But dear . . . you said no fuss.'

'But it's my twenty-first birthday! It's not as though I didn't keep hinting.'

'Where is the hint in "I'm definitely not doing anything for my birthday, if you organize a surprise I will be furious"?'

'I didn't mean it!'

'Well, the surprise is that I haven't organized a surprise!' And she cackled uncontrollably, then coughed uncontrollably and then farted. 'Oops, sorry!' But she didn't look sorry. This was her party trick. It was to do with pieces of crisp going down the wrong way. Oh well. There was wine. There were crisps. There were tricks. So I suppose it was a party of sorts.

I looked at the blouse. How could you know someone from birth and not understand – or notice – what they wear?

As if reading my thoughts, Mum said dreamily, 'I remember when you were born. I was so happy to have a daughter.'

'Why did you call me Edith then?'

Why My Mum Called Me Edith

'Did you know anyone nice called Edith?'

'No, I don't think so.'

'Any relations called Edith? Or Edward, even?'

'No.'

'You liked the name?'

'Nope.'

'I looked like an Edith. You looked at my dear little face and thought, "Ah, Edith"?'

'No.'

'Dad liked it?'

'No, he wanted to call you Dorcas.'

'Jesus! Why then?'

'Sorry darling, I just wasn't feeling very well at the time.'

* * *

I tutted loudly, trying to convey to her how she had ruined my life, but I knew that Me by Any Other Name would be just as miserable.

8

Boyfriend in a Coma

It's a very difficult balance, arranging your facial expression when you're on your own in a pub. You don't want to look morose, because then you look lonely or stood-up or both. On the other hand, too much self-generated gaiety and you look drunk or mad or both.

So, perched at a table at the rear of the Packhorse and Talbot, I was attempting a contented smirk hoping to look as though I were running through some amusing memories in my mind. When I ran out of those I re-read the same joke on the back of the three beer mats on the table:

Old lady 1: It's windy, isn't it?
Old lady 2: No, I think it's Thursday.
Old lady 1: So am I, let's have a cup of tea.

After half an hour of this my smirk had dropped from exhaustion and I was frowning, pretending to work out some long division in my head. I was on my third rum and black and was sitting with my thighs arranged to one side and pressed together like they teach you in finishing school, because as soon as I sat down my short skirt slid up my torso in a stiff, tubular fashion, and became a very wide leather belt.

Steve and I had arranged to meet at 7.00. It was now 7.40

and I was trying to resist calling him from the phone on the bar. I would wait until 8.00 and then I would leave. An hour is an outrageous amount of time to be late. There were two old blokes playing dominoes, one of whom I recognized as an old crony of Jervis's from his drop-in centre. I must have been pretending to do a particularly long long division and frowning appropriately, when I caught his eye for the fourteenth time. He winked at me, 'Been stood up Edie, love?'

He was as deaf as a post and shouted this rather loudly so that the sour-faced barmaid, the three young blokes playing pool and the old lady at the bar with the maroon hair and the bottle of stout all turned to look at me.

I squeezed my thighs together extra tight and laughed gaily.

'Oh he's just been held up, he'll be here soon!'

'What love?!' Edgar bellowed.

'He'll be here soon!!'

At that point all heads swung to look at the swing doors which were opening and closing an inch or two, banging and crashing. There was a pause, then they flew open dramatically just as 'Baby Love' blared out from the jukebox. All heads swung down to see Jervis in his wheelchair struggling to wheel himself in before the doors slammed shut again. Of course, he spotted me immediately.

'Oi, Ethel! Give us a push!' he yelled, just as the door crashed back against him. Everyone looked at me and added 1 and 1 together to make 2. OK. Let them think Jervis was my date for now. It was marginally less embarrassing than looking stood up, so I wheeled him over to the domino table, ignoring the faint sniggers emanating from the far corners of the pub.

At 8.00 I phoned Steve but it just rang and rang. He had obviously left to meet me. But then I had a wave of uncertainty. 'He's got the wrong night,' I thought. 'The wrong pub. *I've* got the wrong night. Was it gone midnight when I phoned him last night? He might've thought I meant tomorrow night. Did we definitely say the Packhorse? Or did we say we'd meet in the curry house?' No, I had been over our call a hundred times. I knew what I had said but would his cannabis-addled brain remember?

I phoned again at 8.10, 8.20, 8.26, 8.32, 8.45, and 9.00. The last time I let it ring 129 times. By 9.15 I was playing dominoes with Jervis, Edgar and Ron trying not to mind that I was spending my twenty-first birthday with a disabled octogenarian who called me Ethel. 'Maybe he's had an accident?' I thought. 'He's a liability on that bike. He could be lying somewhere in a coma. Or maybe he's just forgotten. Oh God please don't let it be that, don't let it be that he's forgotten. Please, please, please let it be the coma . . .'

By 10.15 I'd had seven rum and blacks and was possibly forgetting to press my thighs together quite tightly enough because one of the blokes playing pool came over and asked if I fancied a game of doubles. By 10.40 Martin, with the long hair, and I, had beaten Rob, with the twitch, and Trevor, with the neighing laugh, three times. In my mind Steve was happily settled in his coma and I was playing pool with three hunky blokes.

Anyway, if he suddenly turned up it wouldn't do him any harm to see me looking gorgeous, receiving attention from a crowd of men and playing excellent pool. So in case of his sudden entry I was doing lots of over-the-top laughing gaily.

At 11.15 the lights came on cruelly and in real life Martin, Rob and Trevor looked decidedly unattractive so I tried to phone Steve one more time from the phone on the bar. I let it ring 131 times which was perhaps not quite long enough for someone to wake up from a coma but, well, he could stuff it! When I finally hung up and looked round, the pub was deserted. Even Jervis had left! The sour-faced barmaid was holding the door open for me. I gave her my broadest smile and requested to use the Ladies one last time.

In the loo I staggered bullishly over to the mirror and smiled. But the person who smiled back had no teeth. I looked closer and saw that my teeth were completely black. Or, rather, completely blackcurrant. Oh Jesus. I did a bit of the sort of ready-for-Steve loud, gay laughing I had been doing OUT THERE hoping vainly that I hadn't shown my teeth but no – laughing back at me was a toothless hag in a wide red leather belt. I tried to clean my teeth with water and my finger but with no luck, so I hurried through the pub and out of the door, holding my lips together as tightly as I had been holding my thighs earlier and ran all the way home trying to keep in the shadows.

The next morning I woke up on top of my bed, red leather skirt up round my tits, lilac wrap-around top wrapped around my armpits and eyeliner and mascara all over my face. I glanced at the clock – I was late for Crusties! I had got to sleep at 4.30 a.m. as it had taken me several hours, Lucille's electric toothbrush and a whole tub of smoker's tooth powder to get my teeth to a reasonable shade of grey. And then another couple of hours to blub myself to sleep. The most upsetting moment was Lucille shouting from her bedroom, 'For God's sake, Edie, give it a rest!' How would *she* feel if Barry was in a coma? Well, actually, come to think of it . . . though I still didn't know how she felt about it.

I ran into Crusties wearing the same clothes I'd woken up in and crashed into Moira carrying a bread tray. Our bloodshot eyes met over the Split Tins. She looked like she'd been crying as much as me and her eyes were like watery pink dots behind her thick lenses. Her previous day's flowery purchase was peeking out under her uniform.

'Someone's had a good night!' Kerry bleated from the counter. 'Looks like I'm the only one who didn't get a shag last night.'

Moira and I both smiled weakly.

'I'm sorry I'm late, Moira. You can sack me if you like.'

'Ooh, no love, you're alright. It's only a couple of hours. You're not twenty-one every day. Did the uniform fit?'

Oh shit. I had left my new uniform at home and had no choice but to wear my ever-more filthy old one. No one would see it behind the snack bar though, and I pressed the worst of it against the till. Then in stalked Pollock; Moira did a little leap.

'Gre! Er . . . Mr Pollock!' she chirruped.

'The cream horns should be next to the coconut balls,' he replied.

'Sort it out girls!' Moira called to us querulously as she hurried after Mr Pollock into the back. I eavesdropped from my convenient position welded to the snack bar till. I could hear snatches of their conversation while Kerry rearranged the cream cakes in the window.

'I couldn't get away, Moi, Beverly and the girls . . .'

'Oh, but Greg you promised. Oh! It doesn't matter, you're here now.'

There was a worrying kiss-length pause and an 'Oh Greg!' then Pollock was heard to say, 'Don't call me Greg at work and tuck your hair in your hat.'

Then he whisked out, calling back, 'I said I *might* see you at teatime, Moi, but I've got eight other branches to visit. Bye girls!'

'Bye Mr Pollock!' I said in unison with Kerry's 'Bye Mr *Bo*llock!'

Pollock looked at Kerry, eyes slitty with suspicion. She smiled and waved and, as he turned out of the door and passed the window display, he inspected Kerry's rearrangement.

All the cream horns were arranged with the coconut balls to look like male genitalia. His mouth dropped briefly open, Kerry gave him a saucy wink and he hurried on, his eardrums surely vibrating with Kerry's machine gun laugh. She laughed so hard she disappeared under the bread counter. But then we heard poor old Moira sobbing in the back and Kerry sprang up livid.

'God. The way Moi moons over Bollock Features. He's a bloody bastard. If someone let me down like that just once he'd be out on his ear. I wouldn't stand for it. No fucking way!'

'Me, neither,' I said.

'Moi!' cooed Kerry, 'come on, babes, he's not worth it!'

And Moira came heaving out from the back, wiping her glacé cherry eyes and putting her glasses back on.

'Come on, darlin'!' Kerry put her arm round Moira and led her to the counter. 'Come and look at this, this'll put a smile on your miserable old chops.'

Moira stared at the window display. 'Oh you naughty girls!' and they giggled away at the pastry pornography.

I was enjoying their enjoyment until Kerry suddenly said, ''ere Edie, it's that Steve of yours on his way over.'

And sure enough there he was, a picture of health striding through the doorway. My heart started to thud.

'Right, that's it! He's not in a coma!'

He sauntered up to the counter. He didn't have a scratch on him!

'Hello *Edith!* What you doing in here?'

'It's my new job,' I said sternly, feeling myself flush. 'I told you,' I added, as Moira and Kerry were blatantly listening.

'Nice outfit!'

'Yes, well it would've been lovely to see you but I'm rather busy,' I said, doing a poor impression of a gay laugh.

'What you going on about, you daft bat? I just want a cup of tea.' And he smiled over at Moira and Kerry. 'Strong and milky, like my women,' he drawled.

Kerry and Moira giggled, impressed.

'And no sugar. I'm sweet enough.'

Another titter from the audience.

He turned back to me, his stooge. 'Was that you phoning all last night?'

'No,' I said, ripping the polythene off the top of a new tower of Styrofoam cups.

'Well some arsehole was ringing and ringing. I was in the garage mending the bike and every time I went down the garden to answer it the fucker hung up.'

I didn't feel like admitting to being an arsehole or a fucker in front of Kerry and Moira, so I hardened myself.

'Yes, well, here's your tea. I've left the teabag in. See you around.'

'Yeah, see ya,' and he turned to go.

'Hang on a minute!' I called, my real personality leaking out.

Steve turned to me, 'Yeah?'

Moira and Kerry were completely absorbed, elbows on the counter, heads in hands.

'Um, Moi, can I take my break?'

'Of course love, you two go in the back and have a chat.'

'Oh!' said Kerry, disappointed.

In the back I put on the kettle and Steve perched himself on a stool, drumming his fingers on the formica table.

'You were s'posed to meet me last night,' I said, my back to him.

'Oh shit!' he said. 'Was it last night?'

I swung round. 'You forgot!'

'Yeah. Sorry.'

'I waited in the Packhorse for hours.'

'I thought it was today.'

'Well, it was yesterday.'

In my head I knew what I should say. What Lucille would say, what any normal person would say. And I would say it. I would be a normal self-respecting person. Any minute. I would say, 'Well it's not good enough. I'm finished with you for good. Get out and I don't want to see you again.'

But I was forgiving him because, even as his mouth droned, his blue eyes twinkled faux-intelligently.

'Yeah, this morning, right, Gazzer said, "Oi you two, get out of that van and up those trees!" It was pissing with rain, right, and he goes, he goes, "Else I'm going to report you to the gaffer" and we said, "Ferck erff you c-u-n-t."'

'Hmm,' I said out loud. I thought, 'Maybe I'll say, "Look Steve, I want to know what's going on." No don't say that. "Steve, I don't feel like myself with you anymore – I don't feel natural. I don't want to play games, I . . ."' Oh! this wasn't normal, rehearsing what to say, I thought, re-tuning into Steve's 'story'.

'. . . and, right, when he got back, right, Geoff was skinning up and chatting these two birds up . . .'

'What two birds?' I demanded, stomach lurching.

'I don't know,' he said. 'Two birds.'

'Was it that Julie from Miss Selfish?'

'What?' his eyes burned frighteningly.

'Look Steve, I don't know what's going on anymore. I don't feel like myself . . . I don't want to play games . . .'

'What you going on about?'

'Love is letting go of fear,' I pronounced.

'Where did you get that, some women's magazine?' he sneered.

Damn he was right. I'd read it in Moira's *Woman's Realm* only yesterday.

'I want to know what's going on with us. Our relationship.'

He looked panicky. 'What rel-atio-n-ship?' He could hardly

say the word. 'It's just a bit of fun, isn't it?'

'Yes. But . . . I'm not having any fun,' I said bravely, starting to take off my filthy uniform.

'Yeah?' he said, eyeing my leather skirt. 'Well, don't take it off. I like a woman in uniform.'

'It's horrible and filthy,' I said, leaving it half-on, half-off. 'I've got to nip home at lunchtime and get my new one.'

'Phwoargh! Come here my filthy little nylon love goddess.'

He stood up and stepped towards me, pushing me against the sink and sliding his hand between my thighs.

'Where d'you get that naughty skirt?'

I did feeble pushing him away.

'I had it on last night,' I whimpered.

'You can still have it on tonight, can't you?'

'I'm not seeing you tonight,' I thought as he pressed his hard-on against my pubic bone. My brain slipped down into my knickers and I knew I would be seeing him tonight.

As he nibbled gently across from my ear lobe to my lower lip and down my throat and chest, expertly furrowing into my bra with his perfect little teeth and tongue, my love-goo-ed brain heard faint voices.

A male voice – a Dalek? – said, 'The scones are skewhiff.'

A female voice – Minnie Mouse? – answered, 'Sort it out, Kerry! Now!' and, in a softer tone, 'Would you like a donut, I've cut one u . . .'

And louder, nearer, the Dalek again, 'Hello, hello . . . what's going on here?'

Steve and I leapt apart. It was Pollock, looking like a sex-starved weasel.

'It's not a relat-ion-sh-ip . . .' Steve said.

'Oh, really?' said Pollock.

'What is it then, love?' Moira asked, with genuine interest.

'Just a bit of fun?' I offered up.

'That's what *you* say *we're* having, isn't it? Gre– Mr Pollock?'

'Keep out of it, Moira!' Pollock snapped and Kerry burst out machine gun laughing from the front of the shop.

'I'd better shoot off,' Steve murmured. 'Sorry, mate, you know how it is . . .' (Yuck! He was bonding with Pollock!) and he snaked out.

'Come back!' I demanded and pushed past Pollock, chasing Steve out of the shop, Kerry still hooting with laughter.

He was getting in his van.

'What about tonight?' I shouted through the van window.

'What?'

'We can finish what we started,' I said desperately.

'Yeah OK, Pup. Come round mine, Johnny's away,' and he shot off, hooting his horn in a manly fashion.

Oh lovely, lovely, a whole night – me in this skirt, him in those boxers, baby oil, joints, Bob Marley . . . But, as soon as his van disappeared round the corner, I felt cold and weak and disappointed with myself.

'I've completely buggered it up now,' I moaned, as I re-entered Crusties.

Pollock, Kerry and Moira stood in a row. Pollock's eyes were glaring.

'Oh, no, love. Everyone makes mistakes don't they Gre– er– Mr Pollock. Edie's got O levels and everything. I think she'd make good management material.'

I stared defiantly at Pollock, looking forward to the sack.

But his weasely eyes were scanning my – oops! my wraparound top had unwrapped. I gripped the edges of my uniform together but not before he clocked my leather belt.

'Possibly,' he said, massaging his pointy beard.

'Well no,' I said, 'the thing is, it's just a fill-in job while I decide what to do.'

Kerry shot off a few rounds of laugh ammunition. 'Hahahahahaha! That's what I said, didn't I, Moi?'

'Yes, love, and me,' and Moira and Kerry laughed demonically and Pollock forgot himself for a second. His mouth turned up at the corners and opened a fraction as if he were going to say, 'Me too,' but no, he was too mean to admit it.

'Moira! Kerry! Keep out of it! Get on with your work!'

Then he turned to me, 'I'll give you another chance,' he said. 'And get that uniform washed!'

I was awake all night. It wasn't just the post-coital anxiety. It was the present Steve had given me. A Breville Toasted Sandwich Maker. I tried to be pleased when he said it was so that I could make him toasted sandwiches between popping round, having it off with me and shooting off, but I had a lump of disappointment in my stomach. If I could've been myself, or Lucille, I'd've just reacted how I felt and said, 'What the fuck have you bought me this for?' For my nineteenth birthday he had bought me a fluffy little rabbit (alias Flopsie the Hare/Kangaroo cross) and a pair of lavender suede boots with a fringe down the side that I had admired in a shop in Barnes. For my twentieth he had bought me a shop-lifting mirror. And now this. I tried to rationalize it. I tried to find romance in it. But there wasn't any, plus it was a busman's holiday for me now.

— steve's 'compliments' —

No.18 — you've got a bald patch.

alright shitface?

the trouble with you is you think too much.. NO37

No.138 — you're really good at making yourself comfy aren't you?

you've got a fag in your hand in every photo — No.159

No.201 — you look like Benny from 'crossroads' in those dungerees.

what women's magazine did you read that in? No183

some arsehole was ringing and ringing...

9
Positive About Negatives

So there I was

1)   Still going out with Steve i.e. staying in without him
2)   Being left behind in the growing-up stakes by my
     ex-friend Lucille
3)   In another crappy dead-end job.

Staying in without Steve, in my old man's slippers, I was settling myself down for a night of telly. I'd circled my whole night's viewing from 6.00 p.m. to 12.05 a.m. and plonked a steaming pile of food down in front of me. I then had to run upstairs to get my cardi, rummage about in my bag for my lip salve, arrange my fags, lighter and ashtray on the coffee table, leap up and pull the curtains across, plump the sofa up again, get a glass of water and finally, as the front credits for *Crossroads* were just ending, I scraped up a forkful of M&S Shepherd's Pie for two, aimed it at my mouth and the phone rang. Steve had vaguely mentioned 'next week' last week and the old, faded, stretched recording of 'It might be Steve!' warbled distortedly from the dustbin of my brain.

'Hello?'

'Hello, is that Edith?'

'That's a particularly stupid one, Mum . . . no one speaks like that.'

'Hello? Yes, we've got a cancellation for the photography class tonight!'

'Very good, Buster, you sound like an old lezzer with throat cancer.'

'Is that Edith Dudman? It's Eileen McGlarry.'

'Oh is it, indeed?'

She cleared her throat cancer. 'Are you interested in the photography class tonight?'

Oh God. It really was Eileen Something-or-other. From the evening classes.

'Tonight?' I said, staring at my cooling pile of dinner and Sandy from *Crossroads* possibly saying something interesting.

'Right now, love.'

'Right now?'

'Yes, I know how keen you were so I phoned right away.'

'Um, could I start next week?'

'Ooh, no, love. There's a whole list of eager people waiting to get on.'

I imagined eager young attractive people pushing to the front of life.

'Um, is there?'

'Yes, but you're first on the reserve list!'

Suddenly the eager young people morphed into hunchy perverts. 'I'm going to photograph your boozies!' one of them cackled through brown teeth.

'I'll have to give it a miss. Sorry.'

'Oh, have you got a shift?'

'Shift?'

'At the hospital.'

'Buster, *is* that you?'

'You said you were a nurse?'

88

'Oh yes, shift! Yes! No, I haven't.'

'Well, just get here for 7.30 and we'll enrol you!'

'Um, well, the thing is . . . I might have a shift, let me just check. Hang on!'

I looked at the *Radio Times*. *Hateful Relations* was on at 8.00. The nasty dad was having an affair with the blonde fiancée of the son with the curly hair. The glamorous artist mum, who was doing a series of giant paintings about the seven deadly sins in her paint-splatter-free studio, had just got suspicious. It was going to be a really juicy one. Just then the commercial break started and I caught a glimpse of myself in the momentarily blank screen.

'What's my Mum doing on telly?' I thought, staring gormlessly at my gormless reflection and suddenly realizing it was me! It was A Life of Telly vs A Life. And I had to choose now.

'I'll be there at 7.30! Thanks Eileen!' and I wolfed my dinner down and set off.

From the moment I set off there were signs that I shouldn't be going. First of all I couldn't find my coat, my green old lady's coat with the fur collar that my Mum had taken against. I had to wear a horrible 'smart' navy blue one she had bought me. Then, as I rushed along the communal balcony, I saw my old lady's coat sticking out of my Mum's bin again. I pulled it out and quickly took it home. It had tea leaves all over it. I really should have it out with her once and for all. Didn't she want me to look attractive? But when I hurried back past her maisonette the theme tune to *Emmerdale* was blaring out and that strengthened my resolve. Then, when I came out of the lift, Jervis was lying on the ground next to his wheelchair feigning rigor mortis. I might not be a nurse but I was pretty sure shouting isn't one of the symptoms. He demanded I wheel him to the pub as he'd sprained his wrist (not badly enough to prevent him downing at least ten pints of Guinness when he got there though.) I felt guilty. Maybe it was more important to be a responsible member of society than go off trying to have a self-centred career. But as Maggie Thatcher said, there's no such thing as society. Anyway, I bet Jervis wouldn't wheel me to the photography class if *I* was dead.

Then there were no buses for at least 90 seconds. I nearly gave up, but I remembered Lucille and I throwing away professional gymnastics careers for the sake of seven pieces of Sunblest toast (each). When a bus did show up Dean Rumble was driving, looking like he would squeeze my bum again if he had half the chance. Then, when I got off the bus I saw that old lady, the one who had been queuing up for oil painting classes; she was with 'her Bert', the one who hadn't liked her doing anything, and they were holding hands, she looked really happy. She didn't realize what she'd got. What was a few hours' egotistical oil painting compared to a lifetime of love and companionship? But then what if it wasn't Bert – what if it was a new boyfriend who encouraged her to paint and Bert had got the elbow and now she was blossoming in her Autumn years? Sure enough, as I passed them I heard her say, 'Oh Henry, shall we get some chips?' and I kept on going, despite many other obvious signs that I shouldn't, including a very large puddle right in front of the gates to my old school and a shadow in the shape of a skull and crossbones spreading across the playground.

'Are you waiting for the photography class?' I asked a girl who was leaning against the wall, foot up, reading a big fat book.

'Of course,' she replied in a German accent. 'Olivia is a little late. She will be here soon,' and she went back to her book.

'I could run away right now. £18 – that isn't too bad to do no photography classes . . .' Just then that whatshisname who played Romeo came ambling along the corridor, dropping sleeves of negatives out of a big fat folder all over the floor.

'Edie! Hi. You got on. Great!'

My pleasure at seeing him was exaggerated by nerves.

'Oh hi! God, I'm so glad you're here!' I gushed.

'Really. Well, good. Hi Frieda.'

'Hello Ralph,' she purred, showing her big square teeth in a friendly way, smoothing her hand across her cropped, barley-coloured hair and not being at all frosty. She put her book in her bag. 'Did you stay in the pub long last week?'

Ralph laughed madly. 'Yeah! Alexis and Gavin got really competitive on the pool table, it got a bit tense.'

'Oh, I can imagine!' She chortled unGermanically. 'Gav likes to win! Oh here is Lexy! Lexy! Hi!'

Lexy was tall and rangy-looking with long red hair.

'Hi everyone!'

Someone else came up to the rear of the group.

'Gav! How the hell are you?'

Gavin was tall, Italian-looking, obviously gay.

'Hi guys!' He didn't include me. 'Liv not here? Oh God, yes, she had her driving test this morning. Maybe she's still on her three-point turn.'

'Oh yeah!' and they all laughed in an exclusive, fang-bearing way.

'Oh, here she is!'

Liv came limping down the corridor, heavily pregnant, wearing clogs, stripy tights and a poncho.

'Hi gang! Sorry I'm late!' She got out a big bunch of keys from a big bunchy bag and we all filed in, me last.

'Are you OK, Liv?' asked Frieda.

'Yeah yeah, Winston's left me again and I've got piles but hey, I'm fine . . . But guess what?! I passed my test!!!!'

The four of them started whooping and hugging while I hung back waiting to be scalped alive or put in a big black cooking pot. How could they all have bonded so deeply after one class? How could I be the new girl on only the second week? I glanced at the door. I could still sneak out, run away. I still had my coat on. But then Ralph – dear Ralph, my best friend in the whole class – turned to me.

'Oh Liv, this is Edie. We were at school together. She's a really brilliant photographer.'

'Oh, hi Edie, sorry, my hormones are all over the place, welcome.'

She flashed a workmanlike-smile and turned away before I could reply.

'OK everyone! Let's get printing! Did you all bring a favourite negative?'

Now that really was a valid excuse to run away. I hadn't brought a favourite negative. Of course. So I hung about near the door, worrying about how I could get my coat, which was now on a peg several feet away, and escape without notice. I didn't even like the coat and it wasn't that cold out, I could just run . . . But then Ralph came loping towards me.

'Haven't you got a negative, Edie?'

'Well no, I was thinking maybe I should go – and start next week properly . . .'

'No, use one of mine for tonight – go through this folder and pick one.'

'That's a good idea Ralph,' said Liv. 'Just make sure you bring some next week, Edie.'

So I sat, still occasionally looking longingly at the door, but soon I got absorbed holding Ralph's negatives up to the strip light. I chose one of a landscape. There were quite a few pictures of a pretty girl with long hair looking windswept and interesting in various romantic locations – beaches, dunes, mountains, forests. It stirred my interest. I peeked at Ralph. He wore Green Flash plimsoles with old men's suit trousers in an itchy-looking tweed, a big baggy cream fisherman's jumper with a giant hole in the elbow through which a quite hairy, manly arm was displayed and a mad Hawaiian shirt that peeped over the top of his jersey. His hair was brown and curly and a bit wayward. He was concentrating hard on his printing. I remembered him playing the descant recorder in the Words and Music competition at school, eyes shut, foot tapping wildly, muffled laughter coming from the audience of Fifth Years. He was so brave. I looked back at the negs. There were lots of pictures of large oil paintings – his, presumably, great big confident still lives and life paintings. One, a mural of buses in a bus station, had him standing next to it with a '1st prize' sign pinned to it. He won competitions. I looked at him and he looked round and smiled.

'Chosen one?' He was so nice, so easy, a bit crap like me. Creative, humorous. I bet he could analyse *Othello* or an art house film. That was when I amazed myself by thinking, 'Maybe I might fancy him.' So absorbed was I, I hadn't thought of Steve once. I did a nice print of Ralph's landscape and Frieda the German de-frosted slightly and said it was nice the way I'd filled in the sky to make it darker. At tea break we all chatted and I started to feel positive about my negatives and promised myself that this was the beginning of my new life and I would stick to it despite (or because of) Lucille's low opinion of my ability to stick at anything.

10

Sixteen-pronged Approach

Why couldn't I ever be at stage 1) of a plan and just stay there and not start thinking ahead until I got to stage 2)? All I had to do was stick to the classes, build up a portfolio, apply for college in the spring – I'd already sent off for the application form – go to college in September, stay there for three years and then start on my fantastic career. But no, I had to project myself miles into the future, imagining the whole scenario until the very last scene where I was a miserable, old, lonely, failed spinster-photographer with a monkey in mint-green woolly clothes hawking a meagre living on the streets of some sink seaside town. I bet the monkey would have AIDS and bite me as well . . .

Maybe I should do something else? I'd be happier doing something more useful – veterinary surgery, for example. But then I remembered when Flopsie had that abscess on his foot, and the vet had cut it open and squeezed, and stuff came out like Primula cheese . . . No, God no. What about a writer? Actress? Singer? Lawyer? Politician? Ice skater? If I made the wrong choice now it could be a disaster. Could I face going to college for three years and doing the wrong thing? I told myself not to panic. All I needed was another prong to my approach.

I would carry on with the classes – they were a beacon of light in the intellectual void of my existence – but wasn't there a fast-track to becoming a photographer? I could just *be* one. I had a decent camera. What about children's portraits? Or pet portraits? Or journalism? Or fashion? Or those estate agent photos? Or food photography? Wildlife? I could just start! Or scene of the crime? Passport photos?

'Why don't you just get a job as an apprentice photographer – or just teach yourself, you've got a camera. You could try and sell a little story to Edwina the Features Editor at the *Gazette*, she's always looking for local stories,' Lucille suggested as she floated about the kitchen, making tea in bed for her and Barry.

'Yeah, what could I do it about?' I said, getting excited. 'Loads of things go on round here! "Woman Opens Milk Carton Correctly" or "Local Girl Gets Engaged"! What about "Bakery Runs Out Of Bloomers"? That happened only yesterday! Or "Local Man Gets New Leg". Did you hear about Jervis's new leg? It's coming all the way from Germany!'

Lucille did a fake laugh, 'No, I'm being serious, Edie.'

'So am I!'

'Oh right. Well, the thing is, she likes local media stories, something celebrity based.'

'But there aren't any celebrities round here.'

Then the doorbell rang, and Lucille put down her tray.

'If it's Buster, don't let him in!' I called.

'Hi Buster, come in.' Had *she* gone deaf as well?

'Hi Edie. Guess what?' He was flapping the local paper about. He looked excited; it could only be bad news.

'I don't want to hear about any more deaths.'

'That actor Ed Fallow died. Remember he was in all those gangster movies? His daughter was in your class at school, wasn't she?'

I snatched the *Boxford Gazette* from Buster and continued to read out loud. The news had reached Lucille and she stood in the doorway, all ears suddenly.

'"His daughter Foxy runs an antique clothes shop called 'Clobbered' after her father's most famous film. Ed Fallow died after a long and painful battle with cancer." Brilliant!'

'Edie! The poor man!' Lucille said in a shocked tone.

'Look, if I'm going to be a tough career woman I've got to harden up, and this would make a really good scoop for the *Gazette*, wouldn't it? . . . and I know her!'

'Oi! It was my idea!' Buster complained. He didn't even know it *was* an idea until I had it.

'But isn't it a bit mean? Poor girl, she's probably feeling dreadful,' Mum's eyes looked genuinely watery through the top half of her bifocals.

'Don't try and put me off. There's no room for compassion in the hard-nosed world of journalism!'

'But, dear, isn't she a nervous girl? I read somewhere she had anorexia and drug problems.'

'Rubbish, she's just a drama queen.'

'Poor love.'

'Oh, look, stop it! I'm trying to make something of myself and my empty life and you're trying to ruin it for me!'

And I slammed out and stomped off, not quite quickly enough to miss my Mum say, 'Oh piss off!'

Telling her own daughter to piss off!

I stalked back and looked through the letter box. I saw her get a large bag of crisps out of what was obviously a secret hiding place behind the fish tank, sigh happily and turn the TV back up to distortion level just as I was going to tell her to 'piss off' back.

I stormed across the quad, mentally shoving away the huge guilt-complex my Mum was trying to bequeath to me and deliberately straightening my legs firmly as I walked. Yes, I'd inherited her knocked knees and fine hair, but it didn't mean I had to become soft and squidgy and muddled like her. Mum didn't understand 80s Britain – it was a tough world of shoulder pads and giant hair out there, you couldn't afford to be sentimental.

Edwina the Features Editor had really huge shoulder pads and a massive hair-do and she really liked my photo feature idea about Foxy Fallow and her shop and seemed especially impressed when I said I knew her personally. She said she'd definitely consider buying it when I'd sorted it out.

I rushed to Lucille's desk in the typing pool.

'Guess what?'

She flapped a bit of material at me that she took from a big scrapbook. 'What d'you think of this lilac *crêpe de chine*?'

'What?'

'For your bridesmaid dress!'

'But you're not actually getting married?'

'Engaged to be married. What else could it mean?'

'But you're only twenty!'

'Twenty-one in February. My mum was married at nineteen.'

'But Lucille, we're a different generation,' I tried to explain, 'our mums didn't have careers . . . they had to rely financially on a man.'

'My mum always worked.'

'Yeah, as a typist.'

'That's work,' she said, without a hint of uncertainty.

'I don't want to work, I want a career!'

Lucille smiled pityingly at me and held up the *crêpe de chine* sample to my face, squinting appraisingly.

'What's that book?' I said, pointing at her scrapbook.

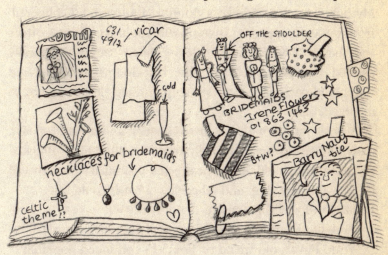

'Oh, it's just where I'm sticking all the reference stuff and ideas for the wedding. Colours, materials, pictures from magazines. Anyway, how did it go with Edwina? You look the part.'

Lucille squeezed my shoulder really hard.

'Ow! Lucille!'

'Nice pads.'

'That's my shoulders, thank you.'

'Oh God. Yes.'

Lucille looked back at her 'wedding book', concerned.

'Anyway, it went really well. She wants the story. I'm a photo journalist!'

'That's great,' she said looking quizzically at my shoulders then back again at her wedding book. 'Actually, maybe I won't go for the off-the-shoulder dresses.'

Poor Lucille. Her wedding book was her only creative outlet. She couldn't help being a bit jealous of my new career.

My heart was beating like a drum as I surveyed 'Clobbered' from the café opposite. It was partly the three Camp coffees and the six B&H's. Eventually I pushed back my naturally padded shoulders, held my fine hair-do high and entered Clobbered without a clear strategy in mind despite hours of mental debate.

A posh fat girl with bright red lipstick and a black, glossy, Lady Di hair-do smiled broadly at me from the till as I flicked casually through old 30s crêpe dresses, wafting a stench of old B.O. around the shop and rehearsing what I would say.

'Hi, I'm Edie!' I practised.

'Edie Dudman?' I imagined her replying, suspiciously.

'Yeah, I'm an old friend of Foxy's,' I continued hopefully.

'Yes, I know about you, you're the one who called her a long nosed c—t and threw rocks at her down One Mile Alley.'

'Well, it wasn't me who actually *threw* the rocks, it was my friend Luc—'

'You know what she said to me?'

'No,' I said, even though it was me making it up.

'She said "My dad dying is the second worst thing that's ever happened to me – the first was Edie Dudman calling me a long nosed c—t."'

'Don't be silly,' I admonished myself, 'she'll never know about that, Foxy would never remember it . . .'

After twenty minutes I was almost dead from asphyxiation from the retro B.O., so I just launched . . .

'Um, hi,' I coughed, 'is Foxy around?'

'No she's orff. She's having a dreadful time with the press.

They're hounding her night and day. I mean her Daddy's just died – can you imagine? They're animals, leeches, scum of the earth.'

She glanced warily at my giant Pentax and my fast deflating shoulders.

'Um, oh, yes,' I explained, blushing, 'I was at school with Foxy.'

'*Really?* . . . Oh, yes, when she had that spell at that crappy comp?'

'Hmm. Well . . . er, poor Foxy. I heard about her Dad. I just wondered how she was?'

She narrowed her eyes suspiciously at me.

'I'm a photography student! Fashion. And I'm doing a project on 1930s B.O. . . . er, I mean clothes, and I wondered if, um, whether . . .?' Her eyes lit up immediately.

Five minutes later I was photographing Foxy's assistant Penny in various outfits from Clobbered outside in the Autumn sunshine. As she posed, squeezed into satin and silk, fur hats perched on her pudgy face, feather boas flung round her plump neck, pointy shoes with wasted heels crammed onto her size 7 feet, I decided Penny was really quite photogenic. The light was magical, I was really enjoying myself, feeling a sense of achievement and starting to believe my own lie about the project.

'I'll get a really good grade!' I thought, as rolls of film flew into my bag.

11

Open-and-Shut Relationship

An hour later I stood slumped at the snack counter at Crusties – a sad, deluded, ex-photo-journalist. After I'd excitedly bid farewell to Penny, told her the photos would probably be in a big exhibition at the Library, may even make the local paper, I wandered off and reality bit me hard in the face. What was I doing? I felt sick with myself. I could easily have wangled a session with Foxy if I'd played my cards right. I had the mind of a hard-nosed journalist but the nerve of a jelly. I was watching Kerry flirting with that horrible Bill the Breadman, the one who kept saying my hair looked like spaghetti and didn't I have a brush? when the phone rang.

'It might be Steve!' I droned mentally. God, I was boring myself.

'Edie! It's Steve on the phone for you!'

I thought I must be dreaming.

'It's Steve! I said you might be in a meeting. You're not going to speak to him, are you?'

I walked over and snatched the phone. 'Hello?'

'Hi, Lamb Chop, it's me.'

'Hi!' I said, not bothering to be cool. Well, if I wasn't going to be a career woman I wanted a boyfriend, even a horrible one.

'Got any gear?' he said. My stomach sank but I ignored it.

My gut and my brain had stopped communicating months ago.

'No,' I said.

'Can you get any for tonight?'

'Maybe.'

'Great. I'll come over about eightish?'

I knew if I could get some dope for Steve I could use it to buy his affection. I knew that was weak and crap but I didn't care. Lucille and Kerry had their techniques and this was mine.

'I thought you said it made you paranoid?' Kerry said, staring into the mirror in the loo, mouth wide open as she separated her blobs of royal blue mascara with a nappy pin.

'I just feel like it! I feel a bit too . . . normal.'

She pronged the remains of her curly perm with an Afro comb.

'OK, come on then! Let's go. My mate Weasel'll sort us out. Moi!' she yelled, 'we're off down the Bush to score, you'll be alright on your own, babes, won't you?'

'Well, ooh, what's the time, it's nearly . . .'

'See ya!' Kerry shouted and we were gone, leaving Moira with the lunchtime 'rush'.

Kerry and I both looked ridiculous in our nylon uniforms, shivering on the doorstep of the huge crumbling Victorian house. Kerry did a funny secret knock, the door opened and out came Edwina. Edwina the Features Editor! Stuffing a bag of grass into her expensive Italian handbag and looking straight at me.

'Goodness, she's a drug addict,' I thought. 'Maybe she will like my photos of Penny?'

We walked into a huge room — more like a village hall — with bare floorboards and rugs, sofas and music equipment dotted about.

People were here and there, smoking, drinking, talking in huddles. Weasel had masses of dreadlocks and greeted Kerry warmly.

Everything she said seemed to make him laugh. She introduced us and I couldn't make out what he was saying but it seemed friendly. I felt very silly and nylon and white.

'Come in Edie, it's brilliant, you get shitfaced just being in here,' called Kerry from the inside of a large thick paper bag which looked like it may have contained a car or a small boat or something.

Apparently, I think Weasel explained, if several of you sat in this paper tent to smoke joints you got 'totally mash-up', what with all the extra passive smoking.

'Um . . .' I wasn't at all sure, but maybe it was a prerequisite to getting some dope. You always had to act like you were merely visiting, coming round to enquire after the dealer's health or to be amused by some of his rambling stories for at least half an hour before any trading could begin.

'Come on, Edie, man . . .' I think Weasel said, laughing. 'Get in here.'

I stood up, bent down and leaned in.

'Well,' I said. It was dark in there and I could just see Kerry's and Weasel's eyes gleaming through a thick fug of smoke. The last thing I remember was saying, 'No thanks' as Weasel handed me a joint of pure weed . . .

The next thing I remember was waking up on my sofa still wearing my nylon dress, mouth stuck together. It was dark.

'Oh my God! Where have I been? What have I done! I didn't go back to work!' I screeched.

'What on earth are you going on about?' Lucille said from Barry's lap on the armchair.

'I must've conked out in that paper bag!'

'Paper bag?'

'I must have been at that squat all afternoon,' I said, heaving myself off the sofa and looking at the clock. '6.51! How did I get home? Was I brought back in an ambulance?'

'I don't know, you were already on the sofa when I got home, I just assumed you'd had another exhausting day.'

My bag was on the floor next to me and I snatched up my purse – the £13 for the grass was gone. I shook the entire contents of my bag all over the floor – no bag of grass either. Barry started to laugh in a high-pitched way.

'Jesus, Edie, what are you doing?'

'My bag of grass has gone! Oh God, Steve's going to be here in a minute, he's going to be really cross. I said I'd get him some dope, to lure him round, and I haven't got it.'

'That's ridiculous! That's the only reason he's coming round?'

'You should dump him, Edie,' Barry said.

'I'm going to, don't worry,' I said, starting to scrabble around on the floor, scooping everything back into my bag. 'I'm going to sit him down and I'm going to say, "Look Steve, I'm not happy with the way things are between us and I don't want to see you any more. Just go and never ever contact me again!" Or, "Look Steve, I'm not happy with the way things are between us, I'm lonely and you make me nervous and I don't want to see you any more. Just go and never contact me again!" Yeah, that's what I'll say and then he'll say, "I'm sorry,

I know I've been a shit. Please don't leave me. I love you, Edie, let's get back to how things used to be, my little Whale Pup. . . . and then we'll get married and have babies . . .'''

Barry, who had been chortling away throughout my rehearsal, now looked a bit concerned.

'No, I'm only joking.'

'If you're only really splitting up with him to make him react in a certain way it probably won't work,' Lucille said.

Lucille and I caught eyes. Isn't that what she had done?' But no, it wasn't, she had merely been mean and unavailable and that didn't work with Steve because he was already way ahead in the mean and unavailable stakes. If you really, really want to split up with someone you don't do a self-pitying speech, you just behave badly until they get fed up. Like Steve was doing with me . . . and I was too feeble to take the hint.

'Right, when he gets here I'm going to tell him it's over,' I said and went upstairs to make myself look as attractive as possible.

Steve arrived at 10.05 p.m.

'Steve, we need to talk about our relationship.'

'Did you get the gear?'

'No, I didn't. Well, I did, but it's all gone.'

'Yeah, you look shit-faced. What did you do, smoke it all?'

'No. Look Steve . . .'

He stared at me with a glazed expression.

'I think we should just . . . have a casual relationship – you know, just see each other when we want to,' I said.

Steve suddenly looked bright, human almost.

'Oh God, Eed, it's like a weight off my shoulders.'

He was like the old Steve.

'I've been feeling so pressurized.'

Now he was articulate too.

'What by?' I said.

'You know, we're only young. We should be having fun, not getting all serious and heavy.'

'Yeah, so . . .' I said, feeling a bit hurt by his sudden animation.

'Come here, my little Lamb Chop . . . bring your cute little peachy face over here,' and he started to plant kisses all over my face. We pressed ourselves against each other and writhed about, snogging like the old days, pulling away to look into each other's eyes and he said was I safe and I said yes . . .

Post-coitally, I felt it was all going so well that I decided to develop my open-relationship technique a little further.

'You can see other people if you like. That Julie from Miss Selfish has always fancied you.'

'Yeah I know. She's thick as shit though.'

'That's rich coming from you,' I thought, staring at his long eyelashes.

'She can't string a sentence together,' he added.

'The pot calling the kettle black,' I mentally murmured, running my fingers along the smooth golden skin on his shoulder.

'She's got a nice arse though.'

I gritted my teeth. 'Well, why don't you go out with her?'

'She asked me out the other day.'

'The cheek!' I thought. 'She knows he's my boyfriend. It's my Mum's fault, letting me walk about in her old dyke shoes. No other woman sees me as a serious contender.'

'Did you tell her to Ferck Erff ?'

'Nah,' he said, without a glimmer of self-knowledge. 'She thinks I look like John McEnroe.'

'You *cannot* be *serious*!'

'No, she does.'

'Right. Great. Well, to be honest, I want to concentrate on my career, I haven't got time for a full-time relationship.'

We ran out of conversation at that point and had sex again.

'An open relationship? Isn't that a bit hippy-ish, Edie?' Lucille said, sticking bits of Callard and Bowser Liquorice Toffee wrapper in her wedding book. She was sitting at her desk in the typing pool at the *Gazette* and I had come in to see Edwina.

'Well, I'm perfectly happy with it.'

'Barry said he saw Steve with Julie Fitchebauer snogging in the street.'

'Yes, I know, and I'm perfectly fine about it. Look, when's Edwina going to look at my photos?'

Just then Edwina appeared from nowhere. 'Right then, Edie, let's see what you've got?' she said, snatching my envelope and heading for the light box. 'Let's pop them on here – oh! they're prints, how sweet. Now let's have a look – ooh, she's a chunky girl, isn't she? – obviously got over her anorexia. There's a lot of flare – didn't you use a reflector?'

'Er, no, she was a bit upset.'

'She's putting on a very brave face I must say. Positively glowing.'

'Shock.'

'Well, these are great, we can sort that out in the printing. Did she agree to an interview?'

Oh, what was the point in lying? I'd get found out eventually.

'It's not Foxy Fallow.'

'Who is it then?'

'Her friend.'

'Ri-i-i-ght. And who is her friend?'

'Penny.'

'And is her father a famous actor who's just died?'

'Not really.'

'Yes or no?'

'He's a bank manager. He did have a heart attack last year. Penny and her mother really thought they might lose him, he's given up smoking and cut down on his drinking and . . .'

Edwina started putting away the photos.

'The thing is, she's really good friends with Foxy and I thought Penny would be a good way of getting to her, if we butter her up a bit . . . and the shop is sort of news in itself . . . maybe.'

I looked into Edwina's cold, dope-dulled eyes and thought of blackmailing her into using the pictures anyway by mentioning her dope habit but, well, I wasn't up to being a press photographer or a blackmailer. I was an artist with a soft, law-abiding centre inherited from my weak and woolly mother.

'Oh leave me alone!!!' And I ran out, leaving her with my photos of Penny Frazier-Smith, Z-list celebrity.

12

Just Do It!

As I approached Crusties for my shift I saw Steve doing 'surgery'
up a tree, i.e. smoking a spliff with Gazza. He looked
annoyingly manly in his straps and ropes so I pretended I
hadn't seen him, did a special saunter and smiled knowingly
to myself. He would be watching me and thinking 'Jesus, I'd
forgotten how beautiful she is' and humming 'Try a Little
Tenderness' to himself – the 'ragged dress' bit. Then he
would climb down the tree and run towards me, grab me and
beg me to forgive him for his affair and propose or
something – I hadn't quite worked out the ending. As I
turned into Crusties I glanced ravishingly in his direction and
he was GONE. Completely gone. But his van was still there.
At the same time, I remembered that I hadn't been back to
Crusties since going AWOL to that drug squat with Kerry
the Thursday before.

'It's OK, Moira, you can sack me. I completely understand.'

'Edie, thank God! Mr Pollock's coming any minute. Do you
know where Kerry is? She hasn't been in at all.'

Still at that squat in that paper bag no doubt, I thought. Then
I had a flashback. Handing Kerry my £13 just before overdosing
on one puff of Weasel's joint. She'd got my £13 or my £13-
worth of grass.

'You two girls were very naughty taking such a long break

the other day but we'll let it go,' Moira said. 'Now Edie, dear, can you get on the snack bar?'

At lunchtime I was on the sixteenth floor of Kerry's towerblock knocking at her dad's front door, no. 115. Blaize, Kerry's two-year-old, answered the door and for a split second I saw in the living room a bit of Kerry's bleached perm swing into view and a giant spliff coming to meet it. Then she was obscured from view as her dad's massive belly filled the doorway.

'Hello, love, what can I do for you?'

'Um, is Kerry in please?'

'No, love, she's not.'

'Oh, right. Could you tell her Edie called round?'

'I will, love, if I see her. Bye love,' and he shut the door.

I looked through the letter box and heard him say, 'Someone called Edie' and heard Kerry mutter something. So! She *had* stolen my £13. And that was a third of the £39 that she earned at Crusties. But it was nearly all I earned because I did 4 shifts a week of 4 hours at £1.23 ph so that was –

1.23
× 16
738
+1230
=£19.68!!!

That was nearly a whole week's wages for me!

As I took the pissy lift down the sixteen floors I resolved that I would not let her get away with it.

I didn't have to wait long.

'Oi Edie! Wait!'

Kerry was sprinting across the grass, wearing a white PVC jacket over her uniform and stretch, bleached drainpipes under her uniform.

'Mummy!' Behind her on the balcony sixteen floors up, Blaize was bellowing wide-mouthed and desperate.

'Blaize! Get back inside! Now! Sorry, Eed,' Kerry said, joining me. 'Give us a fag. Ta. Told my Dad to say I was out cos Danny, that bloke out the army, is giving me grief, hassling me night and day.'

'So your dad mistook me for Danny, who has blond Action Man hair and a moustache?'

'Oh shut up, Edie!' she said and doubled up, machine-gun laughing.

Though flattered, I remained silent, nurturing my £13-worth of steely resentment.

'Kerry,' I said sternly. 'What happened to that £13?'

'Oh yeah! Weasel's, was you alright? You fell akip and then leapt up like a fucking firework and said you had to shoot off. Couldn't find your way out of that paper bag, you made a fucking great hole in it. Weasel was not pleased.'

'The thing is, that wasn't *my* £13, it was for someone else.'

'Oh yeah, your gran's period pains,' she said, winking.

'Arthritis,' I corrected.

'Don't worry, my dad's bought a shed-load and gave us a

wadge. Here are.' And she gave me a bag of grass. As we turned the corner towards Crusties I saw that Steve's van was still parked in the same place and an idea popped into my head. An idea that I mentally wrestled with all afternoon.

Too-nice me: 'Come on it wasn't his fault and you did promise.'

Too-angry me: 'So what? Why should I? He gave me a Breville Toasted Sandwich Maker for my twenty-first and I haven't seen him for four days. Bastard.'

Too-nice me: 'Oh come on. He's just a bloke, and it'd be nice to see him. You just expect too much.'

Too-angry me: 'He's a horrible person, basically. I don't even like him! He's boring, he's nasty . . .'

'He makes you feel alive though, doesn't he? You love everything about him from the very highest golden hair on his head to his little toenail . . . every bit of him is perfection.'

'No, I've had enough of it.'

'But what else have you got?'

'Lots of things!'

'Like?'

''Scuse me, dreamer! Two large Bloomers please, love.'

A large woman with straw hair the shape of a mixing bowl was waving her plump hand in my face.

'Oh sorry,' I said and reached under the counter like Moira had instructed me.

'Look love, I used to work in a bakery, I don't want yesterday's bread. From up there please,' she said pointing up at the fresh Bloomers.

My cheeks burned. 'I wasn't . . . I . . . sorry . . .'

Moira came bustling out from the back with her red rash map of Wales creeping up her neck.

'Moira, this girl's trying to give me old bread!'

'Oh, no, Jan, you know how it is! Me and Jan used to work together at Dylan's in the precinct when we were girls, Edie.'

I smiled heroically under Jan's fierce gaze, though tears pricked my eyes. Once Moira, now maroon, had taken Jan into the back for a free cream cake I continued my dialogue with myself.

'Like my job here . . . and my friends . . .'

'What friends?'

'And my sanity.'

'Come on, just one little fix won't hurt,' and then I added in Steve's snide voice, 'The trouble with you is you think too much.'

'Oh OK,' I agreed, perking up. 'I won't think about it, I'll just do it!' Why was self-destruction so tempting? So attractive? So easy? So addictive? And the thing about addiction is it gives you something to aim for, and once the idea is mooted, it has to be acted on. It was like nicotine. Once

I thought about a cigarette, I had to have one, it was nothing to do with whether I wanted it or not.

'Moi? Can I just nip out one sec?'

I went in the back, tore a page out of the petty cash book – Steve might be impressed, amused by that. But I started the writing off too big and then had to go all weeny at the end.

I fought off the desire to get another sheet – Bill the Breadman was staring at me, and anyway that would be not being myself . . . wouldn't it? Although it was a *version* of me that had the desire to get another sheet . . . I was thinking too much again.

I went outside to his van and popped it under his windscreen and trotted back feeling energized. It was Thursday, the night of my class, and through huge strength of character I had resisted suggesting we meet that night.

Ralph had spent the evening printing an 8 × 10 photo of a

house fly that he had taken with a macro lens.

'Look at the detail on that compound eye!' he enthused.

Mine was taken from my bedroom window, a pigeon in flight. I was rather pleased with it. We were on our second pint of bitter in the Coach and Horses.

'D'you want to see my seal photos?' I said. I had waded into the water on a holiday in Cornwall in 1976 and taken twenty-four pictures of a dot in the water with my Kodak 126 Instamatic camera.

Ralph laughed and said, 'These are nothing compared to my ones of a hawk. I'll show you them one day. If you're lucky. Who's that?' he asked, frowning and pointing. He had found my photos of Penny Frazier-Smith, and was staring at a slightly out-of-focus one of Penny in a peach satin ballgown and fox fur stole.

'Oh, it's a girl called Penny Frazier-Smith. I was trying to . . .'

'Penny Frazier-Smith? I know her! She's a friend of my brother's. Why are you taking photos of Pen?'

'Well, you swear you won't tell her?'

'I swear.'

'Promise?'

'I promise.'

'You mustn't.'

'I won't.'

I was already laughing at the sheer delicious thought of telling him – I hadn't realized how funny it was until then – knowing how he would laugh, how he'd 'get' every bit of it. And he did, he guffawed and chortled at all the right bits and my telling of it got better and better. I got to the bit where I was explaining to Edwina about Penny's dad's heart scare and Ralph was actually crying with laughter, sliding down the padded plastic bench, his trench coat up to his ears.

'Alright?' It was Steve standing over us, helmet in hand. He looked disdainfully at Ralph. 'What's so funny?'

'Oh, Steve. Hi.' My face froze mid-laugh and my stomach clenched. Typical. I was enjoying myself for the first time in about a year and Steve turns up. What I was always hoping – every roar of a motorbike, every scrape of the gate, ding of the phone, ping of the shop door – 'It might be Steve!' The first time in ages I wasn't hoping it was Steve and there he was.

'This is Ralph, from my class. From school, d'you remember him?'

'Er yeah, vaguely. Alright? I'm just going to get myself a pint,' he said, ignoring our empty glasses and swaggering over to the bar.

'Shall I go?' Ralph said.

'No, don't be silly!' I said, trying to gain some control over my complete personality change. But Ralph wasn't being silly. I did think he should go, but . . . why should he? And therein lay my fatal flaw. The 'why should he?' Why did I have to wonder why? Lucille would have got rid of one or both of them in a flash, depending on what she wanted. But I didn't know what I wanted, I just had some vague muddled sense of justice. Steve sat down on the stool opposite, legs wide apart, and sipped at his pint.

Ralph tittered, still looking at Penny's photo.

'That old Gripper next door said you were at your old dear's, your old dear said you were at a class and then some old bird there said you'd gone to the hospital – she seemed to think you were a nurse,' Steve said.

'You didn't say I wasn't, did you?'

'And then some Kraut bird with a carrot up her arse said

117

you'd gone to the pub. What d'you pick this dump for?'

'You can converse in here, it's nice and quiet,' said Ralph, suddenly sounding embarrassingly posh.

'Oh right,' Steve said, eyeing Ralph sarcastically over the top of his pint glass. 'Like a morgue.'

And it did seem like a morgue now he'd arrived.

'Oh look!' Ralph said, 'it's Gavin!' and he waved to Gavin who came over looking moody with an orange juice.

'I thought you said the City Barge,' he said to us accusingly.

'Oh sorry,' Ralph said. 'Gavin, this is Edie's friend Steve, Steve this is Gavin from the class.'

They grunted at each other and then we went back to the Morgue Atmosphere.

Ralph said to Steve and Gavin, 'Edie was just telling me her hilarious press photography story. I happen to know Penny,' he pointed to the photo.

'Who the fuck's that old tart?' Steve sneered. I laughed nervously.

'I agree with Edie, she's quite photogenic,' Ralph said.

'I don't know about all that arty stuff. Who is she anyway?'

'Oh, didn't Edie tell you the . . .'

I butted in. 'Oh it's just that Lucille said I should try and do a little story and photo for the *Gazette*,' I wittered.

Steve stared at me vacantly. 'Wha' the fuck for?'

'You going to sell out, Edie?' Gavin said. 'I thought you were an artist?'

'And you remember that girl at school, Foxy Fallow,' I persevered.

'Oh ye-ah,' Steve raised his eyebrows. 'She was alright.'

'Yeah, bit thin, but anyway, you know her dad was that actor?'

'No.'

'Yes you do, Ed Fallow.'

'Never heard of him.'

'He was crap,' said Gavin. 'Sold out in Hollywood, alcoholic wife-beater.'

'Anyway, she's got this shop called . . .'

And on it went, painfully, unfunnily, Steve's expression blank until the seeing-Edwina-at-the-drug-squat bit when his eyes flickered slightly. Gavin crunching the ice from his orange juice really loudly, occasionally tutting. At the bitter end, Steve told me, 'You should have told her to stick it up her arse, fat old lezzer.'

Gavin yawned and said, 'I think I'll make a move, see ya' next week guys. Ciao.'

'Ciao *wa-nk-er*,' Steve said in his Ferck Erff voice.

So that left the three of us again in the Morgue.

'Just off to the Gents,' Ralph said, then pushed at the Gents' door nine times before realizing it said Pull.

'Who's that mongoloid?'

'Don't be mean. He's very bright. He turned down a place at Ox . . .'

'Have you got the gear on you?' Steve broke in.

'It's at home. We'll go in a minute.'

Ralph was making his way back from the Gents, toilet paper stuck to his Green Flash plimsole. My neck was seizing up at the thought of any more of this threesome.

'Ralph, we've got to go now.'

'Stay for another?' Ralph grinned at Steve bravely.

'Nah mate. We gotta shoot. Come on Shitface.'

'OK Cuntarse,' I replied, laughing to deflect Ralph's shocked look at my nickname. Steve flashed me a frown, I laughed louder.

'Sorry to dash, Ralph, see you next week!' I called and trotted after Steve. I looked back at Ralph. He was leaning down and pulling the toilet paper off his Green Flash. He seemed to have shrunk into his trench coat. Steve had a way of diminishing others, sidelining them with a flick of his icy turquoise eyes or one of his inscrutable putdowns. You couldn't get an A level in that, but it wasn't something to be sniffed at.

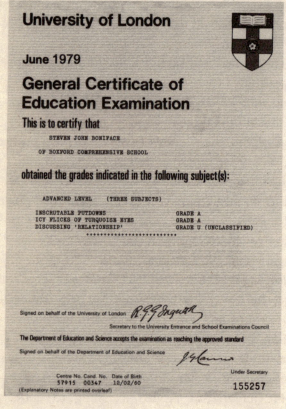

University of London

June 1979

General Certificate of Education Examination

This is to certify that

STEVEN JOHN BONIFACE

OF BOXFORD COMPREHENSIVE SCHOOL

obtained the grades indicated in the following subject(s):

ADVANCED LEVEL   (THREE SUBJECTS)

INSCRUTABLE PUTDOWNS   GRADE A
ICY FLICKS OF TURQUOISE EYES   GRADE A
DISCUSSING 'RELATIONSHIP'   GRADE U (UNCLASSIFIED)
****

Signed on behalf of the University of London

Secretary to the University Entrance and School Examinations Council

The Department of Education and Science accepts the examination as reaching the approved standard

Signed on behalf of the Department of Education and Science

Under Secretary

Centre No. Cand. No. Date of Birth
57915   00347   18/02/60
(Explanatory Notes are printed overleaf)   155257

My application form for college had arrived and now I was sitting in the back of Crusties on my break staring at it. I had filled out my name, address and date of birth, but was stuck on Part 1 a) and had been for several days. It required me to fill in the name of the college and the course. I had waded through some prospectuses at the library and made notes. I kept changing my mind between 2 courses and 2 colleges – Knitting Design at Crewe and Alsager College or Documentary Photography at Newport School of Art and Design – and was using a lot of Tippex. It was so long and complicated I started to make excuses not to fill it out. I didn't *have* to go to college next year, I could go the year after. My life wasn't so bad. I quite liked it at Crusties, in fact I suddenly thought it a completely happy and fulfilling career. I took a tray of meanly-filled rolls into the snack area and looked out fondly at the shop. Kerry was 'entertaining' – and he did actually look totally diverted by her – that new bloke Danny, the squaddy with the Action Man blond hair and ginger moustache, the one that her dad had mistaken me for. He sat at the table mesmerized, while Kerry, slumped down in her plastic chair, stared along her thin mauve legs, white stilettos jigging moodily on the ends.

'Alright, babes?' he said.

'What d'you want, Danny?'

'Just thought it would be nice to see you.'

'Well, I'm having my tea,' Kerry replied scintillatingly.

'Shall I meet you after?'

'If you like,' she said to her mauve legs. Then she did a massive yawn. Then she gave him a beaming smile. Then she shrugged. 'Go on piss off!' she laughed.

It was all very confusing. And not just for Danny. The bit I couldn't master was Stroppy with a Smile. I could only do Weeping or Angry or a terrifying combination of both.

Perhaps if I'd been a bit more like that with Steve he'd still love me, and I wouldn't be having to change my life or fill out this horrific application form.

Danny gave Kerry a big kiss on the cheek and tried to cuddle her but she shook him off, still smiling, and he sloped off.

'Wanna photo?' she said to me and machine-gun laughed.

'No thanks,' I said and looked back at my application form.

'W'a's wrong with you, lemon lips?'

'I've got to choose what I want to do at college.'

'Oh, my heart bleeds.'

'I don't even know if I should be going at all.'

Moira came in from the back. 'Oooh I'd jump at the chance to go to college if I didn't have to work full-time and nurse Mother.'

'Me too,' said Kerry, 'I'd go to college like a flash if I didn't have the kids.'

'Ri-ight. And what subject would you study?'

'I dunno. Books and that.'

They both looked at me and I looked back at them. Kerry's

Crusties hat was at a jaunty angle, Moira's pulled down so it squashed the top of her ears out.

'It's alright for you two,' I told them.

'Oh yeah, how d'you work that out?' Kerry demanded.

'You haven't many options, you've both got excuses to be crap.'

Moira looked quite pleased with that, but Kerry's forehead wrinkled up. 'Oi! Shut your gob!'

'If I was young and free there's so many things I'd do,' Moira said dreamily, staring out at the drizzle.

'Me too,' said Kerry. 'I'd travel, definitely, go to college, set up my own business, definitely, and then . . .'

'I've always wanted to run a safari park,' Moira continued.

'Really,' I said flatly, folding up my form and then my arms. 'Have you ever actually been to a safari park, Moi?'

'No, unfortunately,' Moira said, not understanding the question, 'but I'd love to!'

'I'd open my own beauty salon,' Kerry said. 'Or restaurant! You're mad hanging round here when you could go off and do all sorts.'

'Yes,' agreed Moira, pushing her glasses up her nose.

'Well, it's all very easy to say that from the safety of your imprisonment,' I told them. 'It's not that easy being young and free, you know.' But secretly I was encouraged by their vicarious enthusiasm and slipped out at lunchtime to the library to check out some more prospectuses, leaving Moira and Kerry languishing in their lovely, comfy, genuine-excuse ridden lethargy, drinking tea and reading *Titbits*. However as I made haste along the high street a sudden realization stopped me in my tracks.

13

Through a Visor, Darkly

I'm pregnant, I know I am. I'm only five days late but I just know. No PMT and I feel calm, none of the usual excitement, depression, weeping and plans to run away to Scotland. The thing is I feel (calmly) excited. I'm pregnant! The worse thing is I know I did it accidentally-on-purpose. When Steve had asked me if I was safe that night when we started our open-relationship, I lied. Only slightly. But I was on day eight after my period and officially outside the seven-day Catholic 'safe' period. Not that I was Catholic, just idiotic.

This is how everyone reacted —

Kerry:

Jesus, Edie, you stupid slag! You're going to get rid of it, aren't you? Christ, don't make the same mistake I made — Bloody hell! He's a bastard, that Steve. Gorgeous-looking, though. Mind, those pretty ones lose their looks really fast. Don't let him persuade you to have it, for Christ's sake!

Lucille:

Oh Edie! Haven't you heard of contraception? God, I make Barry wear two Durexes — d'you want me to come to the doctor with you? You've got to get organized. Go private and make Steve pay for it.

My Mum:

Oh darling! Of course, if you want to have it, I'll help all I can. I've told the boys, you don't mind do you? Mark wants to talk to you – I told him to leave you alone. He'll only go on and on about how you should have it. He thinks it'll be the making of Steve if you have it, make him grow up. Mind, Mark hasn't grown up since he had kids. Of course I'll support you . . . Sorry darling, what? Oh, sorry darling, it's just Sonja's getting married in *Emmerdale* . . . just turn the volume up. I can't hear you darling, you're mumbling again . . .

Buster:

I'll marry you if you want but, I mean, what about college, your career? You'd go mad with a baby, wouldn't you, Eed?

The only person I hadn't told was Steve. I'd seen him a couple of times and I'd smiled and nodded encouragingly when he told me about Julie. They were having a lot of rampant sex but she was still 'thick and boring' apparently. I was seeing more of him now than I had done in the whole of the last six months and my stomach was almost permanently knotted. My disconnected brain took no notice however . . .

'I'm pregnant,' I said.

'Well I'm not marrying you, if that's what you think,' was Steve's response.

I don't know what I expected but it wasn't that.

'I don't want you to marry me,' I said.

'You're gonna get rid of it, aren't you?'

'I don't know.'

'Well, what you gonna do? How did it happen anyway? You said you were safe.'

'I thought I was,' I lied.

'Well, at least we know we can both have them.'

And then I didn't see him for four weeks. My stomach unknotted and I went round in a blank state knowing that if I didn't do anything, in seven and a half months' time I would have a baby. The other decision involved doing something. Like so many decisions. You do something or you do nothing. Action or inaction. It's very rarely a choice between two changes. Rather Status Quo vs. Status New. You leave your job or you do nothing. You split up with your partner or you do nothing. You carry on watching ITV or you change channels. The thing was, my body was changing the status quo all on its own.

I quite liked the idea of being pregnant. But everybody else seemed to like the idea of me having an abortion. Or rather they assumed that was what I would do. Not one person reacted happily, they all reacted like I had cancer, except it was the sort that was easily but painfully curable.

Going up the escalator in the tube one day I saw an ad with a silhouette of a down-hearted girl and the words, 'Pregnant? Unhappy?' Well I *was* pregnant. And I *was* unhappy.

Hillary at the Pregnancy Advisory Centre stared at me. 'So the relationship isn't good?'

'He doesn't want me to have the baby.'

'Do you communicate? Have you talked?'

'A bit.'

'Well, that's something, some couples can't communicate at all.'

'He makes me nervous.'

'Can you make demands of him?'

I shook my head.

'You need to make some demands in a relationship. Maybe try and bring him along next time. And think about what you want.'

'Do you have trouble finishing things?' the German lady-doctor with the short, grey hair said, not looking up from her notes. I was at the hospital now. Two students stared disinterestedly at me from behind her. Dr Hopf was interrogating me about my relationship with Steve. It all sounded pretty bad. So obviously she had asked me why I hadn't finished it. Did I have trouble finishing things? I thought of my patchwork with the cardboard bits still in it, my one armed mohair jumper, my application form for college, my empty photo album and my bin-bag full of photos.

'A bit,' I said.

'You have to do this!' she said, coming alive. She beat her fist on her stomach, 'Gut!' and on her chest, 'Heart!' and then on her temple, 'Head! Gut! Heart! Head! You must follow your gut! If this man is bad then you must finish it!' And she looked into the middle distance, maybe wishing she had ended it with Mr Hopf all those years ago. Or wishing she hadn't, perhaps? I had noticed that people always encouraged you to do what they had done, whether they regretted it or not – and then she scribbled something on a form.

I had to be demanding. *I* had to finish things. *I* had to follow my gut. Instead of chasing Steve down the road with a shotgun they were all pointing it at me.

Steve leant on his Honda 250 Superdream and lit up a big fat joint, even though two policeman were strolling our way. We were in town somewhere near Euston, outside the pregnancy advisory clinic, for my second consultation. I had demanded aggressively that he come with me and he had sulkily agreed. He screwed his eyes up against the spitting rain and, looking away, passed me the joint, just as the policemen were about to pass us. Risking arrest, I took a drag – it was our only bond, our only point of contact.

'How long's it going to take?' he asked.

'I don't know.'

'What are they going to say?'

'How would I know?'

'I've got to be somewhere at 5.30.'

Despite the fact that his coldness was so obvious, his irritation so blatant, I thought, Maybe I'm mad? Maybe he's OK? He's not being actually nasty. Maybe it's me? If I was nicer? Cooler? Nastier? Or just – more like him?

While I cried, Steve sat like a stone. Hillary turned to Steve. 'So how do you feel about Edith being pregnant, Dave?'

'Steve,' I corrected her, trying to catch Steve's eye. His eye was like a dead cod's. And so was the other one.

'Sorry. *Steve.* How do you feel about Edith being pregnant?'

'I dunno,' he said. 'I think we're too young to have a baby.'

'How do you feel about Edith having a termination, Dave?'

'*Steve,*' I told her.

'Steve,' she said, not nearly embarrassed enough.

'It's the only thing we can do, isn't it?'

'Well, you could decide to have the baby.'

His cod eyes came alive briefly, his shapely lips twitched downwards like he was going to cry. I felt hopeful.

'Yeah, but Edie's ... we haven't ... I ...'

He looked pathetic, like a boy.

'I'm going to college and everything,' I assisted. 'We haven't any money and ...' then I cried some more.

'What do you think, Dave?'

'Dave thinks the same,' I said.

But what did *Steve* think? I would probably never know.

Steve turned to me and said through his visor, 'OK if I drop you here?'

'Well,' I said, trying to be demanding, 'can't you drop me at home? I thought we should talk.'

'What about?' his voice echoed inside his helmet.

'Well, you know, our situation.'

'We've done that.'

'I want to know what you really think, *Dave.*'

He stared at me blankly.

'The way she kept calling you Dave,' I explained.

'Stupid bitch. Are you getting off?'

I slid off the back of the bike and handed him the crash helmet. We were on the high street near Miss Selfish and I saw Julie peering between two headless naked mannequins. She whipped quickly away out of sight. 'OK, see you,' I said and turned and walked in the opposite direction. His bike revved up and when I looked back he had pulled up outside Miss Selfish and was swaggering across the pavement.

I tried to put one foot in front of the other in a feeble impression of walking, donned a purposeful expression and took a detour into the nearest shop, the Pestle and Mortar chemist, hugely relieved that the girl who had arranged my pregnancy test wasn't there.

Therein I stood and stared at the shelves of shampoos and conditioners, feigning total absorption. I could see Steve and Julie out of the corner of my eye still standing there, watching me from across the road. My heart was thumping with the *Dallas*-style drama of it all.

It was quite a health-foodie kind of chemist, with a whole wall full of vitamins, minerals and homeopathic remedies. A leaflet caught my eye: 'The Bach Flower Remedies at a Glance − Traditionally Prepared for the Following Emotional States' and next to it were all the Remedies in tiny little brown bottles, with teats for dropping the liquid into water. Aha! 'Surely this is where I will find the exact remedy for my exact emotional state,' I thought.

The Guide was divided into seven headings. Fear. Loneliness. Insufficient Interest in Present Circumstances. Despondency or Despair. Uncertainty. Over-sensitivity to Influences and Ideas, and Over-care for the Welfare of Others. It sounded very promising so far. I read on.

'Alright?' It was Buster, sounding like a depressed foghorn.

'Buster! Hi. Oh God, Steve's going to see us together . . . just stand there behind those shelves . . .'

Buster grinned and didn't stand behind those shelves. He loved to think that Steve might think we had something going on. He looked round. 'Where is he?'

'Buster!' I chided, but I was too curious to stop him. 'Over there, outside Miss Selfish . . . with that Julie.'

'Where?'

'Right outside the door.'

'No one there.'

'Jesus, Buster!' *I* could still see them out of my eye corner. I flung round. Just beside the door, at the edge of the window

130

display, were the two naked headless mannequins leaning together conspiratorially. It was actually quite an accurate representation of Steve and Julie. But all that wasted hair-flicking and proud, noble face-making I'd been doing earlier! Deep down, though, I knew it would've been just as wasted on Steve and Julie as it was on the mannequins.

Don't look, there's Edie
shhh..

Buster was already deeply engrossed in the Flower Remedies.

'I need Agrimony,' he stated.

'What's that for?'

'Mental Torment Behind a Brave Face.'

'Yeah,' I agreed, 'but where's the brave face?'

'If you knew the extent of my mental torment you'd think this *was* a brave face.'

'Jesus, you mean there's more?' I laughed. 'You are brave then.'

And my brain, having yet failed to erase the etched images of Julie's and Steve's heads on the mannequins, felt pleased that they would've seen me laughing.

I said, 'Deep Gloom with no Origin, you need. Mustard.'

'No, that's what *you* need,' he said.

'*My* gloom's got an origin, thank you.'

'So's mine,' Buster said, affronted.

The Bach Flower Remedies are 38 homoeopathically prepared remedies, traditionally used for the following emotional states

AN AT-A-GLANCE GUIDE TO THE 38 BACH FLOWER REMEDIES

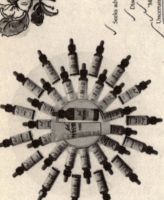

DESPONDENCY OR DESPAIR

Lack of confidence Larch ✓
Self-reproach, guilt Pine *Mum →*
Overwhelmed by responsibility Elm
Extreme mental anguish Sweet Chestnut
After-effects of shock Star of Bethlehem
Resentment Willow
Exhausted but struggles on Oak ✓
Self-hatred, sense of uncleanliness Crab Apple

UNCERTAINTY

Seeks advice and confirmation from others Cerato ✓
Indecision Scleranthus
Discouragement, despondency Gentian ✓
Hopelessness and despair Gorse
'Monday morning' feeling Hornbeam
Uncertainty as to the correct path in life Wild Oat

OVER-SENSITIVITY TO INFLUENCES AND IDEAS

Mental torment behind a brave face Agrimony *B!*
Weak-willed and subservient Centaury *E*
Protection from change and outside influences Walnut ✓
Hatred, envy, jealousy Holly

OVER-CARE FOR THE WELFARE OF OTHERS

Selfishly possessive Chicory
Over-enthusiasm Vervain *E/B* ✓
Domineering, inflexible Vine
Intolerance Beech
Self-repression, self-denial Rock Water

FEAR

Terror Rock Rose ✓
Fear of known things Mimulus ✓ ✓✓✓
Fear of mind giving way Cherry Plum ✓
Fears and worries of unknown origin Aspen ✓
Fear or over-concern for others Red Chestnut

LONELINESS

Proud, aloof Water Violet
Impatience Impatiens
Self-centredness, self concern Heather *Busher?*

INSUFFICIENT INTEREST IN PRESENT CIRCUMSTANCES

Dreaminess, lack of interest in present Clematis
Lives in the past Honeysuckle *E/B*
Resignation, apathy Wild Rose ✓
Lack of energy Olive
Unwanted thoughts, mental arguments White Chestnut ✓ ✓✓
Deep gloom with no origin Mustard ✓ *B EB/B*
Failure to learn from past mistakes Chestnut Bud ✓

'I need most of the ones under "Insufficient Interest in Present Circumstances", like Failure to Learn from Past Mistakes – Chestnut Bud.'

Buster and I were in the park now, foolishly smoking a joint.

'Unwanted Thoughts and Arguments – White Chestnut. Lack of Energy – Olive. Oh, and Sweet Chestnut – Extreme Mental Anguish.' We were laughing now.

'I need Larch, Pine, Elm – all the ones under Despondency and Despair. 'Specially Oak – Exhausted but Struggles On,' Buster said, giggling stupidly.

'Wild Oat – Uncertainty as to the Correct Path in Life,' I wheezed, snot flying out of one nostril.

'Fear of Mind Giving Way,' Buster guffawed.

'Right, I need 27,' I said. 'How much are they? £1.90 each! That's 27 × 2ish – 54ish quid!'

'Just choose one general one. I'm going for Gorse – Hopelessness and Despair.'

'OK, I'll have Scleranthus – Indecision. Or maybe Unwanted Thoughts and Arguments. Oh, I don't know, you choose for me.'

Buster, not laughing now, stared at the leaflet. 'OK, Water Violet.'

'What's that? Proud, Aloof? I'm not proud and aloof, am I? I see myself more as Centuary – Weak-willed and Subservient. I am with Steve anyway.'

'Yeah, well I only see you when you're with me,' he said, looking into my eyes a bit too seriously.

'Right, well, I'm going to go and buy one,' I said, standing up a bit proudly and aloofly. 'Coming?'

'Nah, gotta get back,' he said, and put on his 'brave face'.

* * *

Back in the Pestle and Mortar I spent one hour and seven minutes choosing, until I was convinced I heard the chemist tell his assistant to call the police.

'Don't be silly,' I thought, 'you can't call the police because someone is taking too long deciding!' but swiftly opted for Unwanted Thoughts and Mental Arguments – White Chestnut, and scarpered.

14

Long Distance Dad

'Darling, come on, you'll enjoy it when you get there.'

I was prostrate on my Mum's leatherette sofa.

'I won't, I don't want to go. I can't face the others.'

My Mum was wearing foam antlers on her head in an attempt to be festive.

'Go for Evelyn's sake, she feels funny as well.'

Evelyn was my Auntie, my Dad's divorced childless sister. Nervous, twitchy, kind, selfless, easily pleased. When my Dad ran off to live in Parliament Hill with Pam, his Open University tutor, Evelyn had remained close to my Mum as she found John, my Dad, her brother, intimidating.

'Anyway, I feel guilty about you. Us all together, you on your own.'

'I don't mind,' she said and glanced down through her bifocals at the *Radio Times*, 'I've got Flopsie for company.'

Flopsie was hopping round the living room, one ear up, one ear down, growling at my ankle if I went near him. He'd never forgiven me for repelling his sexual advances two years ago. He'd also started shaking his paw aggressively like a fist.

'Why's he doing that?'

'Oh, he's waving!' Mum said proudly.

'Is he?' I said quite impressed, and my Mum waved back at him enthusiastically, her antlers quivering.

'I wish I could just stay here with you, Mumsie,' I said in my best cute voice.

She looked a bit frightened. Who knew what heights of emotion I might scale during the evening and for how many hours I could repeat myself over my dilemmas?

'They're repeating *Bouquet of Barbed Wire*. It's the last episode. I'll be fine.'

So, she could cope with the repeated tangled emotions of Frank Finlay et al., but not of her own dear daughter. Just then there was a honk of a horn. Maybe Steve had a new horn on his bike! Just like my brother's horn on his old Wolseley! But no, when I looked down at the street there was my eldest brother, Mark, gesticulating for me to come down immediately. I could feel his nervous energy from the balcony and my naturally-padded shoulders crept up towards my ears.

'OK I s'pose I'd better go,' I said pathetically, shuffling towards the front door and away from the comfortingly claustrophobic warmth of my Mum's gas-fired living room. I opened the front door and there was Buster.

'Oh hi, Buster, I'm just going out, I'm afraid.'

'Is your mum in?'

'What?'

'Buster!' Mum warbled, 'It's on in ten minutes, put the kettle on!'

'Oh, I see!' I said.

'I said I'd watch *Bouquet* with your mum. Keep her company.'

'Don't you think it's a bit unhealthy all the time you spend with my Mum?'

'She's lovely, your mum, and we're both a bit lonely.'

'Oh don't! She's not lonely! I feel bad enough as it is without worrying about my Mum.'

'Your poor mum.'

'Buster, is that you, love?'

'Yes it is!' I yelled. 'Hang on!'

'Edie? Haven't you gone yet?'

I could hear Mark honking continuously on his horn. I turned back to Buster. 'Why is she a poor mum?'

'You're horrible to her.'

'I'm not!'

'Buster?!'

'Coming Mrs D!' and he squeezed past me.

I heard Buster say, 'Why are there olive stones all over the carpet, Mrs Dudman?'

'Oh no – that's Flopsie – ooh, he's done a woopsie on the carpet!' my Mum said, doing an appalling impression of Frank Spencer. 'Oh look love, he's waving at you!'

'Hey Flopsie! Gimme five!' Buster said. 'You should enter him for *New Faces*, Mrs Dudman. Like that dog that says "sausages".'

As I approached the steamed-up Wolseley I groaned inwardly. Mark was tapping impatiently on the steering wheel, his door open with his legs hanging out. Standing by the car was his girlfriend, Sandy, looking pained, and in the back my Auntie Evelyn, waving, flanked by my nieces Angelica, seven, and Jemima, nine, AKA Angel and Mimi. In a battered old Ford Escort behind them was Pat, my other brother, his wife Georgie and their three kids, Katie, Tom and Emma. Pat waved and honked his horn.

'What's up with you?' Mark said.

'Nothing,' I answered grumpily.

'Because I've got a crashing headache – girls, can you be quiet!'

'Actually, I'm feeling a bit depressed,' I said.

'What's new?' said Mark.

Mimi laughed from the back.

'Hi, Auntie Edie,' said Angel. She's the quiet, sweet one.

'Hi, Eed,' said Mimi. She's the grown-up one.

'Hello love,' said Evelyn.

'Can you map-read please, Edie?' said Mark.

'Oh no!' cried Mimi from the back.

'Come on Edie, take some responsibility for once.'

'What the fuck's that s'posed to mean?'

Mimi laughed.

'What's so funny?' I said. It wasn't so much that Mimi was grown-up, more that I was childish.

'It's funny when brothers and sisters argue,' she giggled.

'Actually, I'm very good at map-reading.'

Everyone laughed in unison.

'Right,' I thought, 'I hate them all. If only I'd been nicer to Flopsie, he was the only one who ever loved me.'

'Oh fine,' said Sandy, handing me the map. 'You can sit in the front with him. I'll go in the back – budge up, girls!'

'Oh Mum! There's no room!' Mimi whined.

'Just move over, Mimi!'

'Oh don't wind them up, Eed!'

'I'm not!'

I turned to Mark who had been laughing despite his 'crashing headache'. 'We all have to pussyfoot round you when you're in a bad mood.'

'Can you just concentrate on the map-reading – I need to do a left somewhere onto the A406.'

Of course the best thing to help you concentrate is to start blathering on.

'I had this weird dream last night . . . Eed, Eed! Are you listening?'

'Yes! God!'

'It was one of those very short precise dreams – terrifying, this little man with a gnarled-up face, all wrinkled with a leery expression . . . Eed! Eed!'

An elbow landed hard on my arm.

'Ow! Jesus, I'm listening!'

'. . . he didn't do anything, just stared and when I took the girls to that greasy little café behind the town hall, there he was!'

He went to nudge my arm again but I dodged him.

'Third exit!' Sandy called, 'thir . . . Too late!'

'What? What?' Mark demanded, turning off at the next exit.

'Wrong exit!'

'Alright, alright! This is OK, I can cut through to the M25 this way,' and he turned back to me. Oh no! He was going to carry on with his dream!

'It was a premonition . . .'

'Edie!' Mimi said, 'where's Steve?'

'What d'you mean?' I said craning my neck round.

'Er . . .' she said mock nervously, 'I don't know!'

'Well shut up!'

'Charming!' Mimi said and popped her bubble-gum defiantly.

'Steve was off the scene a long time ago, Mim,' Mark told her.

'What d'you *mean*?' I said. 'He's not off the scene at all! It's just – well, I'd hardly bring him to Dad's.'

Silence. Broken only by the pop, pop, pop of Mimi's gum. I wanted to go on explaining – the air was crackling with everyone not mentioning my 'condition'.

'Steve's gorgeous,' said Angel.

'The trouble with our family is we go out with someone and then we think we have to go out with them for ever. None of us seem to be capable of just having a fling,' Mark said.

'Take a right here, darling!' Sandy piped up.

'Don't call me darling when you're giving me directions, Sand.'

Evelyn intervened foolishly at this point in a quavery voice, 'This doesn't seem right to me, Jim doesn't go this way.' Jim was her other brother, eminently sensible beige route-planner.

'This is right,' Mark said. 'It takes us out to the A40.'

'Mimi, don't do that,' Sandy sighed, digging a knee in my back.

'I'm tired,' Mimi said in an elderly voice.

'Yes, well we're all tired,' I told her.

'Some are more tired than others,' said Mark, meaning him. 'Anyway, nobody knows the meaning of the word tired 'til they've had kids.'

'Mark!'

There was a pause, Sandy put her hand on my shoulder and squeezed.

'Well, I'm sorry, it's not *my* fault!' Mark said crossly.

'Don't worry Mark, I didn't take it personally, love,' said Evelyn. More pause.

'Why can't you bring Steve to Grandpa's, Auntie Edie?' a small voice asked.

'Who said that?'

Sandy, Evelyn and Mimi all said, '*She* did!' pointing at Angel.

'I don't know why you're all doing that mock terror.'

'It's not mock, Eed,' Sandy laughed.

'You can't shout at Angel!'

Mimi was right. You couldn't shout at Angel. I smiled at her, her large eyes gleaming in the darkness. She was going to be a man-tamer, like Lucille.

'Why doesn't Auntie Edie ever smile or laugh?' she asked.

'Sandy's right, we should've gone via Amersham,' Evelyn said.

'Look, Evelyn, do you want the map? Look at the map!' I said stabbing at the page. 'We're here and we're going here . . .'

'We are going the most eminently sensible route,' Mark said in a vicarish tone, 'staying on the motorway until the last moment.'

'Everyone shut up!' Mimi shouted.

'Let's all play "first one to speak is out,"' suggested Evelyn.

'Right, I'm out!' said Mark.

'Me too!' I said.

'It's fun not playing this game, isn't it?' said Mark.

'Shhhhh,' said the rest of the carload.

'What did you get Dad?' I asked Mark.

'A bonsai tree kit,' Mark said.

'But they take about 50 years to grow!'

'Grandad's nearly 50!' Mimi shrieked with affected laughter.

'It's just along here,' Sandy said.

'I know! Anyway, Dad'll live to be 100, no trouble.'

'You've passed it!!' Sandy and Evelyn chorused.

'For Christ's sake! Don't bother to tell me!'

As we pulled up outside Dad's house, with Pat amazingly pulling up behind us, Mark got out and said, 'Oh shit!'

He'd trodden in dog shit. He started scraping his foot on the kerb. Behind us Pat started scraping his foot on the kerb as well. He had also trodden in dog shit. Just then Pam and Dad appeared on the drive.

'Welcome, welcome!' my Dad called, waving heartily, their rescue dog, Captain, a severely overweight golden Labrador, wearing a Santa coat and rollicking about on the end of a lead. We all adjusted our expressions and groaned.

'Problems with the traffic?'

'Grandad!' Mimi shouted, '*I* haven't got dog shit on my shoes!' and ran towards them. Pam started to twitch, bending down towards Mimi, her pearls dangling. She patted her stiffly on the head with the side of her hand.

'Dog *faeces*,' she corrected. 'And we have a "no shoe" rule.'

Angel, who had minced shyly up behind them, said, 'Dog's faces?'

'Grandpa's got shoes on!' shouted Mimi, pointing as Captain started skidding into the splits on the gravel, strangulating himself and attempting to bite Mimi's hand off. Mimi began a session of wide-mouthed frog wailing.

'Darling, darling! You'll frighten Captain, he's not used to strangers,' Dad admonished.

'I'm not a stranger! I'm Mimi!' screamed Mimi and ran to her mother's legs.

'Oh God,' I muttered to myself and went into nil-personality mode, which was all my Dad ever saw me in.

'So, what are you up to, Edie?' Pam asked me as she served up the sherry trifle. ('Your Father's favourite.')

'Oh, I'm just saving up, got a little job in, you know, a shop . . .'

'Oh, look, John! Look at Captain! He loves trifle!' They both gazed indulgently at the dog who was tied up in front of a bowl of trifle, because if he was put outside he 'sang' and if he was free to roam, he ate small children.

'Ah yes,' Dad chuckled.

Pam turned back to me. 'Mmmm?' she said. 'Oh! The serviettes!'

'Edie's going to college!' Evelyn said proudly.

'Oh yes?' my Dad said.

'Waste of time at your age,' Mark said. 'You want to get a decent job. Me and Pat never went, did we? And we've done alright.' Mark and Pat still worked with my Dad's window cleaning business, plus Mark drove a mini-cab (hence his poor sense of direction) and Pat was a fireman. Dad had gone back to plumbing, the Water Board having paid for him to do an Open University degree in English Literature in the late 1960s.

'What will you study? Something useful, I hope?'

'Art!' Evelyn spouted. She was a keen clay figurine-maker herself. Hedgehogs mostly. Very fiddly.

Everybody went quiet.

'Not seeing Steven any more?' my Dad asked, chucking Captain a glacé cherry.

'No. I am,' I said.

Everyone went quieter.

'Such a pleasant fellow.'

'She's dumped him, haven't you, Edie?' Mark said.

'She should do,' said Sandy.

'That's right, my dear, play the field at your age.'

'Right!' said Pam, ever on the alert for anything deeper than chit-chat. 'Who's for a cracker!'

'What sort of art will you do, my dear?'

'Photog . . .'

'Oh, John, look at Captain, he's saying "Oh not those noisy cwackers again! They fwighten me!"'

'It's alright lad,' said my Dad to my slobbering step-brother. 'It's only once a year.'

'Bang!' went Mimi and Angel's cracker, eliciting distraught operatic howling from Captain.

'Oh shut up, Captain!' shouted Mimi. 'What a racket!'

'No, dear, Captain's got a lovely voice, haven't you, lad?' Dad said.

'Anyway, I thought I might do photography,' I continued.

'I'll take him out, darling,' my Dad said to Pam. 'It's not fair on the old boy.'

So we all ended up freezing out in the garden for the annual photo.

Mark raised his camera to his eye. 'Say shit!'

'Mark!'

'Faeces!' Mimi said.

'Don't be facetious, Jemima!'

'*Faeces*-ious!' yelped Mimi, giggling.

'Oh, John, look at Captain, he's saying "Aren't I in da photo? I take a lovely snap and I've got my bestest winter jacket on!"'

We all looked politely down at our grinning, panting relation who was obviously at best pointing his paw to his temple and saying 'Durrrrrrr!' and at worst shouting 'Get me out of this fucking poofy coat you bunch of cunts and give me that turkey carcass before I tear the whole lot of you limb-from-limb and make *you* eat Chum and Winalot day-in-day-out, 'cept that time I nicked that catering tub of Blueband margarine off 've the neighbours, luverly, and never getting a shag or even a decent punch up. I woz better off on that balcony in

Walthamstow at least I got to go on the rampage every now and then. Go on, fack off you bunch of Home Counties toffs!'

'Smile, Captain, dear!'

Seeing my Dad and Pam all gooey together and hanging on each other's every word and saying '*we* don't watch soaps' and '*we* don't like this' and '*we* don't do that', and singing duets to the dog made me go into a black mood and start comparing my Mum, and therefore myself, unfavourably with Pamela. What if I had inherited the gene that made men leave you?

On the drive home everyone was asleep except me (and Sandy fortunately, as she was driving). I sat there with cold feet and a distended stomach watching the lights of the oncoming traffic flashing by in the darkness. I had kept my emotions down with seconds of trifle and a large slice of Christmas cake, but I could feel them starting to stew in my gut and rise sourly to the surface.

Once back at my Mum's, on her leatherette sofa, slumped and irritable, I ineffectually tried to stem the rise further with some nuts.

'Oh fuck! I've dropped another nut down the sofa.'

'What, dear?'

'Oh, Christ, do I have to repeat everything!'

'I'm sorry dear, but you were definitely mumbling that time.'

'I wasn't!' I yelled.

'That's better.'

'You're definitely going a bit deaf, Mum.'

'Well, I don't have trouble hearing anyone else.'

'Right. Well no one else thinks I mumble,' I enunciated clearly as I went to the kitchen. From whence I heard:

'A ol am er I.'

'I CAN'T HEAR YOU! I AM IN THE OTHER ROOM!'

Appearing in the doorway, Mum repeated, 'Angel's hamster died.'

'I know, you told me.'

'And Mark told her he'd gone to heaven.'

'Mum you've told me!'

'. . and Angel told me it was OK because Harry had gone to Devon.'

'Ha, ha, ha. Very funny. You've told me.'

And she went back to the living room chuckling, undeterred, to herself.

'Mum! D'you want a trifle?'

'Darling, I can't hear you, I'm in the other room!'

'DO YOU WANT A TRIFLE?!' I screeched, slinging the individual M&S trifle onto her lap and thinking of Pamela's homemade sherry one.

'There's no need to shout, dear,' she said, peeling the plastic lid off and licking it. I wanted to do the same with mine but, determined to keep the moral high ground, managed to resist. I glared at her. She was really enjoying it. Scrape, scrape, scrape. Loving looks at each mouthful. Licking the back of her spoon. Having a good root around and being sure to make it last. She hadn't glanced at *The Great Escape* for several minutes.

'Enjoying your pudding?' I asked nastily.

'Hmm, lovely,' she said, teeth blurred with cream.

'Surely you've finished it?'

'Just one more bit!'

I sighed and took my plasic punnet out to the kitchen where I did some major tongue acrobatics to get the last bits of cream out of the curves. When I came back in, my Mum was doing the same.

'Mum! That's disgusting!'

'Sowwy darlin', it's just so tasty.'

'I wouldn't bother escaping, would you? I mean they get regular meals and play games and they don't have to go back and fight.'

'Yeah well, that's why you weren't running the country in the war.'

'Thank God!'

'It's not clever not to have any ambition you know,' I told her, thinking darkly of Pamela who was a lecturer and had written a book about Mary Shelley and who would never have a trifle punnet let alone lick it out.

'What, you'd go tunnelling off like that?'

'Yes probably. In that situation.'

'Ooh no, I wouldn't. They've got nice bunkbeds and everything.'

'Well, I can't understand that attitude at all!' I maintained. Which was funny, because when *The Great Escape* was on the year before I had had exactly the same conversation with Mark and had taken Mum's point of view. I was arguing for the sake of it. Because we both enjoyed our trifle a bit too much and my Dad had left my Mum and I had been abandoned by Steve. I wanted to cut myself out from some new cloth.

When Mum's friend Betty from number 39 came round for a sherry with her granddaughter things improved, like they always did when we had an audience. That was until my Mum said, 'Why don't you show Angela your rabbit, darling?'

I gave my Mum a dirty look and she said, 'What?' and I said, 'Nothing!' and took Angela out to the balcony where we stood in silence looking at Flopsie. Angela was nineteen.

When I finally flung myself on my bed later that night, I thought, 'I hate my family, they're so critical, and sharp and loud and exhausting. And I'm the worst of all. I like quiet people who don't say anything.' And I thought about Steve, gorgeous Steve, and got out my photo album for a session of regrets and self-torture . . . and decided to go round and see him . . .

Things my Mum does

Jut lower lip out when watch T.V

Put jar away without lid on properly

circle days viewing in Radio times

Feel guilty about people who never feel guilty about us.

Things I'm not going to do anymore

Jut lower lip out when watch T.V

Put jar away without lid on properly

circle days viewing in R. Times

Feel guilty about people who never feel guilty about us.

15

A Few of Steve's Favourite Things

I rang on his doorbell. He lived on the second floor of a house in West Ealing. The lights were off. I knocked hard on the door – maybe the bell was broken. My new ra-ra skirt was blowing about in the wind and I felt foolish. It had taken me 50 minutes to get there, including a 25 minute wait for the E3 bus. I went down the side passage, crunching on broken glass and old fence planks, and across the square of scrubby lawn to his bike shed. No one there. I glanced up – his bedroom window was lit up – and there was Steve with headphones on, nodding. My stomach flipped over.

'Steve!' I shouted, waving.

'Steeeve!' I screeched.

'Steeeeeeve!' I bellowed.

I looked round for something to throw, was just considering a medium-sized rock when a window opened on the first floor.

'Can you keep the noise down, I've got a kid in here asleep!' a woman's silhouette shouted louder than I had.

'Oh, I'm really sorry. Sorry. Could you let me in the front door? My boyfriend can't hear me . . .'

'Who, Johnnie?'

'Steve.'

'Oh right,' she said sighing. 'Hang on, I'll let you in.'

I crept up the linoed stairs and banged on the door.

''allo,' he said, not looking too displeased. 'What you doing here?'

'I wanted to see you.'

'I'm going out in a bit,' he said as I followed him to his room.

'Where?'

'Down the Empress. Come if you like,' he said, sitting on his bed.

'I bought you a Christmas present,' I told him.

'Oh yeah. What is it?'

'I've done you a stocking!' and I pulled a long woolly snake out of a plastic bag. I'd done a stocking of all his favourite things.

It contained:

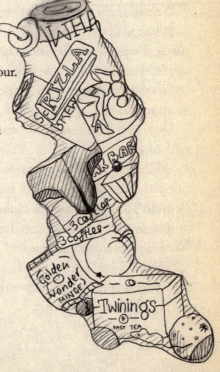

1 × Golden Wonder crisps –
    Prawn cocktail ('minge') flavour.

2 × 3 Castles tobacco

1 × Special Brew

1 × Twinings Breakfast Tea Bags

1 × Star Bar

1 × *What Motorbike?* magazine

1 × black M&S briefs

1 × green King-size Rizlas

1 × Mr Kipling Bakewell Tart

1 × apple

1 × sugar mouse

1 × tangerine

'Oh yeah!' he said gratifyingly at each item and ate his Star Bar immediately, then, when he got to the tangerine, 'Want some tea?' he said and disappeared into the kitchen.

'Yes please!' I called and propped myself up on the bed, plumping up two of the pillows. Why hadn't I thought of this before? No wonder things hadn't been working out. I never gave anything, I just waited for him to come round. He came back in with two mugs of tea and a present under his arm. I could tell he'd used old creased wrapping paper, but who cared?

'Oh thanks,' I said, looking at the toasted sandwich-maker, 'I need two.'

'Do you?' he said. 'I could probably get you another.'

To hide the rigor mortis on my face I plumped up my pillows again.

'You're really good at making yourself comfy, aren't you?'

It sounded like a sneer. I could feel myself going funny, but surely it was a compliment? Then he sat down next to me and started stroking my neck. Thank God I'd kept a grip.

'You've got a beautiful shaped head and neck,' he said. I'd worn my hair up specially, how he liked it.

He crawled on top of me and started pecking my face. 'I've missed you, Pup.'

'Well, you could've come round to see me,' I said. It just popped out, like a toasted sandwich out of either of my Breville Toasted Sandwich-makers.

'Oh Jesus Fucking Christ!' he shouted, leaping off the bed. 'Why d'you have to do that?'

'What?' I said sitting up. 'I . . .'

'Oh forget it, let's go down the pub.'

'Why? What have I done?'

'Don't start whining . . . Get up.'

'I'm really sorry, I don't understand . . . Come on, that was lovely. Come on, Stevie, come back . . . I wasn't . . . Oh please, come on, I really want to. Come on, let's have that beer and joint.'

He looked me over. 'Yeah OK,' he said. 'You are looking particularly gorgeous, Woolly Monkey.'

'I'm wearing stockings and suspenders,' I told him.

'Tell me more,' he said, turning off the main light and putting on the bedside light. He sat on the bed and slid his hand up my leg.

'I love that soft bit there,' he said stroking just above my stocking top. 'It really gets me.'

This was the best bit. If I could just fill my head with now everything would be alright . . .

'Come on,' he said irritably, after lying with his back to me for fifteen minutes and snoring. 'Get your arse into gear. I'm late for Paul and Kev.'

'Y'alright, Eed?' Paul asked in the pub. He felt sorry for me I could tell.

'Yeah fine,' I said. I was squashed in the corner behind a beer-soaked, ash-strewn, shiny brown table, bright light shining in my face. There was a Space Invaders game inlaid in the centre of the table and I watched the space invaders shuttling back and forth. Steve hadn't spoken to me for several hours except to say, 'Here are,' with a half of bitter. I know I said I liked quiet people, but this was a bit extreme. Glued to the seat, knees wedged under the table, I didn't know how to get up and leave. Steve was playing pool and laughing. And I was thinking, 'Go on, get up and go. Save yourself, get up and leave.' But I clung on and stayed at his flat with absolutely no encouragement and was awake all night.

16

Doing Something vs. Doing Nothing

Richmond Park, 30th January.

Armed with the new *Woman* and *Woman's Own* and a ready made joint I walked up Richmond Hill which was covered in grey slush, the remains of that morning's snow already ruined. I was going for a walk across Richmond Park to 'think'. It sounded good. How could you not think walking across Richmond Park? Like someone in a film. I would be thinking and Steve would be watching me somewhere on a video screen feeling bad.

I put a thinking face on but my mind was a blank – what had happened to all my Unwanted Thoughts and Arguments? Maybe I had taken too much of that White Chestnut? Now I needed Clematis for Dreaminess, Lack of Interest in Present.

I trudged across the snowy grass.

'Think!' I chanted to myself, 'Think what to do.'

It must've been the hormones fuddling my brain – no thoughts would come. I don't think nature wanted me to think. It just wanted to get on with it. It didn't want any help, require any discussion or decision. There was no decision. Gut. Heart. Head. I aimed for a group of trees where I planned to sit down on my plastic bag, smoke my joint and look for clues to my life in *Woman* and *Woman's Own*. Maybe my exact problem would be in the Problem Page . . .

Dear Clare

I am 21, my boyfriend is horrible. I deliberately accidentally-on-purpose got pregnant; secretly I would like to have the baby. He wants me to 'get rid of it'. I don't want to lose him, I want him to go back to how he was before it went wrong. I work in Crusties the Bakery and slightly want to go to Art School (although there are a lot of other things I could do, see list overleaf).

Please tell me what to do.

Love Edie Dudman.

My problem was too mad, too freakish, too weird. Even my problem had problems.

'They're pregnant,' a voice said.

I looked across and, walking a few feet away but parallel to me, was a skinny man in his thirties – soft creasy face, sandy hair, beardy.

'The deers. They're pregnant. You can tell by their coats. They'll give birth in April.'

We carried on walking adjacent to each other, the sound of the crunch, crunch of our feet on the hard thin snow, and our breath billowing steam in the sunlight. I wondered if he could tell I was pregnant from my coat, my green old lady's one. But he didn't say anything.

'I'm pregnant,' I announced, though my blank brain didn't actually believe it.

'Are you?' he said, and after a pause, 'Happy pregnant?'

'I'm booked in for an abortion tomorrow.'

Another pause. We had continued beyond my trees and veered together. To have a termination in 1985 you had to be too young, too mad or too ill. Or just act like you wanted one. Obviously they had decided I fitted one or more of these criteria because I was booked into the Charing Cross Hospital on the 31st January. Nobody had showed me a picture of a ten-week-old foetus or even told me what a termination was.

'I'd think carefully about that, if I were you,' the man said.

'I'm trying. But there's no point anyway. My boyfriend Steve doesn't want me to have it. I haven't see him in weeks.'

'Maybe he'll come round to the idea. How old is he?'

'Twenty-two.'

'He'll grow up quickly when he sees his baby.'

'His baby,' I thought, but I couldn't conjure up an image.

'My girlfriend got pregnant when she was about your age – twenty. She wanted to have an abortion but I wanted the baby so I persuaded her to have her. Leanne. She's fifteen now. Liz seemed to take to her and then we had Jason, and then when they were two and four she ran off – couldn't handle it, went to live in Spain with her mother who had left *her* when *she* was twelve. But I've never regretted having them, never.'

Something shifted in my brain. I could have the baby! I could not go tomorrow. Just carry on, just let things take their course. I felt my chest expanding with the very idea.

In the cafe having coffee, Graham said, 'You'd never regret it, you know. Having the baby.'

'I would quite like to have it.'

'Why don't you?'

'I could.'

It was such a simple idea. It suited my simple brain which still couldn't equate anything with anything.

'No one else has tried to persuade me.'

'You haven't taken much persuading!' he laughed. 'You could call Steve and let him know.'

The simple idea immediately got muddied. I felt uneasy. Steve. He would be cross. He would be – worse – cool. And he wouldn't be in if I did phone. But a small hope-fuelled part of me felt excited – he would be pleased, he would be surprised . . . he would be mine. 'I'm going to have it,' I said to Graham. He smiled paternally at me and patted my knee. 'Good girl.'

I felt a huge surge of simple joy. 'All I have to do is not go to the hospital. All I have to do is nothing. All I have to do is just be me.'

'That's right.'

The one chink in my certainty was knowing it hadn't happened completely accidentally. That slightly ruined it. Why did I always have to be so conscious of my every move, my every flitting thought? Why could I never have the luxury of blaming Fate?

Graham drove me home in his lovely warm smooth family car. As we pulled up outside the flats I told him, 'I'm going to go and tell my Mum what I've decided.'

'I'll come with you and then I'll take you out for a meal, to celebrate.'

My Mum's reassuring orange shape appeared through the frosted glass.

'Mum, I . . .'

'There you are, darling,' she said, eyeing Graham. 'Steve's been phoning . . .'

What? Hang on. That didn't fit in with my plan but I felt my spirits rise even further. It was all working out!

'He wants to take you out to dinner,' she said.

Dinner? Steve wants to take me out to dinner? It was like my Mum was a Martian. I glanced at Graham and he smiled and nodded encouragingly, but I could see anxiety and – disappointment? – in his eyes.

'Go on,' he said. 'Call him up.'

'But you were going to take me to . . .'

'Call him!'

'Mum, I've decided to have the baby!' I said, picking up the phone. 'You don't mind, do you?'

'Of course not dear, if you're sure?'

'Of course I'm sure,' I snapped.

'I'd better go,' Graham said. 'Call me if you need anything,' and he handed me a card 'Graham Waddle – Furniture-maker', gave me a quick hug and was gone.

My certainty was, unbeknown to me, ebbing away. 'Steve's been thinking,' I thought. 'He's mulled it over and he's going to support me, discuss it, be the old Steve.' All I wanted – my only real ambition – was for Steve and I to sit down and discuss the situation. I didn't know quite how ambitious that was. He wasn't the old Steve, he was the new Steve, the one in the persistent vegetaitive state.

* * *

Mind, Steve *was* showing signs of life on the way to the Italian pizza restaurant, smiling and almost chatting, but I felt a lonely pang as we passed Le Piaf where Graham had been going to treat me: young, lovely, mother-to-be. After our pizzas had arrived I announced my decision.

'I've decided to have the baby,' I said.

Steve's eyes suddenly looked glazed and sunken like an elderly cat's. A long piece of mozzarella string stretched from his pizza crust to his mouth. He clipped it neatly with a fingernail and folded it back on his plate. He collected himself and brightened his face.

'But what about college?'

He'd never taken any interest in my idea of going to college, only seeing my portfolio as a good place to dry his magic mushrooms.

But I pushed that thought away.

'I mean,' he continued, 'it would be a shame, wouldn't it, to have a baby. You wouldn't be able to do anything. I mean your photography and everything.'

It was nothing to do with his argument that I started to be swayed; it was meaningless. It was the fact that he was actually putting forward an argument at all, that he had thought about it, that he didn't think I should have the baby. If I had it I would lose him. So I put the baby second and I nodded and pretended to myself we were having a nice time.

17

No Going Back

Chiswick House Grounds, 31st January.

Steve sat bouncing on a huge Cedar branch and I wandered about kicking at damp leaves self-consciously. When he was there live and I wasn't imagining him watching me on a video screen I found it so much harder to act naturally. I was speechless. I literally couldn't think of a thing to say. I was so aware of my own responses in relation to him that I wasn't sure if he had just behaved appallingly, but I suspected he had.

At the hospital when I came out of the anaesthetic I felt ashamed under the brisk and breezy nurse's gaze as she gave me hot sweet tea. I had to see a counsellor who asked me how I felt and, as I felt nothing, I said fine. Then I found myself set loose and wobbly in the cafeteria. 'A normal person would be picked up by someone,' I thought. After all I had got there on my own. I phoned Steve. It rang seven times. Relieved, I was about to hang up.

'Yeah?' he answered.

'It's me,' I said weakly.

'Alright?'

'Yeah, I'm OK. Can you come and pick me up?'

'Have you seen the traffic? It's fucking murder.'

'What about the bike?'

'It's fucked.'

'Well, can you pick me up?' I said more firmly.

'OK but the traffic's murder,' he repeated.

'That's OK, I'll wait.'

steve.1

Steve.2

Steve.3

For fifty minutes I sat panicking, turning every unlikely person coming through the swing doors into Steve. He's dyed his hair, he's wearing a dress as a joke, he's put on three stone! Then he turned up, looking like thunder. There was no mistaking him. He marched over to me.

'This fucking place, it's like a fucking maze,' he said turning on his heel and walking away. I got up and followed him. Within minutes we were in some sort of basement passageway, lined with trolleys piled with laundry.

'Jesus fucking Christ, this place is a fucking shit-hole.' He turned and walked towards, and then straight past, me. I did a u-turn and jogged after him.

'For fuck's sake!' he growled. We were now in another cafeteria. Then we were wandering across a walkway from one building to another and, passing the same porter again, Steve said, 'What's that cunt looking at?'

It would've been funny if it hadn't been him and hadn't been me and had been a completely different situation. I was literally running to keep up with him as we wandered all over the hospital, eventually bursting out of a heavy door marked Fire Exit into the darkening afternoon and a mass of dustbins.

'Now where's the fucking car park?'

After we found the fucking car park we drove through the fucking traffic and ended up in Chiswick House Grounds because Steve wanted a smoke and, I suspect, couldn't face my Mum. But little did he know. If he thought *I* was too nice, and thought too much, my Mum was always ready to see the other person's point of view.

'How's Steve feeling?' she said after Steve had dropped me off with a 'Catch you later' and sped off. She had my Aunt Evelyn, my brother Mark and my sister-in-law Sandy round, all wedged into sofas and armchairs. Sandy had recently announced she was pregnant again and was already enormous. They all knew where I'd been but no one said anything, just skirted around the subject. 'I don't know. He's a bloody bastard! He couldn't even not be nasty, let alone be nice.'

'He's not Superman, darling.'

'He's probably feeling upset as well,' said Mark, thinking of how he'd feel.

'Yes, and confused,' my Mum added, looking confused.

'I don't know whether he's feeling confused – if he told me he was feeling confused that would be brilliant. You shouldn't be asking about how Steve's feeling. You should be chasing after him with a big stick telling him not to treat your daughter like that else you'll kill him.'

Mum looked aghast. 'What? But darling, you two seemed so happy last night!'

'Are you feeling tired, Eed?' said Evelyn, yawning.

'No.'

'You look tired,' said Sandy, eyes drooping.

'Stoned, more like,' said Mark. 'That Steve always looks wasted.'

'You're bound to be tired,' Evelyn said. 'Isn't she, Sand?'

'Why don't you have a lie down?' my Mum suggested.

'No. You know I can't do lying down in the day.'

All my family were experts at lying down in the day, but I just tossed and turned and if I ever did drop off for a nanosecond felt murderous, nauseous and like I wanted to crawl back into the womb when I woke up.

'*Is* Steve still smoking that stuff?' my Mum asked.

'*Is* he?' Evelyn echoed.

'I don't know!'

'*You* better not be,' added Mark.

'I'm going over Ali's to get some fags.'

'Oh you're not still smoking, are you, Eed?' Evelyn said.

And as I disappeared into the hall I heard my Mum say:

'. . . probably for the best . . . deformities . . . premature. . . '

I tiptoed back and pressed my ear against the door and caught:

'Such a shame . . .'

'. . . World on her shoulders. . . .'

'. . . Can't seem to be happy . . .'

'. . . Should be free and lighthearted . . .'

'. . . I'm so worried Ev . . .'

'. . . Oh Shirl, you've had so much to cope with . . .'

And Mark's deep drone, 'It was her choice.'

'Stop talking about me!' I yelled and heard a plaintive, 'We weren't, dear!' from Mum.

When I came back with my fags, my Mum's place looked like the scene of a shoot out, like someone had come in and machine-gunned them down. My Mum prostrate on her bed in her room. Mark laid out on the Parker Knoll in full reclining position. Sandy upright but head lolling forward and Evelyn leaning sideways on the sofa with her mouth open. Only Flopsie had been spared the group lie-down, and twitched his nose disapprovingly as I lit up a fag on the balcony and felt the anaesthetic wearing off rapidly. On my way upstairs to my old bedroom I saw a letter sticking out of my Mum's handbag and a bit of my name on the envelope in my Dad's writing.

'He's going to save me,' I thought irrationally. And I waited until I was settled in my room with plumped up pillows, a tea and a fag before I read it.

Darling,

Mum tells me you are in a bit of trouble. She seems to think I could be of help. Though what help a useless old duffer like me could be to you heaven alone knows. Then I had an idea. There is something I could do.

If you really don't want your baby – although it seems a shame and Steven seemed such a nice chap. But you are young, more time to sow wild oats perhaps? I wish I had done – but as you know being older, your mother was very keen to start a family, as I was of course! But we were so young. Well I was.

Anyway as you know, Pamela never had children and time is against her now. We would love to adopt your baby! It might be difficult for Captain initially, being used to being an only dog. But I'm sure the old boy will grow to love his sister or brother.

It would leave you free to pursue your career. You are only 21 – you have

your whole life ahead of you, dear girl.
Have a think and let us know,
Dad x

My heart racing, I tore a page out of an old school exercise book and started to scrawl a reply –

How dare you even think that I would — you're supposed to . . . .

But I just trailed off, it was too painful to articulate. It was easier to think a bad thought about my Mum marrying him in the first place. I replaced the 'She's so crap, she drove Dad away!' with 'How could she choose so badly?!'

I woke up the next day, was happy for $\frac{1}{16}$ of a second and then remembered who I was. I sobbed into my pillow until my stomach ached. I couldn't believe I could be nearly three months pregnant and in a hormone-induced trance one day and no months pregnant the next day, and so aware of raw February reality that I could feel the cold damp air whistling the truth about my life around my brain. I did more sobbing, the noise the only way to drown out my thoughts and when my bedroom door opened slightly and my Mum's face appeared round it I shouted, 'I want my baby!'

Yes, it was theatrical but I meant it in a horrible, base, neanderthal way. I felt empty and *was* empty but I still dragged my deflated body out of bed, got dressed and went home, promising my Mum I was OK.

In the kitchen at home Lucille looked at me sympathetically. I knew Mum had quickly called her while I came along the balcony.

'Has Steve phoned?' I asked pathetically, eyes pickled from crying.

'No, were you expecting him to?' she said in a measured way.

'No,' I said.

'You didn't get rid of the baby because he wanted you to, did you?'

'No!'

'Good. Come on, Eed, why don't you go back to bed and rest? You'd feel better for some sleep.'

Barry appeared in the doorway. 'You alright, chicken?'

'She's alright, aren't you, Eed.'

'I feel a bit funny,' I said.

'Well, you're bound to!' She was trying to sweep my messy feelings under the carpet, as per usual. 'You need to put it all behind you now. Get some rest.'

'No, I've got stuff to do.'

'Well, if that's what you want. See you later, OK?' and she kissed me and they were gone.

I wrote:

1) Library – prospectus – Media Studies?
2) Landscape photos
3) Portfolio – photos/sketchbooks?
4) VSO? need skill?
5) Army?
6) USA Summer Camps
7) Typing – learn
8) Driving lessons
9) Prince's Trust Start-up
10) TEFL – China?
11) Interrail?
12) Cotton wool

18

Not Busking but Dying

Kew Gardens, 1st February.

I paid my 20p to get into Kew Gardens and, with my Pentax camera bouncing about on my chest, went self-consciously round the Hothouse. I put my heavy plastic bag of prospectuses down, took one photo of a rubbery leaf then went to the cafe, bought a takeaway coffee and a bun and headed for a large tree. I sat down and started flicking through *Titbits*. I lit up a B&H, moved on to my *Daily Mirror* and a free *Inspirations Magazine* fell out of it. I immediately recognized the Toasted Sandwich Maker on the front cover. In big yellow letters it said 'FREE GIFT! Receive this stylish Sandwich toaster FREE with your first order!'

Stylish Sandwich Toaster (it said again)
- Perfect for the home or office
- Heat resistant housing
- Ideal for making those tasty snacks
- Thermostatically controlled temperature
- 2 pilot lights
- Nonstick coated plates: easy to clean!
- With fixed cord
- Cable storage
- 700w, 230v ~ 50 HZ

(and then, just in case we weren't concentrating)

• Stylish

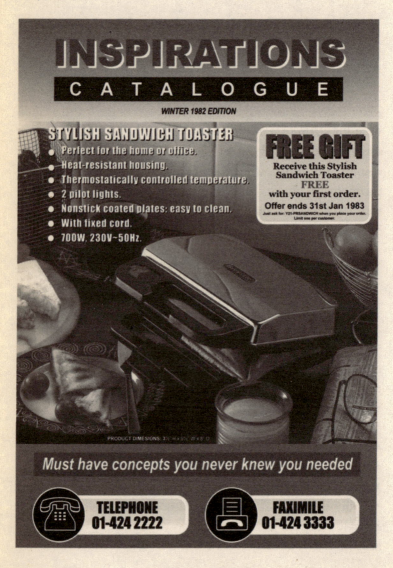

Steve had seen those features and thought of me! Twice! But then I realized he hadn't seen those features and thought of me. It was worse. Steve hadn't actually bought me a Toasted Sandwich Maker, he had bought something else and got the toaster free. Two toasters free. I started flicking through, trying to imagine what he might've bought for himself. The cat radiator basket? No. The giant slipper. No. The Celtic Love Heart necklace? He better not have ... At that point, ironically, I became aware of my own heart thumping and cold sweat dribbling down my sides. I felt boiling hot — I pulled off my hat and scarf — and freezing cold at the same time. My lips were suddenly dry as bone. I rifled in my bag chucking things about looking for my lip salve. Couldn't find it ... started to panic ... my lips dried up more ... Then I noticed I had cramp in my stomach — surely not a period already? I felt faint and white and wobbly.

'I'm really ill,' I thought and looked around for someone kindly-looking to call 'help' to. There was a woman in a stone-coloured raincoat and a headscarf walking determinedly along a path fifteen feet away — I waved, she glanced briefly and quickened her pace. I knew how I must look. My hat was lying turned up on the grass beside me with the change from my coffee slung on top of it. I picked my hat up and — felt terrible, was going to black out — could see two blurry young lads picking their way up the path — surely they would help. I lost my certainty as they passed by and I caught, 'She's a fucking slapper and the other one's tight as a gnat's chuff,' coming from one of their mouths.

I stood up and staggered towards the gate, glanced at the man in the toll booth, thought, 'Help me,' but kept on staggering. I got out into the car park and headed for a thin

Silver Birch, crouched down in the mud and rubbish round its base and tried to focus on a mushroom growing next to an old faded blue Rizla packet, but gave up and closed my eyes.

'Edie?'

'Yes,' I said, not opening my eyes.

'Are you OK?'

I opened one eye and saw Ralph bending over me. I was too ill to dissemble or fluff up my hat-hair or hide my Philistine reading material that lay next to me, flapping open in the damp breeze.

'*Man in BMX Horror Crash*' a headline said in my Mirror.

'Have you got any lip salve?'

'No, sorry. Are you OK?'

'No. I've got terrible period . . . I'm ill.'

'Oh. Can you get up? My brother's houseboat's just over there – you could lie down.'

'OK,' I said.

He helped me up and I leant against his big old man's tweedy coat, and we walked along completely out of rhythm.

In his brother's chemical loo something unfortunate happened, some sort of haemorrhaging. I was in there for ages, sweating and splashing my face with water, and trying not to groan. Ralph tactfully played loud classical music and didn't knock on the door once. Then I lay down in the tiny bedroom which only had room for a double bed and saw a duck swim past the porthole before falling into a deep sleep. An embarrassingly long sleep, as it turned out. My eyes opened to the sound of loud whispering. I looked up at the porthole. It was dark – it must be gone four. I sat bolt upright and caught sight of myself in the porthole glass, one side of my face covered in deep creases and hair flat against my head. My body seemed to have completely recovered however, and it desperately wanted to slide back down into the bed and sleep some more. Ralph put his head round the door.

'Hi Edie, hi, um, how are you? The thing is, my brother and his wife are having people round to dinner and . . .'

'Oh God, sorry. Oh God . . . it's OK. I've got to go anyway. Thank you . . . I . . . sorry . . .' I said, sitting up on the bed and arranging myself, dreading the brother and the wife.

'It's OK, you can go out this way. I'll come with you.'

It seemed there was a secret exit that saved me from having to face brothers and wives.

'Thank your brother for me – see you Thursday!' and I wobbled over the gangplank and ran off into the night.

19

Into the Abyss

I couldn't even have a nervous breakdown without being conscious of it, internally theatrical, imagining everyone else talking about me, worrying about me, film cameras relaying images of me to Steve. So I thought of this era as my semi-nervous breakdown, my very awareness of it seeming to disqualify it as a full one. I phoned Crusties and told them I was ill and even Kerry sounded sympathetic – 'Fuckin' 'ell, you must feel like shit!'. And then Moira came on the phone, 'Hello love, you take as much time off as you want, we can hold the fort.'

Most days I lay in bed until 2 o'clock, then sat in the darkened living room with one ear pressed to my transistor radio and the other ear trained towards *Knots Landing* on the TV. I was still looking for clues to Life. I was also looking for evidence that other people had problems – ideally problems exactly like mine. The people in my life who seemed to be problem-free – Lucille, her mum Wendy, Steve – made up one species, Species A, and made me feel lonely, afraid, alien. The people in my life who were riddled with problems – Buster, Moira, my Mum – made me feel I was with my own species, Species B, inbred and deformed but friendly, infecting each other with self-doubt and inferiority complexes, so that I wanted to run away and mate immediately with someone from the other tribe. Because with the problem-free tribe I put on an act that saved me from being me, which was very unrelaxing but a relief in some ways.

I couldn't talk to anyone about how I really felt during this black time because with Species A I was ashamed and knew that they didn't speak my language anyway. With Species B, although initially relieved and comfy in their company (three minutes) and able to communicate fluently, I soon took the role of a Species A person, Margaret Thatcher for example, and became bad-tempered, refusing to be sucked into their slough of despond, their moaning-and-a-droning. They were just a bunch of workshy moaning Minnies! Why didn't they pull their socks up and get on with it?

So I looked for friendship and companionship in *Knots Landing* and Philip Hodson's Problem Hour on LBC. Typical that they were on at the same time, 2.30 p.m. If Valerie from *Knots* was telling Gary how she felt about the twins being kidnapped, how she loved him and wanted him back, I turned up *Knots Landing*, especially if Philip had a caller saying, 'Hello Philip, I've got a problem with my daughter, she's 11 . . .' (Zzzzz)

Then Philip would get a new caller.

'Hello, you're through to Philip Hodson. How can I help?'

Nervous silence would alert me to a possible ally in misery.

'Hello,' Philip would say softly, 'we've got plenty of time. Why don't you start by telling me your name.'

Pause.

'Susan,' a throttled voice would eventually breathe.

Another pause. Then, 'I'm afraid of life, Philip.'

'Aha!' I would think, turning the volume down on *Knots Landing* and up on my tranny to near distortion level.

Long pause.

'You're afraid of life, Susan?' Philip nudged her.

'Yes,' she would say, her voice thin with terror.

I could relate to that! I turned it up a bit more until I could hear Susan's breath juddering.

'What is it about life that frightens you, Susan?' Philip prodded gently.

'Yes come on! What?! What?!' I urged her.

A bit more shaky breathing and then click – brrrr . . . She'd hung up!

'For Christ's sake, Susan, you traitor!' I yelled and then laughed to myself. Bit more *Knots Landing*, then another call would catch my ear. A man, estuary English, 30s – said, 'It's my girlfriend, Philip.'

My right ear pricked up, my thumb pressed the volume on the TV remote – down went *Knots*. I needed to know what men thought about Girlfriends. 'Girlfriend' and 'boyfriend' were two of my key words.

'She's always fiddling with her hair,' went on Brendan.

'Her hair?' Philip said, his voice rising, eyebrow-like.

'Well, like, you know, if we're going out, she's like in the bedroom and she's doing her hair and holding mirrors up and looking at every angle.'

'Ri-i-ght,' said Philip, eyebrow still up.

'There's nothing weird about that!' I explained to him, defensively.

'. . . and she's looking at it from every angle. And then she starts crying and shouting – it goes on for hours. She threw a set of Carmen Rollers at me last night. She's obsessed with it, Philip. Mostly we don't go out, because it gets so late. She seems to relax then. I don't know what to do, Philip.'

'She sounds insecure. Brendan – what d'you think could be at the root of her insecurity?'

'I don't know, we're very happy together, we love each other to death, she means the world to me, we're getting married in the summer, it's just this hair thing . . .'

Boring. 'Very happy', 'love each other to death', 'wedding in the summer'. I tuned out just after Philip pinpointed a cold, unloving mother.

The thing about being in an abyss is that your survival instinct kicks in every few days and cons you into thinking you feel better. I would get this horrible surge of, 'That's it! I'm better! Hurray!', get dressed, put on make-up and set off on some optimistic adventure – like to the council to enquire about voluntary work – but would get as far as Ali's, where he would do his good old '2p or not 2p' joke or the charity shop where the old lady called me 'Pet', or the Jolly Cafe where they called me 'younga laydee' or the market because I liked the way one of the blokes called me 'Sweed'eart'. I wanted to cling to anyone who was kind to me and ask them to look after me and never leave me and then, panicking in case I did it, I would turn around and hurry home.

One day I managed to drag myself to the library. After all, I had to act as if I was going to college, seeing as that seemed to be everybody else's idea of my *raison d'être*. Ralph had told me there was a course called Media Studies where you studied lots of media-ish things and it all sounded a bit vague and noncommittal which quite appealed to me. I laid the prospectuses and my dog-eared application form on the end of a row of desks and sat down self-consciously. It was 10.27. When I looked at the clock again it was 10.28. I glanced around at the other residents. There was a smelly old tramp next to me, filling in the vowels in the newspaper headings with a biro. A woman shuffled past in slippers and a housecoat. Someone with Tourette's Syndrome shouted, 'Fuck off!' behind the Theatre and Film section.

I wrote 'Media Studies Courses' at the top of my notebook. Then I went over and over it with my pencil and as it darkened and smudged I felt my panic rising. The silence, accompanied by a steady percussion of shuffles and coughs, was deafening. 'I am in the library looking up college courses,' I told myself and opened up the first prospectus – an art school in Surrey – and flicked through pictures of shiny-haired students on campus, smiling over coffee, laughing, linking arms, making jewellery, painting watercolours, spinning pots. My fingers felt clammy. I got to Media Studies. Photography, Animation, Film, Installation, Performance Art. In a photo a young black man pointed a film camera authoritatively. In the background a girl was passing. Not a student, a member of the public – she was out of focus, staring open-mouthed with black, blurry eyes and a fuzz of brown hair. She carried a plastic bag and wore tights with trainers and an old lady's coat. She looked like she might be going to the library. I looked at the students in the prospectus. I looked round at the other library users. 'These are my people,' I thought. 'Who am I trying to kid?'

I needed a cigarette or a coffee, some sort of short-term oral gratification to make me feel different – alive – even if in the long term it made me more nervous and ill. A sign said 'No Drinking, Eating or Smoking.' I glanced at the other pile of prospectuses and back at the one I had looked at.

'That'll do,' I thought. It was my new catchphrase. 'I'll do the rest later,' was my other one.

On the way out I had to photocopy my application form before it fell apart but I couldn't make head nor tail of the photocopying machine. A squat African man wearing bleached jeans and jacket approached me smiling broadly, saying he would help me. He photocopied it huge and cropped on A4, minuscule in the middle of a sheet of A3 and all sizes and styles in between.

Fifteen minutes of this gave me the excuse I needed to get out of there. 'Thanks. That'll do for now,' I told him. 'I'll do the rest later.'

'It's my boyfriend's family, Philip. I don't like them.'

My ear perked up vaguely at the word 'boyfriend'.

'OK, Sophie, what don't you like about them?'

'I don't know. They're so different from my family. They don't talk about anything, they're all stiff and polite – and they're snobs – they make me feel left out and sort of lonely.'

'Lonely.'

My ear fully pricked – down went *Knots Landing*.

'And is your boyfriend like his family?'

Pause for thought.

'Um, no not really. He's fun, funny and he's warm . . . I . . .'

'Because,' Philip said, 'it's more than likely he will end up like his family, people tend to on the whole, so you need to think carefully about how you would feel if he did.'

'Right. I will think about that,' Sophie said. 'He is a bit of a snob now I come to think about it . . .'

I tried to relate this to myself, as I did every problem, book, song, proverb, TV drama, overheard snippet of conversation, horoscope (all twelve signs) . . .

Was Steve like his family? He didn't get on with them and they were furious and disapproving of him. They lived in a large mock-Tudor house, had two Red Setters that they all talked to in baby voices – including Steve, which made me mad with jealousy. His parents were called Ken and Anita – Ken worked for a large insurance company, Anita was a housewife, still pretty but hardened by dissatisfaction and sarcasm. They seemed perfectly OK. Steve was a bit of a disappointment I suspected, and they might have tarred me with the same disappointing brush. I'd been there a few times early in our relationship – Steve had grunted a bit and Anita said to me 'Don't have children, Edie, have dogs', eyes sliding towards Steve with an exasperated but slightly coquettish look. Which reminded me disturbingly of Steve's friend Johnnie saying to him once, 'The trouble with your old lady is she wants to sit on your face.'

His Grannie Enid came to stay once and Ken and Anita were out – a tennis club do. Steve and I went and hung about in his room – it was in the early days when he was still nice and I was still myself and I wasn't repressing insane jealousy of the Red Setters or anything. His room was large and maroon and male – we smoked joints and had it off on his single bed. He went down to get us tea and snacks a couple of times where he must've bumped into Enid in the dark hallway and been too grunty and dead-eyed because the next day he had got home from work to find Anita had put his sheets into a black binbag and tied a note to it:

'*Don't ever bring your little tart back here again. Your grandmother was frightened out of her wits.*'

I didn't see much of them after that. But I always had an image of Anita in a tennis skirt sitting on Steve's face with Enid quaking in her furry boots just outside the door.

Name: Edith Dudman

Address: 24 Kent House Boxford London W16

Date of Birth: 30.9.61

Statement of Personal Intention

How do you Intend to Apply Yourself to your chosen Field of Art?

Through the process of two dimensions as represented by photography I intend to explore three dimensional form as represented by sculptural forms made using random objects exploring the juxtaposition of light and shade and form and function of the human experience of experiencing the modern world. Though my photography and film practise I will attempt to make work which is both accessable to normal people and yet on another level deeply intellectual.

Henri Cartier Bresson is a major influence on my work and I am interested in exploring the people of Newcastle and capturing fleeting moments of their lives in shades of black and white. and as I said before I am also interested in the juxtaposition of light and shade generally. My studies of pidgeons are informed by an interest in nature surviving in the concrete jungle of the city, locked in a tension of opposites and in a maelstrom of ambiguous space.

20

One Step Forward, Three Steps Backward

It is amazing how drink and drugs can take the edge off reality. One half a lager in my high velocity engine and I went from misery to merriment in 0–60. The daytimes were a blur of grey but after 6:00 and drugged I felt OK, almost cheerful.

1) Interrail – come on what have you got to lose!!
2) Stall at Portobello Market £s???
3) Phone Penny – try photos of Foxy again?
4) Portfolio!!
5) Knitted photos??
6) Whale watch?
7) Prince's Trust – 'Meet You at 8' magazine?

I wrote the above list on the night of February 13th after consuming two 2-litre bottles of fizzy red wine with Buster and a bit of hash that I had found down the side of my Mum's sofa that must've been at least three years old. Does it go off? Or mature? Either way we both got very optimistic about our various business ventures, or in Buster's case downright delusional. Buster had been left some money by his Nan and we were thinking up entrepreneurial schemes. And putting each other off. Somehow the other person's idea never sounded as good, and after a while our own sounded pretty crap as well.

'I know, we could set up a cafe!' Buster said.

'Yeah, we *could*,' I said uncertainly.

'A really good one, with mugs of tea and massive portions. There's loads of money in catering.'

'Hmm.'

'We could call it "Buster's".'

'Ye-*ah*.'

'Or "Edie's"!' he tried desperately.

'Hmmm. D'you know what I think would be really good?'

'What? Buster *and* Edie's?'

'A listing magazine for this area! Like *Time Out* but just for Boxford. I'm sure there's loads of stuff going on round here but no one knows about it.'

'Yeah, and we don't know about it either.'

'It can be a trendy listings magazine – weekly. We can write loads of good articles. I'll write the book reviews.'

I tore a page out of my address book and started making notes.

'What shall we call it? "Out of your Boxford"?'

'Nah, that's rubbish. "Time Out in Boxford"!' Buster suggested.

'No, that's been done, idiot. Roll another joint. How about "So Good Boxford."'

'I know "Meet You at 8!"'

'No, that's crap! We can do interviews with famous people . . . and a problem page.'

'Yeah! I'll do that!' Buster said.

'No, I'm doing that ... *and* the interviews. And the photos.'

'I know. Let's start up a band!'

'But we can't play any instruments.'

'We can learn. What shall we call it? "Bust your Arse"!'

'I know "Edie Plus Complex"! You're the complex!' I suggested.

'Oh, what's the point, anyway?'

'Oh come on, Bust, don't give up! The magazine idea's really good.'

'I'm not doing it.'

'OK, I'll go it alone.'

'OK, but it's my money.' His Nan had left him £213.

I was making knitted earrings (maybe I *should* have applied for Knitting Design, Crewe and Alsager?) which I thought I could sell on a stall. We were stoned and consequently when I found my jumper with the one arm I found amusement in it.

'Aren't clothes funny? Bits to put our legs and arms in, which are leg and arm shape.'

'Well, we wouldn't be able to put them on otherwise.'

'No! You don't understand!'

'I do. Leg and arm bits to put your legs and arms in.'

'You don't get the abstract weirdness of it.'

'What?'

'The abstract ... What were we talking about? What did I just say? Oh God, I don't know what we're talking about.'

'Something about arms and legs.'

Then we laughed stupidly for a few minutes but our eyes looked frightened. When we stopped laughing I felt really anxious.

'I feel really anxious.'

'I'm going to Africa!' Buster blurted.

'What?'

'I forgot to tell you. I met this bloke in the pub last night and he said if you've got a degree from Oxford they virtually make you a president or whatever they have, on the spot . . .'

'Yes, Buster, but you've got half an HND from Ealing Tech.'

'Yeah, but they won't know that.'

'They might guess.'

'No. Umbula's got loads of contacts and when I've finished the computer course . . .'

'What computer course? I thought you were going to be a stand-up comedian?'

'Yeah, well, whatever.'

'Which part of Africa anyway?'

'What d'you mean Africa?' he said, looking frightened again. 'Any of that plonk left? Skin up will you? Got any biscuits?'

I had knitted one earring, but by the time I had cast off it had grown and when I hooked it onto a sleeper it was just a large woolly lump not unlike its parent, the original ball of two-ply wool. I had chronic backache and the woollen debris of my enthusiasm was all over the floor and needed clearing up . . . 60–0.

'You're going to have to go now, Buster.'

'Oh, come on, let's have one more spliff and finish off that vino.'

'Oh, alright then.' 0–15.

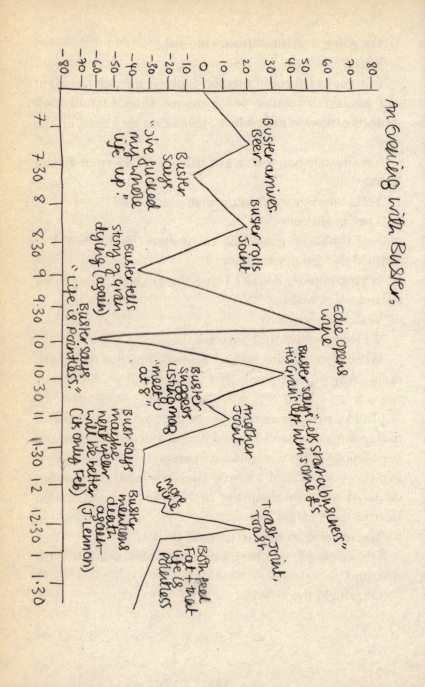

An evening with Buster

Buster arrives.
Beer.

Buster
says
"I've fucked
my whole
life up."

Buster rolls
joint

Buster tells
story of gran
dying (again)

Buster says
"Life is pointless."

Eddie opens
wine

Buster says "Let's start a business"
His brain tells him some £'s

Another
joint

Buster
suggests
using mag
"meet
at 8"

Tasty joint,
toast

Both peel
Fat + that
life is
pointless

Buster says
maybe your
next year
will be better
(it's only Feb)

Buster mentions
death
again —
(J. Lennon)

more
wine

80
70
60
50
40
30
20
10
0
-10
-20
-30
-40
-50
-60
-70
-80

7   7:30   8   8:30   9   9:30   10   10:30   11   11:30   12   12:30   1   1:30

I woke up the next day, looked at my list and went from 0–93. Lucille was banging about outrageously, getting ready for work, running taps, drying her hair, etc.

'*Lucille!* Some of us are trying to sleep!' I yelled, then saw on my digital clock radio that it was 9.42 a.m.

'Sorry Edie! Lucille's gone, it's only me,' Barry cooed laughingly through my door. 'Sweet dreams!' and seconds later the front door shut. My left hand was dead, from my angina probably, and I rubbed it back to life, though it would've been better if I could've rubbed the rest of me to death. I did a bit of deep breathing from my tape 'The Breath of Life' and then – banging! Repetitive banging. Bang. Bang. Bang. I flew out of bed like a torpedo, whipped my curtains open and came face to face with a bloke on a ladder with a hammer.

'Alright love, any chance of a cuppa?' and then, clocking my expression, 'Just fixing the roof!'

'Piss off!' I insisted, whipped the curtains shut and lay back down and tried to relax.

'Someone got out of bed the wrong side this morning!' he called.

'I didn't get out of the . . . Any side of the bed is the wrong side, I didn't want to get out of any side, so either side would be the wrong side . . .' I shouted, not thinking my riposte through before opening my mouth.

He gave up on me after that and I lay there trying to deep breathe in rhythm to his banging. At 10.22 the doorbell rang. I leapt up, flung my jumper and jeans on over my bedwear – stuffing two thirds of my thick grey jersey nightie into my waist-high jeans – and threw myself down the stairs just in time to see a white card plop onto the mat.

'We called while you were out,' it said. 'Please collect

between 10 and 11.30 a.m. at the Main Post Office.'

And then there were a set of boxes –

Excess postage to pay [ ]
Special delivery [ ]
and
Too Bulky [ ]

I opened the door just in time to see Colin Forbes the postman (Two years below me at school, expert at doing Thalidomide and Down's Syndrome impersonations) disappearing round towards the lift with a large sack.

'I was in! I was in!' I shouted.

'Yeah, in bed!' he called back, laughing like a piglet in a postman's uniform.

'Come back!' I shouted from the balcony. 'Why didn't you just post it through the door!' I yelled as he strode off towards his van.

'Too bulky!' he shouted back.

The roof-mender was smirking. 'That's a bit personal!' he said. Mortified, I glanced down at my large low-slung nightie bulge. Then catching sight of the date on the white card I suddenly remembered what day it was, Valentine's Day, instantly cheered up and even smiled at the roof-mender. My survival instinct was kicking in again.

'Any chance of that cuppa?' he said.

'Oi, lad!' Jervis shouted, screeching to a halt in front of me, Kenneth on his lap yapping incessantly.

'It's me Jervis,' I sighed, though the thought of my bulky Valentine's package kept me buoyant. I could still catch up with Colin Forbes, postman extraordinaire.

'You should get your hair cut, you look like a girl.'

'I am a girl,' I said.

'It is the hospital you work at, isn't it?'

Thinking it must be a trick question I looked round for Eileen from the evening classes before answering.

'No. It's the bakery, you know that, I bring you lovely old bread.'

'Could you help me fix my new leg on, it's just arrived from Germany.'

'I think a professional leg-fitter should do that, or whatever.'

'Nonsense, I just need a hand, a nurse is fine.'

'I can't Jervis, I've got to go. I might help you later.'

'I've got an important appointment – with my estranged daughter. I want to look my best,' he said, piling on the pathos. But I knew he hadn't seen any of his five children for twenty-three years and that they all detested him for some unknown reason; I always felt it must be worryingly to do with that ear to ear scar on the back of his neck.

'I'll help you later,' I said.

I got to the post office at 11.29 a.m.. It was quite a trek so I'd had plenty of time to fantasize that it was something big and bulky from Steve, a negligée or perfume, or something from Ralph, something homemade, sweet, clever and bulky. My one fear was that Buster might've sent me something. We'd been spending a lot of time together and I could see him getting the wrong idea. When the man came out from the back with one of those massive envelopes, and I mean *massive*, much bigger than the Crusties birthday card, it was the size of a poster and in a delicate shade of pink, I was a bit taken aback. The writing on the front, tiny in the middle, was pretend child's writing. The postcode was my local postcode.

And I had to pay excess postage. All three things put me reluctantly in mind of Buster the Undiscovered Genius. I carried it awkwardly to an alleyway I knew and, heart racing with renewed hope, set about opening it.

On the front was a big teddy bear. 'Hello Valentine' it said, and inside, 'I like you!' *Like? Like?!* and then bold as brass, not even trying to disguise the handwriting, and in what was unequivocally my Mum's handwriting, it said 'love Mumsie x', in a writing style that could only be my mother's.

I stood there, doing shallow breathing, letting the envelope slide down into a muddy puddle. I lit a cigarette and tried to get a grip. 'Someone really clever has copied my Mum's handwriting,' I attempted. '*Very* clever.'

And then, 'I've never seen Ralph's handwriting, maybe it's exactly like my Mum's?'

It was no good. The card was from my Mum. No one would go so far as to actually write 'Mumsie'. Not even Buster; and I felt irrationally annoyed with him for not going that far.

Hurrying back along the High Street, head down, ginormous card under one arm, hoping even more than usual that I wouldn't bump into anyone I knew, Deidra from Herr Cutt stepped out of Maider's Newsagents right in front of me. I hadn't seen her for seven months – not since she told me to come back for my trim in six weeks. I caught her eye but defocused and tried to look straight through her, thwacking her with my vast card as I passed.

'Edie? That you?'

'Oh Deidra! I didn't see you there!'

She weighed sixteen stone and had pink and yellow hair.

'What you done to your hair!'

'Um, nothing,' I said.

'You've put a rinse or summink on it.'

'Have I? No I haven't – it must be the sun.'

'What sun?'

Oh Jesus.

'I went to Tenerife.'

Why, why, why did I say that?

'Really?'

'Yeah.'

'You look terrible. When did you go? I've just been as well. Did you go to Los Americas?'

'Oh God, Deidra, I'm sorry, I've got to go.'

'Is that a Val Card? Blimey! Someone loves you!'

'Yes!' I laughed. 'Anyway I . . .'

'Oh come on. Who's it from? Come on, let's have a look!' and she tried to wrestle it out of my hand.

'It's from my Mum, if you must know,' I said.

'Oh love 'er. Oh your mum's a love. I wish my Mum was like

that,' and her eyes filled with tears.

'Yes, well look, I've got to dash, Deidra, it's been lovely to see . . .'

'Don't go! Let me give you a trim!'

'No, I . . .'

'Come on Edie, your hair looks really tired, look at those tatty ends. You can't afford to leave it like that – come on, I'll do it at a discount! Tell you what, I'll do it for free!'

'No the thing is. I've . . . got . . . to . . . help my neighbour with his new leg!' I said triumphantly.

'Oh right,' she said. 'You mean that whatsit in the wheelchair?'

'Yes,' I said, surprised at her remembering, 'he's in a terrible state and I'm late.'

'Looks like 'e's late an' all,' she said, flicking her head towards the other side of the road.

And there, letting me down as usual, was Jervis Sponge, being pushed along at the speed of light by one of his old cronies. And he had *two* legs, the one that wasn't usually there sticking out ahead of him with the foot on up the wrong way.

'Jervis! Jervis!' I called, genuinely trying to alert him to my presence. I wasn't doing my usual sneaking-past-him-begging-not-to-be-spotted, I was in fact shouting and waving. But he failed to see me and disappeared into the betting shop, obviously the appointed meeting place for his emotional reunion with his long lost daughter. 'Well, his leg seems to be sorted,' was Deidra's observation, the power of which didn't bode well for my hair. And she linked my arm and frogmarched me across the road. I didn't resist. I was still feeling hurt about Jervis telling me I needed a haircut, forgetting that he'd said that only because I looked like a girl.

'What have you been doing to it?' she scowled at me, once we were in the deserted salon.

'Nothing!'

'I can see that! It's so fine.'

'Oh Deidra, d'you always have to say my hair's fine? I know it's fine!' I said. 'It can't be the only fine hair you've ever seen.'

'No, but it's one of the top finest, definitely.'

Asserting myself, I said, 'Well it's a good job I've got a natural wave else it'd be really bad.'

'Yeah,' she said shaking her head dramatically. 'Blimey if it was dead straight it'd be – well, *really* fine. You'd have, like, one hair on either side of your face!'

'It's not that bad!' I protested.

'So,' she said combing my hair(s) roughly, 'which part of Tenerife did you go to?'

'A really tiny little village, you won't've heard of it.'

'What's it called?'

'Um, Sans Santarianio,' I said.

'Oh yeah, I know it. Dead tatty little place full of Spanish?'

I was really, really, really tempted to tell her I'd made it up and see her big fat chops collapse with confusion.

'Yeah,' she continued. 'W'a's it called again?'

'Costa Delmonte Orangino?' I said.

'Oh yeah, that's it. Horrible. What d'you want to go there for?'

Once she'd finished hacking away at my hair(s) whilst telling me how many babies everyone from school had had, one side was at least two inches longer than the other. It was ruined. It was terrible to start with but now it was ruined. It had taken me years to grow it past my shoulders. But I couldn't risk her 'amending' her mistake – she said it was New Romantic – so I thanked her profusely and went straight into the Oxfam shop. Having parked my giant card outside, I purchased a small black woolly hat for 15p, put it on and hurried home.

'Why are you wearing a tea cosy on your head?' Auntie Evelyn glanced at me from the kitchen where she was pouring out mugs of tea.

'Because I have had a haircut and I look fucking ridiculous.'

'Let's have a look!'

'No!' I said, going into the living room.

'What's wrong with you?' Mum asked.

'A lorry driver said "Hello beautiful" to me,' I said, outraged.

'Ah, that's nice,' Auntie Evelyn called.

'It's not nice! I told him to fuck off! Fucking bastard. And I don't appreciate this card either,' I said, leaning it up against the mantelpiece.

'Why not?' Mum asked.

'Because it's from you!'

'But you are my little Valentine.'

'Oh, I wish lorry drivers would still say things to me, don't you, Shirl?' Evelyn said, coming in with three mugs of tea.

'No. I'm finished with all that stuff.'

'Oh I'm not, I'd love to meet a nice man.'

'Look,' I told them. 'I didn't meet a nice man, a fat old lorry driver insulted me!'

'Make the most of it, love,' Evelyn said blowing on her tea reflectively.

'What? Fat old blokes insulting me?'

'No, being young. You don't realize how gorgeous you are.'

'I'm not gorgeous, I'm vile. Sally Goethem's gorgeous and Jenny Pletheroe. And Rachel Moore. And Emma Cain. Their hair stays brushed-looking and if they get a spot they don't squeeze it.'

'That's the thing, Ev,' my Mum said, going into wise tea-ceremony mode, 'when you're older you think the young have got it all, but they're looking at their peers and comparing themselves. We look at a young person and see the lovely peachy skin and the shiny hair but they don't see that, they take the youngness for granted, they look at the details. To them there's always someone prettier. It's a very insecure time, I'd never go through it again.'

lovely plump skin
+ no wrinkles + all
her own teeth...

longer eyelashes
than me..

bigger
tits

shinier hair

They're all
looking at
my spot...

'By the time you're happy in your skin, it's all wrinkly,' Evelyn said sighing. 'You should show off that nice figure of yours, Edie.'

Then they both stared vacantly at me.

'Carpe Diem!' my Mum said triumphantly.

'What's that, Shirl?'

'Seize the day!'

So I seized my coat, went home and took to my bed again, deciding to resume my semi-nervous breakdown. If that was what the outside world was like, I wasn't going there again.

21

Necessity is the Mother of Cheering Up

All the lights were off and I was lying in my pit, listening to Capital Radio's Love in the Afternoon – I'd done *Knots Landing* and Philip Hodson – when I heard Lucille's heels clacking along the balcony and my heavy heart lifted hopefully. I plumped up my pillows and arranged myself. There was a rustling of bags, clattering of keys and the hall light pinged on. Heels on carpet up the stairs, clomp, clomp, clomp, my door creaked open, light flooded in. I peeped out from under my duvet.

'Jesus Edie! Haven't you moved all day?' Lucille said, leaning over me to open the curtains.

'There's no point opening the curtains, it's dark,' I said, voice croaky from lack of use.

'You're not still depressed?' Lucille said, shocked.

'Depression is repressed anger,' I said angrily.

'You can't carry on like this,' she said.

'Why not?'

'Well, apart from anything else it's depressing for me. It's like coming back to a mental hospital.'

'I feel awful,' I said. I was hot and cold at the same time and wore my woolly hat, two duvets and an eiderdown.

'You look awful. No wonder you feel depressed – it's undignified. Look at your hair.'

My hand reached up. My woolly hat had slipped off during the tossing and turning involved in trying to devise dedications to ring in to Love in the Afternoon.

'It's longer on one side than the other!' I cried.

'I know, Edie, you've said, but apart from that it's all matted at the back.'

'I just don't know what to do. What would you do if you were me?'

'I'd never get myself in that situation because I always get my hair done by my Mum's hairdresser, Eileen.'

'No, I meant I don't know what to do. Generally.'

'Oh right.'

'Anyway not always. You don't *always* get your hair done at your mum's – we had those Page Boys done at Joy's unisex.'

'Oh, so I did! I liked that!'

Oh yeah. Lucille always got the good one.

The good Page Boy hairdo.

The good crocheted waistcoat.

The good boyfriend.

The good pizza.

If I tried to get the same thing as her it never worked out. We both went for Page Boys but they said my hair was too fine to have one that started graduating from the eye-line and I had to have one that started from the chin-line. Lucille had an eye-line one, because her hair was thick. Then a woman in the block, Mrs Wilson, who used to let us do bob-a-jobs in her flat all year round, even without our Brownie uniforms, crocheted us waistcoats. Identical, except Lucille's was trimmed in white and mine was trimmed in petrol blue. Lucille's was just far more exciting. White was so exotic. And once, when I decided to copy her order in a pizza place, hers was still bigger. However, fed up with my whingeing she agreed to swap pizzas and suddenly the one that had been mine, now it was hers, looked bigger. And Lucille always got boyfriends who were nice and I always got crap ones. I didn't know whether Lucille's things just seemed nicer because mine were horrible old mine and, tainted with my ownership, must therefore be inferior. Or was it all in the eye of the beholder?

'When I was little I used to lie in bed and think "I can't believe I wasn't born black",' I said, thinking out loud.

'Edie! That's really racialist.'

'No, it was because people were horrible to black people and so it was a bad thing to be and I couldn't believe I wasn't black. D'you remember when your brother used to make little Robbie shout "Paki" out of the window?'

'No, I certainly don't!'

'That was the sort of thing.'

Lucille put her hand on her hip and sighed.

'Don't you ever have negative thoughts?' I asked her.

'Of course I do. But as soon as that happens I snap myself out of it, shout "shut up" to myself and clean out my knicker drawer or a kitchen cupboard, get my blood moving.'

'Don't you ever get that thing where you can just see the futility of life, where you realize you're just a mass of atoms blobbing about in a never-ending universe?'

'No, Edie, I don't.'

'I'm fed up with being me.'

'Well, who else are you going to be?'

All I wanted was a friend who said, 'Oh, I know exactly what you mean!' Nobody knowing what you mean is the loneliest feeling in the world.

'You used to like discussing things,' I said to Lucille.

'Going on and on about things just makes you feel bad.'

'And you never moan any more.'

'What's the point?' Lucille said with some feeling. At last she was coming round to my way of thinking! But then she elaborated, '. . . in moaning?'

I got out my book of proverbs and quotations that I had been trying to use as a guide to life. It was quite good because you could find one to suit your mood and they all contradicted each other. 'Seize the day!' for example sounded like a good idea but then 'When in doubt do knowt' put paid to that. I picked it up now and read 'Character is fate' – Thomas Hardy. It made me feel a bit uneasy. I thought about my character and felt very worried about my fate. I'd done my tried-and-tested-and-failed technique of drinking tea and chain smoking B&H and 'thinking' so I decided to try Lucille's Tidy Drawers technique. I got up and opened my knicker drawer, which wasn't shut anyway because it had a pair of woolly tights and the sleeve of a jumper from the drawer below stuck behind it, and a festival of knickers exploded out. I started to put them back in the drawer as neatly as possible. It was difficult to know whether to fold them in half or in quarters. So I went in to look at Lucille's drawer. Her drawer was beyond me. How did she do it? Did she fold them every day or did she know the order that she would wear them in so she never had to rummage?

I wouldn't put it past her to have a knicker timetable.

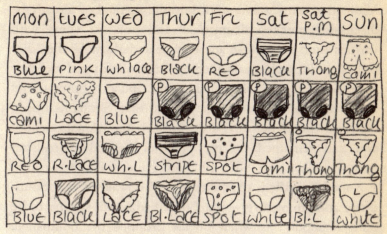

mon	tues	wed	Thur	Fri	Sat	Sat P.m	Sun
Blue	Pink	wh lace	Black	Red	Black	Thong	cami
cami	Lace	Blue	Black	Black	Black	Black	Black
Red	R.Lace	wh.L	stripe	spot	cami	Thong	Thong
Blue	Black	Lace	Bl·Lace	spot	white	Bl·L	white

I went back to look at my own drawer. It already looked messy! I took them all out again, throwing away a pair with a hole in and then feeling sorry for them – they looked lonely in the bin, the two leg holes looking like big sad eyes, and I put them in the high rise pile of period pants – and they *were* period as well – Christmas 1973 from Auntie Evelyn.

I couldn't throw things away. I couldn't finish things off. Dr Hopf was right. My fate was sealed! I would always be in a muddle! But surely it is possible to change your character and therefore your fate?

I was back in Lucille's bedroom doing some last minute revising in her knicker drawer when she materialized in front of me.

'I meant tidy out *your* knicker drawer! Mine's already tidy!'

'I was just . . .'

But Lucille wasn't interested in my explanations and told me I had to get up and dressed because there was a bridesmaids' fitting. Although the *wedding* (said in nasally Midland accent) wasn't until July she seemed to already be discussing chicken drumsticks and vols au vents with various aunts called Jean and Pauline and Mary. All the other bridesmaids had been decided on, Lucille informed me; they were her nieces Kirsty and Danielle and our other friend Shona Gibbons. I was pleased about that, Shona had been my best friend before Lucille joined our primary school and had remained on the periphery of my friendship with Lucille. Sensibly, she had gone travelling round Europe and then to college – she was Down South doing something Arty – but I only had a split second to be pleased about this when Lucille dropped the bombshell. The other bridesmaid was Julie! Julie from Miss Selfish! The Julie Steve was having the affair with. How could Lucille be so disloyal?

'I'm sorry Edie, but she makes bridalwear and it's really nice. So she's designing and making the dresses.'

'When did you decide that?'

'A while ago. I would've told you earlier but I didn't want you to go off on one.'

'But she's awful!'

'Well I like her.'

'But she's having an open relationship with Steve.'

'So are you. Anyway, she's fun and I was good friends with her at typing college and she was thrilled when I asked her to be my bridesmaid.'

'OK,' I said. 'But it'll be really awkward.'

'Try and think about me. It's my wedding,' she said, turning and leaving the room. I leapt out of bed.

'I know it's your wedding!' I said, following her into the

kitchen where Barry was perched on the table looking gormless and Lucille's mum, Wendy, was leaning against the sink in a beige leather jacket leafing through bridal catalogues.

'That hat looks dynamite, Edie!' Barry said.

I tutted and pulled off my woolly hat.

'You sound like you've been thinking things about me,' I said to Lucille.

'No . . .' Barry said, going red. Wendy glanced at him and then at me.

'I meant Lucille,' I said.

Lucille folded her arms, looked at the floor and smiled sarcastically.

'This wedding isn't about you.'

'I *know*!' I wailed. I was probably the person most in the world who didn't want this wedding to happen so how could it be about me?

'OK. Good,' she said.

'Want a cuppa, babe?' Wendy said.

'I'll make it,' Barry offered.

'No, you're alright, love,' said Wendy and made a lot of noise with the kettle.

'Did you look at the flowers, Baz?' Lucille asked.

'What? Oh er, yeah, cracking, babe.'

'Which do you prefer, sweetheart, the Lilies of the Valley or the rose bouquet?'

'Er, whatever you want, love.'

'OK, babe, I like the roses.'

Apart from the endearments, they talked to each other like newly-found pen pals. Maybe politeness and restraint was what kept people together? Maybe that was the secret to a successful relationship? My obsession with 'Talking to Steve' and 'Being Myself' – could that be where I was going wrong?

'I like the roses, love. What do you think, chief bridesmaid?' Wendy said, handing me the catalogue.

'Hmm,' I murmured, still shaking from the between-the-lines row Lucille had had with me.

Lucille tutted loudly and stomped out of the room.

'Lu*cille*!' I said, and to the others, 'What's going on?'

Barry shrugged, quite genuinely I thought, but Wendy said, 'Oh it's nothing, love. I think she just feels you're not that interested in her wedding.'

'What?' I said, horrified. 'I *am*. It's just I've had a crap time recently, I don't know if you know . . .'

'Yes, we all know about your crap time!' shouted Lucille from the living room. 'Trouble is, you're always having a crap time!'

I was stunned. I heard Lucille stifle a sob. Wendy and Barry both rushed in there.

'Oh, come on, babe. It's OK.'

Then the doorbell rang.

'Oh shit,' Lucille said. 'It's the others. Do I look OK?'

'You look gorgeous, pumpkin,' I heard Barry say. I shuffled through to the doorway of the living room. Barry was hugging Lucille.

'Sorry Luce,' I said.

'S'OK,' she said, from behind Barry's blue and white stripy shoulder. But in actual fact I had no idea what was going on or what I was sorry for.

This is what had been happening to Lucille:

Having no doubts,
Being treated like a queen,

Using two Durexes,
Getting engaged.

And this is what had been happening to me:

Doubting everything,
Being pissed about,
Using the rhythm method,
Having an abortion.

And she was the one getting the cuddle.

The bridesmaids' dresses were to be in two colours. Pale mauve and pale yellow. Of course, I was in the pale yellow with the puffy sleeves which was going to clash diabolically with my golden highlights. Julie was preparing to measure us up.

'I'm really glad I'm in the mauve with the off the shoulder, Luce,' Shona Gibbons said, adding quickly, 'Not that the yellow aren't nice too!' and glanced at me and smiled. Good old Shona, she was a Species B type person. I smiled back woodenly. I was still in shock at Lucille's uncharacteristic outburst.

Lucille opened a bottle of warm Asti Spumante.

'Can someone get the glasses?'

'I will!' Julie and I both said a bit too eagerly and jammed in the kitchen doorway together. Julie reached for Lucille's two posh wine glasses while I collected together a tumbler and two plastic cups out of the cupboard.

'Julie?' I said. It was my chance to clear things up with her. And to recover some lost pride.

'Wha'?' she said.

'I just want you to know I'm fine about you and Steve. In fact I actively encouraged him to . . . be with you.'

She stared back at me.

I went on, 'I like to have everything out in the open. I thought it would be good to, you know, talk.'

'Talk?' she said. 'Wha' 'bou'?'

'The situation,' I said.

'Wha' situation?' she said, backing out of the room. 'Steve and me are having a laugh, that's all.'

'Yes, but I didn't want you to think . . .'

'I don't think anything! I'm young, I don't want to get all serious.'

'Yes, I know,' I said, getting all serious, 'but don't you mind about me?'

'Oh, look, don't get heavy Edie – I'm no good at all this stuff.'

I was tempted to tell her that love was letting go of fear but she was already metaphorically zipping up her fly, revving up her motorbike and shooting off.

'Luce, pass that wine, I'm parched!' Julie said. They all cackled away while she measured them, even the nieces, who were only drinking Coke.

'Right, get your kit off Edie, I need to measure you up now,' Julie said authoritatively, avoiding my eye. 'Fing is,' she continued, pins in her mouth, 'I've chose the two different dress designs for the different shapes of the bridesmaids.'

In yellow with puffed sleeves were me (21, brown hair in different lengths, big shoulders, small bosoms, rotund arse), niece Danielle (12, ginger hair, solid block torso, tree trunk legs, sloping shoulders) and niece Kirsty (11, white blonde hair, tiny frame, sparrow legs and prematurely burgeoning bosoms). I couldn't see the correlation myself.

— in pale yellow. —

'And for the colouring,' she added pointlessly. 'Keep still Edie, blimey!' and she measured my chest. '33½ inches!!' she shouted.

More cackling.

'Oh yeah!' Julie exclaimed, 'I got some more of those Celtic Love Heart Necklaces from the catalogue. I got three more, just in case you want to give one to the Maid of Honour. They're quite dear, but worth it.'

'Oh, they're gorgeous!' said Wendy.

'Oh, yeah, so I got some more of those crappy free sandwich toasters with them. I managed to offload the first two but I've got three more now. Anyone want one?' she said, getting one out of her holdall.

'Oh, no ta, love,' said Wendy.

'We've got two of those in the back of the cupboard, haven't we, Edie?' Lucille said.

Damn. On top of the insulting fact that Julie had obviously off loaded a crappy free Toasted Sandwich Maker onto Steve, who had seen it and all its features and thought of me, again, bang went my wedding present to Lucille.

At that point a flapping noise at the door alerted me to Ol' Blue Eyes staring at my semi-clad frame through the letterbox.

'Edie!!!' he called.

'What d'you want, Jervis?' I said, leaping behind the door.

'I've found that old cine camera you wanted.'

'I'll come round later. Go away.'

'Yes, go away, you dirty old coot!' said Wendy.

'I'll let you have it for £50!' Jervis shouted and the letterbox slammed shut.

'Jesus! Poo! I can smell him from here,' said Lucille, wrinkling up her nose.

'Oh, he's alright,' I said.

'He's foul! I tell you, love, you should get the council round.'

'I've called them already,' Lucille said opening another bottle of Asti.

'What d'you mean?' I said. 'Called them? Does Jervis know?'

'Doubt it. But they're going to pay him a visit. I've told them he's a health hazard.'

I felt rage building in my chest and my emotionless depression lifting. I had a reason to live. Jervis!!

Carefree in the Community

I knew I was better the next morning because my list said:

1)   Clean out bedroom
2)   Clean out Flopsie
3)   Clean out Jervis

It didn't say anything about going on a Kibbutz or joining the Foreign Legion. I was feeling more sane. More realistic. Until I went round to Jervis's flat. It hadn't been cleaned since he moved in in 1958 after splitting up with his wife and five children. I had never been further in than his kitchen at the front, and had always managed to hold my breath while I got his teapipe/paper, but now I had to venture further. I rang the bell. Nothing. I looked through the letterbox and called, 'Jervis! It's me! The young man from next door!'

Silence.

Kenneth appeared and yapped at me hopefully.

'Jervis! It's me! Edna, Eddie, Edie, Ethel!'

'You don't fool me! Go away!' shouted Jervis.

Kenneth licked his lips, wiggled his rump and squealed with frustration.

'I know you're all from the council!' Jervis shouted again.

'No! It's just Edie! From next door!'

He wheeled into the hall and opened the door, keeping the chain on, and flapped a letter about.

'I've had a letter from Environmental Health. They're going to come and see my flat. They're going to put me in a home!'

'Let me in, Jervis, I'm going to clean your flat! Then when they come round and see it all clean and lovely they'll leave you alone!'

He looked at me desperately, unlocked the chain and reversed into the living room, bumping expertly over the runkles in the worn old carpet. I stepped in and instantly the smell of unthinkable filth hit my nostrils. I gagged.

'Hangonaminutejervis!' I said with the last of my out breath and ran out. Sometime later I returned, with a wadge of Barry's Mansize tissues sprayed with Blazé and tied round my face with a neon pink chiffon scarf, and a bag of cleaning items from Ali's.

What am I doing? What am I doing? I wondered, but I felt strangely happy and energized. I heard my Mum saying, 'Think about someone else' and Maggie Thatcher saying, 'Think about number one' and knew that I probably wasn't adopted after all.

I started in the kitchen, though scullery seems a more apt word. It, and everything in it, was covered in a brown furry grease. There were tinfoil trays with antique crusts of food on them piled up in a toppling tower. The newspaper under Kenneth's food and water bowls was dated 1979: yellowed and sodden with dried brown dog food stains and crumbs dotted all over it. The lino was cracked, pieces of it lying about like some terrible old jigsaw. It had possibly been blue but was now covered in the same furry grease, but blacker, Jervis's wheelmarks creating a repetitive pattern from sink to cooker to door to Kenneth's bowls. I opened the fridge; it was full of ice and snow from top to bottom.

'OK,' I thought, 'I'll start here but I'd better check out the rest while the Blazé is still active.'

I strode past the downstairs loo and into the living room. It looked like someone had taken several large bin bags and tipped them up all over the floor. Jervis had his bed in the corner of the room covered in ancient soiled eiderdowns in damask pink and sage green, headed with yellow pillows, darker mustard tide marks rippling across them. Dull, dark brown furniture loomed out of the chaos. There was a wardrobe with the door hanging off with a piece of string stretched across the inside with a sad stripy tie hanging off it. A sideboard piled with yellow newspapers stood in front of some shiny brown, leaf-patterned curtains that were firmly drawn across the window. When I poked at them with a washing up brush they disintegrated.

Jervis had managed to heave himself onto his bed and sat with his one leg stretched out. His new tan fake leg stood neatly next to his wheelchair, an incongruous white sock pulled halfway up the calf.

'I can smell something,' Jervis said accusingly.

'I . . .' I began.

'It's my dinner. Liver and bacon. Must be done. Get it for me would you, love?'

I gave him his dinner on a cracked white plate that seemed cleanish and made a start on the kitchen. Which involved standing in the middle of the room looking horrified for twenty minutes. Eventually I donned my Marigolds and piled all the clutter onto the Formica table. Then I opened every drawer and cupboard and tipped and dragged everything onto clean newspaper on the floor – rusty tin openers, roasting tins, saucepans, tea caddies, saucers. Then I covered the sink and draining board with Ajax powder and boiled the black kettle on the ancient greasy gas cooker – a blue speckled affair with legs – and went to ask Jervis what the tinfoil containers were saved for. 'The blind,' he said. 'Don't chuck 'em.'

I wished I was blind at that moment because Kenneth, lying on his front, legs splayed out at the back was helping Jervis to eat his dinner, licking at the gravy whilst Jervis pronged giant bits of meat with his fork.

'Where do I take them?'

'The blind home. They'll be pleased with those. Don't know what they do with them, melt them down and make spectacles with them, maybe?'

'Hmm, probably,' I said, and went to chuck them away.

When I had a cleanish sink of boiling water, I inspected every item in the room. If it was so coated in furry grease that I couldn't identify its nature I chucked it into a large grey industrial sized bin bag.

'Don't throw anything out without asking!' Jervis called.

'I won't!' I called back, flinging an unmentionable rusty cheese grater in the bin bag with a clink. I then started cleaning the more recognizable items. Within minutes, the boiling soapy water was lukewarm, slimy, brown soup and I had to start all over again.

Five and a half hours later Jervis had seven clean items of cutlery, two dinner plates, a cracked cup, a saucepan with a brown, white and orange flower pattern, a gravy boat and a Double Diamond beer glass. That would do him for now. The kitchen looked scruffy but brighter. I'd rubbed at the windows, grunting and sweating, and you could see through them now, though the outer edge was still impenetrable. I was soaked through from slopping water about, and dust and grit stuck to my sweaty skin. My hands were red raw and bloated with brilliant white, soggy nails. My hair was tied up with a tea towel, the Blazé mask long gone. I was exhausted and shaking from the physical effort, particularly the hoovering with Jervis's sucky stick – a hoover without attachments. It was like the ancient art of Cupping and Jervis's threadbare carpet thought it was a load of old New Age claptrap. But I felt great and thought seriously of becoming a professional cleaner.

I went in to see Jervis.

'I'll finish off tomorrow, Jerv–'

I stopped in the doorway. He was fast asleep with Kenneth on his chest. Kenneth eyed me and his tail flicked Jervis's chin.

On my way out I held my nose and peered into the downstairs loo to prepare myself for the next day's challenge. Something horrific lurked in there, something orange – the same orange as the flowers on Jervis's 70s saucepan. Large orange fungi was bulging from the U-bend and cascading out from the rim of the bowl.

I left our flat the next day and bumped into Jervis on the balcony.

'Oi laddy! You left a right mess in my kitchen yesterday and where's my cheese grater?'

I shoved him out of the way with my squeegee mop, and three days later his whole flat was, I won't say clean, but it was habitable. For an alcoholic, one-legged, octogenarian miser anyway.

I left for my first Crusties shift in three weeks the following morning and saw Tony Jackson, the man from the Social Services, standing on Jervis's doorstep holding a clipboard. Jervis's new leg was just visible and I noticed his foot was on back to front again. 'Damn,' I thought, 'they'll be worried about that and put him in a home for sure,' but hurried away as I heard Jervis complaining loudly that his neighbour had shortchanged him on some Ajax. Then five minutes later, from the bus stop, I saw Tony Jackson coming out of Ali's with a Toffee Crisp and a *Radio Times*. It later transpired that he hadn't even stepped inside Jervis's flat, conducting his inspection entirely from the doorstep. All my efforts for nothing! Then Lucille got a call the next day from that Tony Jackson the Fraudster, saying he had given Jervis's flat a thorough inspection and everything seemed in order, but they were going to start providing him with Meals on Wheels.

Maybe I should be a social worker? I thought. Then did my usual leaping ahead in my imagination, past the three-year course, past the exams and straight into a vision of me fighting off a mad axe-wielding bloke who I was trying to care for in the community with only my clipboard as a shield. I was then shut in a hole under the floorboards and brought out for sexual abuse every now and then. No, I'd gone off that idea.

23

It's My Party and I'll Kill Myself if I Want To

Clothes were all over my bed. I had outfit number 8 on – an above the knee skirt that was also a pair of shorts, in a viscose rayon, white polka dot on black, and a flowery wrap-around top – both from 'Everything She Desires' in the market. I no longer patronized Miss Selfish. I had scraped my neither long nor short hair back into a bun the size of a raisin, held in place by 17 Kirby grips, creating the sensation of wearing a vice on my head. I had on the requisite 40 denier black opaque tights that stretched across the front of my pelvis and thighs in an enraging twisty fashion and didn't quite meet my crotch.

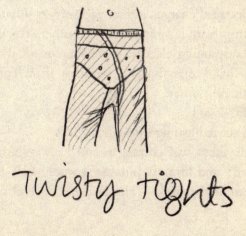

Twisty tights

In order to change outfits, I had to leap over a sheet of my mounting board on which lay rows and rows of magic mushrooms Steve had asked me to dry for him nine days ago, each leap from wardrobe to bed challenging the crotch of my tights further.

I was going to Penny Frazier-Smith's party, at her parents' pile on Richmond Hill. Ralph had invited me, in his ambiguous manner, to 'Come along, it'd be really nice to see you'.

He had come round to see me in my abyss one day to enquire if I was OK and to show me his pictures of a 'hawk' – a dot in the sky × 36, reminiscent of my famous seal shots. He suggested we do an exhibition called 'Disappearing World' or 'Endangered Species', which made me laugh.

And then I told him about being made up of atoms and he said, 'Did you know that atoms are made up of protons, electrons and neutrons? And with atoms that are made up of, say, one proton and one electron – that's hydrogen . . .'

This was less amusing. But as he continued I wondered if, maybe, he was making some weird, roundabout pass at me?

'. . . they stay together because they're like two magnets, the opposite electrical charges attract each other. What's weird is how they stop from crashing into each other. The centrifugal force of the spinning electron – they're constantly spinning, you see – that keeps the two particles from coming into contact with each other.'

'Oh, right,' I said.

Then he started leafing through my LPs.

Whenever Steve was coming round I always arranged my records to try and impress him. So I would hide the ones I actually liked at the back – The Nolans, Dr Hook, Boxford

DISAPPEARING WORLD - An exhibition of Photographs

By Edie Dudman.

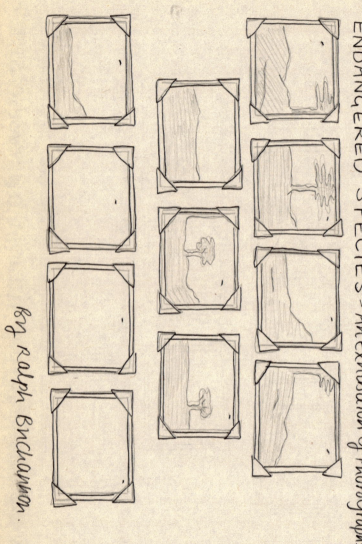

ENDANGERED SPECIES – An exhibition of Photographs

By Ralph Buchanan.

Comprehensive Sing Joseph and the Amazing Technicolor Dreamcoat (with me on the triangle), Don McLean, Cats and Dogs Sing the Beatles, John Denver (Steve was particularly scathing about that once) – and put the 'impressive' ones at the front – Black Uhuru, The Clash, Bob Marley, Gregory Isaacs. But Steve never noticed. That day, however, my records were in their natural arrangement and Ralph noticed them immediately.

'Oh, marvellous, I love this Don McLean album!'

After he'd gone Lucille said, 'Edie, Ralph really fancies you!'

'What? I said, blushing beneath my woolly hat. 'D'you think?'

'You've gone all pink!' Lucille said, thinking it sweet and funny the way only resolutely pale faces do. But it is not sweet and funny. It is humiliating and life-ruining and stops you doing anything potentially embarrassing (potentially everything) in a pretend cool way, because you cannot look even pretend cool with a beetroot face.

'I haven't! Don't!'

'Why haven't you mentioned him? He's lovely.'

'D'you think?'

'Yeah!'

'D'you think he's nice looking?' I asked her.

'Well, it doesn't matter what I think, it's what you think that matters.'

'I'm not ready for all that,' I said. But my interest was restirred.

Consequently when he turned up during my cleaning out of Jervis's flat the following week, I had already gone a bit confused and moody and was toying with the idea of trying

Lucille's unavailable technique again. But he asked me straight out if I'd like to go for a kebab with him that night. 'Kebab? Tonight? With me?' were his exact words, with such terror in his big green eyes that I softened and said I would. After our sit-down kebab at the Dervish (he asked to taste the wine even though there was only House Red and House White) we stood outside stiffly, looking in opposite directions down the High Street. It seemed ridiculous so I said, 'Well, I s'pose I'd better go . . . I . . .'

But he leapt in, 'I've got you something – a gift – but it's back at my bedsit. What about a coffee?'

Back at his bedsit, which was right down the Brentford end of the High Street, he gave me some blackberry jam with the pips in. 'I remembered you saying you could never find it.'

It felt to me like a romantic gesture in my very thin book of romantic gestures. He was standing over me, very close.

'Thanks,' I said, tensing up. I had a fear of people making moves or sudden declarations because of my blushing problem. But nothing intimate or embarrassing followed. Instead, he plonked himself down on the floor several feet away and told me that he wanted to adapt old water tanks into living spaces.

'Get hold of an old water building with tanks in and saw them up – they'll be like miniature one-person living spaces: sleeping area up here, and storage, with a kitchen here in a separate bit, then a communal shower area and latrine here.'

'Hmm,' I said, lowering myself onto a cushion on the floor by the gas fire. His bedsit was a large room with a single bed in the corner and a kitchen in a cupboard. He'd attempted a bit of a tidy-up but from my new vantage point I could see a tangle of books, underpants, unopened junk mail and shoes rammed under the bed and under the wardrobe.

'Would you live in one?' he said, pointing at his Biro sketch of a converted water tank.

Was that a come-on? It was way past last tube and bus time. The single bed was throbbing in the corner of the room.

'Yeah, I might!' I said. It was quite hard to be coquettish about water tanks.

'I've found this site down in Cornwall that I think I could rent off the Water Board.'

I felt possessive and hurt that he might go and live in Cornwall and felt myself going even more moody and confused when he made himself up a bed on the floor and offered me his.

Then I became obsessed, plotting and planning ways of being alone with him again. Quite a good opportunity presented itself, but unfortunately it involved Jervis.

In a bad mood one day I had met him on the balcony.

'Jervis, surely Kenneth doesn't still have to wear that lampshade on his head?' I said irritably.

'Oh, yes, love, he does. He's got that flesh-eating disease.'

'What flesh-eating disease?'

'He eats himself if he doesn't wear it. Then he gets a bald patch and the vet paints him pink – it's all very embarrassing for me.'

'And the lampshade isn't? He's probably got fleas, Jervis. I could de-flea him,' I said, inwardly praying for him to say no.

'To tell you the truth, love, I've gone off him.'

'You've gone off Kenneth?'

'I used to have a Doberman, Eleanor – loved her to pieces, before your time, lad.'

'No I remember her, Jervis, she bit my arse. And she bit my niece's arse too.'

'Wouldn't hurt a fly, Eleanor, lovely lass, wonderful with children. Kenneth's a liability, he shits in the house.'

'He doesn't! He shits in the passageway! And only because you don't take him out.'

'I want rid of him. Can you take him down the pound?'

'Jervis!'

Jervis turned away to get his pipe, thwacking Kenneth on the way. 'Get away, you terror!'

I eyed the ear to ear scar on the back of his neck. A backal lobotomy perhaps? Had he been a psycho? A wife beater? A child abuser? That would explain why none of his three wives or five children ever visited him. Or . . . pet abuser? That was an image I chose not to entertain.

'I'll take him for now, Jervis.'

'You do that, I'll be glad to see the back of the both of you!'

'Come on Kenneth!' I said, and he trotted after me quite happily.

'Go on Jezebel!' Jervis shouted after one or other of us.

I looked at Kenneth and hatched a plan.

A few days earlier I had been deliberately wandering past where Ralph's mum lived, down by the river, knowing that he was often there on a Saturday helping her with chores, when I 'bumped' into him and he invited me in to meet his mum. Bunty Beardsly-Buchanan was wearing a Viking outfit when we were introduced.

'She's very involved with the church,' Ralph explained.

'You're not the Dudmans of Wisbech are you?' Bunty asked, bustling out of the room and coming back in with a framed school photo. 'What was her name? We had a Dudman at school . . . Pamela or Patricia – where is she? Ah, that's her! Petronella Dudman-Didcott. Is she? She looks a bit like you!'

I stared at the face in the black and white photo. Petronella had brown curly hair and glasses like black Polo mints and a face like an out of focus potato.

'She was a bit backward,' Bunty continued.

'Thanks,' I said.

'Relation?' she persisted eagerly.

'I doubt it. No one in my family went to a school like that.'

'I never would've sent Ralph to that horrific State school, but after Trebe died and we had to come back from Keenya – well, no funds – both the boys had to go to that terrible school. Of course Ralph had a good few years at Marlborough. He's a terrible disappointment to me. I wanted him to be a lawyer or a doctor but he's got all these peculiar ideas! Edie, could you do me a favour and go out in the garden and get me some rosemary and some thyme?'

I stood in the garden panicking and staring at the plants. I didn't even know which ones were herbs. Ralph saved me. He took the dandelion leaves out and filled the flat basket with some leafy stalks.

'Take no notice of Bunty, she's a terrific snob. It's all she's got left,' he said before we went back in.

'I'd rather like a dog again, although this house is so small,' Bunty complained, squeezing herself into an armchair, the horns on her Viking helmet getting entangled in a spider plant.

It was a three-bed Victorian semi, three times the size of my Mum's maisonette.

'Space! That's what I miss! When Trebe was alive and we lived out in Africa we lived in a vast place – the hall was the size of this room – ceilings way up there . . . yes, a dog. No, a bitch. A shitsu maybe?'

I phoned Ralph and he came over to my Mum's, Kenneth's temporary home, and helped me prepare him. Kenneth was a small white fluff-ball of unknown heritage. We shampooed him and he behaved perfectly, only shivering whilst his eyes gleamed trustingly. Then we conditioned him and towel-dried him and he shook himself a few times. We waited for him to dry but time was running out so we blow-dried him and he turned into a dandelion clock.

'Oh my God!' I said. 'He's a poodle!'

'Maybe that's good,' Ralph laughed, 'he'll look more pedigree.'

We arranged Kenneth as if for Crufts, new collar, new lead, we even brushed his teeth. Then we waited down in the quad for Bunty to arrive, Kenneth's fur blowing about revealing pin pricks of pink skin in the centre of pure white rosettes. The brownish tint on the fur around his eyes and chops was more obvious against the white, and one eye watered a little, leaving a slithery brown duct.

Bunty pulled up in her Renault 4, her mouth already pulled down in disappointment as she zoomed her large brown eyes in on Kenneth. She rallied a beaming Viking smile and came hobbling over without saying 'hello' to either of us as she bent down to beautiful, sweet Kenneth.

'She's got a gammy eye. It puts me orff rather.'

'Right fine! You don't like him!' I said and began to drag him off.

'Well . . .' she started, grimacing. 'Him? I thought she was a bitch?'

'Oiii!!' a voice bellowed.

Bunty jumped.

'What you doing with my dog? Oi, get away!'

Jervis was swinging his fake leg about with one hand and wheeling towards us with the other.

'Where've you been Kenneth, you naughty boy? Come 'ere!'

Kenneth ran and leapt onto Jervis's lap, licking him all over and looking whiter than white in contrast to Jervis.

'What've you been doing to him, you perverts?'

Bunty yelped, 'Oh!'

'She looks terrible, oh my poor little baby!'

'Oh, you like him again now, do you?' I said, folding my arms.

'What you talking about lad, of course I like him!'

Oh well, I'd rather see Kenneth with a potential pet abuser than with someone who says 'orff' when all around her say 'off'. So I let it go.

'Imagine living here,' said Bunty clutching her handbag to her chest.

'Hmm. Imagine,' I said.

Ralph and I went to see an arty movie that night which we analysed at some length but he still didn't make a move.

'Oh, God, my outfit's so adjustable! When I put my arms up my top slides up my waist and when I put them down, it stays up.'

'Don't put your arms up then,' Lucille said in her matter-of-fact style. She was sitting on her bed doing her toenails. She had two perspex boxes with 'Pedicure' and 'Manicure' written on them, filled with various files and clippers.

'But what if I have to reach up to get a cereal packet or something?'

225

'At a party?'

'Or . . . you know . . . something on a shelf?'

'Oh Jesus Edie, you'll be fine when you get there and forget about yourself.'

'I never forget about myself,' I exclaimed as I stomped back to my room, stepping on two and a half magic mushrooms. 'And not in a good way!' I called back, unnecessarily.

My shoe collection consisted of 1 pair of my Mum's brown lace-up dyke shoes, 1 pair of too-white trainers, 1 pair of black court shoes (size 6, too small), 1 pair of Roman-style sandals with a strap round the ankle (size 6), 1 v. dirty pair of floppy suede lavender boots with the fringe down the side chopped off. And, of course, the tartan size 11 slippers. The court shoes were so tight they made my head ache even when I wasn't wearing the vice. In the shoe shop they had been bordering on loose, even in fishermen's socks! – how does that happen? I was a size 6 in shoe shops but a size 7 or even 8 in real life. And I had wide feet as well. I never had the luxury of buying shoes I liked, only ones I could actually get on my feet. Roman sandals with black tights was not a good look and anyway my feet squelched over the edges and scraped on the floor. The lavender boots were too dirty – I must dye them black, I thought, so that they go crusty and I have to chuck them away.

The other footwear was eliminated for reasons too obvious to list. I was down to the white trainers with the black tights. At least I could walk in them; even jog if pushed. I finished off the outfit with an old man's M&S cardi to cover my bum and because Jervis had said I looked 'smart' without it. Then I pushed my shoulders back because Shona Gibbons had been reading a book about body language and told me my shoulders said 'Go away'.

I took my first steps along the balcony and, on about step five, one leg of my shorts went up my bum so I had to splay my thigh inelegantly to release it. I should've turned back immediately and changed but the human capability for hope is unbelievable: every time I released the offending shorts-leg from my bum I truly believed it would stay like that. Thirty-five minutes later, walking up Richmond Hill, the leg of my shorts was still in the same bastard bum-hole-loving rhythm, working its passage up my inner thigh every five strides. I tried leaving it up there but it was intolerable. I even hid in a side alley and took my tights off but it made no difference to my arse-adoring shorts.

I hung about just inside the hedge outside 18 Hampton House, a double-fronted white villa with a long, dark, front garden. 'That's it. I can't do it, now.'

I didn't want to walk in. I didn't mind the party. I just didn't want to enter and live through that moment when everyone looks round. My plastic bag containing two cans of lager rustled and clunked. I could hear babbling voices, strains of music and through the closed curtains I could see orange light and shapes moving about, which produced the effect of a tropical fish tank, everyone exotically swimming around. I heard a voice shout, 'Amazing!' and saw that it was Helen Cox who I had worked with at the Lyric coffee bar. Well, I worked and she networked and I always felt she was scrutinizing me at the same time as being completely disinterested in me. I turned to leave just as Buster appeared round the hedge. He had a spotty red and white scarf round his neck and a collarless shirt circa 1875/1975 plus new jeans called 'Huggers' – too blue, too stiff, too high-waisted, too from Millet's and not hugging him nearly enough.

'Buster!' I cried, feeling immediately less like the weirdo. It was all relative.

'I can't go in,' Buster said.

'Come on,' I said. 'Let's go in together.'

'No! Penny already thinks we're an item – all the time we spend together, our business plans.'

'Penny? You like Penny?'

'Yeah, she's nice,' he said defensively. 'What's wrong with her?'

'Nothing, she's really sweet. Why didn't you tell me?'

'I don't have to tell you everything.'

'Is that why you're all dressed up like a fop?'

'Yeah, I've been collecting stuff from all the charity shops and selling it to her at her mate's shop. She's so lovely, always laughing and smiling.'

I felt a stirring of jealousy. 'You'll soon wipe the smile off her face,' I said.

I was jealous of anyone fancying anyone else. If a man who I found totally, repulsively, unattractive told me he fancied someone, I was immediately outraged. Why didn't he fancy me?!

'Oh, come on Bust, let's go in together,' I said, now relishing the possibility of making Penny jealous and dragging Buster up the path, 'I fancy that Ralph.'

'Ralph? Oh God Edie, you'll eat him alive,' Buster said as I rang the doorbell.

'What d'you mean?' I cried, as Penny came steaming towards us.

'Edie! Buster! Come in! Those horns look brilliant!'

Buster and I opened our mouths to say something but she had taken my bag of lagers and was off again – 'Alexis! Emma!

Come in!' – sashaying along the hall wearing a red satin 50s ballgown, a red feather in her black glossy hair, her cheeks scarlet to match and her black eyes gleaming dangerously. She didn't ask for the 57th time if I'd remembered the photos. But I had, they were in my bag and I'd framed the one she'd said she liked of her in the white 30s Romanesque gown, full moon bosoms squelching over the brim and a white feather boa slung across her arms, which were plump and pale as raw sausages. I went and handed it to her wrapped in tissue but she cast it aside with another gift, a bouquet of yellow tulips ('Oh lovely, bananas!') on the hall chest, her eyes darting about distractedly.

'Is Ralph here yet?'

I shrugged my shoulders casually, scanned the corridor behind her and saw Steve and his friend Johnnie, hunched together with cans of beer. Steve had a beard, but still my stomach turned over. I didn't want Steve to see me with Buster – he might think we were an item – so I mounted the grand staircase towards the bathroom and stared at my burning cheeks. They would be tattooed to my face until morning now, no amount of Penny Frazier-Smith's mother's Yves St Laurent foundation would conceal their maroon existence. I still tried though, got an allergic reaction and had to wash it off, merely making myself ruddier. As I dismounted the stairs, pulling my grey cardi down over Mr and Mrs Bum-Shorts, I spotted Ralph lurking on his own. He saw me and waved. I waved back, briefly, coolly, aware that even my wave said, 'Go away' and immediately made my way to the kitchen, bumping into Frieda from my photography class.

'Edie, how are you?'

'Oh, hi Frieda!' I said, far too enthusiastically. Anything to put off speaking to the only person I wanted to speak to. 'How are you?'

'Oh, I am OK, fed up with this British weather.'

'I don't see how it can be any better in Germany?'

'It is much better in Germany. And this British beer! Yuck.'

'Yes, sorry. Do you know Penny then?'

'Of course. She is in my millinery class.'

I glanced up where she pointed. Frieda was wearing a pill box hat with a peacock feather sticking out of the top.

'Oh right,' I said and noticed Buster out in the garden helping Penny with a bucket of ice, AKA looking down her cleavage.

'So who did you come with? Ralph?'

'No.'

'Are you and Ralph an item?'

'Er, not, no.'

'You are not having a love affair?'

'No. I . . .'

'You are crazy, you spend all your time with him. He is fabulous and handsome.'

'I s'pose so,' I said, taken aback; Ralph was weird and eccentric, surely I was the only one imaginative enough to find him attractive?

'So you don't mind if I pursue him?'

'No! Do what you like!'

'He is very sexy. See you later,' and she was gone, her peacock feather like an antenna, searching for her prey.

I stood panicking, half relieved, half devastated, and then, in a self-destructive moment and because it is easier to be a martyr, decided to approach the most brain-numbingly boring jabbermouth in the universe. Helen Cox the networker.

'Hi Helen,' I said. I could see the peacock feather zig-zagging above a throng of people like the aerial on a dodgem car.

'Edie! Hi! How are you?'

'Oh fine . . . I . . .'

Then Helen leant her arm against the door frame and hemmed me in. She scrutinized my outfit whilst pointing at her lip.

'I've had the most terrible flu and cold sore . . . Look!'

'Nope, I can't see anything,' I said.

'Are you working?' she said, staring at me buggle-eyed with competitiveness, her padded shoulder now obscuring my view though I could still see the peacock feather shimmying towards me again.

'Well, no, not . . .'

'My sister told me about this fantastic job and got me all excited, I phoned the guy up and he seemed really interested so I filled out the application form – it took me ages! Up all night, got a cold sore . . . did a brilliant interview, flirted outrageously and didn't get the job – guess who did?'

I had gone into tape recorder mode because Ralph had just passed the doorway meerkat like, and I somehow knew it was me he was looking for, so perversely bent my knees so my face was completely concealed by Helen's shoulder pad.

'Edie!' Helen insisted.

'Er, I don't know. What?'

'Guess!'

I rewound the tape recorder, *weeeeeeeeeeeeeeeeee* and pressed Play, "didn'tgetthejobguesswhodid?"

'The other candidate?'

'My *sister!* The bitch!'

And then, 'Oh Ralph, I am looking for you,' I heard Frieda say.

'Oh, hello, Frieda,' Ralph said warmly. Why was he so nice

to everyone? It was infuriating. I peeped over the shoulder pad as Frieda's 'So!' coincided with Helen's 'So!'

Frieda's feather could be seen coming straight out of the top of the back of Ralph's head, vigorously quivering like a tomcat's tail. His greatcoat concealed everything else. She might spray him at any moment!

'So! *Anyway* Edie!' Helen continued, her big lips flapping in my face. 'You always were a bad listener! So anyway, *then*, you'll never believe it, I landed on my feet with a styling job at *Moo Magazine*! Brilliant dosh, bit boring.'

'Hmmm,' I said, knowing my eyes were wide with the effort of tuning her out and eavesdropping on Ralph and Frieda.

'Ralph! You are crazy! I'd live in an old water tank if I could live there with you! Of course!'

I heard Ralph laugh nervously. I looked at Helen, said, 'That's brilliant Helen, so how's Chris?' and looked back over at Ralph. They'd gone!

'Oh don't get me on the subject of Chris, the bastard, d'you know what he did?'

I looked at Helen's watch. 12.35 a.m.! I had spent hours putting off the party, waiting for it to start and now suddenly it was nearly over. Then I saw the back of Ralph's greatcoat receding towards the bottom of the stairs and sighed agitatedly into Helen's jawing face.

She continued, 'He's not here tonight because we had a row because I asked him to take my skirt, this lovely red raunchy thing, to the cleaner's and do you know why he didn't collect it? *Do you know why Edie? Edie!?*'

'Look no, I don't know why . . . I've got my own problems . . .'

Her mouth went slack and her eyes dulled with the effort of me talking.

'Helen,' I said, shaking her shoulder as though she were unconscious, 'I'm going to have to go and talk to someone quickly,' and I yanked her out of the way and started to push through the jabbering throng in the hall. Ralph and Frieda had obviously sat down on the bottom of the stairs because the feather was flicking in and out of the banisters.

'He said he had no cash and he was too nervous to write a cheque in case he couldn't spell Sketchleys!' Helen called after me and added with a yell, 'Unbelievable!' just as I got to the end of the stairway and, through the banister, caught a flash of Frieda and Ralph sitting together and heard, 'Well, do you fancy me or not?'

I took one step back and froze.

'Er, ooh,' said Ralph.

Frieda did a German version of giggling. 'You must know, Ralph!'

'Well you're very . . .'

'Yes?'

'Attractive . . .'

'I am going to kiss you,' Frieda announced to him.

At that point I shamelessly bent forwards and, clutching a banister in each hand, gawped at Frieda gobbling at Ralph's mouth.

But then 'Penny's got a knife!' I heard someone shouting from the kitchen and hurried over to the doorway. There was Penny standing in the middle of the kitchen, bread knife to her ample bosom. A small eager crowd had gathered, all pleased, no doubt, at a reprieve before bulging night buses and kebabs had to be negotiated.

'Go away!' Penny screeched. 'Get away from me all of you! I don't even know *you*!' she spat, pointing at a poor girl in a pink cardi and glasses.

'I'm Celia!' the girl croaked. 'Your cousin from Maine!'

'I'm going to kill myself, Celia!' Penny told her, eyes black and wild, and rearranged the bread knife. 'And then the world will be saved!'

Someone opened a can of beer at this point, perhaps to celebrate the securing of the world's future, and a jet of beer spurted up to the ceiling, showering the audience with spray. I looked up at the ceiling and down at the beer can and up to the face of the beer drinker with the bad timing. Buster. Looking aghast. I felt an urge to laugh.

'What's the point? I don't want to live!' Penny cried. Apart from ruining her parents' ceiling, what had Buster done? He did tend to have a bad effect on people – maybe he had told her his Kierkegaard-influenced philosophy on life? I started pushing my way towards him through the gawping throng. A girl with a large bow in her hair, with a mug in one hand and a glass jug sploshing with steaming black coffee in the other, shouted, ''Scuse me all!' in a plummy accent. It was Pookie Lloyd from school, the one who once came into the girls' bogs and shouted,

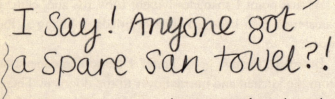

I say! Anyone got a spare san towel?!

in an even plummier voice. The most frightening girls in the school were so taken aback they just stared at her through their fug of smoke. She seemed to have the same effect now and there was a parting of the waves as she shouted, 'Any of you guys got a spare laxative or any other kind of purgative?! She needs to get it out of her system.'

I heard someone say, 'Bad trip' and someone else say, 'Acid'.

'Pen! Drink this, come on, give me that – maybe you could get Ralph to come and talk to you?'

'R-a-alph! Ra-a-lph!' Penny wailed with her funny r's and fell to her knees, blubbing again. The knife slid spinning across the black and white lino. So! Penny fancied Ralph as well. We were all at it. Attraction is very rarely original, I realized. She must've seen the banister moment with Frieda as well.

Now I'd arrived at Buster's beer-spurting area but he had vanished, which was unfortunate for him because Penny was just taking off her red dress and shouting, 'I weigh seven and a half stone!', which was blatantly the drugs shouting. She then changed her mating call from 'Ralph!' to 'Romeo! Romeo!' and went running out of the room with her dress round her waist, several loyal debutantes hot on her heels with cardis and shawls. She bumped into Buster, who decided to take his chance. 'Juliet!' he answered, taking her in his arms.

'Romeo? Wherefore art thou Romeo?' she cried.

'I just am,' Buster said.

I couldn't take any more of this and decided for once not to be the very last person at the party.

As I came out of the coat room I saw Steve with Johnnie, leaning against the wall on the lower landing, ogling people as they filed past, scoffing nastily at blokes or plain girls and giggling lasciviously at pretty ones. I heard Steve say '. . . look like without her clothes on?' Just as he clocked me, Ralph stepped in front of me, obscuring Steve with the bulk of his coat.

'Edie,' he said, and by the look on his face I knew that something was about to happen.

'Edie, I've got to talk to you about something. If I don't, I'm going to throw myself off a cliff or something.'

'Cliff?' I said stupidly. I didn't want Steve to see me, which was odd as previously I had yearned for him to see me with someone else and feel jealous.

'Or a bridge,' he said motioning towards Richmond Bridge.

'Come out here,' and I led him onto the roof terrace at the back.

The moment Ralph kissed me it was wrong.

'Edie? Can I put my arm round you?'

'Of course you can,' I said.

And then he loomed towards me and kissed me and my lips felt sick. Subtly, tingly sick. 'Give it time,' I thought, 'I'm just used to Steve.' But the thought of Steve in the hallway only yards away made me push Ralph playfully away.

'God I'm starving. Shall we go and get some chips?'

'Yeah,' he said, a little too eagerly, 'and a battered sausage?'

24

New Friend Who's a Boy

'What happened with that geezer?' Kerry said, the second I entered Crusties.

'What geezer?'

'That bloke you've been after, that water tank geezer, did you get off with him?'

I hesitated. 'Yeah,' I said lightly. 'Yeah, we're seeing each other.'

'You don't look very pleased about it.'

'Of course I'm pleased. I'm just tired,' I said in a dull voice.

'Oh yeah, tired, been spending a lot of time in the sack? I love that beginning, shagfest bit. Only good bit.'

I did a fake coughing fit.

'Oh God, wait 'til you see Moira's chops. She's ecstatic. Her mum's died, no that's not why she's ecstatic – it's 'cos Bollock Features said they could get married when her mum died, 'cos now Moira's got no responsibilities.'

'What about Bollock's responsibilities?' I said, ever the daughter of the abandoned mother.

'He's gonna leave his wife and kids.'

'Edie, love!' Moira burst into the shop from the back. She was clutching a white wide-brimmed lacy hat.

'Sorry to hear about your mum, Moi.'

Moira dissembled and put her hand to her heart. But she was dry-eyed.

'I am too. I really am. My poor old Mum, she had Parkinson's for 35 years and she's been about to die for about 34 years. I've been her sole carer since I was 12 years old! Don't get me wrong, girls, I didn't want her to die, but I can have my life now. John, my brother, he only lives down the road but he's a real bachelor, never lifted a finger and now he thinks he'll get the house! No, it's my turn now.'

And she plonked the hat on her head and reverted back to twelve years old, full of hope and ready to start her life again.

Later on I was slicing a donut — funnily enough the way Bollock liked it — and Moira was putting her hat away in its box on top of the freezer for the 12th time.

'How are you, love?' she said with the generosity of the happy.

'Oh, I'm fine, Moi.'

'Kerry says you've got a new young man?'

'Oh yeah.'

'When will we meet him?'

I just had time to register a slither of fear at the thought of Ralph meeting Kerry and Moira when I was saved by the bell.

'Moi! It's Nige!!'

'Hell-o Miss Sweeney! Are we going to get you settled this time?' said Nigel Weaver from Barnard, Weaver and Graves, in his sing-song Valleys accent. He was tall and stooped, with brown curly hair flecked with wiry white hairs that sprang out. He helped Moira on with her mac and they were off.

'Jesus!' Kerry said. 'That Nige has actually gone grey since he's been helping Moira. He's found her flats every time

Pollock said he'd leave his wife when Whatsit turned thirteen or Thingy done her O levels. She'd get her mum sorted in a home, put her house on the market and go through the whole flat and hat thing – she's had that hat years!'

Later on in the evening I set off to meet Ralph down at the river in Richmond. I spotted him before he spotted me. He was looking round anxiously, not even trying to pretend to do long division in his head. His collar was tucked in on one side and one of his shoes was flapping open. Though he was tall, over 6 foot, he looked small and vulnerable. I liked Ralph so much; he was bright, he was funny, I even liked the way he looked once I got used to it – he was rather beautiful really – tall (if he'd just stand up straight!), big dark green eyes, dark floppy hair. But he always looked a bit scared. As though if I said 'Boo' he would jump out of his skin. Which just made me say 'Boo' rather a lot. And sorry quite a lot.

Boo! Sorry. Boo! Sorry. Boo hoo. Sorry. **Boo!!**

Sorry . . .

I tugged at his arm. 'Hi.'

His face lit up. 'Hi. What's up?'

'Nothing.'

'Sorry.'

'Oh, Ralph! There's nothing to be sorry for!'

'Sorry. How was your day?'

Ralph put his arm round me but we banged against each other unrhythmically, unlike those protons and electrons he had told me about, and we soon gave up. I spoke fast, occasionally glancing at him, trying to adjust my eyes to his dramatic looks.

'My boss Moira's looking for love nests for her and this married bloke, he's our area manager,' I gabbled, 'and she came back from seeing this one and said she couldn't take it because there was no fishmonger in the vicinity and she had to have fish on Fridays for him. I don't think he even knows about it yet. She's already got her wedding hat.'

Ralph laughed. I looked across at him and his looks had mellowed with use and he didn't look so alien. He took my hand and turned me round to look at him, pushed a bit of hair from my face and loomed towards me, eyes shut.

'Oh! Ralph!'

'What's wrong?'

'Well, there's something . . . well I feel you ought to know. I was pregnant. Only recently and had to – well I didn't have to – anyway, I'm not pregnant now.'

'Oh, you poor thing!'

I pressed my head against his rough tweedy chest and he put his arms round me and I spoke into his coat and told him all about Steve, the abortion, the way he'd treated me. I was hurt, emotionally battered – it wasn't his fault, things would be OK,

I just needed a bit of time. Things would get better.

And they did improve immediately as soon as we were both supping at a pint of bitter in the Bull's Head, eating pork scratchings and putting loud songs on the jukebox. Then Ralph slid his arm round me and I tensed up as he stroked a patch on my neck over and over. He continued to rub the same patch until it was really quite sore, so I shot up to go to the loo.

We decided to go for something to eat after that. It was snowing, a thick layer already covering everything, blunting the sound of the traffic so that Richmond High Street felt eerily quiet. The first restaurant was too empty, the second a bit orange. In the third one they tried to seat us by the men's toilets and I walked out and in the fourth there was a stinking gas heater, though we sat down for a few minutes and then ran out. There was a too bright one, a too busy one and a clattery one. Then there were quite a lot of shut ones. Then there was Kentucky Fried Chicken. We were starving and freezing by now. We bought a Family Bucket which consisted of 5 pieces of chicken, 5 portions of chips, 5 portions of coleslaw and 5 portions of beans. We sat in the gutter and tucked in.

'Hi you two!'

It was Lucille and Barry looking down at us, faces flushed and fresh, arms linked, matching black coats.

'Oh hi,' I said with a mouth full of roll (oh yes, 5 roll and butters, I forgot).

'Peckish?' Barry asked.

'Yeah,' Ralph laughed.

'We've just tried that new wine bar down there, Fouberts. It's quite nice.'

I couldn't think of a reply. There was just the sound of me and Ralph munching, steamy breath coming out of our nostrils like two carthorses at their trough.

'See you then!' and they walked off with that silence that is waiting to get far enough away to talk about us.

'Blimey, what have you done to yourself?'

'You're not the first person to say I look good today,' Buster replied.

'I didn't say you looked good.'

'I've been cycling and I've had a haircut.'

'So, how's it going with Penelope?'

'Why d'you have to say Penelope in that silly voice? She's no posher than Ralph.'

'Right.'

'Jesus, Edie . . .'

'What?' I waited hopefully for some doom-mongering.

'It's so nice having sex again – I feel alive, connected, I feel attractive. All my women friends keep saying I look better than they've seen me look for ages.'

'What women friends?'

'Well, you . . . and Lucille said I looked well. And Jervis called me Miss.'

I laughed despite myself. But I was determined to knock that new, never-seen-before cheesy grin off his face.

'And contacts,' he said.

'Yes, you've said about the sex, thank you.'

'Contacts. Contact lenses. Make me look younger.'

'Yeah, well the beginning excitement never lasts. Enjoy it while you can.'

'So you're making Ralph sleep in his jeans?'

'No. Look we were fifteen when I made you sleep in your jeans. I was a virgin.'

'Liar.'

'Anyway,' I said, cranking up the drama, 'I have just had a terrible time as you know – I don't want to leap into bed with him. It's much better to take it slow, I mean if you have sex straight away you know each other intimately immediately and one day you wake up and look at each other and you don't know each other at all and then you've got to try and get to know each other with all the sex stuff in the way.'

Buster was not impressed. 'God, I couldn't wait to get Pen's pants off. We can't look at each other without leaping on each other . . .'

'Yeah, yeah, alright, you don't half go on,' I said. 'Anyway d'you want a coffee?'

'Oh, I can't, I'm meeting Pen,' and he cycled off, waving.

His wave said, 'I can't wait to get Pen's pants off.'

'Yeah, well I don't see why I have to leap straight into bed!' I called after him. 'Why can't we take it slow like in Jane Austen's time – the wooing is the best bit!'

But deep down, buried in my subconscious under layers of excuses, rationale, muddled thinking and essays on Jane Austen was the fact that I just didn't want to have sex with Ralph.

'You and Ralph looked so happy when we met you the other night,' Lucille said from behind her wedding book.

'He's got dirty fingernails. I don't know why. He hasn't got bad eyesight – he must see that he's got dirty fingernails. I don't know what to say to make him clean them without being horrible. I thought I could say, "Oh, have you been doing some gardening?" and he'll say "No, why?" and I'll say "Oh, it's just you've got dirty fingernails".'

'You're so picky, Edie.'

'I'm not, how would you like it if Barry had dirty fingernails?'

She looked across at Barry and stroked his hair. 'Barry's different, he's more clean cut. Ralph's more your sort of bloke – arty and messy and stuff.'

'I'm clean cut!' I said. 'How about if I say "Ooh, what've you been doing? Your nails are filthy!"'

'Yeah, whatever,' she said, sighing.

'What? Why are you being funny?'

I wanted to believe that she might be jealous of my sexless relationship with an eccentric weirdo but knew I was clutching at straws.

'Ralph seems really sweet, Edie. Can't you just accept him for who he is?'

'Of course I can!'

'The gardening one's good.'

'Thank you, Barry.'

And then he added casually, 'Saw Steve today.'

My stomach vaulted.

'Barry,' Lucille said, 'I told you not to say anything.'

'I'm not interested anyway,' I said in a high voice.

'Good.'

'Did he say anything?' I asked Barry.

'He asked about Ralph. He'd seen you in the City Barge or something, he said, "How's Edie?" and I said you were fine and he said "Is she going out with . . ."'

Lucille interrupted, 'No, Barry, that's wrong, isn't it? "Is she seeing that spaz from her class?" was what he actually said.

Like the nasty piece of work he is.'

'He seemed genuinely interested,' Barry said kindly.

It didn't help my sexual feelings for Ralph that night in bed that I kept going over and over what Lucille had said Steve had said, 'Is she seeing that spaz from her class?' The fact that Steve was interested, that he remembered I went to a class, and that the spaz was from it. You couldn't not deduce that he minded, that he was thinking of me. Consequently, I had taken my eye off the ball regarding the gardening line. Instead, the second I felt Ralph's hand on my waist through my layers of clothing it just fell out of my mouth.

'Have you been gardening?'

'What?' he laughed.

I sat up. I had on my vest, giant pants, old yellow Blondie t-shirt and leggings.

'Your fingernai . . .' I trailed off as I grabbed his hand.

'Gardening?'

'Your nails look so clean!'

'I've been washing my clothes in the bath,' he said, looking puzzled.

'You smell nice and earthy,' I said by way of explanation.

'Hmm,' he said, 'you smell of ladies.'

'I don't!' I giggled nervously.

And he started to snuggle into my neck.

'Ahahahah!' I shrieked, spiralling up, up and away until I was kneeling in a protective pool of duvet.

'Am I tickling?' he said and leapt on me and tickled me hard on the belly and then blew a raspberry on my stomach. I laughed loudly and painfully, momentarily proud that Lucille and Barry would think we were having a laugh if not wild sex.

'Do—o—on't!' I cried and then got superhuman strength,

pinned him down, pushed the pillow on his face and leapt from the bed. Then, for want of any other way to divert him from my lady smells, I started to cry. It was genuine-ish and so was the reason.

'Oh Eed don't cry. I can't bear it.'

I remembered Steve's 'Not the old water works,' or 'Give it a rest Blubberwoman.'

'It's just I still feel all messed up – you know, with what happened.' *True*. 'And I do really like you.' *True*. 'It's just I don't know what's wrong with me.' *Slight lie*. 'I think I'm tired.' *Lie*. 'It's just I still feel sore.' *Deliberate ambiguity*. 'You know, emotionally.' *True*. 'As well as physically.' *Lie*.

'Oh, God, sorry, there's no rush. Come on. Shall I make you some toast and hot choc?'

'Yeah,' I said, nestling into the bed like a toddler all cried out and sleepy.

We sat up and ate three pieces of toast each and Ralph told me the story of Sonja Perkins, the strongest girl in the school, challenging him to an arm wrestle behind the bike sheds and then offering him money to see his penis. Then I told him the story of Shona Gibbons when she fancied Mr Nork our history teacher and he said to her at the end of the class, 'Are you doing anything over the weekend?' and she blushed and said, 'We've got a family do on Sunday but I'm free on Saturday' and he said, 'You think I'm asking you out! I just thought as your grades are so bad, you could do some extra work over the weekend.' And then, as we settled down into this lovely, platonic, fully dressed snuggle, laughing and talking, I fantasized that Steve could see us on the TV screen and was sick with remorse. So for his benefit I added an extra scene . . .

'Right!' I said.

'What?' Ralph said, looking scared.

I'd read in a Marje Proops problem page earlier that day that if you don't fancy sex with your partner you have to force yourself – you might even enjoy it.

'Give us a snog,' I said, trying for Frieda's approach, and pressed my lips to his and immediately his tongue was in my mouth – hard and immobile – my lips had that sick tingly feeling again but I persisted, pushing his tongue back with mine and trying for a more nibbly approach. But he won the tongue wrestle, planted his hand on my bosom and pinched my nipple too hard.

'Ow!' I said, which was difficult with his tongue in my mouth.

'I'm nervous. Sorry,' he said.

'Try not to ram your tongue in.'

'Sorry.'

'Where's it gone now? No, that's ramming!'

I tutted loudly and pushed him down on the bed and sat astride him. Then I leant over his face, our wobbly bellies squashed together. I started to feel for his willie whilst pecking at his face. I couldn't find it.

'Hold on, Edie,' Ralph whispered.

'What?' I said, happy to halt the proceedings.

'I don't know what's wrong with me.'

'Don't you fancy me?'

'I think you're utterly gorgeous.'

'Did you ever have this problem with Laura?' That was the girl in the photos in the scenic locations – his girlfriend of three years, now departed to America to train to be a concert pianist.

'No, but . . .'

'Oh, I see! It's because you still love her.'

'No Edie, it's not . . . I love you.'

'Hmph,' I said, turning the light on, finding the twisted stick of my knickers, putting them on, turning the light off again and curling up in sleep position.

'Edie?'

'What?'

'I'm sorry.'

'S' OK,' I said, and it was, especially as it wasn't just my fault that we couldn't have sex. 'I can understand why you feel like that – Laura was really beautiful and skinny and brainy . . . Night, Ralph.'

25

Do Be Do Be Do

o

o

oooooom

I was up and down on an hourly basis. I can't carry on, I can't go on any longer, one minute; La la la la la, euphoric joy accompanied by song the next.

Coming along the balcony I was thinking really good thoughts about Ralph – I always did when I wasn't with him – he was bright, he was encouraging, he was handsome, I could talk to him about anything, we were having a Jane Austen-style courtship, soon everything would come together. 'La la la la do be do be do' but then I would visualize the moment of sex, 'Do be do be dooo-oooo-oo-*oom*.'

'You sound jolly!' Mum said, appearing from her doorway with her hair all sticking up. She was always there to prick my delusional balloon.

'I am not jolly!' I shouted. 'If you must know – I am feeling very muddled up.'

'But I thought . . .'

'Yes, never mind what I said yesterday. I'm just not sure about Ralph.'

'But you said . . .'

'Maybe I've rushed into it. I need to be on my own.'

'But I thought you said . . .'

'Never mind what I *said*.'

'But the water tank?'

'I don't know if I want to live in a water tank.'

'And your pottery, I thought you and Ralph were taking your clay down to Cornwall, you seemed so keen on those pottery seascape thingies you were going to sell . . .'

'Oh stop it! I've changed my mind, it's all a pipe dream, I'm going to do TEFL and go to China.'

'By the way,' she said casually, obviously in shock from my China revelation, 'this came for you.'

She handed me an envelope. It was thick, white and typed. 'Miss E. Dudman' it said and the postmark read 'Newcastle-U-Tyne'.

It rang no bells from where I stood, gabbling away in fluent Mandarin in the Zhejiang province of my mind. I vaguely tried to think of a possible northern admirer. Then I remembered my application form, the heap of Tippex with the wobbly, skinny biro writing on the very last and final layer that said, '1st choice Newcastle-U-Tyne Polytechnic – Media Studies'. I opened the envelope. The letter invited me for an interview for the media studies course on the 1st of April. A Thursday. In three weeks.

26

Everything I Know About Mounting

'What the fuck do you know about mounting!' I shouted at my Mum, who had foolishly made a suggestion and was now quivering in the doorway with a strip of photographic paper stuck to her slipper.

'And you!' I shouted at Ralph.

I had been banished from Lucille's for getting Pritt Stick on the carpet and had taken over my Mum's. It was now the actual night before the actual day of my actual Interview in Newcastle.

I had all my old photos, mostly of people walking along the High Street or sheep from my old Saturday job at the City Farm, spread out over the floor. I'd also taken quite a lot of photos during my semi-nervous breakdown of the interior of my bedroom – close-ups of the duvet, cups of tea with mould in them, candles etc., plus landscapes out of the window (all of the quad) and some portraits of Lucille, Barry, Jervis, Buster, Mum, Flopsie and Kenneth. But I was also supposed to have a portfolio showing a strong background in drawing. And sketchbooks.

As well as knowing the answer to any general knowledge question, Ralph was really good at being pretentious – it was probably something to do with the few years he had spent at public school. *He* said it was from listening to *Woman's Hour*, and Radio 4 generally, with his mum. He had arranged my photos in series and called them 'Agoraphobia', 'Urban Agriculture' and 'DNA'. A load I'd taken of Kenneth's bone he'd called 'Untitled 5' and told me to say I was interested in the juxtaposition of light and shade, the inevitability of death, and exploring sculptural form within a two-dimensional framework.

'I know a bit about mounting,' Mum said, 'I have had three children.'

Mum and Ralph laughed.

'I'll make some tea!' Ralph said sucking up to my Mum, tea addict of the century.

'Good idea Ralph,' she said.

They were enjoying the war spirit camaraderie, in the same way as the Home Guard in the Second World War, knowing they weren't going to have to climb aboard a train and, armed with only a cardboard portfolio, invade Newcastle Polytechnic.

'Blokes that get on with my Mum are not right for me,' I thought as I spotted a 10 × 8 photo stuck to the back of Ralph's fisherman's jumper.

'You've got a sheep on your jumper,' I said.

'Baaa!' went my Mum.

'It wants its wool back,' said Ralph.

I leant across and snatched the photo off Ralph's jumper as he left the room. 'Hilarious!' I shouted and could hear them giggling in the kitchen.

There were giant pieces of mounting board everywhere, some still monoprinted with Steve's magic mushrooms. There was glue all over me so that everything I touched stuck to my fingers, I was dehydrated, I needed a wee, I had only eaten biscuits for hours, there were criss-cross strips of white photographic paper all over the carpet and I could never find the scissors. When I did find the scissors I trimmed my photos, Herr Cutt style, wonkier and wonkier until they were snapshot size. One, originally of Kenneth, now of only his left ear and eye, was passport size and still crooked. I'd even gone through in my mind the idea of going to the Adult Education College, breaking in and printing them all again. But it was too late. It was all too late. I'd had weeks to prepare but had only panicked and procrastinated. I'd told them all this but they still seemed to think it a great laugh.

'I've got to fill this sketchbook by the morning!' I screamed, holding out a brand new black sketchbook, A5, the first three pages already badly sketched on and ripped out. '*And* make it look old!'

'Keep still, for Christ's sake!' I was drawing my Mum watching TV, trying to fill my sketchbook with quick one minute poses, even though she was basically in the same position, give or take a cup of tea at lip or lap position. Ralph was mounting my photos onto the sheets of card. It turned out he did know about mounting after all. Of course.

'Oh this is hopeless!' I spat. 'Put your lip in!'

The more juicy *Dynasty* got, the more her lip jutted out.

'Oh, I'll just have to stick loads of things in that look like I'm interested in their shape and form.'

'*Shape and form*' I wrote next to a Rizla that I stuck in the centre of a page, and then I stuck photos from magazines, fag packets, food packets, a tea bag (I wrote '*implies water – form, shape?*' next to that). Bits of material, sweet wrappers … rubbing the pages to distress them, and smearing tea here and there. It looked atrocious.

Things Lucille Does	Things I Do
Put hair thingys round hair brush.	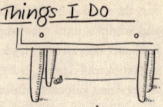Drop hair thingy behind chest of drawers.
Tie scissors round wrist.	Sling scissors aside casually – (well I've used them now!)
Write out each track on cassette cover neatly in Biro.	Write something vague in big fat silver marker (I'll remember what's on there!)

I checked Ralph's mounting technique. He had mounted so eagerly, piling them up so quickly that they'd all got stuck together and when pulled apart left little white tears on the black areas of the photos.

'For Christ's sake, you imbecile!' I shouted. 'Look what you've done!'

'Darling, honestly, the way you speak to Ralph!' my Mum rasped at me in the kitchen.

'Oh, I don't mind, Mrs Dudman!'

'Well you should mind,' I told him, coming back in to see him kneeling on the floor.

'Sorry Edie. Look, I can fill these bits in with a black felt pen. Look.'

'Oh darling, did you have to give me that double chin,' my Mum said, flicking through the one-minute poses.

'No, I could've done a triple chin but I left one off to be kind.'

To give her her due, she did laugh and as I stuck in a Mentoes wrapper ('waxy *texture*, epidermis?') I had an idea. This reminded me of something. What? Lucille's wedding book! It was old and battered, it was stuffed full, it even had drawings — not bad ones I have to admit — it was brilliant! I would pretend it was reference for a Postmodernist, Postfeminist, abstract animated film about the shape and form of marriage!

We left my Mum's place looking like a bomb had hit it, and went back to Lucille's to procure her wedding book. I had decided not to ask her if I could borrow it as

a)   It was 2.35 a.m,
     and
b)   She would say No.

I snuck in very slowly to the sound of loud snoring, pretty sure the book would be by her bed in her bag. Sure enough, I caught sight of its silver cover gleaming, upped the pace a bit and immediately my foot hit something. Barry bolted up in front of me. He was wrapped in a duvet on the floor.

'Edie?' he whispered.

'Shh,' I mimed, putting my finger to my mouth.

'What you doing?' he whispered.

I pressed my finger harder to my mouth and widened my eyes pleadingly, reached over him and took the wedding book out of her bag. I looked at him pleadingly again. Lucille continued to breathe softly. I noticed she had cotton wool in her ears.

'I'm just going to borrow it,' I mouthed, 'I'll explain later,' and Barry stuck his arms out and pulled me down by the neck and kissed me hard on the lips.

'Ba-ee!' I said, ventriloquist style, 'ot u nooing?'

'Edie, please . . .'

'Wo!' I whispered and snuck out again, only vaguely registering Lucille and Barry's sleeping arrangements and not giving my full power of analysis to Barry's behaviour.

'I don't want to go! Go away!'

I was in the bathroom, the cabinet doors open, creating a two-way mirror. My hair had tipped me over the edge into hysteria. I should've just left it looking sort of alright after I'd blow-dried it. Now it was half done in a French plait, with a huge cow's lick sticking out of it. Ralph peered round the door.

'Woo! That looks nice!'

'It does not look nice!' I shouted and threw a hairbrush at

him. 'My bald patch is showing!'

He laughed. 'You haven't got a bald patch!'

David Kenton said I had a bald patch at school and, although I knew it was just my crown, I had never got over it.

'I don't want to go to college!'

'You haven't got in yet.'

'Yes, but if I go to the interview I might get in and then I'll have to go.'

'Just calm down, Eed.'

'You calm down! You make me like this – because you're so ineffectual, you turn me into a hysteric.'

'*Turn* you into?' he laughed dangerously.

'Go away!'

'Come on, we've got to get you to the station, I've ordered you a cab. D'you want me to make you some sandwiches?'

'Stop helping me, stop focusing on me, you're suffocating me. I feel like I can't breathe. I think you'd better just go, it's just not working between us.'

Ralph's face crumpled.

'You're doing my head in!' I screamed and locked the door.

Ralph knocked gently.

'Edie, come on, the cab's here.'

'Go away!' I shouted and kicked at the bathroom door. My foot went straight through it.

'For Christ's sake, I only tapped it!' I yelled.

Ralph's face peered through the hole. I sat on the edge of the bath trying for a defiant expression.

'Come on Edie, you're just nervous!' then Ralph's face disappeared and I heard, 'What's going on?'

'Oh, hi Lucille – er, Edie's . . .'

'Jesus, what's happened?'

Cloink cloink cloink. Rat a tat tat!

'Edie! What's going on?'

'I'm on the loo!' I fibbed.

Lucille's face appeared in the hole. 'Are you indeed?'

'I tried to walk out of the bathroom not realizing the door was shut and my foot just went straight through, it's like paper.'

'I thought you had your interview?'

'I'm not going.'

'Right, well have you seen my wedding book? I got to work and hadn't got it in my bag. I need to show my cutlery reference to Janet.'

I could see my bag behind Lucille's head on the landing carpet, with her wedding book poking out.

'Have you looked in the kitchen? I think I might've seen it in there,' I said woodenly.

I heard the minicab honk.

'I've got to go, I'll sort the door out later. Sorry,' I said, coming out of the bathroom, clutching my bag to my chest and barging past her. I would rather go to Kings Cross with a greasy French plait and a suffocating boyfriend than explain to Lucille about her wedding book. She'd've been bound to ask to search my bag if I'd hung around.

'Sorry Ralph, I didn't mean what I said,' I told him, once my broken portfolio, tied up with Ralph's belt, and all my bags were piled onto the train.

'I know,' he said, 'you're just overwrought. Have you got your ticket?'

'Oh, don't be so motherly, Ralph, it's really off-putting.'

'Sorry,' he said.

'Sorry!' I called, as the train pulled out of the station.

'Sorry!' he called back.

'Oh for Christ's sake,' I muttered through a gritted-teeth grin, but Ralph, obviously teeth reading, looked anxious and shuffled away, holding up his old man's beltless trousers.

I sat down in my four-seater and watched London go from Victorian to Edwardian to 30s to 70s to 50s to mock Tudor and real Tudor, fields and cows and sheep, and felt myself relax. All my selves that I was, with all the people in my life, faded away and I was left with a Me that I hadn't been with for a while. I smiled at my flattering reflection in the glass and felt in my bag for my tinfoil package of sandwiches that Ralph had made me. 'I love you Ralph,' I thought. 'As long as I don't have to spend any time with you.'

27

The Actual Day of my Actual Interview

After my Super-8 animated film of Sandy's pregnant tummy, alternating with time-lapse rotting veg and fruit, and edited together with Sellotape, had leapt off the projector a few times, I did the speech, verbatim, that Ralph had taught me, and they looked impressed, but they were quite insulting about Lucille's wedding book.

A woman with a moustache, a big black t-shirt and a soul-boy haircut said, 'I like the way the drawings look like amateur fashion drawings, reminiscent of knitting patterns from the 50s ... echoing the rigidity, repression and inequality of intersexual relationships.'

A girl, the student representative, wearing a 50s dress and old man's Long Johns with Doctor Martens, her hair much longer on one side than on the other and shaved at the back said, 'And the bridesmaids' dress fabrics clash! Classic!' and laughed, pushing the long side of her hair out of her face. I immediately regretted my French plait.

'I know,' I said, 'and I'm in that foul yellow . . .'

I think they thought I was being postmodern, and they all laughed.

'I think you'll look very fetching in it,' said the bloke with the beard.

The woman with the moustache was looking at my one-minute poses.

'Is this your mum?'

'Yes.'

She turned it round to show me and pointed at the mouth, lip jutting out.

'Something around the mouth.'

I pulled my lower lip in and frowned.

'OK, well, thanks Edie. It's all very interesting. Thanks. Great. Oh, almost forgot, what is it about Newcastle that attracts you?'

They all sat staring, pens poised.

'The bridges,' I said, feeling very original. 'And the light.'

'Ah,' he said. 'Well, thanks, Edie, great, have a good journey back,' and he shook my hand vigorously.

'Enjoy the bridges,' the student rep called.

'Yeah!' I said. 'Bye!'

'Maybe she might be my new best friend when I get up here,' I thought.

It was Ralph I wanted to phone as soon as I got out of my interview but Steve who I was hoping had found out the time of my train (even though he didn't know I was going anywhere) and would be there to meet me at Kings Cross. As I stood in the phone kiosk in the refectory dialling Ralph's number I saw the student rep from my interview go past with some bloke with a Mohican. I caught, 'God, if one more person says "the bridges" or "the light" as their reason for coming here I'll scream. It's because it's all they've seen on the way in on the train.' And all my confidence dwindled away.

'Hello?' Ralph said.

'I've messed it up!' I replied. 'I don't want to go anyway. It's miles away, it's too far from home. I think I'll just put it off for a couple of years.'

'If you're worried about me, Eed, I can find some tanks up there and join you,' he said.

Lucille looked furious.

'How dare you!' she said. Barry was shuffling around behind her. He looked pleadingly at me.

'What?'

'How dare you go rooting around in my stuff?' She held out her wedding book which she had obviously found by rooting about in *my* stuff, but I decided to let that go. She wanted to know why it said 'Anatomy of a Modern Marriage: The Repression of one Woman's Creativity and Independence, by Edith Dudman', on the front cover.

'What the fuck does that mean?'

'Look, I'm really sorry. I was desperate, and your book's so brilliant, the panel on the interview thought it was brilliant, and said the drawings were really amazing, like professional fashion drawings.'

'Why didn't you ask me if you could borrow it?'

'I tried, but you had cotton wool in your ears.'

Barry looked panicky again.

'Oh whatever!' Lucille said and slung it on the kitchen table, but I could tell she was flattered about what the panel hadn't said.

'Thank God for Crusties,' I thought arriving for my shift. 'Maybe I'll just work here and I'll save up and do Interrail!'

'Hi everyone!' I called. Kerry came out looking uncharacteristically grave. I could hear Moira wailing in the back.

'She's on the phone to Bollock. He's told her they're closing down this branch of Crusties.'

'Oh no!'

'It's alright for you, it's all Moi and me's got.'

'It's all I've got as well,' I said dramatically. 'I messed up my interview.'

'Yeah, well, we've got a week left. So I'm looking for another job.'

'If only I'd done the trainee manageress training maybe I could've saved it!' I said.

'Yeah, right,' Kerry replied and she started circling ads in the *Gazette* with a blue eye liner.

Moira came rushing into the shop.

'Girls! It's alright girls! Everything's OK! Greg says he's going to help me buy the franchise on the shop and I can carry on running it, but it'll be my business. Greg and I will be living together anyway so it doesn't matter that he won't be the area manager! I've always wanted to be a business woman! So Kerry, I'll make you Manageress and Edie you can be Head Sales Assistant! And I want you both to come out with me at lunchtime to celebrate, I've got something to show you both. We'll shut the shop up for a bit.'

* * *

Kerry and I both stared at the large black dildo on the pink satin bedspread.

'Whoops!' Moira cried.

Moira had taken us round to the flat she had bought as a love nest for her and Bollock.

'Shall we have a drink?' Moira said, as we crossed over the threshold.

'Ooh, er,' I said, looking at my watch – 12.46 – then looking around the flat, 'Moi, it's lovely!'

And it was, in a frilly, pretty Moira way.

'I've bought this,' she said, pointing at a chunky pine table with six matching chairs, 'so Greg and I can entertain. You girls can come round!'

'So when's Bollock moving in then, Moi?' Kerry asked.

'Oh, just as soon as they've got some family wedding out of the way! Then he's going to tell Beverley,' she said, bustling through to the hall. 'Come and see the bedrooms! That one's for us and this one in here is for the girls if they want to stay. Apparently Jessica likes horses so I bought that poster from Athena – only room for bunk beds but that's OK.'

'How old are the girls, Moi?'

'Er, now, let me . . . ooh, 17 and 19 now. Goodness! And this is our bedroom. What d'you think?'

Our mouths fell open.

'Whoops!' and she threw the big black dildo into a drawer by the bed.

'Blimey Moi! It's a right shag pad!'

Black satin sheets, mirrored ceiling, white fluffy carpet, leopard throw, candles galore, a water bed and Karma Sutra pictures on the wall.

'Well, I . . . the mirrored ceiling was already here, so I

thought I'd go with the theme. Greg likes sexy environments.'

'Alright Moi,' Kerry ordered, 'don't go on, for Christ's sake.'

I imagined Mr Pollock's dandruff collection on those black satin pillowcases. I was stunned. Moira was a traitor! I thought she was in my crap-with-men gang, the weak and weedy division – the Laura Ashley and the pandering to his every whim – but now I saw she probably sliced Mr Pollock's donut exactly how he liked it in the bedroom too. She'd wanted him for years – took every kind of rejection imaginable – and now she'd got him. Was that how it worked?

'Has he seen it yet?'

'No, not yet,' she said blushing. Kerry and I glanced at the bedside drawer. There was a silence with Moira and the dildo in it.

'Let's have a drink to celebrate!' Moira said, getting a large bottle of vodka out of the other bedside drawer.

'But it's only ten to one,' I said.

'Oh come on!' she said and we sat round the pine table drinking vodka and orange.

Things that haven't put Ralph Off.

going on about my bald patch

Having 'Turkish slipper' tits

Licking Plate

wearing grey 'contraception nightie'

Annie's song

Having a John Denver Album

peeing in a mug

saying 'Period fart'

repeatedly pulling at that 1 black hair on chin

28

Hey Fatty Boom Boom

'D'you think I always want to have sex with Barry?' Lucille said.

'Oh. Don't you?' I said.

'Of course not. If I'm not in the mood I do it for him. With a lot of blokes it's their cuddle.'

'Is that what your mum says?'

Lucille sighed. 'Don't forget about Wednesday – I've got to be measured up again because I've lost so much weight and yo–'

'And I've got so fat. I know. All Ralph and I do is eat.'

'Why don't you have a bit of restraint?'

I was just putting butter on top of my peanut butter which already had butter underneath and
toast underneath that.
And table underneath that.

'Use a plate, Edie, please.'

'Weight always drops off me in the summer, it'll be OK.'

'You and Ralph are starting to look like two Weebles.'

'You mean the ones that wobble but don't fall down?'

'Yes. That's probably not helping your sex life.'

Ralph and I lay bloated on my bed with our trousers undone. Lucille and Barry were in Paris for the weekend so we had the flat to ourselves. Ralph had made a roast and, having both had seconds and thirds and licked our plates, we had collapsed on the bed.

'Look at me! They're having to let out my bridesmaid's dress.'

'I think you look gorgeous,' Ralph said, lifting his head up briefly and accentuating his new chin.

'Look at my stomach!'

'I like it.'

'Yeah, you like it, but no normal person would.'

'They would,' Ralph said, 'it's womanly.'

'And my tits are horrible.'

'Small and perfectly formed.'

'They're like Turkish slippers!'

'Small and perfectly formed Turkish slippers.'

As he talked his stomach quivered like a puddle of white blancmange, black hair circling his disappearing bellybutton like water down a plug hole. 'If he did some sit-ups and got a tan he'd have a good body,' I thought irritably. 'But it would be too mean to say that.'

'Jesus, I'm boiling,' Ralph said, leaping up and peeling his clothes off down to his Y-fronts. He was allowed to wear just his pants in bed now, though I still wore my contraception nightie – the full length grey thick t-shirt one with the pockets on the hips, the one deemed 'too bulky' by Colin Forbes, the laughing postman.

'If you just did a bit of exercise and got a tan you'd look fantastic, Edie,' Ralph told me.

I stared at him. Right, that was it, he'd done it now.

'How come you never moan about *your* body?' I asked him.

'Well, it's alright, isn't it?'

'You feel alright about it?'

'Yeah.'

'Yeah?'

'Well, I haven't got any particular complaints.'

'What none?'

'Not really.'

'Not really?'

Ralph laughed nervously.

'You're too smug, it's unhealthy,' I said, knowing really that he wasn't smug, just not vain. 'Anyway, you've got short arms.'

Ralph glanced down. 'Have I?'

'And a massive belly.'

Ralph glanced across at the wardrobe mirror. 'It's not "massive", is it?'

'And you've got a slightly bosomy look about you.'

'Bosomy?'

'A bit.'

Ralph stared at himself in the mirror. 'Oh God, I'm disgusting.'

'See! How do you like it?' I replied.

And then we both laughed like a pair of Weebles. But Ralph's laugh was a bit short-lived and hollow. He looked so dejected and was holding his stomach in, Charlton Heston style, that I felt enraged with guilt.

'Oh, look, I'm fed up talking about this!' I said. 'I've eaten too much. For God's sake don't let me eat any more of that chicken.'

Ralph put his t-shirt back on and sat hunched on the bed.

'Sorry Ralphy,' I said, my mood lifting as his deflated. 'Come here,' and I held out my arms.

'What about my bosoms?'

'Never mind them . . .'

And we were just pressing our t-shirted bosoms together in a sisterly hug when the doorbell rang.

'Oh no! Who's that going to be? The place is a wreck.'

'Lucille?'

'No, they're not due back 'til tomorrow.'

The bell rang again more persistently. And then in the rhythm of a football chant.

'For Christ's sake!'

I threw on my old lady's rabbit fur coat and ran down the stairs.

''allo Edith Dudman.'

It was Steve. I left the chain on.

'Fur coat and no knickers?'

'What d'you want, Steve?' I sighed.

'I've come for my mushrooms.'

'I chucked them out.'

'What for?'

'They were in the way.'

He looked astounded. I waited for the onslaught.

'Can I come in?'

'No, it's not convenient.'

'Edie! Who is it?!' Ralph called, all pipe and slipper-ish. Embarrassed, I closed the door to a crack.

'Who's that?'

'Lucille. She's got a sore throat. Anyway, I'm going now, Steve, see you.'

'Hang on, Pup, I need to . . .'

And I closed the door firmly and watched his shape through the frosted glass until it slid away.

On my way to the kitchen I called up to Ralph,

270

overcompensating, 'Want some tea, Ralphywalphy?'

I put the kettle on. I couldn't find any clean cups so I looked in a lesser cupboard for some cracked or handle-less ones and found Lucille's wedding book hidden right at the back instead. I flicked through abstractedly to make the kettle boil quicker and came across a page of close writing. My name sprang out at me.

'Edie's always flirting with Barry,' it said. *'Doing her "I'm so cute and muddled" act. She's so self-centred.'*

Me! *Me* self-centred!

'She gets these really nice sweet guys and then turns them into bastards. Like Steve – he was such a lovely bloke and she destroyed him . . .'

My heart was banging at my ribs. I destroyed *him*!

'It'll be Ralph next – she wants people because other people want them. That poor Frieda, she seemed a really nice girl – and then she gets them and messes them up – she'll be dropping him like a hot brick soon. I'm fed up of them lying around the flat like a pair of tramps – Ralph sleeping on the sofa like a rotting log or humming his nervous tuneless tunes . . . Poor guy.'

So it was the sofa era. 3–4 weeks ago. What about Barry? He was a Poor Guy, having to pour over cutlery and invite designs. Ralph and I had a really good honest relationship – the mystery she liked to shroud herself in with Barry meant they didn't really know each other. I went back to reading.

'I can't wait til it's just me and Ba . . .'

'Edie!!'

I jumped out of my skin.

'Put that down!!! Come on, give it to me!'

'No!'

'Come on, give it up,' Ralph laughed.

'Geddoff!'

'You told me not to let you eat any more,' he said, trying to grab the chicken carcass off me. Unbeknown to me, I had been tearing at it while I read. There was a greasy struggle and it slipped out of our grasps and landed on the floor by some black suede court shoes.

'Jesus you two! What is this? Some sort of Iron Age reconstruction?'

I still had a drumstick in my hand and stepped across to cover the wedding book with my rabbit fur coat. I saw that Ralph's willie was peeping out of the leg of his paisley Y-fronts and flicked a meaningful glance at it but he mistook my eyeline and pulled his stomach in.

Lucille turned away. 'Get it tidied up please.'

'Hi Edie! Hi Ralph!' said Barry as he followed Lucille into the living room.

'Hi Barry,' we grunted, keeping in Iron Age character, me particularly trying not to sound flirty.

I popped the wedding book into the cupboard, managing to get greasy fingerprints on it, and hurried in to Lucille.

'Sorry Luce, I'll tidy up. What happened to Paris?'

'It was cold so we came home.'

I only noticed then just how thin Lucille looked. They both looked gaunt and nervous.

'You two OK?'

'Yeah, just tired, we'll turn in in a minute,' and they stared ahead together.

29
Loofah Madness

WOO-OOO . . .

'Right, come on Charlton!' I said when we got back in the bedroom. Lucille and Barry's zombie-like behaviour and my cavewoman outfit had given me renewed confidence, and I decided that Ralph and I should have a bath together. Barry and Lucille were always having baths together. Laughing and sploshing, that's all you could hear.

But once Ralph and I had tutted and sorry-ed our way into an uncomfortable position, with Ralph's feet by my ears and my knees cold and dry as a bone above water, there wasn't much to laugh about. I showed him the ghost face on the end of the loofah and went 'Wo-oo-ooh!' and did a bit of enforced laughing. Ralph looked a bit worried. Then I splashed him and he splashed me back and half the bath water went on the floor.

'Sorry,' he made the loofah say.

'S'alright,' I said, getting out and swirling the towel around on the floor with my foot. 'I think I'll make some tea.' And I left Ralph and the loofah trying to relax in four inches of water.

'Edie!'

'Jesus Christ, Barry! You frightened the life out of me.'

'Sorry.'

'I'm just making some tea, d'you want so . . . Barry!'

'I'm sorry,' Barry blubbed, 'I just . . . I don't know what to do. Sorry, Edie.'

How could someone produce that much snot so quickly? He sat down in a heap at the table and buried his face in his hands.

'Barry, what's the matter?' I said, patting his shoulder in a soldierly fashion – I was unable to move my arms from my sides in case my towel fell off. I shoved a tea towel in his direction.

'Don't tell Lucille about that – what I did that night . . . I don't know why I did it.'

'I know I'm ugly and unattractive,' I fished.

'It was you I fancied, you know.'

To cover my embarrassment I reached for the fridge door, elbows pressed tightly to my ribs, and busied myself with the milk carton, opening it wrong like my Mum.

'When I first met you and Lucille in that pub I didn't know about Steve and I fancied you.'

'Yes,' the back of my head said, 'but it's Lucille you fancy now.'

'Yeah, obviously, who wouldn't? But you're more of a laugh. You're easy to talk to. You've got a spark.'

'No I haven't.'

'Anyway, you're probably a bit complicated for me.'

'Yes, probably,' I said, pouring milk either side of the mug.

'I'm not very bright,' Barry said.

'You are!' I said, protesting too much. 'You are bright! Very bright!'

'I keep thinking I don't want to get married but I can't analyse why. Can you help me Edie?'

'Well, you are a bit young.'

'It's not that. I don't know if she loves me.'

'Of course she does.'

'Why? Why does she love me?'

That was a tricky one. I re-did my towel extra tight.

'You're really nice, Barry. Anyone would love you. Have you asked her?'

'Yeah, all the time. She just says "I don't know. I just do." I know I'm a bit boring and that,' he said, eyeing me hopefully.

It was my turn to be fished.

'You're not a bit boring and that, Barry!' I said. 'You are a lot boring,' I thought. I was virtually dropping off on the spot but I didn't want my towel to slip off.

'You remember that time you said I looked cute in my old man's slippers?' I went on.

'No. Did I?'

'Yes. Those big tartan ones.'

'No.' He looked as though he was going to cry again.

'Well, you did and I was quite attracted to you after that.'

He did a big sniff and smiled a bit, but then his lips did a down-turned banana shape and started quivering.

'Lucille's just not very good at showing her feelings,' I said, remembering the bit in the wedding book. 'But I know she thinks the world of you. She adores you.'

He did a big nose-blow into the tea towel.

'OK,' said Barry, 'I feel better now. Thanks Edie.'

And then a voice came trundling down the stairs, 'Barry!'

'Oh, shit, it's Lucille, I don't want her to know I . . .'

'What's up?' Lucille said from the doorway.

'Oh, I found Edie crying, she's a bit upset.'

'What's wrong *now*?' Lucille said, folding her arms.

For Barry's sake I sniffed. 'Oh nothing. You know, just the usual.'

'Oh right. Come on Baz, we've got an early start if we're going to get down to your parents for lu . . . Oh, Edie! That's a new tea towel!' she said, picking up Barry's snot-filled tea towel by the very tip of a corner with her nails and slinging it in the washing machine.

30

High Street Blues

The doorbell rang the next morning as I was trying to find some clothes that still fitted me. I opted for a baggy white Lady Di blouse and some giant dungarees.

I opened the door. It was Steve. Again. Petting Kenneth.

'Alright little lad.'

Kenneth lay on his stomach and squealed. He loved Steve.

I remembered the time I had dog-sat when Jervis was in hospital and Steve had thought it amusing to empty Kenneth's water bowl and put pepper in it instead. That dog had such a short memory.

'Hello,' I said and waited for him to comment on my weight gain, even though I only had my head round the door.

'Hi, alright? Can I come in?'

He always said I looked like Benny from *Crossroads* in my dungarees and I wasn't in the mood.

'Er no, I've got to get to work, Kerry said Moira's poorly.'

'I'll give you a lift.'

'No, it's . . .' then I heard Ralph doing that honking throat-noise that he did in the morning, weighed up a Confrontation Between Steve and Ralph vs Being Likened to Benny from *Crossroads*.

'Oh fuckit,' I thought. Benny wasn't so bad and he *was* in that Shakespeare production, so I slipped out of the door and

Hello Miss Diane

shouted 'Bye!' as I closed it behind me.

Some honking drifted out of the bathroom window.

'Who's that?' Steve asked.

'Oh, it's Lucille, her throat's much worse,' I said, hurrying along the balcony. 'Hang on a sec, I've just got to pop this round my Mum's for Flopsie.'

Mum eyed Steve suspiciously as I handed her the dandelion leaves, but with Steve's warm hand pressing briefly on the small of my back I didn't feel the urge to comment on her Parker Knoll hair.

'Hi, Mrs Dudman. How is the chinned wonder?'

'Who?' my Mum said, touching her chins.

'Flopsie he means!' I laughed.

My Mum wasn't so amused.

'I hope you're not taking my daughter anywhere on your motorcycle?'

'Mum! Steve's just going to drop me off! It's fine.'

'Right, well, not on the motorcycle.'

'No, in the van!' I said.

'Oh, OK,' Mum said, gratefully shedding her don't-darken-my-doorstep persona. 'But be careful, dears.'

Just as we turned to go, the laughing postman came loping along the balcony.

'Alright Benny?' he said, smirking. 'Got a letter for you. Don't worry, it's not too bulky.'

He handed it to me. It *was* quite bulky actually, at least several sheets of paper. The postmark was Newcastle-U-Tyne. I tore it open, Steve, my Mum and the laughing postman staring.

Dear Edith Dudman,
We are pleased . . .

I didn't need to read on.

'They're pleased!' I exclaimed.

'Who?' Mum said.

'What about?' the laughing postman enquired.

'I've got into college!' I said.

'Oh darling!' my Mum squealed, 'That's marvellous! Isn't it Flopsie?'

Flopsie's low-slung cheeks chugged away, reeling in a dandelion leaf.

Hearing a faint honk from the flat I said, 'I must go and tell Ra . . . Lucille!'

'I'll wait for you,' said Steve.

'Oh, I'll tell her later,' I said.

As Steve zoomed along and I clung to his leather back I became aware of summer. The air was warm and had the tangy smell of freshly mowed lawn with creosote undertones, the sky was infinity blue, cottonwool ball clouds skirting the rooftops, the tarmac shimmering wobbly with the heat. I took a deep inhalation of baked leather and was immediately back in those halcyon days after my A levels, when Steve would collect me from my Sales job in the lamp department at Harrods, when 9–6 was spent just counting the minutes in time to my stomach flipping. I heard an ice-cream van and felt the same carefree summer shedding of control. My acceptance letter was throbbing in my dungarees pocket. 'We're pleased to offer you a place on the Media Studies course . . .' I kept repeating to myself, and I imagined phoning Ralph and telling him.

When we pulled up outside Crusties, Steve folded his leg over so he was facing me and leant his visor against mine. Big drops of rain started plopping onto the pavement creating that unmistakable London summer smell of damp, warm dust.

'Alright?' he smiled, his eyes Mediterranean turquoise in the sunlight.

'Yeah! Thanks for the lift.'

'S'alright,' he said and looked me over. 'You've put a bit of weight on – very Nell Gwyn.'

'Yeah, I know I'm a right fatso at the moment.'

'You know I don't mind.'

I averted my eyes and saw Moira's new silver Mini parked skewhiff outside the bakery.

'Oh, shit, I'd better go. Thanks for the lift!' and I skipped off across the road. I felt for my acceptance letter in my dungaree pocket and my stomach did a little flip. And then I didn't eat the cheese pasty that I had mentally earmarked for myself.

Halfway through the afternoon I noticed that Kerry was doing something weird with the till. She was taking the money from the customers but ringing nought on the till. Moira was slumped in the back, drunk, with her wedding hat on. We had had to lock her in because she kept coming out and frightening the customers.

'Why are you ringing nought on the till?' I asked.

'£1.34,' Kerry read as she added a figure to a load of other figures on a piece of paper she kept in her hat. 'It's brilliant. I can take all this money out of the till at the end of the day and no one's the wiser. I do it every other customer.'

'Girlsh!' Moira shouted. 'Lemme out!' and she banged urgently on the door. 'I need to get shome ishe cream, my throat's shore, I promish I wone buy jink . . . pleeeaaash, girlsh . . .'

'Oh, OK, Moi,' Kerry said, unlocking the door, dipping in the till and giving Moira a pound note.

'It's Moira's money you're nicking,' I said to Kerry after Moira had gone.

'It's not, it's Bollock's.'

'No, he lent her the money to buy the franchise . . .'

'Look, I need it! Anyway I heard her saying that he's bought the franchise for her but he's still the owner – he's buying her off 'cos he's not leaving that Beverley.'

'He is! After that holiday he's got to go on with his brother!'

'Yeah, yeah. He's done her over so I'm going to do him over. Right, £36. Not bad for a morning's work.'

'But the accounts!'

'I'm fiddling those too. Me and me dad and the kids is going to get evicted otherwise – we owe eight months, rent. D'y'want some? Go on, have this fiver.'

'No!'

But I was prepared to help her smoke a Thai Stick, obviously purchased with the same dirty money. 'Come on, let's celebrate your college place!' We put 'Back in 5 minutes' on the door and went out to the back alley. It had stopped raining but everything was wet and gleamed in the sunshine. I had two puffs and said, 'I've gone all weird.'

'What d'you mean, *gone* weird?' Kerry said and machine-gun laughed at me.

I stood up. 'Don't speak to me. I'm going to die. I'm going to die, just when things are looking up. Typical! No, don't come near me. I can see all the molecules, oh God, I need some orange juice, I've OD'd.'

Kerry clutched her stomach. 'Ha ha ha ha ha ha ha hah!'

'It's not fucking funny, Kerry. That stuff's spiked with something. Call my doctor, his number's in my address book . . . Hurry!'

'Wha-ha ha ha ha ha ha-t? Oh don't, my stomach's going to split open.'

'Oh, Jesus, what's that noise? It's an intruder . . . he might rape us!' I said, pinning myself against the wall.

Kerry was pointing, her mouth wide open in full laugh position, unable to catch her breath. 'I ho-ho-ho-ho-hope not!'

I looked round expecting a machete-wielding madman. It was Pollock in his day-off gear, which was almost as frightening. High-waisted jeans and a Persil-white sweatshirt with 'Queen – Wembley Arena 1979' on it.

'What's going on?'

That sobered me up.

'Edie's sick, Mr Pollock, I've got to call an ambulance.'

'What's that smell? Have you been smoking?'

'Only cigarettes, sir,' Kerry said.

I snorted at the 'sir' and we caught eyes and started to giggle.

'What d'you mean "only cigarettes"? What else would you be smoking?'

Kerry did a bigger shrug in between her already shrugging shoulders.

'What are you laughing at girl? Get up!'

'Yes, oh Queen.'

'What?'

'On your shirt. Que-e-e-e-ha-ha-e-een.'

'Don't be silly Kerry. Where's Moira?'

'Um,' and we both started another painful bout of giggling.

'She's gone to get ice cream, sir.'

'Ice cream?'

'She'll be back in a minute,' Kerry said, just as Moira came crawling out from a bush in the alley, with dirt all over her face and clutching a bottle of vodka.

'Moi!' Kerry shrieked, 'I only gave you a quid!'

'I nicked it,' Moira said and keeled over.

'Right, get back in the shop you two! Now! I need to look at the accounts, there's something amiss.'

That should've sobered Kerry up but she still shook and giggled her way back into the shop. Mr Pollock closed the door behind us and we bent up double behind the counter laughing, but it soon petered out now it was allowed.

Then we heard, 'Look at you, you pathetic old drunk!'

Kerry stood up straight, her hackles visibly rising.

'Pleash, Greg, don't . . .'

'Get off me, you smell like a brewery!'

'But vodga's indetec-ive-able, ishn't it?'

'Get off, woman!'

Kerry moved closer to the door to hear better.

'When are you leaving Bevly? When th'oliday's over?'

'I'm not leaving Beverley. I just don't feel the same about you any more Moi. I'm happy to help you with the business but that's it, the other stuff 's over.'

Moira let out a long, low moan like a whale in labour.

'Now be quiet. I need to look at the accounts.'

Moira did some more whale song.

'There's nothing been going in the bank, Moira! Look, no deposits . . . Or, OK, one here for £18.51 and that was three weeks ago. You've been too busy drinking, I s'pose? Right, let's look in the safe box.'

'I want to die-ieee-ieeee,' Moira sang.

'There's £144 in here . . . For five weeks' takings?'

We heard a bang and a splat.

'Moira! Look what you've done – there's mayonnaise all over my sweatshirt! Now, I want you to explain about the money?'

'Shuddup about the money!' Moira said. 'We don't need money we've god eash other . . .'

'Get off me, you disgusting old slut, look at you, no man would want you . . . I don't want you . . . ow! Right!'

'Aaah! No! Greg!' Moira screeched in a different tone.

Kerry went leaping in there. 'You leave her alone, you cunt! I knew you were bashing her! You fucking bastard . . .'

As I arrived on the scene, Kerry was pushing Bollock backwards with such forceful shoves that he went flying onto the bins and clunked his head on the brick wall. Moira was clutching her already blackening eye . . .

'Greg!' Moira screeched, bending over him. She turned to us, 'What have you done, Kerry? You've killed him!'

'Good!' said Kerry, grabbing her bag and coat and the rest of the day's takings, running out of the shop and straight onto a number 27 bus. An enormous rainbow curved over the High Street.

'Hello, hello?' said a cheery Welsh voice. 'Is Miss Sweeney around? I've come to see how she's settling in!'

Fallout

After the Pilfering Sales Assistant had fled, and the ambulance had whisked the Comatose Area Manager away, and the Estate Agent had stuffed the Alcoholic Manageress into a minicab, I locked up Crusties, that well-known and trusted family bakery, and took the keys home with me. A spell of really boiling weather had begun and, having not heard anything from Kerry, Moira or Pollock and not wanting to tempt fate, I lay low, sunbathing on our balcony. I didn't even know if Pollock was dead or alive, and I didn't really care. Slathered in Ambre Solaire suntan oil and listening to Radio 1, I lay there fantasizing about myself brown and glistening, drinking champagne and laughing somewhere in Newcastle. Possibly on one of those lovely bridges. I was imagining celebrating my twenty-second birthday properly to make up for the black-teethed debacle on my twenty-first. Maybe a disco on an open-topped bus? The buses were yellow up there, and of course it would be filled with a bunch of exciting new art school friends, so just a minor adjustment needed to the mental image that swam about on the orange insides of my eyelids.

'Edie!'

It was Lucille, leaning against the railings and blocking the sunlight.

I looked up at her. 'What? Move out of the way!'

'It's Mr Pollock on the phone.'

'Is he alive?'

'Of course he is, I've just spoken to him. Are you going to be lying out here all day? I need to dry my pants.'

At Charing Cross Hospital Pollock looked wasted and pathetic in his smooth, narrow bed, with a bandage holding his cracked skull together.

'Thanks for coming in, Edie,' he said, gripping onto my hand.

'S'alright,' I said. He had tears in his eyes. I gritted my teeth.

'Mrs Pollock is divorcing me. She's changed the locks on the house.'

'Really?' I said flatly.

Then he told me that Moira had come in when Beverley was visiting and told her straight – well, drunk – about their 12-year affair. Then she threw her Crusties uniform at his head and stormed out and by the time he'd managed to get the uniform off his head – a buttonhole had got stuck on the safety pin – Beverley had gone. He got a call from her solicitor the next morning.

'I've had no visitors since,' he said, in a quivery voice.

'Oh dear,' I said, popping a wrinkled grape in my mouth.

'The thing is, Edie, I need to get back to Crusties – I'll have to take over the managing of it, I've got a lot invested in it. I wondered if you'd consider coming back for a bit?'

'I'm going to college in September, I'm afraid,' I said.

'Just until then, or even just for a few weeks?' he said, clutching feebly at his head.

'Well . . .' I said.

* * *

'You're a good girl, Edie, for helping me out like this,' Pollock said two weeks later. He was tucked up behind the bread counter wearing a Crusties hat on top of his bandaged head and a creased short-sleeved Crusties shirt. Mr Pollock was now living in the bedsit above the shop. I had agreed to go full-time while he looked for another manageress. Knowing the job was now finite, just until I went to college, made it almost enjoyable. I was kept to a busy schedule doing a brainless job but without that gnawing feeling that I should be trying to do something else. It was a proper summer school-holiday feeling, not like before when futile, dead-end days just stretched ahead until futile, dead-end death.

Kerry had vanished. I'd gone up to her high rise to try and negotiate getting Pollock's money back,

but it was all boarded up and her Spanish neighbour, Meli, with the two wigs, said they'd done a moonlit flit. So it was just me and Pollock and a new girl, Susie, who told me defiantly that it was just a fill-in job for her. I told her we all said that and Pollock and I laughed meanly. Well, that and being caned never did me and Pollock any harm.

32

Ooh

Weekends only have meaning if you do something boring and tiring during the week. It was Saturday and I was happy just because I wasn't at Crusties. Ralph and I had had our tea in bed with morning telly and he'd just set off to his new 'studio'. He'd rented the boys' toilets in an old closed-down school and was spending his days either sawing away at a small water tank that he'd got from somewhere or phoning Mr Block at the North Cornwall council to see if he was going to be able to rent the building with the big tanks in. We'd settled nicely into our mutually supportive, fully clothed, cuddly relationship. There seemed to be an unwritten agreement between us to keep things unsexual. I knew I should probably finish with him according to the laws of Tribe A, but neither of us seemed unhappy and the lack of sex, and all its accompanying emotions, seemed to be keeping things on an even keel. My stomach only flipped over about going up to Newcastle now, and that was a nice, healthy, butterfly feeling, not like the furry moths with dysentery that seeing Steve used to induce and that I had confused with excitement.

I was just sighing happily to myself as I settled down for a whole day roasting on the balcony when Lucille came flouncing out.

'I'm getting my hair done at the Vera Lassoo Training Academy,' she announced.

'But you always get your hair cut at your Mum's hair-cutter, don't you?'

'Eileen's in Lanzarote so I thought I'd give it a go – I feel like something new for the wedding.'

'Ooh,' I said admiringly.

'Come on. Come with me!' She had a new, slightly wild look in her eye.

'Ooh . . . no . . .' I said.

'Come on, we could make a day of it! Have lunch!'

'Where's Barry?' I asked. Barry was the sort of boyfriend that accompanied Lucille everywhere. Clothes shops, the Family Planning clinic, even the hairdresser's.

'He's playing golf.'

Slightly offended that Lucille only sought me out when Barry was absent, I covered up with a sneer in my old nasally Northern accent.

'Playing go-o-olf?'

'Come on, Eed, you could do with a decent haircut.'

'It doesn't look that bad, does it?' I said, fondling my thin oily ponytail.

'It's just it's not really saying anything, is it?'

'Yes it is, it's saying "please don't get me cut again it was horrible and hot under that woolly hat . . ."'

Lucille gave a high-pitched giggle. 'Oh Edie! Come on, it's only £5, the students do it – top international students under the direction of top art directors.'

'Ooh,' I said. 'Do they let you have what you want? Or do they just *do* something?'

'They do a complete restyle!' she gushed.

'Ooh,' I repeated.

'They're really good at colour there and perms. Your hair

would look great permed, Edie.'

'Yeah, I had that perm before . . . it was quite nice,' I said, sitting up and sipping at my warm lemon barley water.

'Come on, I'll treat you, it'll be a laugh!'

So I agreed, knowing that in several hours she would be having a laugh and I would be in the ladies' toilet crying and splashing my hair with cold water. Well, maybe it would be worth it to see her laugh again, she'd been so tense recently.

At the academy we were all called into the salon, where each of the student hairdressers, all very trendy and international-looking, stood next to a chair, waiting for a model to be assigned to them. They eyed us and we eyed them.

I whispered to Lucille, 'I hope I don't get that Japanese bloke with the geometric hairdo, he looks a bit dangerous.'

'Yeah,' she laughed, 'or look at that one with the ribbons!'

Then Ronny the Art Director waltzed in and allotted us one by one to particular stylists.

'Hello,' I said to the Japanese bloke with the geometric hair-do, 'I'm Edie.'

'Harro,' he said, as he helped me into my nylon cape, 'I'm Yash.' Then, sitting me down and looking at me in the mirror, he said, 'Your hair very fine.'

I took a deep breath and looked down the line at a Dutch girl who was rifling admiringly through Lucille's luscious locks. I looked back at my own sorry hairs.

'D'you think it's too fine to have a perm then? I have actually had it permed before. Twice actually.'

Yash remained in silent contemplation of my hairs. He pushed them up to neck length.

'Yes vey fine. Need body. Suit you shorter.'

'Er, I don't really want it any shorter.'

'You no want hair cut?' said Yash.

At that point Ronny the Art Director, who was meandering along the row, arrived. He lifted up a bit of my hair disdainfully. 'So Yash, what d'you think?'

'Messy Bob?'

'Excellent idea!'

'The thing is, I don't want to lose any length,' I informed them.

They both looked at me in the mirror.

'I thought . . . a perm. Maybe?' I said.

'On your hair!' Ronny said. 'No way, couldn't do it, madam. It would just fall out. Crumble up and drop right off! You wouldn't like that would you?'

'No, but I have had a perm bef–'

Ronny ignored me. 'OK Yash, cut along the natural wave here and pull the hair upwards like this until the hair runs out and then continue in the same way for the next section, etcetera, etcetera. Then just wait for me to come back . . . OK?'

'I thought maybe just some long layers . . .' I said, but Yash had already started snipping furiously at the back of my neck. I saw some long wisps of hair drift onto the floor by my feet and, panicking, tried to look along the row to Lucille.

I just caught a glimpse of her smiling and her hands demonstrating 'longer at the front and shorter at the back' before my head was wrenched back into position.

Then Ronny the Art Director was gliding past again and saying to Yash, 'Great, lovely. Really classic, Yash. I love that wave. How about if we cut this section right round to the base of the ear?'

'Base of the ear?' I shrieked. 'Excuse me, you're not cutting it too short at the back are you?'

'And then some light layering on top . . .'

'I don't really want any off the top because . . .'

'Else it won't stick up otherwise.'

'I don't want it to stick up!'

''Cos your face is so close set, it'll open it up, see?'

'I . . . What?'

'Hey,' said Ronny with a dead-eyed smile, 'relax! You'll look fabulous!'

'The thing is . . .' I said as he floated off and a hairdryer started whining next to me. Oh what was the point? And I started trying to remember where I'd put my woolly hat.

'After finish I do some highlight,' Yash said.

'Yeah, whatever,' I said, looking down at the *Cosmo* problem page on my knee and taking a slurp of my cold, hairy tea.

Yash snipped away and eventually I surfaced from Irma Kurtz and focused on my still damp hair. It looked . . . quite good! I didn't dare believe it, so I kept my sullen expression even though it was like looking at a horror film or Ena

Sharples – must remember not to look sullen in real life – and said to Yash accusingly,

'It's too short to have a perm now, isn't it?'

'I not blow dry,' Yash said. 'Dry inside infra red . . .'

And as it dried and Yash scrunched away it looked better than quite good . . . it looked . . . good!

But, still not daring to believe it, I said sulkily, 'I won't be able to put it up now . . .'

And Ronny who was back said, 'Hey, what's the matter with you guys, there's a girl over there having a really neat style looking like the world's just ended.'

I looked down the row of weird geometric hair-dos and right at the end, wearing the weirdest geometric hair-do of all, was Lucille, her face crumpled into sobs and saying, 'Not what I wanted, that's all.' She was being shown the back of her hair in a mirror by the Dutch girl, whose grasp of English was obviously not as good as I had imagined. Even I, from miles away, had understood Lucille say she wanted it longer at the front and shorter at the back. But the Dutch girl had cut it shorter at the front and then it went down towards the back in chunky steps and ended in a square tail in between Lucille's shoulder blades.

My mouth was wide open with horror (thank God Lucille hadn't seen me) as Yash gently pulled my head back round to face the back of my own hair-do in the mirror . . . and the sides and the front . . . it was . . . could it possibly be . . .

Gorgeous! I swung my head about – mine *was* slightly shorter at the back and it had gone a bit wavy and I had golden highlights! My face lit up and my haircut looked even better – wondrous, in fact!

'Thanks Yash! Thanks!' I whispered.

Yash smiled. 'It vey fine. It vey good. Soft.'

I felt tears prick my eyes.

'Oh, what now? Ronny said. 'Honestly, one starts and they're all off!'

'No, I really like it!' I said.

'Thank the Lord,' said Ronny.

I looked guiltily along the row.

'Is my friend alright? She's getting married in three weeks.'

I could see Lucille blowing her nose and repeating, 'Not what I wanted, that's all.'

'We're going to give her a free colour downstairs with our top colour expert. A deep mahogany – it'll look fabulous with that cut.'

'Ooh,' I said as I watched Lucille being led by the elbow down to the basement by the now distraught-looking Dutch girl. Lucille was blubbing uncontrollably.

I tried to be tactful on the way home and not admire myself too much in the bus window. My response to Lucille had gone from:

'It's *nice*. Honestly Lu, it looks really nice.'

to:

'It's different, that's all, you need to get used to it. It's definitely a statement.'

to:

'It'll look better when it's had a chance to settle down. I'm not laughing!'

to:

'Yeah, maybe the mahogany is a bit severe. You can change the colour though, can't you?'

to:

'What about a veil? You're wearing a veil though, aren't you? I'm just trying to help!'

to:

'Yeah, you're right, Lu. Get it recut first thing. Well, when's she coming back from holiday? A week's not too long … Jesus, what the fuck was that Dutch girl thinking of?'

When we got off the bus on the High Street Lucille went straight into Maider's Newsagents to see if they had any foldaway rainhats. I didn't patronize Maider's since they'd told me off for using it like a library, so I loitered outside pretending to check out the small ads but actually slyly checking out my new hair. I could hear Lucille explaining in a cross voice what rainhats were and Mrs Maider's low mumbled denials of their very existence. Just as Lucille flounced out rainhatless and I turned to trail after her, cantering slightly to keep up, I thought I saw Steve across the road leaning against a tree and peering across at us. He put his hand up to shade his eyes. The sun was low and dappled through the London plane trees but still dazzling and I looked back for longer than usually socially acceptable. As we proceeded along the High Street I came into shadow and saw it was definitely him – he was hoovering a big blue stream of joint smoke from his mouth up to his nostrils – and he saw it was definitely me and put his hand up to wave. But I swung my Messy Bob away because Lucille was sobbing again. We were passing the bathroom shop with all the mirrors in the window.

* * *

Coming along the balcony I saw Jervis see us. I put my finger to my mouth.

'Is that the woman from the Residents' Association?' he bellowed, pointing at Lucille.

'It's Lucille, Jervis! With a new hair-do!' I said brightly.

'Looks like Mary,' Jervis said as Lucille got closer. 'Same bike helmet.'

'No, it doesn't, silly!' I said, in a trying-to-keep-the-peace, mummy's voice, 'Mary's helmet is blue . . .'

'And you look like a horrible old, smelly old, one-legged old man!' Lucille told Jervis.

His slack, bristly, old mouth hung open. He couldn't argue with that.

'Edie, I need some new underpants,' he said to me by way of a reposte-by-proxy. 'They only do my size in British Home Stores in Ealing. Size 48 waist and you've got to go and get them.'

Barry was in our flat wearing a yellow golf jumper and having a cup of tea with Ralph. His eyes lit up when he saw Lucille.

'Don't say anything, I'm having it recut as soon as possible.'

'It looks no different,' Barry said.

'Looks no different!' Lucille screeched. 'It's completely different!' and she stomped upstairs.

'Jesus,' Ralph said after she'd gone.

'Look, it's not that bad and she can . . .'

'No, your hair . . . you look amazing, it's gone all wavy!' Barry studied me. I swung it about proudly.

'Yeah!' I said, 'it's not a perm!'

'It looks fantastic, Eed!' Ralph said.

'What have you had done to it, Edie?' Barry asked earnestly.

'It doesn't look any different.'

That night, as Ralph and I lay in our cosy platonic cuddle, we heard low mumblings from Lucille and Barry. High-pitched complaining tones from Lucille, peppered with staccato grunts from Barry. Ralph and I widened our eyes at each other and Ralph turned down the World Service. Listening at the wall with a mug, I could only decipher the occasional word.

L: '. . . you mean?'

B: '. . . any difference . . .'

L: '. . . two weeks away . . .'

B: 'Sorry . . .'

L: '. . . disaster . . . face everyone?'

B: '. . . won't mind . . .'

Ralph was giggling and saying, 'What? What?', but then it all went softer and I heard some cooing and then it went quiet. So Ralph and I went back to our game called 'Or'. We were on, 'What would you rather eat, a frilly-necked slug or white dog shit?'

When I woke up in the morning I leapt up, and looked at my hair in the mirror to make sure I hadn't dreamt it. It still had that magic hairdresser's spring in it and I just sprayed it with water from the plant spray like Yash said, did a bit of scrunching and it was superb. I was going to look fab in my newly taken-in bridesmaid's dress, I thought, as I scampered downstairs. Lucille was sitting at the kitchen table, fondling a fraying knot of damp tissue. Her face was all swollen and white beneath her burgundy helmet.

'Hi,' I said, getting my bag from the kitchen table while Ralph lurked in the hallway. 'OK?'

'Yup,' she said.

'Booked into a hairdresser?'

'Not yet.'

'Is it growing on you?'

'What?' she said.

I heard Ralph drop his keys in the hall and suppress a giggle with a cough.

'Your helmet,' I said. But miraculously she didn't seem to hear me and just stared ahead.

Ralph called in a strangulated voice, 'I'm going to go, Edie, I'll see you later,' and I could hear him fighting to get out of the door, then saw him staggering past the frosted glass, staring straight ahead and laughing openly.

The phone rang and Lucille snatched it up eagerly. 'It's for you,' she said, sighing.

'Hello,' I said.

It was my Mum telling me something was wrong with Flopsie, news which would normally elicit a guilty outburst, but I was so desperate to get out of the flat that I put on my siren and went rushing round there.

33

Summertime and the Living is A Bit Easier, Actually

Ninety degrees in the shade and I was squashed on the very edge of my Mum's balcony, my new sun spot. I was wearing a pair of her giant flowery pants rolled down into bikini bottoms. I couldn't stand it round at Lucille's because she was redesigning her personalized serviette holders and kept tutting loudly at anyone who wasn't doing anything i.e. me. I had Radio 1 blaring from my tranny, competing with Wimbledon which was blaring equally from my Mum's TV. Mum was panting, wrapped up in wet towels on her Parker Knoll.

'I cannot believe it!' shouted John McEnroe, again.

I sat up to take another slurp of my lemonade and swung my hair about. It brushed in a satisfyingly chunky way on my coconut-oiled shoulders. My messy bob seemed to have changed my personality. I ran my fingers through it and they didn't get stuck in a tangle. I sat up and opened the net curtains with my foot, towel-pattern and grit pressed into my oily back.

'I s'pose I'd better do Flopsie,' I said to my Mum, peeling myself off the balcony and going blind as I left the bright sunlight and entered the black living room.

Flopsie was living in the bath on a crocheted blanket and I was injecting him twice daily with penicillin. His paw shaking had had nothing to do with fighting, 'Gimme 5' or wanting to go on *New Faces*. He'd had an abscess again but so big that it had broken his toes and he was shaking them with the pain. My poor Flopsie. We had fallen in love again. He'd had a personality change as well and seemed to genuinely appreciate my veterinary care and was a softer, kinder sort of rabbit.

'Dear, the phone for you!' Mum called and I padded down the stairs, Flopsie's silky fur soft on my bare chest.

'Oh shit, sorry . . . oh shit, 11 o'clock! Sorry! I'm on my way . . .'

What was wrong with me? I never forgot anything, it was always on a list. Several lists. But inside, I was proud I had forgotton. I quickly showered, the dribble of water and my Mum's spec of soap making little impression on my oily skin and hair.

'Edie! Phone again!'

I threw on my dress, and raced downstairs again.

'Yes?'

'It's me,' said Steve.

'Hi – oh look, I'm really late . . .'

'I'm downstairs, in the phone box by Ali's.'

'I've got to go to the *Gazette*.'

'I'll give you a lift.'

'Gotta go,' I said and slammed down the phone.

My Mum was standing with her hands on her hips in the living room doorway. 'It's too late for that,' I told her, and slammed out of the flat. I knew I'd accept the lift, it was like the cigarette again, the one you've thought of and have to have. As I reached Steve I could still see Mum standing like a trophy, hands on hips, looking through the net curtains.

'Penny arranged for me to take some photos of that Foxy

Fallow and I've got to go to the *Gazette* and show them to this woman,' I told Steve as I mounted the back of his bike.

'Nice one.'

'As long as I don't mess it up.'

'You won't. I've got faith in you, Pup.'

When we pulled up outside the *Gazette* I slid off the bike and gave him back the spare helmet, fluffing up my hair again.

'Hair looks nice,' he said.

'Really? Thanks,' I said, conscious that Lucille might be able to see me out of the window. She would be very off with me if she saw me with Steve.

'What time you finishing?'

'Oh, I'll only be an hour or so.'

'I'll wait for you – I might go and get my hair cut at No Boys on Saturdays.'

'Oh, no, it's OK, I might have lunch with Lucille. And then I've got my Crusties shift.'

'Alright, Pup, don't panic,' he laughed. 'What time d'you finish there?'

'Four o'clock.'

'I'll pick you up.'

He was offering me another cigarette and I'd only just put one out. This time I showed some restraint.

'I can't, I'm meeting someone. Thanks for the lift though!'

'Yeah, see ya, Pup.'

Edwina's shoulder pads were extra giant today and up round her ears.

'Oh, sorry Edie, I'm really tense. Sit down, love. Does your bloke know where that dealer Scruff's gone? I need to get some blow and Weasel's gone AWOL. I'm going mad, can't sleep . . .'

'I'll ask him,' I said.

'Great!' she said, tearing herself back to my contact sheet of Foxy Fallow.

'These are fabulous, Edie! Fabulous! You couldn't ask your boyfriend straight away, could you? Or, like, as soon as possible and get back to me? I tell you what,' she said, getting one of those giant purses with YSL written on them, 'I'll give you this £30 in case he can get anything straight away.'

'OK!' I said. 'Oh, and Edwina, she gave me a little interview, I've written it out here.'

'Fabulous!' Edwina said, with joint signs swirling around in her eyes. 'I tell you what, I'll pay you for the photos and the article now because I'll definitely use them. Here are . . . £50 in cash. You couldn't track your bloke down now, could you?'

I went to find Lucille but Fat Martin said she called in sick. So I went and had a nice sandwich and coffee in the graveyard on my own and wended my way to Crusties.

'D'you think Moira's happy with that estate agent, Edie?' Mr Pollock asked me, not for the first time.

He was in Snacks, overfilling the rolls, for which I had been forced to reprimand him.

'She seems fine, honestly,' I said, trying to be tactful.

'As long as he's good to her,' he said.

'Yeah, he's a really nice bloke.'

'Does she ask about me?' he went on.

'Um, I think she did ask how you were. I'm not sure.'

In fact, Moira was ecstatically happy. She was getting married to Nigel Weaver of Barnard, Weaver and Graves. He'd sold her love nest for her at a profit and was moving her into his 30s semi in Hounslow. But I didn't want to tell him the details and hurt his feelings.

'Good,' Mr Pollock said. 'She deserves to be happy.'

And he deserved to be utterly miserable because he was a horrible, slimy, selfish bastard. And he *was* utterly miserable. And I, weak and weedy, always rooting for the underdog, felt sorry for him. His beard was a lot less pointy these days and had a selection of crumbs in it. They were all over his shirt too.

'I'll take your uniform home tonight if you like, Greg,' I said, 'and wash it in our washing machine. I'll bring it back Monday.'

When I got home I started stuffing Pollock's unsavoury uniform and half the contents of my wardrobe into the washing machine. I heard a whimpering noise and assumed it was Lucille about to tell me off for overloading the machine. But she was crying stiffly onto her mum's shoulderpad in the corner of the kitchen and hadn't even seen me. She gasped for air. Wendy didn't say, 'Come on, have a good cry,' like my Mum, or squeeze her tight until she couldn't breathe and say it was, 'A watering of the soul'. Instead she winked at me. 'Make some tea would you, Edie, love?'

I put a teabag in each cup and put away the tea caddy knowing I hadn't put the lid on properly. Lucille was always accusing me of not putting the lids back on properly and I didn't want to upset her further. 'Character is fate,' I reminded myself and forced myself to reopen the cupboard and screw the lid on tightly. I put it back in its place in the row of storage jars, each with labels saying 'Rice', 'Pasta', 'Sugar', 'Coffee', 'Barry's mints' in Lucille's square, confident writing.

'Come on, love,' Wendy said, holding Lucille at arms' length, 'dry your eyes, you don't want Baz to see you like this.'

'Yeah,' Lucille said bravely, dabbing her eyes with a screwed-up tissue. I noticed her nails were bitten to the quick.

'Hasn't he seen it yet?' I asked, referring to her hair, but they ignored me.

She had had her hair redone – it was now short and bulbous, and Eileen had stripped off the mahogany and dyed it Natural Straw.

'Luce, it really doesn't look that bad,' I persisted.

'It's not that,' Lucille said, aiming her onion eyes at me, 'Barry's cancelled the wedding.'

'What? But it's only in a week . . .'

'He just isn't ready. It's fine,' she said, with a tight-lipped smile.

'But . . . oh my God . . . that's terrible!' I said.

'We're still getting married,' she said firmly, 'just not now. Next year probably.'

'Did Barry say why he wanted to cancel? I didn't flirt with him I promise!' I blurted.

I saw Lucille glance at her wedding book hiding place.

'Well, of course you didn't, Edie!' said Wendy. 'Lucille would never think that, and anyway you're not the flirty type. He just got the jitters, poor love. He's very, very upset, poor lamb.'

'It just got too much for him,' Lucille agreed, 'the Aunties, the chicken drumsticks. He said he'd prefer a quiet wedding, so I've nodded and smiled but I'll get my way again next year.'

I was amazed and baffled and impressed by Lucille's responses to things.

'Oh, Luce, you're so brave,' I said admiringly. 'If Barry had said he didn't want to marry me, well not me, because obviously he would never want to marry you, but if I was you and Barry said he didn't want to marry me, and I was you, I would've been enraged, rejected, furious, proud – had a screaming fit – Please marry me! Or – Go fuck yourself then, I don't want to marry you anyway! And I'd've thrown his special mints all over him.'

Lucille and Wendy stared at me.

'Why would you want to do that, love?' Wendy said. 'Where would that get you?'

'I love him,' said Lucille.

'How could you love him when he's treated you like that? Cancelled the wedding at the last minute! After all the work you put in and he just sat about like a tree sloth! Want him maybe, but not love-him-want-him-to-be-happy love him? Surely?'

'Of course she wants him to be happy,' Wendy said.

I knew my mouth was hanging open in a confused ape-ish way but I couldn't close it. 'Oh,' I said, 'right. I don't understand.'

'Of course you do, Edie! Goodness, I thought you were bright! How would you like it if someone was wailing and blubbing, it's not very attractive, is it?'

'But . . . Lucille's been upset in front of Barry before.'

'Men don't mind you being upset as long as it's not about them.'

'Oh right,' I said. 'I didn't know that.'

Lucille sniffed and went back to her list of things to unorganize.

'OK, that's A to J guests for you to call, Mum, and I'll do the rest. Just got to cancel the vicar now. And the flowers. Yup that's it.'

'Ah, here's our boy,' Wendy said.

'Hi girls,' Barry said, winking at me. 'Sorry about this, Wend.'

'Don't you worry, love. Want a cuppa, love?'

'Yeah, please, Wend. You alright, babe?'

'Yeah, you?'

'Yeah.'

And they puckered their lips up and kissed, lightly, fluffily.

'Yeah, and if you decide to do it next year, Baz love, you can do it much simpler,' Wendy said.

'Yeah, don't worry, love, we'll just see how it goes,' said Lucille.

'Liars! Liars! Liars!' I shouted in my head and escaped to my room.

Even though they were liars I still wrote, 'Men don't mind you being upset as long as it's not about them', albeit a bit half-heartedly, under 'Wendy Jenk's Stuff About Blokes' in the back of my book of quotations.

Wendy Jenk's stuff About Blokes.

'Let him stew for a bit'.

'Persuade him it was his idea'.

'Laugh at all his jokes.'

say:—
"It would've been lovely to see you but I've made other plans!" (idly voice)

"Never sleep on an argument"

"Edie!! you don't do that in front of your fella do you?"
(Blow nose on leaf / lick plate etc)

'make him feel like the most important person in the room'

"Never let him see you without your face on"

"men don't mind seeing you upset as long as its not about them"

34

Down by the Riverside

'Wow, Eed! You look amazing!'

Penny and Buster were welded together as usual, arms round each other's shoulders.

'Your hair looks amazing! Where d'you get that tan?' said Shona.

'Boxford,' I replied.

'You're browner than me,' Shona said, pressing her beige, freckly arm to mine, 'and I've been to Crete!'

Ralph sat to one side and Shona Gibbons the other.

'Hey, Edie,' Ralph said, 'tell Shona the good news!'

'What good news?' Shona said expectantly. I felt for her, she was hoping it might be something to do with her. She fancied Steve's friend Johnnie, had had a snog with him at Penny's party and always hoped I might have news of him.

'Edie got into college,' Ralph said.

'Edie, that's brilliant!' Shona said bravely.

'Yes, well, I haven't decided whether to go or not yet.'

'For Christ's sake, Edie, you must go!' Buster said.

'I'll get a bottle of champers!' Penny said.

Everybody looked up behind me. Buster's eyes simmered. I knew who it was.

'What's the celebration?'

'Oh, hi Steve.'

'Edie's got into college!' Penny squealed.

'I know,' Steve said.

'How d'you know?' Buster asked aggressively.

'*I'll* get the champagne,' Steve said.

'Oh brill!' Penny said, 'I'll give you a hand.'

I glanced at Penny and Steve at the bar. Penny was roaring with laughter.

'We can go somewhere else if you want,' Shona said, patting my arm.

'No, it's fine,' I said.

'You sure, Eed?'

'Yeah, it's fine.'

'Arsehole Creep,' said Buster.

'No champagne,' Steve said, standing over us.

'Tell you what, we can all go to my Mum's house, she's away at my brother's. We've got some booze in the cellar,' Ralph offered.

'Nice one, Ralphy boy,' said Steve.

Ralph looked pleased.

'Yeah!' said Penny. 'This is a dump anyway!'

'I agree,' said Steve and Penny batted her fat black eyelashes at him.

'Anyway, Edie,' Penny told me, 'Foxy really liked the photos and wants you to take some more at her new production company's office. She's going to give up the shop and let me take it over. Buster's going to invest that money he inherited off his gran in it . . .'

'Oh great,' I said, only listening with my normal-sized ear. My other one was like a giant, flapping, ear trumpet trying to tune into Steve and Ralph, who were walking up ahead together, Ralph flaying his arms around enthusiastically. Shona was scootering along on her bike and Buster was sloping along in Kierkegaard mode. Ralph was making a shape with his hands that I just knew represented a water tank. I heard him mention Mr Block. Heard Steve tell Ralph to tell him to 'Ferck Erff!' Heard Ralph laugh nervously . . .

'What's it called?' I asked Penny, not quite sure what I was enquiring about.

'Way to Go! After that rock musical her dad was in. So she said either Tuesday or Friday?'

'Yeah, good,' I said. Oh God. Ralph was now climbing on the back of Steve's bike.

'We'll go ahead!' Steve called, and they screeched off doing a wheelie, Ralph screaming like a banshee.

Steve was by the stereo looking dismissively through Ralph's mum's music collection. I cringed when I saw him pick up the same John Denver one that I had.

'What did he have to come back for?' Buster growled at me. I shrugged my shoulders.

'Has anyone got any drugs?' Penny asked, bringing in a tray of various bottles and glasses.

'I've got some oil,' said Steve, getting out a bottle of brown goo. 'And a few mushrooms.'

'No mushrooms for you, Pen,' said Buster.

'Oh Busty, but can I have some joint?'

'Don't call me Busty.'

'But you are busty, Sweetiepie!' and she grabbed his bust affectionately.

Ralph smiled weakly at me. I knew he thought I was a traitor, I'd got thin and he was still a Weeble.

'D'you want some Angel Delight, Eed?' he asked.

'No.'

'Why not?' he said, hurt. 'You love the Butterscotch one.'

'I'm not hungry.'

'But why?' said Ralph.

'I'm just not!'

'Anyone else?'

Everyone ignored him and eventually he ate the whole basin-full. Steve was spreading oil on the Rizlas, elbows on knees, legs confidently astride Bunty's African stool. Hunched over the chessboard he was using as a tray, he was making no contribution to the conversation but his stage presence was immense.

Penny and Shona were dancing to 'Rumours' by Fleetwood Mac in that we're-dancing-but-we're-a bit-embarrassed way, so we'll lean towards each other and whisper in each other's ears and do loud laughing and a bit of jokey ironic dancing holding our noses and wiggling and doing the bump. Steve was leaning back on a squidgy sofa smiling across at them sardonically. Buster looked on moodily.

'Pen! We've got to go!'

'Oh why?'

'I'm tired. We've got to get to those jumbles in the morning.'

Buster was using his Gran's money to help Penny restock Clobbered now Foxy had found a new hobby.

'Oh don't be boring, Busty – ooh, sorry . . .' and she and Shona burst out laughing.

'I might turn in,' Ralph said, 'I feel a bit sick.'

He did look a bit green. He'd been doing amateurish joint smoking, managing to look the part as he took a drag, doing major eye squinting etc but nothing came out when he blew.

'Hold it down,' Steve said. 'Oh right,' Ralph said, and held the joint out

in front of him and turned it upside down.

'No, hold the smoke down in your lungs,' Steve explained.

Ralph giggled foolishly, and took a massive drag. That's when he went green.

'You coming Eed?' he said now.

I looked down at my puzzle ring. 'Um, in a minute,' I said. 'Actually, Ralph, I might go home – I've got to do Flopsie's foot in the morning and everything.'

'We can get up early and go over and do that.'

I could feel Steve studying us coolly. 'Um yeah maybe.'

Ralph stayed put.

'I'll make some tea,' I said and gratefully escaped.

Buster came in the kitchen.

'Want a hand?' he asked gloomily.

'Yeah, OK, get the mugs out.'

Instead he sat down with a thump.

'Steve's trying to steal Pen away from me like he did you!'

'He didn't steal me away from you. We'd been split up years.'

'You might've been, but I was still attached. Anyway he's got the hots for Pen. Why d'you think he's always hanging around? If he lays a finger on her . . .'

'Buster! I really don't think so . . . try not to get jealous and aggressive, you'll drive her away.'

'Well, he's after her, I can see the way he looks at her. She's got a perfect body and he keeps looking at it. Why else would he be hanging around here?'

Right. That was just too annoying.

'It's not Pen he's after. He thinks Pen is fat, ugly and loud.'

'Really? He said that?'

'Yes.'

'Thank God for that!' He got up to go back.

'Mugs, Buster!'

Steve came in then.

'Need a hand?' he said, and although I shook my head, feeling my messy bob swinging about, he still put his hand on my lower back and pulled me towards him. I hung limply and my groin melted. I stepped onto his feet and he walked me backwards into the downstairs loo, locked the door behind us and we did desperate clothes-clawing. Then, half naked and somehow on the floor of the three-by-five-foot room, twisted around the U-bend, I heard, 'Edie?'

It was Ralph. Nearby.

We froze.

'Edie! Where are you?'

I mouthed and motioned for Steve to go out of the loo now and I would hide behind the door. Quick! Ralph's footsteps were coming nearer.

'Alright, Ralphy?' Steve said, emerging into the kitchen.

'Hi, have you seen Edie?'

'Nah, mate. She might've gone to get some milk.'

'Right,' Ralph said. 'D'you think she's alright?'

'Yeah, she's a big girl now . . .' And I heard their voices drift away.

As I came back into the living room with the tray, Steve was changing the tape and silence hung in the air. A police siren went past loudly. Trying too hard, I said gaily, 'That's probably my Mum thinking I've been killed on your motorbike, Steve!'

Everyone went even quieter. Steve kept his knowing back to the scene and continued selecting a tape.

'What d'you mean, Edie?' Shona grinned stupidly, still dancing to nothing. I panicked and started to laugh. Painful ugly-face-making giggles. Everyone stared at me for a bit and then the music started up again. The John Denver. Penny and Shona continued dancing, a bit of desperate waltzing, and Buster, despite my reassurances, went back to his brooding. He would have caught the implication of my comment in his old crush-on-me days. As I giggled on in stops and starts only Ralph went on looking at me. I thought I could see realization building in his eyes.

'Right, who's for tea?' Steve said, taking the shaking tray out of my hands.

'Sorry,' I said, and then laughed some more.

'What *are* you laughing at Edie?' Shona cried. 'Is it my dancing?'

I glanced at Ralph, who was still looking daggers at me, and I was off gurning again.

'Actually, I'm going to shoot,' Steve said.

'Oh, can you leave some of that stuff?' Penny said.

He gave her the bottle. Buster gave it back.

'Come on, Pen, we're going.'

'S'ow!' Penny wailed.

'Yeah, I'd better go too,' Shona said.

'See ya!'

And they were suddenly all gone.

Ralph turned down the music and looked at me.

'I wasn't on Steve's bike!' I said, in a voice gruff from laughing. I cleared my throat and tried to wipe the stupid grin off my face.

'What d'you mean?' he said.

'I'll help you tidy up.'

'Like a mountain in springtime, like a walk in the rain . . .' added John Denver.

'I'll do it in the morning,' Ralph said, quite authoritatively.

'Actually, Ralph, look, I'd better get back – Flopsie and everything . . .' and I made for the front door, letting out an involuntary spurt of laughter. 'Well, I'll see you tomorrow,' I said. 'Um . . .'

Ralph filled the door gloomily and I backed away down the shady path. I heard, 'Yeah, have a nice life,' drift across the damp air.

'Don't be silly! I'll see you tomorow!' I called back. 'Right . . . 'bye then!' and I hurried out of the clunky wrought iron gate onto the dark riverside walk and started to run. The others had vanished. As I passed the church and turned away from the river and towards the roundabout I saw a shape at the end of the road by the subway. A potential rapist at least. But I was drunk and drugged and mad and thought, 'Yeah, come on then! I can take you on,' and walked boldly towards him. The shape waved. There was a motorbike shape next to it. Steve.

'Oh Jesus,' I cried as I got close, 'that was a complete nightmare!'

'Uh-oh,' said Steve and started walking away. I looked behind me. Ralph was approaching, hunched and determined. Steve had gone but the bike still stood there.

'That's not Steve's bike,' I said.

'Just wanted to see you safely under the subway,' he replied.

'Oh, right, thanks, I'll be fine.'

I hurried under the subway and came out the other side, waved across at Ralph and then continued away. After a few strides I looked back and Ralph was gone. I could see Steve further up the road, round the bend. He waved. There wasn't much traffic so I ran across the roundabout.

'What's wrong with him?' Steve said.

'Oh nothing. He's jealous.'

'What of?' he asked, eyes glinting.

'Oh I don't know . . . Oh, Jesus.'

Ralph was back by the subway staring at us.

'Well, 'bye then Steve!' I shouted. 'Thanks for bringing me my cardi!'

But Ralph had disappeared into the shadows again.

'Come on, I'll walk you home,' Steve said. 'I can collect the bike in the morning.' We started walking in the wrong direction, even though we both knew full well where I lived. And we walked and walked, until we were down by the river at Hammersmith. We walked over Hammersmith bridge and all the way along Barnes towpath to Barnes bridge, over Barnes bridge to Chiswick Park, where we climbed over the wall. At five o'clock we lay down on the cricket pitch and fell asleep. We'd barely said two words to each other. The sun woke us at nine, and we bought a plastic bottle of strawberry milkshake to share from the garage. Then he did finally walk me home.

35
Oh

Damn. Damn. Damn. Damn. Damn. Damn.

A few days after the roundabout episode I lay in the bath and felt really cross with myself. Steve had met me every day from Crusties and we had wandered about the riverside in the warm evenings holding hands and kissing in a love-drug-induced trance. I stayed at his flat every night and put my brain into neutral. But now I was over-tired, back at home and coming down with a thud, and even though it was boiling hot I shivered slightly in my cooling bath. I had been really horrible to Ralph. I phoned him up as soon as I got out of the bath.

'Ralph, I . . .'

Slam!

And again. 'Ralph! Don't . . .'

Slam!

And once more. 'Ralphy!'

Slam!

And then just endless ringing. I didn't want him to not like me. I didn't want to never see him again. I knew what he'd be thinking. How would it feel being cheated on, and with someone who I'd described as thick, nasty, unfeeling, unimaginative, inarticulate, rude to my Mum and selfish? How would it feel to be second best to that?

Ralph caught sight of me loitering nearby as he came out of his place, and looked annoyed. I felt my heart lift.

'What?' I said as I approached, hoping to continue the theme.

'Sorry, sorry. I'm being horrible,' he said, irritably.

'I don't blame you for being annoyed with me.'

'I could never be annoyed with you Edie,' Ralph said.

'Why not?' I remembered the 'Have a nice life' from the other night. 'You seemed annoyed the other night. You said "Have a nice life."'

Ralph looked at me, his brain cogitating.

'Did I? Why would I say that? No . . . Have a nice *night*, I must've said.'

Yeah, good one, I thought.

'You kept slamming the phone down on me.'

'Have you been phoning?'

'Yes, loads of times.'

'Oh, Mum's been over sorting my place out.'

'What did you tell her?'

'I didn't tell her anything.'

I sighed, and looked down at Ralph's feet. He'd got new, shiny leather Chelsea boots on.

'I don't blame you for hating me,' he said.

'I don't hate you!'

'Oh good.' His whole face lit up. I'd thrown him the weeniest crumb and he'd turned it into a bucket of fried chicken. 'Edie? Is there someone else?' he was heard to say.

'No, there's no one else,' I told him.

'There is someone else,' he told his new boots.

'No! There isn't! For goodness' sake, I've told you!'

'There's someone else . . . for me,' he said, louder and looking straight at me.

'What?'

'I'm involved with someone else.'

I stared at him.

'Someone you know. Someone from our class.'

'What? Who? Frieda? Oh, that's so Germanic! Doesn't she ever give up?'

'No, Gavin.'

'What d'you mean, Gavin?'

'Gavin and I are seeing each other.'

'Who's Gavin?' I said, running through all the girls in the class.

'Gavin. Italian looking, takes photos of dogs,' Ralph said.

'Gavin? But he's gay!' I said stupidly.

'I know!' he said, with a nervous guffaw.

'But . . . I . . . are you gay?' I said, blushing at the fact that I was already blushing. I remembered with horror all the things I'd said about Gavin. Head Boy, Pompous Pilot, Joke Free Zone, Humour Transplant.

'Well, I s'pose I must be a bit. But, Edie, I don't want it to affect our relationship.'

'But . . . how . . . when?' I managed to ask.

'You know that night you missed the class because you had that bridesmaids' fitting? Gavin asked me if I wanted to go back to his for a coffee, he wanted to hear about my water tanks . . .' (*I bet he did*, I thought) '. . . and we were sitting about chatting and I suddenly thought, he's going to try and get off with me . . . it went all quiet and then I leant over to get my wine, and he said, "I want you to be mine", or I thought he did, so, to be polite really, I touched his hand and then we rolled about a bit, you know. Anyway, later on when we were talking about how it started and who did what, it turned out he'd said, "D'you want some more wine?" or something. Sorry Edie. I'll stop if you really want me to. I don't even actually like him very much.'

'Hmph,' I said, remembering the way Ralph and I both laughed at the pictures of the 'seal' and how Gavin and Steve had sat there stony-faced.

'I don't know what it is, he doesn't understand me at all . . . but I feel insanely nervous and excited about him . . .'

So Ralph had got the same disease as me. He had fallen in love with someone he didn't like.

'I'm going on holiday with Steve,' I told him.

'Steve?' he said, looking perplexed.

'You knew, didn't you? That time, by the roundabout, I thought you saw us.'

'I thought he was just giving you your cardi.'

'But you were acting all weird and suspicious.'

'Oh, I was just checking you'd really gone, sorry, because Gavin phoned after you left and said he had to come and see me and I didn't want you to cross paths. Sorry.'

'Oh,' I said. 'Well, anyway, Ralph, I'm going on holiday with Steve for a few days, he's taking me away. We're going to try and make a go of it.'

'He's a nice guy,' Ralph said, with a faraway look.

'Sorry,' I said.

Ralph started to twitch, 'Oh God.'

'Are you alright?'

'Here's Gav!' he said with a tremble.

'Who?'

I looked round and saw Gavin on the other side of the road. As he caught my eye he looked briefly venomous. I suddenly knew who it was who had been clearing out Ralph's place, and slamming the phone down on me, and taking Ralph out to buy new boots. Then he was waving, looking right and left for traffic and skipping across the road to join us, breathless, bosomless and smiling in a tight white t-shirt.

'Hi Edie,' he said, looking at Ralph.

I had an unwanted image of him fondling Ralph's breasts.

'We're going to eat at the Italian, d'you want to join us?' Ralph said.

Gavin's eyes burned.

'Oh, no, it's OK, I've got to go ... somewhere ...' I explained.

'OK, see ya!' Gavin said, too quickly and excitedly, taking Ralph's arm.

'I'll call you tomorrow,' Ralph said, looking a little desperate.

Gavin steered him away whilst picking a bit of Sellotape off his shabby, blue, warehouseman's jacket.

'Oh,' I thought, standing there in the dark. I'd gone all out to put him off but now he'd told me about his gay experience I couldn't help feeling I'd gone too far.

'Not all women are as vile as me!' I called in a reedy voice, as they vanished into the distance.

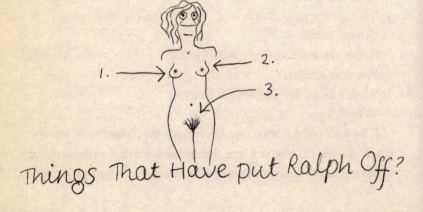

Things That Have put Ralph Off?

36
Being Yourself . . .
But Which One?

Lucille and I sat in the Jolly Cafe. She didn't look very jolly but I took a deep breath.

'Steve's taking me on a little holiday. A surprise.'

'You are joking?' she said crossly.

'What's wrong with that?'

'Edie, you seemed so much happier when you were with Ralph.'

'I'm happy now.'

'So am I,' she said.

'Good,' I said, 'I'm so pleased. Can't you be pleased for me?'

'He treated you like shit, Edie.'

'Well, everyone deserves a second chance. You're giving Barry one.'

'That's different.'

Everything was going right for me – college place, haircut, tan, surprise holday – I felt I shouldn't rub her nose in it when her life was going downhill.

'Yes, I know, I'm an idiot,' I said, to please her.

That night Lucille and Wendy were unorganizing the wedding downstairs, with Barry slouching about looking guilty and asking Lucille if she was all right every five minutes. Lucille is the sort of person who gets constant enquiries as to whether she is all right – 'Alright, Lu?' – which she nearly always answers in the affirmative. Whereas no one ever asks me whether *I* am all right, presumably in case I tell them. So I snuck upstairs to pack. I had just got my suitcase on wheels out of the wardrobe when Lucille called up, 'What time are you going?'

'First thing!' I shouted dramatically (11.30 in fact).

'Where's she going?' I heard Wendy ask.

'Dorset.'

'Who with?' I heard Barry ask.

'Steve. He's taking her away for a few days.'

And then Wendy saying, 'Oh, he's a nice fella. Nice looking.'

And then some negative muttering from Barry.

'Oh Edie!' Lucille called. 'Can you clean the bathroom before you go? I feel like I've been doing all the cleaning!'

I went to the bathroom and started scrubbing and wiping, even though I hadn't packed yet. I did it so thoroughly that I even found some traces of golden henna round the back of the cold tap.

Later on I was trying to decide whether to take two jumpers and a cardi or two cardis and a jumper when there was a rat-a-tat at my door. It was Lucille in her fluffy white dressing gown and mules, with a rope of wet hair over one shoulder. The comforting smell of Vosene came off her. She always bought a family-sized bottle of shampoo and used it to the bitter end. Whereas I, convinced that a shampoo could change the basic properties of my hair, usually had several bottles on the go with only a squirt used of each, the rest rejected for not giving me blonde curly hair.

'Hi,' I said, which wasn't the speech I'd rehearsed earlier.

The one I'd rehearsed went; ~~Lucille. Look, Lucille.~~ Lucille, I feel a bit upset with you. You know I'm going away and I'm really excited. Unlike you, I don't always get my own way all the time and asking me to clean the bathroom just seemed really nasty/weird when you know I've got to pack.'

'Hi,' she said. 'All packed?'

'Yeah!' I said. There was no point drawing her into my warm layer dilemma. She sat on my bed and twisted her rope of wet hair.

'Didn't you see the note from Ralph?'

'No. What note?'

'He called round earlier, asked if he could leave you a note.' She pointed at the bedside table. There was a lined A4 sheet of paper folded into quarters. She handed it to me.

Dear Eed,

I'm sitting on your bed and I feel so sad about everything that's happened. I want to be the one comforting you when you're down and tired, or rubbing your feet – pressing in the instep how you like it. And hearing your story again about Mr Nork falling off the desk. You in your Blondie t-shirt, me in my knee-less Long Johns. I want to be the one who makes your tea strong and milky with 1 and 4/5ths of a teaspoon of sugar in it. You make things happen, you're exciting, you're tortured, you're complicated. I've loved basking in your warmth and honesty, I'm so happy to have known you. I feel like I've known a real woman, thank you for that.

Love Ralphy X

PS I wish I could press your Turkish slipper breasts to my chest and cuddle you forever and ever . . .

I handed it to Lucille and she read it.

'Oh Edie, I'd love someone to write me a letter like that.'

'Yeah,' I said, 'it's lovely . . . but . . .' *He's a bit gay*, I was going to say, but Lucille interjected.

'Barry's not very good with words. He's a bit boring . . . and he snores really loudly, but I can wear ear plugs.'

'He's not that boring!' I said, but then, eager to agree in some way, 'Oh yeah, God, though, I think *I* might wear ear plugs when he's really droning on about work!'

'Ear plugs when he's *snoring*,' Lucille corrected me, before continuing, 'But he's really kind . . . I do love him.'

Oh my God, Lucille was *talking* to me! I froze, giving her air time, not wanting to break the spell.

'. . . my Mum loves him as well. The whole family do. I want to marry him more than anything.'

But then she didn't say anything for a few seconds and I couldn't last out the silence.

'The thing I don't understand is,' I said, 'how you could look someone in the eye and say "I do" and mean it 100%.'

'You don't mean it 100%, do you. Barry's the best I'll get,' Lucille answered.

'How d'you know?'

'My Mum told me. She said you always think there's someone better round the next corner but there isn't.'

'But she's had loads of boyfriends!'

'Exactly. She said they're all the same or worse. But you get addicted to looking round the corner. Mum wants to see me settled and happy. She loves Barry. She wants to be a young Granny and she thinks it's good to be a young mother, like she was.'

I thought about the time Lucille and I went on a two-week

school trip when we were eleven and she wrote a letter home to her mum every day. I found a whole load of them screwed up in the bin in our dormitory. First she wrote the letters out in rough and then she copied them out neatly, starting again if she went wrong. My one letter to my Mum went like this . . .

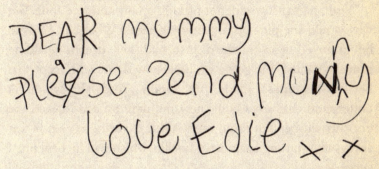

DEAR MUMMY
PLEASE SEND MUNNY
LOVE EDIE × ×

Lucille couldn't even be herself with her mother. And if you had a mother to impress/win over that didn't leave much time to obsess about blokes/career choices etc.

'You don't have to please your mum all the time,' I said.

She shrugged. 'I don't mind. It's OK. I'm not all brave and adventurous like you. I'm just a coward.'

'You could do all sorts of things – you could go to college, we could do something together, like Interrail . . .'

But her lips were pursing shut again.

'I don't want to do Interrail. You haven't got any puff, have you? I really fancy some.'

I had, because Steve had given me a big lump, so Lucille popped over and got some of Ali's lethal cider on tap and we spent the rest of the evening laughing and making faces into my shoplifting mirror. Then Lucille said suddenly, 'I'm going to bed.'

A bald statement just like that. And she got up to go.

I would never say that. I would say:

'Oh, God, it's quite late, maybe we'd better go to bed?' or 'I'm quite tired, are you?'

'Night then,' I said, in a slightly annoyed voice. And added a giant sigh for good measure.

'Yeah, night,' she said, not picking up my annoyed tone. But why would she pick up my annoyed tone? What had I got to be annoyed about? She'd just had her dream wedding cancelled and I was going on holiday with Steve. Except that her un-neediness made me lonely. And she wouldn't understand that anyway. I knew the next time we talked the door would be shut again as if it had never been ajar. It was always like starting again with Lucille, which had its benefits, I suppose.

At 1.15 a.m., pissed and stoned, I packed two jumpers and two cardis and zipped my case shut. Then I went downstairs, made a pile of toast and watched several hours of telly. It was the World Gymnastics Championships and I allowed myself a little scratch at one of my old regret scabs. Why didn't I go to that bloody gymnastics class? That could've been me doing back flips! I could've saved British women's gymnastics! It was all Lucille's fault – it was definitely her who suggested giving up waiting for the bus and going home to eat toast first.

In bed, I re-read Ralph's letter. It brought a tear to my eye. But I decided it was good for me to be around people who weren't like me. Like Steve – his cool was so alien to me – and Lucille – her control was unbelievable. I liked myself better with them, I was well behaved with them, because I couldn't be myself. Was I really myself with Ralph? If I was, then I couldn't cope with me, warts and all. Me letting it all hang out. Maybe being yourself is only a case of choosing to be with people who make you be a self that feels nice. Or comfortable. Or, if you really hate yourself, miserable.

I put Ralph's letter away and snuggled down to think 'Mmmmmm' about my trip with Steve.

37
Magic Moments

I'm wearing my dirty, ex-lavender boots that Steve bought me for my nineteenth birthday. I did dye them brown and they didn't go crispy. That's what it's like when you have a run of good luck. I'm wearing an orange-checked Ra-Ra skirt that Steve used to call a tablecloth but he hasn't said it this time. I've got it pulled up just above my boobs like a sundress. My legs are golden and toned and I'm as brown as a berry. I'm tramping along the beach at Durdle Dor with a towel, some orange squash, a tranny and a packet of B&H in a plastic bag. Steve tramps behind me. There's hardly anyone on the beach but we instinctively keep on walking for about half a mile and stop and sit on the big white chalky stones which press into our bum bones. The sea's flat and navy blue, little white ruffles crawling back and forth where the stones are smaller, only a couple of centuries from being sand. Or decades? It crosses my mind that I could ask Ralph whether it would take decades or centuries for those stones to turn to sand and he would probably know the answer, but I don't bother mentioning it to Steve. Gulls are calling. The sun is hot but there's a weeny tinge of autumn in the air. Despite that I struggle into my black halter-neck bikini under my Ra-Ra skirt, determined to swim. But then 'Oh fuckit,' I think, 'No one can see and anyway I want them to see.' I throw off my Ra-Ra skirt/dress, roll my knickers off, push my boots off with my heels and ouch my way to the edge of the water. It dips right down, so I plunge in, giving little yelps, then swim out and turn and wave at Steve who is watching me. I float on my back and can hear the whoosh and crackle of the current in my ears, a distant gull and nothing else. I close my eyes. 'I am happy,' I think.

I come hobbling back along the stones, tingling all over, salty droplets sitting on my oiled skin and all the little transparent hairs standing on end. I'm pleased with my nipples which are like frozen bullets. I lay down next to Steve on his leather jacket. He splashes out the little pool of water from my belly button and dabs me with the towel. Then he crawls on top of me, all warm and dry and puts the towel over us like a tent. I nestle my head between two large stones and he kisses me with his spongy lips.

'Prepare to be severely adored,' he says and then applies his warm dry hands to my shivery hips and his warm wet lips to one of my icy nipples.

38
Black Magic Moments

I remembered the exact moment when Steve went off me
after six months of lovely spontaneous togetherness.

'Don't go,' I said. And that was the moment the balance
tipped. That was the moment I eventually obsessed about.

I had stayed the night at Steve's flat in West Ealing. We
smoked a joint in the morning. Everything was normal, apart
from me. The excessive dope-smoking was sending me mad,
thoughts were flying about my mind that I felt too afraid to
express to Steve. Thoughts like, 'I'm mad, I'm mad, I'm mad.'
I was going for my second interview at a children's home in
Acton. The first interview had been all very casual. I'd met
Mrs Barrowe, the manager, and a couple of the girls, it didn't
seem to matter that I wasn't qualified or experienced. I just had
to go back for another visit. I wanted the job, I really did. Steve
dropped me off at my Mum's.

'Don't go.'

'Well, don't you want to get ready?' he said through his
visor.

'Oh, come in for a cup of tea while I change.'

'Yeah, OK,' he said and climbed off his bike.

After he'd gulped his tea down he was by the front door,
hand over the handle. My Mum was hovering.

'I think I'll shoot off now, Pup.'

'Oh! Can't we have breakfast at the Jolly Cafe before I go?'

His eyes darkened a little. The balance tipped a few more millimetres. Or, maybe that was the actual moment? Maybe I had still had a chance then. If I'd let him go.

'Yeah, OK,' he said and plonked himself down on the leatherette sofa.

'I don't know if I want to go!' I exclaimed suddenly.

'Oh darling!' Mum said.

'Oh Mum, shut up!' I shouted.

Steve looked shocked.

I started to cry. I ran up the stairs. Looked at myself in the mirror. Saw my limp, flat hair. Sobbed some more. Ran back down the stairs, where Steve considered me from the leatherette sofa, his opinion of me dying in his eyes. I had started to self-destruct and now I had to finish the job off. It was like having over-eaten at Christmas, and not knowing what else to do except eat another date.

'one more date.'

I flung myself on the living room floor, got out my spindly beige plastic fork . . . aimed for the date . . .

'I don't want to go! Don't make me!'

'Darling . . .' my Mum bent over me.

Steve stood up. 'Maybe I'd better go.'

I clung to his legs. 'Don't leave me!'

He looked down at me. It felt just like those dreams where you've murdered someone and there's no going back.

'Dear, if you feel this badly about it maybe you shouldn't go?'

'Oh keep out of it, Mum, for Christ's sake! I do want to go! But I want Steve to come with me!' I yelled.

I managed to pull myself together after that and decided not to go – yes, 'If only I'd gone for that job at the children's home!' became a regular regret – and Steve and I went to the Jolly Cafe where you are guaranteed to be cheered up by the jolly Colombian family and their jolly employees. But Steve's eyes had a matt finish and I couldn't swallow my egg and bacon and kept saying sorry and smoking. He said I was disgusting when I put my cigarette out in my fried egg, in a new, nasty voice. I should've said, 'I don't care if it's disgusting!' but I watched what I said for the first time. The new game was suddenly him being as nasty as possible to make me end it and me being as nice as possible to try and stop him being nasty. It was a lose/lose situation.

Instead of seeing the whole build-up, the part the other characters played, and chance, I blamed it all on me and that one moment instead of seeing the whole intricate, interwoven plot of the play. Looking back, I *had* got a little clingy before that, but I thought it was OK, romantic. When he left me at the doorstep some week-nights I always said, 'I don't want you to go.' Once he said, 'Eed, I don't like it when you say you don't want me to go,' but I didn't really understand so I added that I wished I could zip him open, get inside and zip him shut again.

I remembered the fear and the absolute knowledge that I had messed up. That he had gone off me, that the balance of power had shifted.

So, sitting in the passenger seat of Steve's van nearly three years later, it was fascinating to watch the balance tipping the other way. And what had I done but given up, let go and gone wandering off in the other direction? All those times I'd wished I'd said fuck off, been cooler, been nicer and now I hadn't had to do anything.

'I don't want you to go,' Steve said, clinging on to me in the petrol station forecourt.

I kissed him on his lovely spongy lips. 'Come on we'd better get moving, it's spitting.'

Steve's mum, Pamela, had helped him plan the holiday to Dorset and had written out a list of suggested trips and tips. It was based on a holiday she and Ken had been on when they were young. It took in Durdle Dor, Corfe Castle, the Blue Lake, Studland Bay. Steve was paying for everything. Every B&B was booked ahead. We were having a nice time. We'd had sex on the beach under a towel, in the sea clinging to a buoy, in the bath, in the pub loos up against a wall, in a haystack, on a golf course, behind a lorry, in a front garden. We'd had it off all over the place but we hadn't had it out. The air was crackling with unsaid things. But then on the last night, driving to our last Bed and Breakfast, Steve said, 'You know when you said you didn't mind about that Joooolie?'

He said her name in his 'Ferck Erff' voice, to diminish her, presumably.

'I wanted you to mind. I wanted you to tell me not to. I wanted you to, you know . . .'

'Go mad?'

'Yeah, like go really, you know . . .'

'Berserk?'

'Yeah. You always know the right words, Pup. I couldn't stand it when you were seeing that Ralph bloke. I was eaten up with jealousy.'

'Really?' I said. 'Left here.'

'You looked really happy.'

'Did I?'

'Yeah.'

'But you said it was like a big weight off your chest when I suggested the open relationship,' I pointed out.

'You just seemed so miserable all the time. I felt like I made you miserable. And then when I saw you that time – you'd gone all gorgeous and brown and had your hair cut in that, you know . . .'

'Messy bob.'

'And you were lively and laughing and I fell in love with you again. I'm desperately in love with you, Messy Bob.'

I looked across at Steve in the orange darkness, car headlights illuminating his face every few seconds.

'What d'you love about me?' I asked.

'Everything.'

I looked at the itinerary with Steve's petrol lighter. It was funny looking at his Mum's writing in the half light as we zoomed along. Her curly grown-up writing saying at the bottom, 'Have fun kids!'

The last time I'd seen her writing, it had said 'Little slut'.

'What's this place called? Swanwich?'

'Swanage.'

'Your mum's spelt it "I-C-H", isn't it "A-G-E" at the end?'

'I C Haitch, I think.'

'Why d'you say Haitch and not aitch?'

'Aitch is the cockney version, isn't it? My mum taught me to talk posh, like,' he laughed.

'It's Aitch.'

'It's the letter Haitch so it must start with an Haitch. Right, Pupling?'

'Well, it doesn't. OK, we need the next right, at the next junction.'

We pulled up outside the B&B and went up to our room, flung our bags on the floor and ourselves on the bed and had wild, desperate, sweaty sex. It was still our clearest form of communication. Steve didn't turn away afterwards but stayed welded to my back.

'I'm madly in love with you, Bob Dudman.'

I thought about the letter from Ralph.

'But what in particular do you love about me?' I asked him.

'Everything in particular,' he replied, stroking that soft bit on the inside of the top of my thigh.

'Look at that fucking prat!' Steve said.

We were in the bar downstairs of the pub we were staying in. It was too late to go anywhere else to eat.

A big bloke with a paunch, messy blond hair, a ruddy complexion and a donkey laugh was ruling the pool table. He'd been the winner who stays on for a dozen games.

Steve put a 20p on the table and sat supping at his pint ('in a straight glass, please, mate') and eyeing the proceedings. When it was his turn, he was as cool as ice, started to play pretty well. There was a hush, people began to watch. Steve stalked about the table and finished off the game with a super cool, cue-behind-his-back shot.

'Shot,' said the ruddy-faced local admiringly. Then Steve said he wasn't staying on and left the table. I felt proud and ashamed at the same time. I wouldn't have dared piss off the locals but I could see they were quite in awe of him. And now he was in awe of me. The balance was back.

All the way back to London he had his hand on my knee any time it wasn't on the gear stick or the steering wheel. It was heaven.

EDIE DUDMAN
STEVE BONIFACE (Hate)

EDITH DUDMAN
STEVE BONIFACE (marriage!)

EDIE DUDMAN
NEWCASTLE POLYTECHNIC (marriage)

EDIE DUDMAN
BOXFORD GAZETTE (marriage)

EDIE DUDMAN
INTER RAIL (LOVE)

EDITH DUDMAN
STEVE BONIFACE   LOVE!!
Edie Boniface

39

Edie Dudman for the Defence vs. Edie Dudman for the Prosecution

'You look happy, Edie!' Evelyn said.

'Yes, I am quite, thanks Auntie Evelyn. Is Mum back?'

My Mum poked her head round the balcony doors.

'Oh we're so glad you're happy, aren't we Flopsie?'

Flopsie looked straight through me with his boss eyes.

Telling Evelyn I was happy was one thing, but telling my Mum meant I had to keep it up.

'I'm not that happy!'

Mum ignored me. 'Get that bubbly out of the fridge would you?'

I sloped off to the kitchen. 'Mum! You never put the lid back on the marmalade properly! And the bread. Look! It'll go stale open like that! And the cheese! Look! All rindy!' I called.

'Oh, stop going at me!'

'It's for your own good. That's why you've got those little moths.'

'Oh, they're quite sweet.'

'They're not sweet, they're disgusting.'

'OK, dear, I'll try.'

'You could try moth balls?' I heard Evelyn suggest.

I nipped in the downstairs loo, hoping there'd be a drip on the seat.

'And there's always a drip on the toilet seat where you've rushed with the wiping!'

'I know, I'm always on to the next thing,' she said. 'In my mind, anyway.'

'Tut!' I called. But that was how I was too.

The day before, Edwina had offered me a filing/trainee staff photographer job at the *Gazette*. Just like that. I hadn't even asked for it. My picture of Foxy was quite good and the scoop about her new production company Way To Go was featured on the front page of the Saturday edition. 'Photo by E*ddi*e Dudman' it said up the side of the picture and my Mum crossed out one of the d's and had it framed sideways, so you could read the writing but not the picture.

I screwed all my Mum's lids on properly and went back in to the living room with the Pomagne. I'd got a new plan, and I wanted to test it out.

'I might not go to college now,' I announced.

'Oh Edie! Why?' Evelyn asked, looking distraught.

'I've decided that I'd be much better off staying here and taking that job at the *Gazette* – in three years' time I'll be doing what I want anyway – photographer. Also I'll be earning money if I stay here, and all my friends are here and my family. Having a degree doesn't get you anywhere in art. Your work's more important – like a portfolio – and experience counts for more in the world of work. I can go to college any time in the future, it's better to go when you're older, you appreciate it more. I just don't feel ready.'

Mum and Evelyn stared swirly-eyed at me.

'I think you're right,' my Mum said, 'if you're not ready.'

'Yes,' Evelyn said, 'I agree. And it'd be lovely for us if you stayed. Let's open this Pomagne!'

I held out my hand in a 'Halt!' position.

'But I'm young, now's the time to go to college, I'll never get round to it if I leave it any longer, I'm already older than the others in my year, life will get in the way and I'll never go. I'll just get stuck in that job at the *Gazette* – Fat Phil's been there eight years, he'll never become staff photographer. Mitch will never leave or die, college will give me all sorts of opportunities, I might find I don't want to be a photographer. And I'll make friends from all walks of life. It's cheaper to live up there and if you've got a degree the world's your oyster. I think I should go!'

Mum's and Evelyn's mouths hung open.

'Well?' I demanded.

'Yes, I think you're right, don't you, Ev?'

'Yes! Yes I do! You must go Edie! It'll be marvellous!'

Evelyn pealed a strip of foil off the top of the Pomagne but her fingers froze as I launched into an edited version of the first argument.

'But the job at the *Gazette*'s an opportunity of a lifetime! People give their right arms for a job like that. If I work at it I could be an editor in five years.'

My Mum: Hmm, maybe that would be . . . oh darling, go for the job!

Evelyn: Yes! It sounds really good – I mean they must rate you. Yes, the job definitely!

Evelyn's fingers twitched tentatively on the cork.

'College will be fun!' I announced. 'It'll be an experience that I may never get the chance to have again. I'm young, I should be free and mixing with people my own age!'

My Mum: OK. I'm for college. Definitely.

Evelyn: Yes, I am. Edie you must go. Let's get this Pomagne open!

'Oh, you two are useless! You just agree with anything I say, you're swaying about like two brainless palm trees.'

'But dear, you're so persuasive. I just don't know.'

'I'm all muddled up. You make it all sound good . . .' Evelyn said.

'And bad . . .' added my Mum.

'Maybe I should be a lawyer! That's it! I'm a Libran, I'm really good at seeing both sides of any argument. I'll cancel the course and do Law!'

'Oh, what a brilliant idea!'

'Edie, I'm so glad you've decided on Law. That's wonderful!'

'Fancy! A lawyer in the family!'

'Don't be ridiculous!' I said. But I was pleased to see they were so persuadable. Because there was another option that I hadn't mentioned to Mum and Evelyn. The Steve Option. Steve wanted to talk about 'the relationship'. He'd learnt how to pronounce it now and was using it in his sentences quite a lot. He wanted to see me all the time, he kept asking me not to go up to Newcastle, he said Johnnie was moving out and did I want to move in with him? Everything I'd wanted over the last three years was being offered to me on a plate.

'Really, what I want to do is have a simple life, stay at Crusties and move in with Steve,' I practised.

Then their mouths really dropped open. They didn't look so much like brainless palm trees now.

'You're joking,' my Mum said.

'Well, if it's what you want, Edie,' Evelyn said, looking anxiously at my Mum.

'She's joking,' Mum said, and Evelyn giggled nervously.

'Why can't you two give me wise old-sageish advice about what the right thing to do is?' I cried.

'Well, we don't know any better than you,' Evelyn said.

'But you've been on this earth ages! Why don't you know?!'

'There is no right thing to do,' my Mum said, trying to be an old sage. 'You think you make choices – once I've done this, once I've sorted this out, once I've got that – that you'll get to this plateau where everything will be alright, but you never do. There's always another thing.'

'Oh for goodness' sake!' I yelled, reaching for my coat. Lucille was right, going on and on about things did just make you feel bad. And as I left I heard them forget all about me and start debating whether to have tea with *Corrie* or wait and have it with *Dynasty*. And then I heard the Pomagne pop open.

As I strode along the balcony I thought, 'I just want someone to tell me what to do.'

And there was Jervis waiting for me outside my front door. He'd been on this earth the longest of all. Surely that counted for something?

'Jervis, if you were young and you had the chance to go to college or get a job with quite good prospects, what would you do?'

'I'd join the Foreign Legion, love.'

I considered this briefly. They would definitely tell me what to do. All the time.

'No, that's not one of the options. You see, I'm trying to

decide what to do, I don't want to make any more mistakes and regret them.'

'What mistakes can you have possibly made, young man?'

'Is there anything in your life that you really regret, Jervis? And don't say not learning to play the piano, because that's what everyone else has said.'

'Oh, I wish I had learnt to play the piano!'

'Is there anything else?'

'There is one thing. I should never have split up with the first Mrs Sponge.'

Ah, this was more like it.

'She was my first love and she had a cuddle with a neighbour when I was in the Far East during the war. I went mad when Mr Snodgrass in the corner shop told me. I left her even though she was expecting. You never get that again, your first love. No, you never recapture that. You've got to stick with it. I should never've gone off with the second Mrs Sponge. She was violent, you know. Gorgeous looking woman, great big arms. She hit me on the back of the head with a frying pan because I left the spoon in the soup, that's why I'm a bit funny in the head.'

I stared at him. 'Hmm, I wondered about that.'

'I'm not funny in the head, thank you very much!' he said.

'No, of course you're not, you're not at all funny in the head!'

'That's nice of you to say so, Edward.'

'In fact, you've given me the best advice of all,' I told him.

40

What She Wants

It can be embarrassing to want something really badly and then be offered it. There's a pride thing, a certain hesitation, you want to grab at it but it looks foolish, greedy, base. It reminded me of a day back in February when Kerry came into Crusties wearing a really nice, dark brown leather jacket.

'That's a lovely jacket,' I told her.

'Oh yeah, it's alright. My brother's girlfriend gave it me.'

'It's really nice.'

'Have it!' she said, taking it off. 'Go on, have it!

'Er,' I said. Had I sounded like I was hinting?

'I want you to have it, I don't really want it.'

'Oh, no, Kerry, you can't just give it to me, I mean your brother's girlfriend gave it to you. No I couldn't take it.'

She shrugged and slung it on the chair.

That night I felt a bit regretful. I should've just taken it. She'd offer it to me again the next day. Or I'd tell her I'd changed my mind. I came in the next morning all leather-jackety. No sign of it. Kerry wasn't wearing it. It wasn't on the chair.

At lunchtime I said, 'Kerry? I . . .'

And out came Moira on her way to the bank. Wearing the leather jacket. Squeezed into it. Looking really pleased about it.

'What?' said Kerry.

'Oh, nothing.' Yeah, exactly. Nothing. That's where it got me. I had my pride but I didn't have the leather jacket. Maybe Moira would give it to me further down the line? I coveted and regretted that jacket for weeks. I even told Moira it looked a bit tight on her.

Of course I wanted to live with Steve – it's what I'd wanted for ages – but I was so used to being in a state of longing and dissatisfaction and feeling like an abnormal weirdo that it all felt a bit unusual and awkward. I remembered how much I'd regretted not moving in with him when he first got his flat. I had said I wasn't sure, assuming that he'd ask me again and then I had my Black Magic Moment not long after and of course the opportunity had gone.

Lucille would've just taken that jacket if she'd wanted it. Because she was the sort of person who knew what she wanted. But people like me, who don't know what they want, often have to wait and see how they feel when they do or don't get something. And I felt relieved when I heard that Edwina had got fed up holding the job open for me and had employed someone else. And, having accepted the place at Newcastle straight away but done nothing about it since, it was too late to get in the halls of residence and I hadn't sorted out my grant. And it was the 13th of September – I should've been up there on the 16th. It was slipping away and I was letting it . . .

Making decisions always left me deflated because I did so much pro-ing and con-ing that whatever choice I made came with a great list of real or imagined cons attached. In the back of Crusties at the end of the day, washing the soup urn, a thought kept going through my head. A horrible, destructive thought. It was the old me trying to sabotage the new me's happiness.

'Once you've thought something five times you mean it,' Lucille had told me her mum had told her. But when you are a person who thinks a lot, it's difficult to know which thoughts to take notice of. So I tailored that rule to my personality and decided that once you have thought something 500 times you mean it. And then I employed one of Lucille's negative-thought banishing techniques.

As I went out the front to wipe down the glass display cabinets, chanting 'shut up, shut up, shut up!' Mr Pollock and Susie were standing round a small table with a bottle of Leibfraumilch on it. Pollock had combed his beard and Susie had some chalky pink lipstick on her thin lips. Then, just as I was chanting my final 'shut up' a certain till-dipping person with her hair newly bubble permed came clacking into the shop.

She machine gun-laughed Pollock and Susie in the back.

'Oh, tha's a nice welcome,' she said, in reply to my final 'shut up', 'I haven't said nothing yet!'

Pollock and Susie turned round and we all stared at Kerry.

'What's the matter with you lot? You look like you've seen a bleedin' ghost!'

Kerry stood there with her hands on her hips, chewing gum loudly. I waited for Pollock to throw her out or call the police but he didn't.

'Hello Kerry,' Pollock said in a measured way, 'why don't you join us for a glass of wine.'

'Yeah, alright, I will in a minute, but the thing is I need my job back,' she said, eyeballing Susie.

I looked at Bollock, expecting an explosion of spittle and beard crumbs. Susie's pink lip quivered.

'Hang on, where's Moi?' Kerry asked.

It was Hurting Pollock's Feelings vs. Seeing Kerry's Disbelief but I couldn't resist it.

'You'll never guess! She's getting married to Whatsit from the estate agent's and she's . . .' I glanced at Mr Pollock, 'Sorry, but . . . she's having a baby!'

'Blimey! She's ancient!'

'I know! 46! It happened the first time they had sex together!'

Mr Pollock was very brave about it. He cleared his throat, 'Do give her my best regards if you see her,' he said. 'Anyway, Kerry, Susie here is going to be the new Assistant Manageress.'

'Oh, I see, and Edie's going to be the Manageress, I s'pose?!' Kerry said.

They all looked at me. 'No, Edie is leaving. This is her leaving do. I do have a vacancy for a Manageress, as it happens.'

'I promise I won't do any nicking,' Kerry said, raising the level of her interview technique a notch.

'Well I am a bit desperate,' he said.

'Oh great! When do I start?'

'The money will be better. I know you've got two young children.'

'Bleedin' hell! Have you been visited by the ghost of Christmas past, or somink? How much better?'

'Better enough for you to pay me back the money you owe me.'

Kerry's eyes darkened. 'Oh yeah . . .'

'And you'll have to do the day release training.'

'Yeah.'

'Come into the back with me and we'll discuss the arrangements.'

'Yes siree!'

And Kerry marched into the back with Pollock, winking at me and Susie on the way past.

'Maybe I *should've* done the manageress training?' Susie whispered to me.

'But you want to be a dental nurse,' I reminded her, secretly having a weeny doubt myself.

'Yeah, but . . .' Susie trailed off. I heard a horn honk.

'Oh, look there's your boyfriend!'

Kerry and Pollock agreed that she would pay him back 37p a week and the job was hers. Steve joined us and we all stood round drinking Leibfraumilch and Susie and Pollock gave me a set of cheap gold jewellery that was bound to set off my nickel allergy. Later, in the pub, Kerry did loud machine gun laughing at one of Steve's 'Ferck Erff' work stories and I felt happy and proud. I was normal! I was, I was, I was!

'D'you want to come back to mine?' Steve asked, outside the pub. 'I want to show you something.'

'OK!' I said.

At the flat, Steve proudly showed me he had bought a king-size bed and said that he could adapt the utility room into a dark room for me. I noticed he'd got a photo of me from Dorset framed on his mantelpiece. He came towards me and started to kiss up my neck. His spongy lips came towards mine. My face involuntarily turned away. His lips sought mine, but my lips led my face away again.

'What's wrong?'

'I don't know.'

'You've always been ready to kiss me,' he said.

I'd never noticed what fat cheeks he had before. Like a hamster.

'Sorry,' I said and I turned away. 'I'm just tired.'

'Tired of me?'

'No, of course not.'

Sex is a private language that two people can either speak together or not. You can't skirt around it or change the subject – it is the subject. My lips wouldn't kiss him and that was it. But I could talk them round, I was sure. I wasn't going to give in to doubts. I was just tired. I fell asleep and when I woke in the morning he was propped up on his elbow staring at me. Hamsters are really sweet. They are, they are, they are!

But then, just like that, the unwanted thought that I had told to shut up came back.

'I don't love him anymore.'

It kept playing on my brain tape recorder. Just the words. A sentence in my head. In quite a good impersonation of my voice. I kept erasing it and it kept coming back. I had gone way over the 500 mark.

'It's ridiculous,' I told myself. 'Of course you love him! You can't stop loving him just because he now loves you! That's the old cliché. You're just afraid of happiness, like Shona said. Come on! He's the old Stevie back again, like you wanted. Don't be one of those people who only wants the unobtainable – that's pathetic! Just stop thinking – yes, you can give that up right away! – everything's OK now. I love him, I do, I do, I do!'

And I closed my eyes and clung to Steve's warm naked torso as he slurped his tea. He did a comforting pat on my rump.

'Alright, Babycakes?'

'Hmmm,' I thought. 'I'd have given my right arm for that a year ago.' And then my Mum wouldn't have been able to tell me that at least I had all my arms and legs. And she wouldn't have needed to, because I would've been happy. 'I love him, I love him, I love him .. .' But on the back of my eyelids a banner went past pulled by a small determined aeroplane, and written on it in a poor copy of my handwriting:

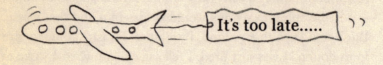

And then it came back the other way.

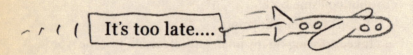

But I wasn't fooled. I opened my eyes and the image pinged away. Steve kissed me, his lips still hot and metallic from his tea. I found his M&S black briefs with my feet and pushed them down his lovely hairy legs and opened my thighs wide.

'I love you, I love you, I love you,' I said and kept my eyes wide open as well, in case that aeroplane came back.

Steve gave me a lift to Queen Charlotte's Hospital to see my sister-in-law Sandy and her new baby. The second I saw Dora kicking her legs in the air that was it. A feeling came over me. I tried to fight it off. No! Not after all this – no, I don't feel like that! The feeling was harder to fight off than the thought. Steve held the baby and we all oohed and aahed and as I looked at him his features drained away. Suddenly his lips didn't look particularly full, his hair didn't look that golden, his eyes looked sludgy grey. He just looked like a bloke who I didn't really know. Like that pink shell I found at Durdle Dor and I said 'Look at this lovely shell' and put it in my pocket and then I saw there were thousands of them all over the beach, realized it was just an ordinary shell and chucked it away. Poor old shell, it almost had me fooled.

Because it wasn't just me that had a Black Magic Moment. Steve had one as well. Way back in January. When I told him I wanted to keep the baby and he said, 'What about college?' That was the reason he gave for me not to have the baby. Of course there was the whole intricate plot of the play, but that's what flashed through my mind now. In that Italian restaurant, 9.45 p.m. on the 30th of January 1983, the moment my opinion of him started to die in my eyes. But I was too busy looking into his for my own reflection.

41
Somewhere in the Middle

Boxford looked lovely the day I set off. I don't know if it was because I knew I was leaving and was happy and giving off happy vibes. Two neighbours I had never exchanged words with said 'Good Morning'. Jervis gave me his super 8 camera. It turned out to be a standard 8 camera and totally useless to me but I accepted it gratefully. Lucille gave me a new set of Boots No. 7 make-up and a really warm hug and said she was going to miss me and she was really sorry she had been such a bitch. Buster told me that that actress off *Crossroads* had died of heart failure, but I knew he meant well, and Penny and Shona gave me a compilation tape of all their favourite songs. Ralph gave me the new John Denver album. Both my brothers' eyes looked watery and Angel and Mimi and my new niece Dora gave me a great big card with loads of kisses on. The sky was blue, the air was blowy and fresh and hopeful, the birds were tweeting, and I'm sure I saw a woodpecker in the quad. Ali in the corner shop gave me a bag of goodies for the journey and my Mum gave me £100 and squeezed me very tight indeed. Evelyn told me she was absolutely certain that I was doing the right thing, but I knew if I told her I had changed my mind and was going to be a taxidermist her certainty would waver.

Then Steve honked his horn and pointed at his watch and I dragged my suitcase on wheels over to his van.

At Kings Cross I leaned out of the train window. He must have been able to see the distance in my eyes. They were looking up the road that said N for New Life and he was already on the periphery of my vision.

'I don't want you to go.'

'Oh, come on, you'll be fine. I'll write as soon as I get sorted out.'

'I wish I was in your head, Messy Bob.'

Because my head was empty of him and his head was full of me. Mine was empty and free, not full of rehearsing speeches, analysing reactions, imagining responses, empty and free to absorb now, the future, my new life. I wasn't exactly enjoying watching the balance tipping the other way but it was relaxing. I understood Steve's cool now. I'd done all the caring so he just hadn't needed to care. And in the role of the non-carer you go into a kind of empty-headedness. Instead of being paralysed with fear you're paralysed with a kind of 'I dunno-ness'. You just don't know. You just don't know. You can't put your mind to it.

As the train pulled away, Steve mouthed, 'I love you'. I couldn't forgive him. But I knew how it felt knowing you've messed up, that it's too late, and, having a weak and woolly centre bequeathed to me by my mother, I genuinely did feel sorry for him. And pity is a kind of love. So I mouthed it back.

It was all a bit last minute, going up to Newcastle. My grant was going to be delayed and I wasn't even sure where I was going to stay when I got up there. Once Steve was a dot and

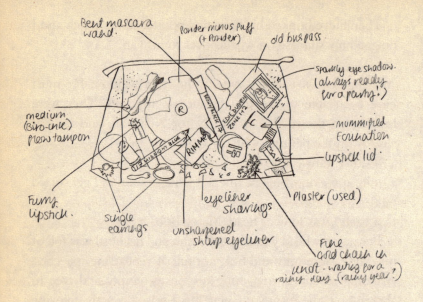

Bent mascara wand.

ponder minus puff (+ ponder)

old bus pass

sparkly eye shadow. (always ready for a party.)

medium (Biro-ink) prew tampon

mummified foundation

lipstick lid.

Funny lipstick.

single earrings

eyeliner shavings

Plaster (used)

unsharpened sharp eyeliner

ring and chain in
unot - waiting for a
rainy day (rainy year?)

I'd settled in to my four-seater all to myself, I sighed. After a bit I got out my make-up bag. I had nothing better to do. It needed a good clean out and contained:

1 unsharpened eye liner that scratched my eye ball every time I used it

1,050,987 specks of sparkly eyeshadow escaped long ago from their plastic container, lining the bag and everything in it and always on my face so that, 'Going to a party?' had been a commonly asked question of me. At the bus stop at 8.30 a.m. During my afternoon shift at Crusties. At 12.10 at night watching telly in my grey contraceptive nightie

1 lipstick, with its broken lid always at the opposite end of the bag. The lipstick a shade of red I would never wear and covered in fluff, sparkly eyeshadow and eye-pencil shavings (I did sharpen it once – into the bag)

1 ancient foundation tube cut in half with scissors to get at the last
    smear and long since mummified
1 dried up old mascara with a bent wand
1 Tampax released from its cardboard tube and absorbed in
    medium flow biro ink

I had two other make-up bags as well. They were retirement
homes for all my other sad old cosmetics, stuffed into the
bottom of my wardrobe.

Lucille's make-up bag was another story. The lining was
always clean. Each bit of make-up was new and regularly used.
Lucille liked to be on top of things. Lucille was on an
Autobahn – no turnings off, no roundabouts, no dead ends or
traffic lights stuck on amber, no wrong ways or surprises.
Single vision and a clear target. Whereas I was somewhere in
the middle of page 64 in the A–Z, and I was holding it upside
down. Deliberately. But I was enjoying being in the middle,
where I didn't know how it was going to end. For the moment
anyway. And as I finished cleaning out my make-up bag and
put all the new stuff Lucille had given me in it, I comforted
myself with the thought that Lucille would never know the
intense joy of having a clean make-up bag after having a messy
one for four years. Even if it didn't last it was worth it, I
thought, eventually deciding to keep my five-year-old bent
mascara for back-up. And, as I celebrated with a cup of tea
and a B&H, it felt OK to be me. And it felt OK to be a bit like
my Mum.